My Dying Breath

Copyright © 2002 Ben Reed
Cover art by Robert Tracy
Cover design by Mike Ritter

All rights reserved.
ISBN: 1-58898-814-7
www.mydyingbreath.com   .

My
Dying Breath

A NOVEL

Ben Reed

NORTH CHARLESTON BOOKS
CHARLESTON, S.C.
2002

My Dying Breath

Ben conveys images that, for many of us, will be our first uncluttered look at what happened to our fighting men on the ground, while at the same time depicting what was happening among the enemy and on the home front. The Vietnam War, in all its dimensions, has never before been so honestly portrayed. Ben brings the reader so close to the physical and emotional action, that he can smell the cordite and feel the pain.

Richard B. Purdue, President of SuperiorBooks
Author of *MSS: The Real World of Books*

Tremendous! My Dying Breath ranks up there with Body Count by William T. Huggett, Sand in the Wind by Robert Roth and James Webb's Fields of Fire. The three best works of fiction about Marines in Vietnam.

Billy Myers, former Marine
Author of *Honor the Warrior*

Engaging, emotional story of Marines, war, family and the culture that revolves around all. The reader will share the experience and it will seem like you're standing with the platoon in boot camp or along on a patrol in the A Shau Valley or waiting for that letter from a loved one. Damn, I enjoyed this book.

Lt. Col. David W. Couvillon
USMCR Commanding Officer 3rd Bn, 23rd Marines

If you want to know what Vietnam was like in the northern I Corps for a Marine Rifleman in 1969, read this book. After you have rushed through it the first time, relax, and read it again. It's that good.

Roger T. "The Walrus" LaRue
Delta Co., 1st Recon Bn., 1st MARDIV, 1969-70

Table of Contents

PART 2: THE NAM

PART 3: THE CRUCIBLE

Please see Glossary on pages 493-498

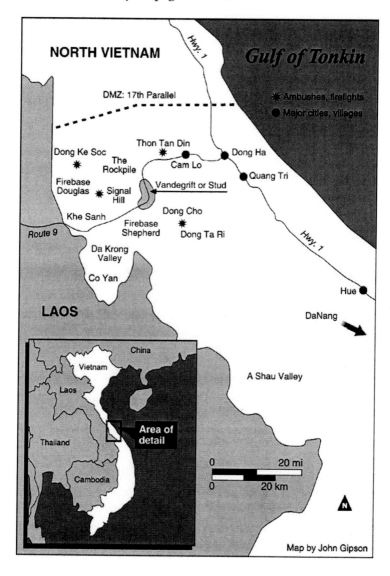

Map by John Gipson

For Curry and Rose

Acknowledgments

My Dying Breath began as a seed planted in the mind of a 19-year-old Marine more than 30 years ago in a distant land. But it did not blossom until 2000 when friends of a 50-year-old veteran began nurturing its roots. And there are so many to thank for the fruit that it has borne.

In the formative stages, great friends like my brother Michael, my buddy Scott Rabalais and strategist Bill Sierichs were indispensable. Jessica Schiefelbein, Richard Deshotels, Tony Brown and Dean Roper added support in the difficult early stages.

Bob and Linda Tracy, and Mike Ritter with their artistic talents became new friends during the arduous rewriting days. Old friends were on hand as well and *My Dying Breath* could not have survived without the aid of Glenn and Gail Adcock, Phil Amy and Sammy Fusilier.

And then there were the experts—military adviser Roger T. LaRue, military writer/editor George Morris, former Marine Commandant Gen. Robert H. Barrow and retired Maj. Gen. Ron Richard. The Vietnamese technical direction of Bao Nguyen and the Rev. Than Vu helped keep it real. Editor Richard Purdue showed me how to find a voice to soften a journalistic style.

To the young ones, those who never knew Vietnam and know little of its legacy, I thank for lending their time and support—daughters Lesley, Allison and Kayla, and friends Richard and Leigh Ann.

And, finally, to my loving and beautiful wife Clarese, and my dear friend Vana Plaisance—thanks is simply not enough. You were there.

The Author

Dedicated To St. Joseph The Protector
As An Installment On A Debt
That Can Never Fully Be Repaid.

In Memory Of The Donnie-boys:
Donald Webster David
James Donald Feucht
and
Donald Charles Reed

PROLOGUE
Firebase Douglas, Republic of South Vietnam
Spring 1968—9 a.m. local time

Strewn about the coiled wire and smoking bunkers, the bodies of a score of U.S. Marines lay like children's old toys, twisted and abandoned. A North Vietnamese Army officer stepped among the dead and dying, his fists propped on his hips as he patiently searched the ruins of the artillery base. He soon paused and kicked the helmet from an American's head. He studied the shattered young face, shook his head, and then moved on through the smoke and fog.

The NVA major searched for another minute. His scowl curled into a thin smile. "Ah, here. This one will do," he crowed in his native tongue. He straddled the body, its arms and legs pointing unnaturally. Drawing his American-made Bowie knife from its black leather scabbard, he squatted and grabbed the youth's shock of blond hair with the slender fingers of his left hand. With a deft slice and a twist that sounded of shucking corn, the major scalped the Marine. He wiped the blood dripping from his new trophy onto the blouse of its former host, rolled it up, shoved it into his trouser pocket, and then smiled again. "Lt. Dang?" he said without looking up.

"Yes, sir?"

The major pointed the knife at his aide, whose eyes flitted about, searching the skies. "Dang, go and find me paper and something to write with."

The major stood and again walked among the massacred. His tactics, which could no longer be doubted by his superiors, had exceeded expectations. Nonetheless, scores of his soldiers lay stiffening in the dry ravine at the hill's edge.

Sacrificed for victory in the hour-long battle, they could be replaced. It was the dozens of warriors who now scurried atop the firebase that earned his admiration. For the first time in five years of fighting the Americans, they had defeated the Marines.

Dang emerged from a bunker and offered his superior a half-melted ballpoint pen and a yellow ledger pad, its edges slightly browned. "Major, as you ordered," Dang said with a cough and a rapid blink. He again glanced at the sky. "But please hurry, the American jets will be here soon."

The major frowned and dismissed the lieutenant with a wave. He scribbled a note in English, ripped the paper from the pad, knelt and then stabbed the note onto the back of the dead Marine.

"But, sir, that knife is your prized possession. You can't leave it here," Dang observed, puzzled by the major's actions.

"No, Dang." The major stood and spread his arms like he was about to conduct an orchestra. He postured, smiling as if the corpses had risen in a collective ovation. "This is my prize." He paused, stroked the pocket bearing the blond scalp, stared into Dang's eyes and then nodded toward the knife. "I have more of those. But this…" he again raised his arms high, "…this is victory."

Dragging his mangled legs through the red clay toward a sandbagged wall, another Marine, his skin blackened and muddy, whimpered. Dang drew his pistol and pointed it at the head of the helpless man. In the manner of a school-yard bully, he asked, "Should I shoot this one?"

"No. Let him live," the major commanded, not bothering to look at the youth. "That one will remember. He will tell others." He shook his head and grunted, "No."

Darting about the firebase, scavenging for whatever munitions and supplies they could use, the NVA soldiers looked up at the sound of their leader's voice, one they had learned without reservation to trust and obey.

"Let's go," he shouted. "Our work here today is done."

A breeze funneled up from the valley. Whistling, it slid the smoky veil from the hilltop. The major's note, stabbed fast to the back of the Marine, rustled in the morning wind.

Get out of MY country! Or DIE! – Major Pham Van Bui

PART 1

The Corps

On the first night of the first day of boot camp,
you ask yourself why.
On the morning of the last day of boot camp,
you know why.

Darkness.
It leaves the minds of men uncertain.
Time shifts, focus blurs.
It disturbs the soul.

CHAPTER 1

Precious Air
Da Krong Valley, R.S.V.N.
May 16, 1969—11:45 p.m. local time

The first sound, as subtle as two blades of grass rubbing together, preceded a sudden rustling that startled Tuck. His head snapped up and his fingers fumbled for the pistol grip of the black rifle leaning against his thigh. Finding the grip, he pulled the M-16 to his shoulder and tapped his finger against the side of the trigger. He slowly inhaled the night air. It was thick with the scent of freshly turned earth and damp fern. The grass moved again. He pointed his rifle toward the sound, and waited in the darkness.

Beads of sweat forming near his scalp grew into droplets and streamed down his forehead. Tuck wrinkled his brow and then blinked as they paused at the scar above his right eye and then glided to the tip of his nose. He reached up and swiped his face with the tail of his T-shirt, stiff with the dried salt of a day's sweat.

Fighting through the ringing that masked his hearing, Tuck strained to detect the sounds of twigs snapping or metal clanking and to sort them from those of an animal foraging in the night. It was a difficult skill to learn. The ringing in his ears made it even more difficult. A rat, he soon decided. Not a tiger, too small. No, must be a rat. He lowered his weapon and slowly exhaled.

Sitting cross-legged on the edge of his fighting hole, Tuck leaned forward and looked toward the top of the jungle canopy. He searched for any hint of a breeze—the sway of a branch or the quivering of a leaf. There was none, but the Vietnamese night reminded him of home. He longed for Louisiana nights and Anna's warm embrace. The memory of her kisses, especially the first, and her consuming gaze still made him smile. After nearly 40 days in the bush, only the thought of returning to her prevented him from succumbing to despair.

He had earlier watched the half moon set below the crest of a nearby hill. Now only the stars and the jungle floor's phosphorescent decay illuminated the darkness atop the peak where he and his buddies stood vigil. In the pitch of the night, Tuck, like the others, felt alone.

He glimpsed a bat flitting in the starlight and mumbled a prayer for time to quicken. The physical demands of being a "mountain Marine" had sapped both his energy and courage. Fatigue had given way to weariness. Doubt filled Tuck's mind as Donnie-Boy's orders nagged. Why had he obeyed the command? Had he proven his loyalty, but bartered his soul? He dared not tell anyone of his doubts.

His friend, Danny, would relieve him in 15 minutes and the notion of a few hours of sleep beckoned seductively. Perhaps sleep would this time bring solace, if only for a while. But the dreams loomed. Dreams? No, nightmares— the kinds in which the dreamer utters unheard screams and then awakens, only to remember the dread. Tuck feared they'd never go away.

Tuck twisted about and glanced up the gentle slope toward his sleeping friends, whose three lives he guarded, and heard their gentle snoring. Dozens of other grunts slept around the perimeter. Soon, each would, in turn, stand a two-hour watch.

Tuck felt a prick and slapped at a mosquito on his neck. He peered down at the radium dial of his watch, its accuracy waning as tropical corrosion slowly devoured its inner workings. He wiped away the grime with his thumb and noted for the hundredth time how the face of the Timex glowed the same green as that of the ground's eerie sparkle. A bracelet of dirt coiled beneath the damp leather wristband, which stank of sweat. It was 11:50 p.m., 10 minutes to go. He again wiped his brow, squeezed shut his eyelids and shook his head. "Hang in there," he encouraged himself—too loudly.

"Huh?" Danny grunted from 10 yards up the slope. "My turn yet, Tuck?"

"Nah, you still got 10 minutes. Sorry I woke you, man."

"That's OK, little bro, don't mean nothin'," Danny said. He yawned and rubbed his eyes with mitt-like hands. Tuck was their leader now; he'd proven his mettle and would be the one to get them through this latest ordeal. "Damn, shouldn't be this hot anywhere." Danny yawned again and then scurried down the slope to Tuck's left side. "Any movement?"

Tuck pointed to the edge of the saw-toothed elephant grass. "Few minutes ago I heard some rustling. Probably a rat." He slowly rose to his knees, closed his eyes and stretched. "Oohahhumm, it's gonna be nice to get some slee…"

CRACK! The report from an AK-47 rifle split the night air.

Tuck's yawn hissed into a gasp as a bullet ripped through his upper chest. Like a sledgehammer's blow, the impact slammed him to the ground. The evening stillness erupted into confusion. His arms flailed at terrors unseen. Spasms shot through his body. Writhing, he sought air—hot, humid, any air. It did not matter now. He wanted it; needed it. Gasping brought but little air to his lungs. Confusion mounted. Familiar sounds—somewhere, just not sure where. Close, no—distant. Voices, too. Anna's? No.

"There he is. Get him, the sneaky bastard! Turn that 60 loose," Tuck heard Danny cry out...or, was it Donnie-Boy?

A string of automatic weapons fire stuttered in short bursts. Tuck couldn't tell from where it came—it didn't matter. His lungs sought the thick air. Precious air. Anna's face drifted before his eyes and then vanished into the starlight. He struggled up onto his right elbow and saw a shadow—that of a fleeing man, not a rat—fall hard. The hill fell silent.

Tuck's head drooped. A smoking hole marked his T-shirt. He fell back again, gasping. His body chilled beneath the strange dampness spreading across his chest. It smelled and felt like warm honey.

The shooting had stopped in less than a minute, but Tuck had lost concept of time—a lifetime might have slipped by. What? Hours since he'd wakened Danny? Had they spoken at all? The more he gasped, the more confounded his mind became. "Dear God, more air, please," he pleaded silently. But was it silent? Or, was he shouting?

Danny dropped his rifle into the grass, turned and then cradled Tuck in his strong black arms. There was a debt to be repaid. "Corpsman, corpsman," Danny hollered, "Man down over here. Damn it." He whispered to Tuck. "Hang in there, little buddy, I ain't gonna let you die, man. I ain't gonna let you die. Come on, man, don't close your eyes. Look at me you dumb Cajun."

Silhouetted against the onyx sky and bright stars, Danny's face appeared heavenly to Tuck. An ebony angel, he mused, slowly losing grip on the present, mumbling, *"O, St. Joseph..."*

CHAPTER 2
Gung Ho's Child
San Diego, Calif.
July 15, 1968—9 p.m. local time

From the small round window, he watched the glimmer sprawl to the edges of the north, south and east, stopping only where San Diego waded into the Pacific Ocean. To Benjamin "Tuck" Richard, the coastal city lying in the darkness below had been placed on earth as his personal gateway to the United States Marine Corps.

Tuck—only his mom called him Benjamin—elbowed the two sleeping giants poured into the seats on either side. They merely squirmed and grunted at his prodding.

"Wake up, we're about to make our final approach. We'll be real Marines, real soon," Tuck urged. The sound of the word "Marine" filled his mind with thoughts of glory and his ears with the cadence of marching drums. He could almost taste the word, and it smelled of honor.

He wriggled in his cloth seat, growing hot from a long night's flight, to claim a better view of the rising land. The portal reflected a boyish face trimmed with sky-blue eyes that when he smiled nearly disappeared beneath a squint. Standing barely over 5 feet, 7 inches, Tuck looked like his mom—fair complected with soft brown curls that hung loose and tended to be unruly. His friends likened him and his temperament to that of a baby bull—stocky and trusting.

"Yeah, just think," Johnny Robert mumbled, slowly turning to look through a bleary eye out the starboard side of the Boeing 707. *"Mais*, yeah. Just think."

Johnny, a pale blond with a rich Cajun French patois that tended to make "this and that" sound like "dis and dat," struggled to sleep off a hangover. A farewell blitz in the New Orleans French Quarter had punished the unflappable ox with a churning stomach and a thick, dry tongue. His green eyes were yellowed and bloodshot.

"All I want to do right now is dream about them Bourbon Street gals," Johnny said with a Jack Daniels whisper and a grin. He twisted in his cramped seat.

Tuck turned and shook the shoulder of the man on his left near the aisle of Row 37R. "Donnie-Boy, wake up. Come on, man."

"I'm awake, how can anybody sleep with your fidgeting," Donnie-Boy replied, shrugging his shoulders to shake off a chill, "…always the fidgeting. Can't you ever keep still?" He, too, struggled to find comfort in a flight nearly four hours old. "I'm just trying to catch a few more Zs while I can. I gotta feeling we ain't gonna be sleeping much the next eight weeks."

Donald Charles Hebert—"Donnie-Boy" to Tuck—was someone to look up to, figuratively and literally. An athlete, he stood a solid 6 feet, 3 inches and weighed at least 220 pounds. Charismatic and called a natural leader, he was ruggedly handsome with high cheek bones and a thick nose set in a dark bronze complexion he'd inherited from his dad, a half-blooded Chitimacha Indian. He had earned all-state honors in football and baseball, but the state colleges had passed him by because he didn't hit the books like he could hit a curve ball.

Tuck and Donnie-Boy had grown up in the town of Eunice— "The Heart of Acadiana" as its 12,000 residents and one billboard boasted. Johnny hailed from nearby Mamou—even smaller and located some 10 miles north along Louisiana Highway 13. Both of these Eunice natives had met this giant for the first time only yesterday. He stood over Donnie-Boy by at least two inches and carried another 20 pounds of muscle.

Already 19—a year older than Tuck and Donnie-Boy—Johnny had used the early hours of the flight to relate the exploits of his one season of freshman football at LSU. A badly injured shoulder, suffered while tackling an Alabama halfback, had cut short his gridiron career, and his collegiate experience. And Johnny didn't hesitate to pull down his T-shirt to show the girls the seven-inch scar adorning his right shoulder. "Some day I'm gonna think of a tattoo that'll enhance its beauty, yeah. Maybe even with your name on it, *cher*," Johnny had told more than one girl the evening before.

A soft tone preceded the flashing "Fasten Seat Belt" light at the front of the coach section. "Please fasten your seat belts, we're now on our final approach into San Diego. The weather is clear and the temperature is 74 degrees. We hope you enjoyed your flight and that you'll fly United with us again," the stewardess purred into the hand-held intercom.

Donnie-Boy buckled up and flashed Tuck his customary smirk of a smile, the kind that hid the truth from most but never from Tuck. "I'd like to fly united with her."

"Ha. Ha," Tuck mocked succinctly. "You can do better than that. Just say you want to ball her or something." He didn't have to look. Tuck could feel Donnie-Boy's smile.

"Don't make me think about it," Johnny whispered through a raspy cough. "I think my head's gonna explode already, yeah."

The whine of the engines that had held their ears captive changed to a roar when they strained to slow the jet's approach into San Diego. The aisle dipped precipitously forward. A clunking sound announced the locking of the landing gear. They were about to become Marines.

•

9:35 p.m., San Diego: Bound for the Marine Corps

Recruit Depot (MCRD), the olive-green bus seemed to wander in circles. Tuck looked out the window, trying to get his bearings. He felt engulfed in the darkness, as did 30 other wide-eyed recruits nestled within. They sat like timid children.

Tuck's palms strangled the pitted metal bar atop the seat in front of him. It helped steady the lurching ride. His mind knew of neither the destination, nor what trials lay ahead. He only knew that the sergeant who had greeted them with bellowing at the airport 10 minutes ago had mastered nearly every dirty word Tuck had ever heard—and he wove them into sentences with gusto. It would take a case of Ivory to wash out that man's mouth.

Even the stalwart Donnie-Boy now fidgeted beside him. Tuck nudged his lifelong friend and nodded toward their new chum, slouched in the seat to the left. "Look at that." Johnny slept, either unfazed or simply too hung over. "Nothing seems to bother him," Tuck whispered. He looked around the bus and appraised the other recruits. "What a collection," he murmured, again feeling Donnie-Boy's smile in the darkness. It comforted him.

Tuck noticed a few colored guys, too. No trouble spotting them, their large hairdos silhouetted against the city lights that shone through the windows. What might they be thinking? He and Donnie-Boy had attended an all-white Catholic school and had lived in a largely segregated town. His experience with colored people was limited to the likes of Soco, the old maid who cleaned their home on Fridays; and Charlie, the hired hand's son on his uncle's farm.

Tuck had always known he would someday mix with other races. What lessons might he learn? He wondered if the word "colored" was still appropriate, or should it be Negro, or Afro-American, or black—the latter two becoming more the style on the television news.

The bus leaned to the right when the driver slowed and

turned left through the gates of the MCRD. Another 10 minutes had passed, according to Tuck's brand new Timex wristwatch, a gift from his mom on the day he left home. Its green face and white hands glowed in the dark.

The bus squeaked to a stop. The time had arrived.

CHAPTER 3

The Arrival
Marine Corps Recruit Depot, San Diego, Calif.
July 15, 1968—10 p.m. local time

The recruit depot—the West Coast version of its more infamous cousin at Parris Island, S.C.—lay sprawled over a 482-acre tract adjacent to the San Diego airport and the Navy's basic training center. Rows upon rows of Quonset huts and white stone buildings with red-tiled roofs stand as sentinels around a gigantic, asphalt parade ground. The recruits, who march about it for endless hours upon innumerable days, know it as "the grinder."

Since 1921, nearly 230,000 recruits had passed through the arching main gate leading to the MCRD's administrative complex. Seventy-five more recruits now joined that proud number.

"Ohhh, myyy God," Tuck whispered, combing his fingers through his curls and watching the barbers shear his friends. Donnie-Boy's straight black hair fell to his shoulders and then to the cluttered floor. A single drop of blood trickled past his left ear. His dark brown eyes stared widely ahead. He was not smiling.

Smoke spiraled slowly from the tip of a barber's hand-rolled cigarette and mixed with the smell of over-heated clippers. The scent filled the room with a stench that pinched the nose. Tuck hoped, that before he took his turn in the chair, the barber would flick the ashes from the cigarette that lolled from his lips. He did not. Unsmiling and with a full head of salt and pepper hair, the barber called out, "Next."

"That's you asshole," a wiry sergeant shouted from only inches away. "Get your fat ass on the chair, boot. And we don't have time for you to tell him how to cut it."

Tuck flinched, bolted toward the chair and sat down in it upright. He dared not budge.

Using clippers, damp with the sweat from the scalps of nervous recruits, the barber couldn't match the touch of ol' Mr. Fontenot back home. Tuck had to admit it, though—the guy was quick. In less than a minute but without a nick, his curls mixed with the heap of assorted blonds, reds and blacks on the tiled floor, a veritable salad bowl of shorn locks. He knew better than to pass his hand over his head while the wiry sergeant glared nearby. Feeling a breeze across his scalp, he assumed only stubble remained. His dream was rapidly becoming real.

Johnny sat next to Tuck. Having arrived with short hair, his coarse blond follicles had hardly added to the ankle-deep pile.

"What the hell are you looking at private? Get your ass off the chair and get outside with the rest of the maggots," the wiry sergeant again shouted, shoving Tuck toward the door. "You've been here 10 minutes and you're already pissing on my beloved Marine Corps."

The wiry sergeant—not much taller than Tuck—had a red face with neck veins that bulged like a chicken's toes. He had met the recruits when the bus arrived at the Depot and had been chewing them out ever since. Tuck found comfort that the sergeant had taken equally big bites out of just about everyone else's butts, including the big guys, Donnie-Boy and Johnny.

Standing near the end of the group outside the barbershop, Tuck searched the faces of glassy-eyed teen-agers. He did not recognize anyone from the bus. Amazing how a haircut equalizes people. "They'll break you down to a common denominator before they build you back up," Tuck remembered his recruiter's honest admission.

Tuck peeked at his watch. It would soon be midnight and he had not slept since 5 a.m. Johnny and Donnie-Boy had been the smart ones after all. He wished he had been so smart.

"OK, you sorry ass civilians, let's get you out of those civvies and into some utilities." The voice belonged to a taller, somewhat older sergeant with a less abrasive tone. He had been lurking in the shadows.

The two sergeants hustled the 75 recruits—now designated as Platoon 2080—into the white stucco Receiving Building where empty cardboard boxes waited on a series of gray tables in a room that smelled of fresh paint.

"OK, this is the drill," the tall sergeant bellowed, walking among the recruits. "Strip and put your clothes and valuables into the boxes, complete the mailing labels and form letter supplied and seal the contents. They, and all contraband, will be mailed home along with whatever short note you can write in the next 10 seconds." He slammed his hand on a table. "Do it!" The recruits, surprised by how the man's anger was breaking down their pride, responded quickly. Was this what they had signed up for? Though they had been warned, it was still a shock.

After an hour of processing and clothing issue, Platoon 2080 was ushered back into the darkness. Tuck and the neophytes could not yet march but the drill instructors seemed to not care less. "Run, you maggots," the wiry one shouted. "I don't have all night to waste on you collective mosquito turds. I've got poontang waiting for me in town."

Stumbling in the night with a sea bag slung over his shoulder, Tuck ran with the confounded herd for what seemed like hours. Glory was a concept already fading from his mind.

They passed endless rows of corrugated Quonset huts

that looked like half-buried drainage pipes. Tuck could only estimate it to be 2 a.m.—the sergeant had ordered him to mail his new watch home. Up ahead he saw three barracks, washed in a dim yellow glow from surrounding security lights. Seconds later, the sergeants halted the panting recruits in the shadow of one of the two-story structures.

"Stand up straight and quit breathing so damn hard. We've only begun to start working your pitiful little peckers into the dirt," the taller man said. He strutted around the formation with his hands clutched behind his back and looked almost too soft to be a drill instructor. "My name is Staff Sgt. Jim Thomas, and this is my Marine Corps you've broken in to, so don't screw with it and we'll get along just fine. I, and Sgt. Jerry Gaines here, will be your drill instructors for the next eight weeks," Sgt. Thomas said, pointing to Gaines, whose veins seemed to throb in his red neck.

Tuck watched the two men exchange glances and grins. "And, tomorrow you'll meet your platoon commander," Thomas said with a voice that seemed to forewarn of worse things to come.

On command, the recruits hustled into the brick barracks—clean, almost antiseptically clean—that was bracketed by windows so clear they appeared to have no panes.

"Now grab a rack, you pecker-heads," Thomas hollered, his voice echoing across the 100-foot long room. "In the next hour, you will need whatever sleep you can get."

The recruits filed quickly through the barracks and chose their "racks." Tuck and Donnie-Boy grabbed a bunk halfway down the center aisle. Johnny pushed away a challenger for a lower rack next to his friends.

Striding to the center of the barracks with clenched fists, Thomas shouted, "I am your drill instructor and will be addressed as 'The Drill Instructor' when you are referring to me. And, when answering me you will say 'sir, yes, sir' or 'sir, aye aye, sir.' You donkey turds are privates, not very worthwhile ones just yet, but you will still refer to yourselves as 'The Private' and not 'I' and I am definitely not a 'You.' A ewe is a female sheep and unless you want to stick it to me in the ass, you will not make the mistake of calling me a YOU. Understood?" Thomas spun on his heels so everyone in the barracks could hear the message. A healthy amount of "sir, yes, sirs" erupted, mixed with a handful of sheepish "yeahs," "OKs" and nods. Some of the recruits still refused to yield their civilian independence. That would soon change.

Thomas glared in the direction of the improper replies and started to shout, but caught himself. Tuck noticed a snarl forming on the right upper lip of the sergeant's mouth. "Tomorrow. Tomorrow you will learn. When the Gunny arrives...you will learn."

"Gunny? What the hell is a gunny?" Tuck whispered to Donnie-Boy, who only shrugged.

"OK, maggots," Thomas said. He turned to march toward the DI's office at the front of the barracks, "you've got five minutes to piss, shit or whatever and then get your asses to bed and to sleep—no jerking off. It's 0300. Reveille is at 0500, that's five o'clock for the titty-babies still on civilian time. Enjoy your sleep, ladies."

Tuck, after a quick trip to the head, which he learned was the term for bathroom, squirmed into his bunk and then probed the sagging mattress above. "Donnie-Boy, Donnie-Boy." There was no reply. There would be none.

Tuck closed his eyes, shielded them with his forearm from the glare of a security light, and ran his hand over the sandpaper that used to be his hair. "Oh, my God, Tuck, what have you gotten yourself into?" The cadence of marching drums was ebbing. And with sleep approaching, his mind drifted back to a spring day on the patio of his home in Eunice.

They stood beneath an old rain tree, its branches bent

and gnarled by too many climbing feet and dangling arms. "Dad, I guess I'll just spit it right out. I'm joining the Marines. I want to do my part. You did yours in Europe, now it's my turn," Tuck had proudly said with a tone of defiance. "You've always said you were never prouder than you were then—in Europe, I mean."

"OK," his dad slowly said. "That's a pretty tough outfit, Tuck, those Marines. You sure that's what you want? With Vietnam and all going on, you might give the Air Force a thought like Mark did."

"Yeah, Dad, I've given it a lot of thought. It's the Marines." Tuck felt better, having finally declared his decision and independence. His father's eyes had glowed with a mixture of admiration and fear.

Curtis Richard, a decorated World War II veteran, cautioned his eager son. "You know, it's not like playing war in the neighborhood. People get hurt in war. I know for a fact. Men do die, without glory. I've seen it." He paused to let the advice sink in. "And you know, Tuck, uh, I'm not sure how to say it. But, you're not doing it just because Donnie-Boy's joining up?"

Donnie-Boy had enlisted in the Corps two days earlier and too often Curtis had watched Tuck follow Donnie-Boy's lead. Having grown up as next-door neighbors, they were closer, perhaps, than brothers, Curtis knew. An only child, Donnie-Boy had practically adopted Curtis' five children as his own brothers and sister.

"No, that's not it," Tuck assured him. "Donnie-Boy rushed ahead just so he could say he'd done it first. But we're going in on the buddy plan. We'll still be together."

Tuck thrust his hands into the pockets of his jeans and looked down at the leaf-stained concrete. "I feel like I need to do something. I don't know. A lot of the guys say we're crazy. Some don't. But, after watching hippies protest on TV and head to Canada and all...well, somebody's got to do it, go over there, you know.

"And I know you—and what you're thinking. You're thinking, that I'm still just a kid and I need to grow up some more. Look, I'm not ready to go to college, Dad, even though I'll go this summer for mom."

Tuck paused and glanced over the backyard. The thick St. Augustine grass needed mowing again. Louisiana's subtropical climate could quickly turn a lawn into a suburban jungle. He thought about how he would miss the smell of freshly mowed grass. The backyard had also served as his and Donnie-Boy's base camp during their "playing army" days. Donnie-Boy, always the general, and Tuck, his faithful lieutenant, seldom lost a battle on those summer afternoons that often played out into the fringes of the night. He had always enjoyed victory in the lowering darkness, and he wondered what the real thing—battle—must be like.

"Dad, I want to help my country. I know that sounds corny and all. But, is there anything wrong with that? Really. You tell me," he asked, still craving the confirmation only his father could give.

"No, not at all, Tuck. Maybe a bit gung ho, but then again you're picking the right outfit for that attitude." His dad laughed and then wrapped his arm around Tuck's neck. "Come on, let's go inside and break the news to your mom. There's gonna be a fuss."

Walking back into the house, Tuck turned and saw the dread on his father's face and his eyes turning shiny. Tears filled Tuck's eyes that day, like they did on this first night.

CHAPTER 4

Gunny Hill
Marine Corps Recruit Depot, San Diego, Calif.
July 16, 1968—5 a.m. local time

Mornings arrive early at the MCRD. Reveille trumpets across the grinder at 0500, but smart Marines rise at 0445 to make their racks and attend to personal needs before the lights come on. Such wisdom, however, is lost on tenderfoot recruits with less than six hours in the Corps.

Tuck frowned when he heard there was not a real Marine playing reveille. Instead, a recording blared through a loudspeaker. Despite a mind still wanting for sleep, he could tell the difference. He also noticed a different voice booming across the barracks like a bull in a barrel. It lacked the flat Midwest tones of Sgt. Thomas, or the slight Southern twang of Sgt. Gaines.

"Is this what I get for all my toiling in the Marine Corps, a bunch of sleepy-eyed faggots scratching their balls with morning hard-ons," the voice boomed. "Well, kiss my emancipated ass. Get out of those sleep-soaked racks. NOW!"

Tuck scrambled to his feet, only seconds before Donnie-Boy crashed to the tiled floor and onto his back—quite unlike Donnie-Boy. Tuck strained to help him up.

"It's too damn early for any branch of the service," Johnny said, rolling out of his rack. "And whoever that emancipated ass is can kiss mine too, *cher.*"

"What's the matter with you, Paul Bunyan?" Tuck heard a voice growl and grow closer with the sharp click of each footfall echoing across the barracks. "Too damned early? Two hours sleep not enough for mama's little boy? Too damn bad, tomorrow night I'll make sure you get one hour, and I'll have MY emancipated black ass in your face for you to kiss when you wake up. Got it, asshole?"

The voice had grown a face and its wild, bulging eyes were staring down at Johnny's nose. Surely Johnny had never looked up to any man, or beast.

Tuck peeked to his left at Donnie-Boy, whose mouth hung slightly agape. His bronze complexion began to pale. In all of his life, Tuck never knew Donnie-Boy to fear any man.

But this was altogether new. Could it get any worse than this?

Gunnery Sgt. John "Gunny" Hill had just crashed into their lives. He leaned over and whispered into Johnny's face. "Well, are you gonna move it, or you're just gonna stand there and hope the next eight weeks blow past in the next eight seconds." After a frightful pause, he shrieked, "It's too early in the morning and too early in your career to start pissing me off like this. So keep your mouth shut, big wad, because I have too many other maggots in here to stomp on...What's your name, puke? I want to remember it so that when I'm feelin' like pickin' on someone close to my own size, I'll know who to look for."

"John R. Robert," Johnny replied with a slight smile. "But they call me T-Johnny."

Looking down at Johnny's nametag, Gunny Hill tried to mock Johnny's accent. "Well, well Pvt. Robert..."

"Not Robert like them Yankees say it," Johnny corrected with a smirk, interrupting Gunny Hill's retort with his flat, French accent that only a Cajun, or perhaps a Canadian, could produce. "It's said like this, ROH-bear"

"Robert?"

"No, ROH-bear."

Tuck closed his eyes and slowly shook his head. This was going to get ugly.

"Are you some kind of French queer or something?" Gunny Hill challenged.

"No, sir, a Cajun—you know, a coonass," Johnny said.

"A what?" the gunny hollered.

"A coonass, from south Louisiana. We're Acadians who traveled down from Nova Sc..."

Gunny Hill cocked his head. "I don't give a damn about your heritage. But what the hell does the 'T' stand for, Titty-baby?"

"No. It means 'little' in Cajun." Johnny flashed a smile Tuck had not seen since Bourbon Street. He guessed the sudden change in Johnny's demeanor from taciturn to gregarious might be a sort of defense mechanism.

The conversation abruptly ended with a loud slap to the left side of Johnny's face—a blow that drew snot from the nose of the unsuspecting recruit. "Shut the shit up," Gunny Hill hissed, his open hand now a balled fist.

Tuck could only figure that if one carried about 250 chiseled pounds on a 6-foot-6 frame, a person might get away with talking to Johnny Robert like that, not to mention slapping the snot out of him. Gunny Hill was, could and did.

Following Johnny's best "Sir, yes, sir," Gunny Hill did an about face and hunted his next victim. Johnny was left trying to figure out what had just happened.

"Man, I thought nothing would ever get to big Johnny," Donnie-Boy whispered.

"Any more COON-asses in here?" the platoon commander boomed.

"Sir, yes sir," Tuck shouted. The big man would soon find out anyway.

"And what's your name, half dick?"

"Sir, Benjamin Richard, sir."

"Well Pvt. Rich…no, wait." Gunny Hill looked down at the nametag. "Did I hear right? It's REE-shard? Is that right, REE-tard? I bet they call you T-turd, right?"

"Sir, yes sir, I mean, yes, but no sir. They call me Tuck." He grimaced at his clumsiness.

"And why may I ask—no, let me guess," Gunny Hill said. "You couldn't say 'tuck' when you were a little boy with no front teeth and that it always came out 'fuck,' like you couldn't 'fuck your shirt in' or your front tooth was 'fucked under your pillow' awaiting the fuckin' footh fairy who was probably a big faggot like T-Johnny. Right?"

"Why, yes sir, that's pretty much the way it was," Tuck admitted, wondering how the man knew the story behind his nickname.

"Of course it was, and I bet T-Johnny gave you that name, snot-lick."

"Well, no sir, actually another friend of mine gave me that name," Tuck said, unable to keep from looking at Donnie-Boy. Things just got worse.

"And, you," Gunny Hill said, turning to Donnie-Boy. "You looked pretty chummy with Mutt and Jeff here. What does mommy call you when she cuts your meat, scumbag?"

"Sir, Donald Hebert, sir."

"I ain't even gonna guess, I…"

"Sir, it's H-E-B-E-R-T, pronounced AY-bear, sir," Donnie-Boy interrupted.

"My God, what are they doing to my blessed Marine Corps? We got any Smiths, Browns or Washingtons in here? I'll even settle for a Jones? Well, I've had Cajuns before and I've stomped them just the same. But three of you at the same time may be a bit too damn much for me and my Marine Corps. We'll have to watch you three—coonasses," the gunny said, his voice trailing off, searching the barracks for more prey.

Johnny turned and looked at Tuck with glassy eyes and a snotty lip. "This place is gettin' serious, yeah."

From across the room, two black recruits tried to stifle laughs with fists to their mouths. Their snickering lingered a few seconds too long.

"And what in the living hell are you two Ubangi-lipped mothers looking at? Enjoyed watching the white boy get slapped around, huh? Do you think you're something special? You think you're my 'brothers' right? Think again you stupid pair of bug-eyed eight balls," Gunny Hill hollered, grabbing the men by their throats and driving them backward 20 feet into the wall of the barracks. Nearby recruits scattered, windows shook and the barracks itself trembled when Gunny Hill made his point. Dangling from his lobster-like grasps, Gunny Hill walked the gagging torsos back to the center of the barracks.

"Nobody, and I mean nobody, in here is different. You're all the same to me, you're all shit beans ready to be fried and dipped in worm piss. Marine recruits are not fit to lick the sweat off a snake's nuts, be it a white snake—or a black snake," he shouted, staring alternately into the teary eyes of the gasping pair.

"Yesssss zzzzzzir," came a hiss from one of the men. The other's eyes had already rolled back into his head. Suddenly both tumbled to the floor like the scarecrow in *The Wizard of Oz*.

Apparently, Gunny Hill knew when to let go. And, now, having watched the biggest guy he'd ever known humbled and two black guys throttled like rag dolls—Tuck wondered what would become of him should he ever cross Gunny Hill. He vowed not to.

"And wipe the snot off your face, Pvt. Robert," Gunny Hill shouted over his shoulder. He stormed out of the barracks. The door slammed behind Gunny Hill with a thud.

"We knew you'd just love your new platoon commander," Gaines said with a grin.

Tuck noticed something more. Gunny Hill had pronounced Johnny's last name correctly.

CHAPTER 5
The Letter
Eunice, La.
July 20, 1968—9 a.m. local time

Curtis Richard ambled to the end of the driveway of his suburban home. The grass needed trimming—but not today. His leg ached a bit more than most days, and he limped more noticeably than usual. Though some 25 years had passed since a 20-millimeter slug had bitten an inch from his left thigh, twinges lingered. On this bright morning, however, Curtis focused on neither the limp nor the pain. He even ignored the summer heat and sweat beading on his brow despite the short walk.

Having bid Tuck farewell more than a week ago, he and Mary had received a package containing Tuck's clothes and watch, along with a three-line note indicating he had "arrived safely, am in good hands, will write soon." Curtis smiled at Tuck being "in good hands."

Curtis was eager to read some real news from the second of his four sons. Mark, the eldest, was an Air Force captain serving in Korea; Dave, his third son, was a junior in high school; and Winston—named for Curtis' admiration of Winston Churchill—neared his sixth birthday.

A car accident a few years earlier had taken the life of Brenda, his oldest child. Tuck's two-year enlistment, virtually guaranteeing a trip to Vietnam, gnawed at their wounded hearts.

Curtis opened the mailbox and found two envelopes. The telltale red and blue border of an Air Mail envelope indicated one hailed from Seoul. The other was a small, light blue envelope emblazoned with a gray image overlay on the left side. It depicted World War II-era Marines raising the American flag over Mount Surabachi on Iwo Jima.

Curtis shouted and waved the letters overhead. "Mary, Mary, a letter from Tuck. And Mark, too." He strutted now, the limp hardly noticeable. He picked up the pace toward the carport. "I told you we'd get a letter from Tuck today."

Mary emerged suddenly from the doorway and snatched both envelopes from his hand.

"Hey, give me those back," Curtis said. He wrapped his arms around Mary, teasingly trying to wrest the letters from her. He stole a kiss.

"Here, you read Mark's first." She shoved her eldest son's letter into Curtis' chest. They entered the house and the welcome cool of the air conditioning. Mary sat at the kitchen table and slashed at the envelope with her long nails, nearly tearing it in half. Tears immediately welled in her eyes when she began reading Benjamin's letter.

"Something wrong, Babe?" Curtis asked, reading Mark's letter. "Tuck didn't get himself kicked out already, huh?... That damned Donnie-boy."

"Oh, don't be so foolish," Mary fussed before shuffling the two-page letter. "Of course he didn't. It's just that, well, he's still my—oh, never mind. And don't call Benjamin THAT name around me. You know I don't like how he got that name."

Her smile faded with a sigh. "Here," Mary said curtly, "Read YOUR son's letter."

Curtis grabbed the letter with a good idea of what had caused her sudden turn of emotions. He rifled through it to the last page. It was signed—*Your loving son, TUCK.*

Hanging on every word, Curtis read:

Dear Mom, Dad, Dave and Winston,

As my first short note said, we got here late in the evening of July

15 and haven't stopped yet. I don't know if joining this thing was such a good idea. It's tough and is gonna get tougher.

Our drill instructors are all mean as hell but seem to be fair if you do what's told, and do it right—and fast. But that's hard to do.

They put me on a diet even though I told them I was at my playing weight. But, that didn't go over too good and I know I must have done a couple of hundred push-ups for that wisecrack. I hope my big mouth doesn't get me into too much trouble like it always did back in school. There are no class clowns here.

Donnie-Boy is doing OK and is already advanced to platoon guide, the lead position. As always, he does just about everything right and is a favorite, if you can call him that, of the DIs.

Dad, Donnie-boy and me met a big guy from Mamou who played freshman football at LSU before getting hurt. His name is Johnny Robert. Y'all might look up his dad. His name is Wilfred. He and an uncle Alcide own an old appliance and repair store or something like that.

Mom, I'm learning to make a bed real good and learning how to mop a floor. Maybe I'll be a bigger help around the house. That's all for now, but the letters will be coming regularly since that's all I got to do with my free time, the little time I got. All I ask is that you pray for me and keep those letters coming. Your loving son, Tuck

CHAPTER 6

Birds and Brotherhood
**Marine Corps Recruit Depot, San Diego, Calif.
Aug. 15, 1968—5 a.m. local time**

Platoon 2080's progress through Phase I of boot camp was in step with most first-month platoons and showed a modicum of resemblance to a Marine Corps unit. They had begun to march and drill as one and perform ably the simplest of military tasks.

Regular physical training made Tuck realize how physically weak he had been. Four pull-ups had become 11 and 25 push-ups had grown to 75. Despite better conditioning and loss of 10 pounds on the strict "hogs" diet, his muscles ached. If exercise had not yet found a place to leave sore, then the jabbing of needles and peppering of pneumatic guns had.

Tuck, who'd learned to rise before reveille sounded, was dressed and lying atop his rack awaiting the scratchy reveille recording. He slipped into the nether land between consciousness and deep sleep—oblivious to what the day harbored. Just when the bugle's first notes reached his ears, so did the familiar voice. It rang out and the barracks lights blinked to life.

"Get up, girlies. You don't want to miss the little jaunt we've got planned today," Gunny Hill sang out. He'd taken his turn "baby-sitting" the platoon for the past two nights. "Now get your cheese dicks outside and form up."

Seventy-five pairs of boots hit the floor in unison. Pausing for a last-second tightening of bunks, they dashed outside where the California cool greeted them. Making sure not to tread upon the immaculate lawn—little more than cleansed, raked and cleansed again dirt—the recruits formed four straight columns on the sidewalk and waited at attention with the platoon guide, Donnie-Boy, at the front.

Gunny Hill, meanwhile, made a walk-through inspection of the barracks and soon exited towing a rumpled sheet and blanket. He dropped it to the ground.

"Where's that little Cajun turd we got out here? Richard?"

"Sir, here, sir," Tuck shouted, fear gripping him. Was that his bedding lying on the ground?

"You're my new housemouse," Gunny Hill ordered. "Just make sure you 'tuck' in my sheets when you make up my rack.

"Roper, you're fired as housemouse," the gunny said, pointing at the heap of rumpled linens. "You can't make up your own rack; you can't make up mine. Get down and give me 50.

"Friar Tuck, you join Brown and Larsen on the house crew."

A housemouse's duty, maintaining the drill instructors' quarters, was a double-edged sword, Tuck would learn. A housemouse benefited in the long run, usually a promotion to Private First Class at graduation. But he's always under the DI's thumb.

"Not bad, ladies. I almost saw a hint of unity here—about damned time, too." He saluted them with soft applause. "Are you hungry?"

"Sir, yes, sir," the collective reply snapped back.

Gunny Hill marched 2080 a short distance to the mess hall, where it stood at ease while another platoon worked its way, one deliberate step at a time, into the mess hall. With the red sun starting to rise, dozens of mourning doves darted about and pecked at the ground. A pair of the grayish-brown game birds wandered within inches of Tuck's boots and he flashed a smile toward Donnie-Boy. Like telepathy, Donnie-

Boy twisted around, saw the birds, looked up and returned that knowing smile.

The day was starting out well and Tuck recalled their many fall weekends of dove hunting. "Back home, those would be some dead birds right now," Tuck whispered. He felt one of the birds brush the cuff of his trousers. "I've never been this close to live ones. I can taste mama's dove gumbo."

Suddenly, a whack to the back of Tuck's head sent his cap falling over his face.

"Why are you talking in my chow line, asshole?" shouted Gaines, who had slipped up behind Tuck unseen—DIs were good at that. "You want to kill those birds? Go ahead. I don't care if you do, at least you'd know how to kill something."

"Sir, no, sir." The day's start took a sudden turn for the worse.

Gaines turned, grabbed Tuck's cover from his face and then flung it upon one of the doves. He stomped the bird with a squish that sounded like a naked fart.

"And, I guess you would want to eat them, too?" Gaines shouted.

"Sir, no, sir." Tuck's mind reeled. He knew he was in for a world of shit.

Gaines retrieved the quivering bird. "Well, tough shit, numb nuts, open up," he ordered, preparing to shove the dove into Tuck's mouth. "I SAID. 'Open up.'"

Tuck shut his eyes tightly and opened wide. He reluctantly obeyed the direct order. His cheeks flushed with embarrassment.

"Stick out your tongue, bird brain, so you'll get a good taste." Gaines shoved the dove head first into Tuck's mouth. Only the feet and tail feathers protruded.

"Now, CHEW," Gaines ordered, his nose nearly touching Tuck's left ear. "Because that's all the chow you're going to get this morning."

Chewing the bird proved to be a challenge. Tuck gagged on the blood and feathers. His stomach revolted and nausea swept over him when the nerves of the bird shuddered one last time. Blood splattered across his cheek. He began to choke, and cough feathers.

"OK, that's enough. I think he's learned his lesson. He won't be messing with the birds no more, none of these guys will," Gunny Hill said, pointing with his thumb toward the recruits. "Private Richard, get that damn bird out your mouth and get in the chow line for some juice or something." Gunny Hill waved him toward the mess hall.

Tuck tossed the remains into a waste bin when he walked toward the double doors. Nausea, however, overwhelmed him and he spewed blood, feathers and the remnants of last night's stew onto the manicured lawn at just the moment Thomas joined the platoon.

"Gaines, you been dove hunting again?" Thomas said. He shook his head and looked into the waste bin. The carcass was headless.

Gaines smiled and shrugged as if it was just another day on the job.

•

By 1100 hours, and after a morning of ushering 2080 through history and protocol classes, the drill instructors prepared a fitness test.

The recruits stood at parade rest outside the barracks. "We're going for a little run, sweethearts. Today it will be with full web belts, including canteen with water and slung M-14s. We're going to find out who can cut it, who can't and how well you assholes work together," Gunny Hill advised. "So get inside and get your gear on. We're going for a stroll."

Tuck, his stomach still queasy, hurried into the barracks and gathered his gear and M-14. This was his chance to prove his worthiness.

"Hey Tuck, how you feelin', man?" Johnny asked,

joining him at the rifle rack. "That was a shitty thing to do, what Gaines did."

Tuck did not reply, his mind was focused on the run.

The big guy put his hand on Tuck's shoulder. "You OK? You don't look too good, *non.*"

"I'll be OK, just leave me alone right now," Tuck mumbled. He pushed Johnny's hand away and then headed to the door.

"How is he, Johnny?" Donnie-Boy said. Tuck passed him without a word or a glance.

"I don't know, Donnie-Boy, I think we're gonna need to watch him today. He didn't eat no breakfast...'cept that bird."

•

The 10-foot wide path meandered for nearly three miles along two-thirds of the back perimeter of the Depot. Its surface glowed in the sun like a Gulf Coast beach with just enough sand to make the footing soft and unstable. Failure was a turned ankle away.

Undulating past the confidence course, the trail skirted the fence of the San Diego airport. Tuck saw the airfield as one of distant hope. Once his portal to the Corps, it now looked like an escape route. Only a high, chain-link fence separated him from the "freedom birds."

Each day he watched the big four-engine jets lift off, their destinations unknown, only imagined. Soon, he'd read, the new and bigger Boeing 747s would be in service. He hoped to catch a glimpse of one some day, or perhaps ride one home in the fall.

Today, Tuck ignored the jets' gleaming skins, their thundering echoes and the scent of fuel trailing from their exhausts. He had a mission—conquer this conditioning run. He had lost weight and his endurance had improved beyond his expectations. His confidence soared despite the morning incident and the tickling he felt with each deep breath. Damn feathers.

Donnie-Boy strode just ahead of the platoon's four columns, carrying its banner and staff across his chest. Johnny led the fourth squad, running in the right, outermost column. Tuck trailed Johnny in the seventh row.

With their 11-pound rifles slung over their right shoulders, the run began without a hitch. Only the heavy canteen's monotonous slapping at his left hip distracted Tuck. It was a snap.

Sgt. Gaines ran just to the right of and behind Tuck. So close, he could feel Gaines' shit-eating grin. Sgt. Thomas led the platoon, just ahead of Donnie-Boy—2080 had never before run this route. Gunny Hill, decked out in a white T-shirt swollen at the sleeves and chest, trailed the formation by 50 yards.

A mile and a half into the run—PING! The metal hinge fastening the sling to the top of the M-14's wooden stock snapped. The rifle spun backward off Tuck's shoulder like a wayward baton. The flash suppressor at the end of the 44-inch rifle struck the trail with a thud, kicking up a spray of sand and gravel.

Tuck snatched the flapping sling and yanked, not accounting for the rifle's momentum. It somersaulted upward and the barrel struck him across the face and above his right eyebrow. Blood spurted from his brow and ran down his cheek. The pain momentarily paralyzed him.

Tuck battled to keep pace, but as fast as he recovered, Gaines attacked.

"Pvt. Richard, how dare you drop my Marine Corps rifle, you puke," Gaines shouted. "We didn't give you that weapon to draw lines in the sand. We gave it to you to cross lines in the sand, asshole. And, what's this, blood on my Marine Corps rifle? Who gave you permission to hit my Marine Corps rifle with your ugly puss? Who told you that you could bleed?"

Tuck frantically tried to repair the sling. The hinge pin, perhaps repaired in the past, had worn loose from the wooden stock and would not fit tightly. He gasped, feeling a wave of panic wash over him.

"If you can't fix it, then carry the bitch," Gaines hollered from inches away. He grabbed at the sling to examine it. Both men continued to run, barely breaking stride.

Blood and a ballooning eyelid impaired Tuck's vision. His heart pounded. Confusion set in. He needed more air.

Gaines, cursing while trying to repair the sling on the run, threw the loose end at Tuck. It struck him across the bridge of the nose before falling and becoming entangled between his thighs. As if hog-tied by a champion cowboy, he stumbled. The rifle slammed into the ground and then caught between his shins. He collapsed onto the trail. He wanted to cry, but didn't.

The private running just ahead looked back in time to maintain his balance—but not before his boot kicked Tuck's forehead. Anthony Williams, a lanky recruit trailing one row back, hurdled Tuck. But when he landed, his boot forced a cloud of dust into Tuck's face.

"What now private bird-eater, laying down on the run? Get your ass, make that your coon-ass up, and get back in formation. We can't wait on your sorry cooooon-ass. Aaaaagh, and what's this? My Marine Corps rifle. It's filthy. You asshole. How dare you treat my Marine Corps rifle like this…"

Donnie-Boy and Johnny, not fully aware of Tuck's dilemma, heard Gaines' fussing but didn't dare turn around. They ran on, waited and listened to the ranting. But the shouts continued and Gaines' voice grew distant.

"I'm going back for him," Donnie-Boy said to Johnny, breaking ranks and handing him the platoon standard. He then sprinted to the rear. Johnny shook his head, looked to the heavens, handed the standard to the leader of third squad and then turned to join Donnie-Boy.

"What the hell..." Sgt. Thomas groaned, looking back. "Where are you cheese dicks going, get back..."

They arrived after Tuck had stumbled for a second time and was crouched on his hands and knees. He still gripped his rifle, nearly buried in the sand. Donnie Boy wrapped his arms around Tuck's waist while Johnny grabbed Tuck's right armpit with his huge left hand.

"Let's go, man, run best you can," Donnie-Boy whispered. "Suck it up. It's the fourth quarter." Tuck looked up at Donnie-Boy, who then saw the bloody gash across his brow and the scrapes to his nose and forehead. Donnie-Boy shook his head. "Aw shit, Tuck."

Stunned, Tuck finally dropped his rifle to the sandy trail and gasped. "It's OK. It's OK." His wound had stopped bleeding but his bludgeoned eye was fully shut. "Get my rifle, OK?"

"And what do you two assholes think you're doing?" Gaines hollered. "Drop that worthless piece of crap and get back in formation." He motioned toward the platoon, making its last turn for home only a half-mile away.

"Sir, no, sir," Donnie-Boy replied with a cold and dark-eyed stare. "The private can't leave his buddy, sir."

"That goes for me, too, sir," Johnny shouted.

"Who in the hell are you two? Mounties or something? Drop him and haul ass..."

"That's enough, Sgt. Gaines, they got the message," Gunny Hill, who had been observing, ordered. "You two privates get your man back to the barracks."

They trotted away with Tuck supported on either side. Cajun bookends.

"Let's go, Gaines, we've got a busy night ahead," Gunny Hill said, pausing to watch the trio turn for home. "Oh, yeah, and pick up that rifle and see if you can fix it. You know, I'm gonna have to punish those guys for breaking ranks. But I've got to admit, those Cajuns stick together. Jerry, you need to learn that's what a lot of this training is about. I like those guys."

"Aaaa, screw 'em," Gaines said, leaning over to retrieve the rifle.

Sandy-faced and bloodied, Tuck had caught his breath and recaptured his bearing when Gaines and Gunny Hill arrived.

"Privates ROH-bear and AY-bear, front and center," Gunny Hill bellowed with exaggerated emphasis. "Next time you fail to obey an order and choose instead to help a fellow recruit in need, it's going to really get bad. Now get down and give me one push-up each." The big man flashed his first genuine smile after a month of training. "Pvt. Richard, get in the head and clean up that ugly mug of yours. And, don't forget about this." He pointed to the broken rifle in Gaines' hands. "Come by my quarters to get it after you stop bleeding."

Standing in front of the mirror, Tuck saw that the gash was again oozing blood down his cheek. He braced himself on the sink with his left hand and forced several handfuls of water over his face and brow. He knew his washing had best not leave a trace of dirt or a drop of blood on the sink. He closely examined the wounds, none appeared deep enough to require stitches and hoped they wouldn't leave scars. He nearly panicked, however, when he saw for the first time a large tear in the right knee of his utility trousers.

"Oh, man, I can hear it now. That skinny asshole Gaines will be all over my ass, 'My God, scumbucket, what's the matter with your trousers?'" Tuck mumbled while leaning over to examine his trouser leg. "'Did you make a hole in my Marine Corps trousers while praying too hard that mama will come take you away,' or some bullshit like that."

"What is that you said, private? Did I give you permission to talk in my head, asshole," said Thomas, who had slipped in behind Tuck to use the urinal.

"Sir, nothing—I mean, sir, no, sir. Just telling myself what a skinny asshole I'll be when I become a proud member of the Marine Crops, sir," Tuck rattled off, hoping his lie worked.

"Yeah, right, asshole. You've stopped bleeding, get out of here," Thomas ordered with a jerk of his thumb.

"Sir, aye aye, sir." He then turned and sighed. It worked.

Tuck exited when the remainder of the platoon was filing into the barracks. He proceeded to the DIs' quarters, as ordered, and prepared to bang on the frame of the door when he heard a loud clanking noise inside. Was that his rifle?

"Damn it, the mother just won't stay in the damn hole," Gaines swore. He picked up Tuck's rifle. "It's all worn out like a whore on Sunday morning. That's three times the son-of-a-bitch has come out on me. It can't be fixed."

"Well, how about trying to fix it while running in formation?" Gunny Hill sarcastically replied. "Now, go down to the armory and get Pvt. Richard a goddamn M-14 that won't goddamn fall apart on him. OK?"

"Yeah, I'll get it first thing in the morning."

"No, go now, he's going to have to clean it up before lights out."

"OK, Gunny." Gaines turned and opened the door, nearly running over Tuck. "Out of my way, asshole, I'm going to get you another of my precious Marine Corps rifles, and you had better not...My God, scumbucket, what's the matter with your trousers? Did you make a hole in my Marine..."

"Gaines, get going," Gunny Hill again admonished his underling with a pained expression. "We ain't got time. OK?"

The gunny then turned to Tuck. "Pvt. Richard get in here and get those other two housemouses Brown and Larsen in here, too. I want these quarters cleaned up immediately."

Cleaning a DI's quarters was like mowing the green on a golf course. It was already clean. It just needed touching up.

After completing his chores, Tuck returned to his bunk and found Donnie-Boy and Johnny sitting on the floor, studying their Marine handbooks. Tomorrow they would leave for a two-week stint at the rifle range, and another chance for him to prove himself.

"You know, guys, I really don't know where to start," Tuck said, fumbling over the words. "To thank you for this afternoon, if I ever get the chance to repay you…"

"Pvt. Richard, report to my hut on the double," Gaines shrieked.

Tuck looked toward the door of the DI's hut and saw the beady-eyed sergeant standing with his new rifle in hand. He ran to meet him.

"Repeat after me and remember this serial number, not every slime-dick recruit gets a second weapon."

"Sir, yes, sir." He geared up his mind for the seven-digit test.

"OK, remember this number, 1-2…Aw, for Jesus' sake," Gaines whined. "I can't believe it. Just maybe your day's luck is changing after all, Pvt. REE-shard."

"Look at this number, Gunny," Gaines sighed. "Just look at this lucky ass number."

Gunny Hill looked, chortled, shook his head and puttered away to the latrine with the current issue of *Stars and Stripes* rolled up in his hand.

"OK, asshole, don't break any brain cells remembering 1-2-3-4-5-6-7. Asshole."

"Sir, yes, sir. 1-2-3-4-5-6-7, sir," Tuck replied and then smartly slapped the weapon from Gaines' grasp. He dared not smile.

Before locking the rifle in its stand, Tuck inspected it for dirt and grime. His luck seemed to be holding. He found it immaculate. Had the armory kept their rifles in that good of a condition in storage? Surely not. His first M-14 was full of grit and grease. Had Gaines taken the time? No, Gaines couldn't have been that human. Or? He dared to smile.

Tuck returned to his cohorts. "Like I was saying, thanks for the lift. I couldn't have..."

Again, Gunny Hill's bellow resonated across the barracks.

"Listen up, ladies, tomorrow we'll be heading up to Camp Pendleton for qualifying at Edson Range. It's not going to be an easy two weeks. Mostly snapping in, or dry-fire practice for those of you who hadn't studied yet, live-fire qualifying and a lot of PT. That's right, and you thought today's run was fun," Gunny Hill said, glancing toward Tuck and his buddies. "Just wait. There's nothing much else to do over there when you're not on the range. So get to sleep early tonight, you're gonna need your rest...Lights out in five minutes."

Tuck couldn't let it go. Feeling like he had let 2080 down, he had to tell Gunny Hill something. Just his walking to the hut required guts. Tuck pounded on the frame of the door.

"Who's that I hear tapping at my door?" Gunny Hill hollered from his rack.

Tuck rapped even harder. "Sir, it's Pvt. Richard, sir."

"Enter. And it had better be worth it."

"Sir." Tuck paused, suddenly at a loss for words.

"Yes, what is it, private?" Gunny Hill sighed deeply and then rolled over, his back now facing Tuck and his feet hanging over the end of the cot.

"Sir, I...sir, the private could have made it, sir. The run I mean, I, I, uh, the private had the courage, the stamina, he could have completed the run, that's all, sir." Tuck's voice trailed off. The ensuing pause seemed like a lifetime.

Gunny Hill opened his eyes and stared at the wall inches away. "I know, son—I know," he softly replied.

Tuck silently slipped away.

CHAPTER 7

News from Home
Edson Range, Camp Pendleton, Calif.
Aug. 22, 1968—10:30 p.m. local time

Johnny sat on the floor slumped against his rack, clutching a letter as if it might contain his own obituary notice. His eyes were glazed.

The light inside the Edson Range barracks was diffuse compared to the florescence flooding their cavernous quarters back at the MCRD. Hanging incandescent lights cast odd shadows across the long room of bunks. Tuck did not see the tears in Johnny's eyes. Yet, he sensed something amiss. Mail call, the most anticipated time of a recruit's day, turned solemn.

"Nonc Alcide est morte," Johnny mumbled.

"What's that?" Tuck replied, sitting near his Mamou friend and opening a letter postmarked South Korea. "I didn't understand you, big buddy."

"I said...I said my Uncle Alcide is dead. He died three days ago of a heart attack at the shop. Daddy said he died in his arms." A single large tear rolled out of Johnny's left eye. "According to this, they buried him today. Daddy said he tried to call me, but...but since Bub wasn't exactly immediate family, they told him it was against policy. He was like a second daddy, you know."

His friend's pain touched him. He nodded and placed his hand on Johnny's knee.

"What are you two so quiet about?" Donnie-Boy asked. He sat beside them. "Y'all look as if somebody died or something. Y'all can't be that tired." Their eyes shot stares that could have hit a bull's eye on his chest from a mile away. "What? I say something wrong? What gives?"

"Johnny's Uncle Alcide died this past week of a heart attack."

"Oh. Tough break, man. Losing your uncle's gotta be hard. At least it wasn't your daddy," Donnie-Boy said without looking at the pair. "I know all about that."

Clenching the letter in his left fist, Johnny wiped away the tears before the approaching Gunny Hill could see his face. The platoon had arrived at the rifle range a week before, but all the recruits had done was physical training, dry fire, study course safety and more PT.

"Fifteen more minutes of free time to read those letters sweethearts, then it's lights out. We've got a big day tomorrow, so no chokin' the chickens tonight. First day of live fire, I don't want no sleepy-eyed maggots puttin' new holes in my ear. Puttin' some in Sgt. Gaines' ass I could understand… " The recruits laughed and elbowed one another. Gunny Hill was easily becoming their favorite.

Johnny straightened up, threw his head back and let out a deep sigh that sagged his shoulders. Tuck and Donnie-Boy waited.

"*Nonc Alcide*, everybody just called him Bub, and my Daddy, Wilfred, are not many years apart. They married the Berzas sisters, Julie and Joan. They was only two years apart and inseparable, too, just like Bub and Daddy—or maybe you two, even," Johnny explained, pointing to Tuck and Donnie-Boy. "Bub was older and married the older Julie. So, Daddy got to marry my Mama, Joan. There was a much younger sister, too, Marie, and later she married a Carlisle. Anyway, they tell me them gals was fine, too."

They exchanged grins. This might be another of Johnny's preposterous stories—like versions of his football exploits.

Taking a deep breath, Johnny continued. "When I

was seven years old, Mama and Aunt Julie left Mamou to go shopping in Alexandria. It was around Easter, I can just remember, and they wanted some new clothes and stuff. But before they could get five miles up the road, a pickup truck ran a stop sign and hit 'em. Aunt Julie was dead in the car, and my Mama, she was driving, died just after they got her to the hospital. Both their necks was broke, I found out years later. They wouldn't tell me no facts before I got to high school.

"I cried for Mama and Aunt Julie. But I stopped hurting a lot sooner than Bub and Wilfred did. Those two must have cried for weeks. I suspect they still cried some. I'm sure Daddy's crying today." Johnny dabbed his eyes with his T-shirt. "Anyhow, Bub and Julie didn't have no kids, and since Bub and Daddy already worked together at the repair shop, well, Bub just moved in with us. We live next door to the shop.

"They didn't never remarry. Just us lived together for 13 years. Bub's the one who taught me to play football so good. He was big like me. Daddy's big too, but not like ol' Bub. You know, Bub played football at LSU in the '40s—just like me before I tore up that shoulder.

"Ol' Bub, he was a heck of an uncle, just like a daddy. He was only 51. Now if y'all don't mind, I need to be alone now. Got to write me a quick letter to Daddy, you know."

Tuck patted Johnny on his "tore-up" shoulder. Donnie-Boy ruffled the growing fuzz on Johnny's head. The pair hopped into their racks and settled in. Tuck heard sobbing in the bunk below.

CHAPTER 8

Something in Common
Mamou, La.
Aug. 28, 1968—9 a.m. local time

The drive from Eunice to Mamou is an easy 10 miles north along Louisiana Highway 13. Tawny rice and soybean fields, grazing cattle—chiefly red and white Herefords and silver-gray, humped Brahmans—and rich oil fields filled with tirelessly nodding pumps dot the flanks of the straight road that breezes through the northern portion of the south Louisiana prairie. Less than 10 miles north of Mamou the "piney woods" begin to take over where the prairie gives way to the heavily forested lands of central and north Louisiana.

But it is the prairie, the flat agricultural land whose horizons end abruptly at tree lines snaking along the banks of numerous bayous, that make up most of what is known as Acadiana.

A gentle S-curve to the right signaled Curtis' arrival to Mamou, a town of about 2,500 that boasts of its raucous Courir de Mardi Gras—a celebration the Catholic-dominated region eagerly awaits before it enters the Lenten season.

Unlike the drunken revelers who beg for beads and trinkets from float riders in the New Orleans French Quarter, drunken revelers on horseback in Acadiana celebrate Mardi Gras by begging from farm to farm for chickens and rice for their evening gumbo—a dark Cajun soup.

Though a bright bluebird day, Curtis Richard knew from Tuck's letter this trip would not be a pleasure visit. He had reluctantly agreed—at Mary's insistence—to visit Wilfred

Robert, who had just lost his brother, Alcide. Numerous attempts to reach him by phone had resulted in a persistent busy signal.

Robert's Appliance and Repair Shop stood out on the right side of La. 13 only a half-mile into Mamou. It was a gray-brick building 50-feet wide with a flat roof. Two picture windows flanked either side of the single-door entrance where a black and red "CLOSED" sign hung crookedly from an unseen hook. The tires crunched in the gravel when Curtis pulled his tan, '63 Chevy Impala into the small, empty parking lot.

"Oh, crap," Curtis muttered, seeing the sign—he was either too early or the shop was still closed because of Alcide's death. Curtis waited 10 minutes and passed the time by reading Bud Montet's sports column on LSU football in the *Baton Rouge Morning Advocate*. Curtis also checked off a mental note to mail a copy of the Tigers football schedule to Tuck, whose latest letter lay folded on the seat nearby. He looked at his watch. He had time to review it.

Dear Mom and Dad,

We've been at the rifle range almost two weeks now and tomorrow is qualifying day. I've been shooting real good. Dad, you taught me well with a shotgun and that old .22 single shot. Gunny Hill says I'm among the top three in the class. Big Donnie-Boy and Johnny Robert have been having some problems hunkering down in their stances. They'll shoot good, I'm sure.

I have enjoyed the rifle range and will not like going back to San Diego in a few days. Here, the PT (that's physical training, Mom) is going well. I'm in the best shape of my life. I must be down below 160 and can run for miles and miles without getting pooped. The other day Sgt. Gaines had us in a group pressing huge wooden logs. He said it was to teach us group unity. But I think he's just an ass (sorry Mom) and wanted to punish us for something silly we did. Sgt. Gaines is a thorn in my side. Heck, he's more like a boot in my butt. Maybe he's a better guy when he's not a DI, but I'll probably never know.

Sgt. Thomas is almost as mean as Sgt. Gaines, but he's fairer. Sometimes he looks like he's tired and not happy, but it's hard to tell. Gunny Hill is without a doubt the best colored man I've ever met. Any man maybe. Not only is he huge and powerful but also he's got one loud voice. Sure, he'll slap you around if you mess up. But he doesn't get in your face unless it's real important and he thinks it will save your life or something. And he never hits someone or grabs them unless they deserve it. He lets Sgt. Gaines do most of the harassing.

Mom, I've been getting all your letters regularly. Keep it up. I heard from Mark last week, he says it's already getting cold in those Korean mountains and he's getting lonesome.

Also, please ask my friends from school not to quit writing. I know a lot of them don't like the military, but we're still friends, I hope.

Oh, before I go. Johnny got some sad news the other day. His Uncle Alcide died at Johnny's daddy's shop of a heart attack. Johnny was really down and says his daddy, Wilfred, is all alone. Dad, maybe you could go over and visit Mr. Robert. I'm sure y'all could talk about the Tigers. Doesn't the season start next week? Do they open with Texas A&M or Rice, I forget? Let me know. Gotta go now, it's almost lights out and Sgt. Gaines is on duty. Remember me in your prayers—only about two weeks to go—Your loving son, Tuck

Curtis pulled out his pocket comb and smoothed his curly black hair, which was starting to gray at the temples. He got out of his Impala to stretch his legs, particularly the left one. It ached more than normal and a short walk might do it well.

Strolling around the right side of the building, he saw a large white-frame house with a black-shingled roof set back about 20 yards. Rows of dark green azaleas bordered the property along both sides. Weeds and tall grass choked the neglected lawn. A blue Ford pickup truck sat idly in the side garage on the right side of the house.

Maybe there would be someone home who could tell him if the shop would open today. Curtis limped along the short sidewalk toward the house. Walking up the three steps of the front porch caused him to wince. He tapped on the door with the brass knocker and noticed a half dozen letters bulging from the mailbox on the wall. Several more envelopes, dampened by the morning dew, had fallen onto the porch.

Curtis heard movement inside the house, but no one answered. He knocked again—still no answer. Oh, well. I'll tell Mary I tried, Curtis thought. Maybe I'll come back later. He shrugged and headed back down the sidewalk.

"Hey, what you want?" a thick Cajun voice yelled from the door. "If you're sellin' something, go away. And don't come back, *non*." The voice came from a burly man standing behind the black screen door of the entrance.

"Excuse me. No, I'm not," Curtis called back. "I'm just trying to find out if the store here is going to open today."

"No, it's not. So just go on away."

"Well, do you know when it might?" Curtis tried again.

"What the heck is it to you? You need somethin' fixed? Go on down to Fontenot's repair place on down the road on the left."

"Hey, I hate to bother you, but…"

"Well, then don't," warned the man, who Curtis noted was twice his size and younger.

He looked to see if the way to the car was clear, then shouted, "My name is Curtis Richard and I live in Eunice. My son is in the Marines with a Robert kid and I'm looking for his dad, Wilfred. Can you help?"

The man stood silent for several seconds. He rubbed his chin and stared absently at Curtis.

"The store'll be open Monday at 7:30. You can come back then…" the man said, his voice trailing off before picking up again. "Oh, hell, I'm Wilfred. Shit, come on in,

I'll get you a cup of coffee." Wilfred Robert slowly opened the screen door.

Curtis warily approached the porch and noticed a week's worth of whiskers on Wilfred's face and a shock of unkempt salt and pepper hair. He wore a pair of faded blue jeans, a sleeveless undershirt and was barefoot. Dark circles framed his reddened eyes, as if sleep had dodged him for days. Curtis extended his hand but Wilfred cast him a vacant look, and then turned and guided him into the house. Curtis shrugged and then followed.

"Come on in the kitchen. I'm sorry it's such a mess. It's just that I've been kind of crazy lately," Wilfred said, fishing a coffee pot from beneath a sink piled with dishes. After rifling through his cupboard, he reached up and scratched the back of his neck with a huge, roughened hand accustomed to heavy labor. "Got no more coffee, shit, and I need some, yeah."

"Water'll do just fine," Curtis grinned. "I don't think you've misplaced that just yet."

"Guess not, I hope," Wilfred smiled back weakly. "Ice?"

"Yeah, it's getting pretty hot out there already, probably gonna hit 98 again," Curtis advised. He pulled up a chair and cleared a spot at a table crowded with papers—mostly insurance documents and business records. A few envelopes with the Marines' familiar eagle, globe and anchor logo were scattered about. "Love your filing system. There's a lot more letters out in the mailbox, you know."

Wilfred placed two glasses of ice water on the table. "Don't know if you're a comedian or just tryin' to cheer me up."

"To cheer you up, of course," Curtis assured him. "My boy, Tuck, wrote to us saying you lost your brother recently. I thought you might like to talk to somebody whose son was going through the same thing. You know, I lost a daughter in a car wreck a while back. It's tough."

Wilfred rubbed his face and his eyes began to tear.

He took a gulp of ice water and let out a satisfying sigh. "Ummm, first water I've had without a touch of ol' Jack in near two weeks. Tastes good. Guess I'll get around to eating soon, too."

He then fumbled through the stack on the cluttered table. "They're here somewhere, let's see. Johnny don't write too often. Spelling's always been tougher for him than blockin' and tacklin'. His mom, God rest her soul, was supposed to handle all the education."

"This what you looking for?" Curtis said, tossing toward Wilfred four letters emblazoned with the Marine logo.

"Yeah, that's them," Wilfred replied. "Not many, huh? Just those four, that's all I got so far, other than that first one that said 'I got there OK,' you know."

"Yeah, we expected more too. But Tuck's been a faithful writer since the second week. That's what the Marines like to say, 'always faithful.'" Curtis took another sip of the cold water.

"Yep, 'Semper Fi, Do or Die.' That's how we always said it in the Corps back in Korea."

Curtis started at the remark. "I was in the Army Air Corps back in WWII, turret gunner on a B-17. We named it the *Belle Ami* after the pilot's pet boxer. Caught one through the leg in '43. Nearly blew it half off," he offered in exchange, lightly slapping the side of his left thigh.

Wilfred tossed a letter toward Curtis. "This was the first real letter I got from that boy of mine." Curtis unfolded the letter and read.

Dear Daddy and Bub,

This place ain't worth shit. The food ain't no good and there's not much of it. The boss sergeant is a big colored boy who could even whip my ass. But I like him. Met two nice guys from Eunice, can you imagine that. Donnie-Boy is almost as big as me. And a little guy called Tuck, he's kinda smart. I like both of them. Tell Bub I love him, too.—Your son, T-Johnny

"Well, he sure doesn't waste time getting to the point, huh?" Curtis handed the letter back to Wilfred. "What about Bub?"

"What you mean, what about Bub?" Wilfred quietly replied. He caressed Johnny's cryptic letters, staring at his son's handwriting as if it spoke out to him.

"Did Bub go into the Corps and to Korea with you?"

"Oh, no. Me and Bub barely got out of high school." Wilfred looked up and straight into Curtis' green eyes, an almost perfect match to his own. "We was good football players, but Bub was really good, all-state team and all that stuff. He went right on over to LSU and played a couple of years just after World War II ended. He hurt his leg pretty bad in a game and the Marines wouldn't take him to fight, plus he was gettin' a little old for the military."

Curtis took his last sip and felt a kinship growing. "How'd it happen, Wilfred? You know, how'd Bub go? If you don't mind me asking."

Wilfred got up, took Curtis' empty glass and returned to the sink. He added extra ice to both glasses and momentarily stared out the kitchen window. "I just rocked him in my arms, like he'd just gone to sleep." He returned and sat, again staring Curtis in the eye.

"Bub had just taken a call from ol' Mr. Spence. He was never happy with our repairs. Bub had fixed his old icebox for about the fourth damn time and it still wasn't working right. We told him he needed a new one, but he insisted we fix it. He told Bub he wasn't gonna pay until we fixed it again. It made Bub get real mad. He hadn't paid since the second time we fixed it. Hell, it was a piece of shit, you know. And, he didn't like that old man. He was mean and tight."

Wilfred and Curtis both took a long drink, nodding and smiling.

"Well, ol' Bub, he finally said good-bye real nice and hung up the phone real soft like. He just stood there looking out the window for about a minute and then he turned and looked at me funny and smiled. I was fixin' a toaster. But his smile didn't look right, and then he said, 'You know Wilfred, I sure do miss the girls, yeah. Sometimes I wish...'"

Wilfred's eyelids drooped and his cheeks sagged. "He just stopped right there. His eyes kinda turned up and he went to his knees. I caught him before he hit the floor. He was so big, a lot like T-Johnny. He knocked me to my butt and just slid into my arms. I held him there just like a big ol' baby. His eyes had closed and it didn't look like he was breathing. I shook him real hard and screamed in his ear a bunch. But he didn't move. He kinda coughed one time, I think, and I saw some blood come out.

"I might not be all that smart, but I knew for damn sure my big brother was dyin' on me. I opened up one of his eyes and all I saw was a big black pupil...

"I just rocked him...and rocked him. Right there in my arms. I wish I'd knew a song I could have sung him. So, I just hummed an old lullaby I used to hear Joan sing to Johnny. I didn't even know the name of it. Ol' Bub was gone by then. No use in calling out an ambulance. He was already gettin' cold. I tightened my arms around him, thinkin' I could warm him up.

"Finally, after about 20 minutes or so, I guess, I put his head down real gentle-like on some old newspaper. And then I went ahead and called the sheriff's office to send a coroner." Tears trailed down Wilfred's cheeks and his fingers nervously flitted through the papers on the table. "I tried to get Johnny to call me back home from boot camp. But they said Bub wasn't immediate family. I was gonna argue, but I was in the Corps and understood. So I just wrote him a letter."

Curtis rose, walked over and stood behind Wilfred. He squeezed his broad shoulders.

"Thanks, Wilfred, for telling me. I know how it is. Like I said, I lost my little girl a while back. I understand. OK? I'll be going now. But I'm sure we'll be seeing each other as the boys move on." Curtis turned and walked to the front porch. "Hey, look, there's another letter from Johnny in this stack out here—fat one, too."

Wilfred perked up and hurried to Curtis' side. His face was alight with the first real smile Curtis had seen during the visit. He slowly reached out with an open palm, childlike.

"Curtis, thank you. Can't say I feel a whole lot better because I know what that letter's gonna be about. But if it means anything, you and T-Johnny are the only ones who know the truth. Most people think I found ol' Bub just lying on the floor already dead."

Curtis bid good-bye to his new friend, whose thick fingers rapidly tore at the envelope. He walked away from the Robert home with a spring in his step.

CHAPTER 9

Family Treasure
Village of Cam Lo, R.S.V.N.
August 30, 1968—7 a.m. local time

Pham Thuc Trai knitted his slender fingers over his head and quietly wept. Squatting on calves knotted like those of an athlete, he watched the trucks roar past the big bull's vacant eyes.

The ancient bull, lying dead by the roadside, had served the Pham family for more than a dozen years. Its brute strength provided them with the means of producing their own food and, thus, security. Untiring in its toil, protective of its turf, yet gentle enough to allow children to hitch rides upon its back, the massive beast had earned the devotion of its family.

The stark angles of the early morning sun shaded its noble head from Trai's view. Too many drivers had gone out of their way to run over what remained of the bullet-riddled carcass. Dust from the convoy billowed and spread a thin layer of red over its slate gray hide. One of its mighty, swept-back horns was driven into the earth.

Occasional rifle shots rang out, fired by Americans riding in the rear of the trucks. They shouted what sounded to Trai like obscenities each time their shots hit the mark. The words were new to him, but the inflection was unmistakable. Trai's 16-year-old legs and arms flinched at the sound of each blast of the guns.

There was no flinch remaining in the ancient bull.

An hour earlier, shortly after dawn, Trai's hobbled

father, Pham Van Loi, had routinely placed a small kiss on the foreheads of his sleeping twin daughters and on the cheek of his wife, Minh. He then went out to check on the water buffalo, penned in the rear of the small home. Loi found the stall empty, looked about and frowned. The beast had escaped before this, but had never wandered out of sight. Usually, Loi had found it munching on some patch of tender reeds, or trying to gnaw its way into the locked feed box. Now concerned, he awoke Trai and told him to seek out Trau Gia, as the family had long ago named the bull.

Not finding Trau Gia near the farm, Trai padded along the hard-packed, earthen road often used by American convoys hustling through the nearby village of Cam Lo. The hamlet was one of several along Route 9 in Quang Tri, the northernmost province of South Vietnam.

Cam Lo also lay near the American artillery base known as The Rockpile. Vandegrift Combat Base also was not far away—the sight of American convoys was common.

Normally, the Marines passed without incident. Often they would stop and pay top dollar for cold soft drinks and distribute candy and other treats to the swarming children who eagerly lined the route.

Trai found Trau Gia lying next to Route 9, a quarter of a mile from their home. It had been shot a half dozen times, as best as he could tell through the tears gathering in his eyes. Strange cuts had been made into its flanks.

Trai tenderly brushed one of its regal horns with the back of his hand. But the trucks soon approached and roared precariously close. He no longer dared to reach out and touch his old friend. He heard laughter when the driver swayed to catch Trau Gia on the rump. The sound of bone shattering assaulted Trai's ears. He could not stay longer.

Hurrying home to advise his father, Trai recalled distant gunfire in the hour before dawn. Gunfire before dawn, however, was common in Quang Tri. Picking up the pace, he realized there had not been a day that he could remember in which Trau Gia had not been part of the family. Approaching home, tears flowed freely from Trai's large black eyes.

"Can you tell who did this injustice to us, Trai?" Loi addressed the last of his surviving sons. They stood on the back porch of their home, gazing hopelessly into each other's eyes. Trai could see the dread in his father's stare but did not know how to help him.

"No, father. As you've said before, bullets leave no names. It could've been the army from the North or the Americans; or perhaps both, as they came upon one another in the night. All I know is that Trau Gia is dead and the Americans are having sport with his body."

Loi bowed his head and clenched his fists. "We needn't care, the damage has been done," he sighed. "Return to the roadside and wait for me. I'll get help. We'll bring Trau Gia back home for a fitting end. And then I'll pay a visit to our American friends."

When Trai returned, he found even less remaining of the carcass. He briefly watched three waiting dogs—circling and nipping at one another as if determining which would go first.

Trai initially believed Trau Gia had wandered into a crossfire and had become another casualty in this endless war. After the morning's spectacle, however, he was convinced his family's treasure had met its fate at the hands of Americans. He did not know if it was fact. But today, this is what he wanted to believe, and in his heart he knew it to be true.

In the midst of the heat and dust, Trai watched the dogs feast on Trau Gia's entrails.

Trai turned toward home. He never looked back.

CHAPTER 10

Curtis and Mary

Eunice, La.

Sept. 5, 1968—9:30 a.m. local time

Curtis Richard reached across his desk and popped the paper tape from his electric adding machine. He neatly folded it and placed it in the ledger assigned to Joseph's Oilfield Sales, Inc. He removed his black-rimmed reading glasses and rubbed his eyes. He glanced at his watch. Just where was that mailman anyway? The truck was 30 minutes late.

It had only been a few weeks since Curtis, a private accountant, had taken on the JOS account. Curtis was doing well for his family but the success of JOS might mean the difference between just getting by and real financial success.

"Maybe when Mark and Tuck are finished their tours, they can help me do some renovating," Curtis said to himself, a bit loudly. He looked around the room.

"What was that, Babe? You talking to me?" Mary was in the kitchen, next to the laundry room. "If you are, you'll have to speak up because I have the washer and dryer going full blast."

"Oh, nothing, just talking to myself again. Wondering... oh, never mind."

Mary breezed into the dining room with a cup of coffee in hand. "Oh, I see you've been working on JOS," she said. "How are those guys doing anyway? I know their young wives are spending money, that's for sure," Mary said. She placed the cup on his desk.

"These guys are on to something, I think," Curtis

observed. "They've been doing their homework, researching Middle East politics and world oil stocks. They think there's going to be an oil shortage in the next five years and that the U.S. is going to be doing a lot of exploration. So, they're setting up clients now and stocking their warehouses with implements. There's gonna be a heckuva lot of drilling here and in the Gulf."

"Oh, bull. There's plenty of oil to go around," insisted Mary, the daughter of an offshore oil worker. "But I hope they're right, it'll mean good business for us too. Right?"

"Umm, hmmmm," Curtis smiled. He was glad to see Mary returning to a semblance of normalcy. It had been a rough three years since Brenda's death in a graduation-night auto accident. It had devastated the family, but the loss of her only daughter, at 18, however, had exacted a particularly heavy toll on Mary. The tears still came, usually late at night and muffled by her pillow, but the days of deep depression had passed.

"Finally," Curtis shouted when he saw the mailman arrive with a fistful of letters. "I'll get the mail, Babe."

Curtis walked smartly up the driveway, gathered up the mail and headed back to the house, waving quickly to the kids playing in the yard next door. His leg was not hurting today and his limp was barely noticeable when he reached the kitchen.

"Boy, this is going to be another scorcher. Summer ain't nearly ready to give in. And to think, the Tigers gotta play football in this heat Saturday. Those boys are gonna die." Curtis said, sorting the mail. "Oh, damn, I forgot, I was supposed to send Tuck an LSU schedule."

"Already did it," Mary said, whizzing by and quickly planting a peck on Curtis' cheek. "I mailed him one last week. What'd we get from the boys?"

"One from Tuck; nothing from Mark." Curtis fished

Tuck's letter from the envelope. She soon joined him and leaned over his shoulder.

Dear family,

Well, we've only got about a week to 10 days to go and things are starting to improve. Well, kinda. They're not hollering quite as much. The DIs are real busy getting us ready for our final inspection, it comes right before Sept. 15 graduation. I sure wish y'all could make it, but I understand. Heck, I don't think the old Chevy could even make it all the way to San Diego.

"What's he mean old? That Impala can still go anywhere," Curtis objected.

"Yeah, right. I've been telling you we need a new one."

Dad, I'm proud to tell you I scored the highest marks on the rifle range last week, a 249 out of 250, that's Expert. I hear that the top shooter usually gets to make PFC out of boot camp. Plus being a housemouse ought to help me get a stripe as well. Donnie-Boy also qualified as Expert.

Dad, your visit to Johnny's father must have been a good one. He says his dad wrote him a letter right after you left and just talked and talked about your visit and how it made him smile and how he went out and cleaned up the yard and all. He says his dad plans to call you to go to an LSU game with him one Saturday.

"See I told you it would be best if you went over there." Mary elbowed Curtis in the ribs.

"Yie yie" he yelped, feigning pain.

Oh, yeah, mom, thanks for the little schedule. Go, Tigers. When I get out of boot camp and move to ITR (that's Infantry Training Regiment) you'll be able to mail me some newspapers about the Tigers and Blue Jays. How is Dave doing in football so far? Has St. Ed's played their first game yet? I would think so. Let me know.

Yesterday they taught us how to kill and maim people with our bare hands. You really learn some useful stuff here (ha, ha).

Mom, I'm down to 150 pounds and will need some new clothes when I come home on leave. That should be sometime in early November. I think leave will be 20 days or so. Well gotta go now, it's nearly lights out. I need my beauty rest (ha, ha). Keep me in your prayers.

Your loving almost-a-Marine son, Tuck (Benjamin)

"He's something else, huh, Babe, that boy of ours," Curtis said. "He's going to be OK."

"Yeah, yeah, he'll be OK. And so will you," Mary replied with a big hug.

CHAPTER 11

DIs' Decisions
MCRD, San Diego, Calif.
Sept. 10, 1968—6:30 p.m. local time

Platoon 2080's drill instructors sat around a small wooden table in the corner of the NCO Club. It was dim and blue-gray layers of cigarette smoke lilted near the ceiling. A jukebox played the tunes of a mournful western ballad. They each nursed a bottle of beer; Gaines and Thomas drew long, hard drags on their Camels. Except for the cigar he allowed himself at the end of each training period, Gunny Hill did not smoke.

Master Sgt. Phil Stagg, head of the training battalion, was drilling Platoon 2080 to get a first-hand look at the new Marines. It gave the trio a chance to socialize for the first time in eight weeks. Hill and Thomas had trained several platoons together over the past five years. Gaines, in his second year, was going through the paces with Gunny Hill for the second time.

"This is it for me," Thomas said, blowing out a streamer of smoke. "I'm tired and I've had my fill with nursing these kids. I'm retiring at the end of the year." He took a final drag and then snuffed out the cigarette in an overflowing ashtray. His pause was met with silence. "I've got enough time in to pull most of my pension, plus my cousin's got a spot for me in his insurance business. Oh, I'm sure I'll hate the work, there's nothing like the Corps."

Thomas reached out and patted a copy of *Stars and Stripes* folded on the table. "But this job's eating my heart out."

Gunny Hill slowly turned a bottle of Schlitz in his massive paws. He looked up and stared into Thomas' eyes, but said nothing.

"What you mean, Jim?" Gaines said. "You're not too old to do this job. I've seen you on the runs and in PT. You're in great shape and I've seen the way you handle the pukes. You're one of the best. C'mon Jim, you don't want to sell no damn insurance. What you going to do, slap 'em up the backside of the head if they don't buy a policy? Tell 'em to drop down and give you 20? That'll go over real big at Mrs. Smith's kitchen table. Ha."

Gaines took the last swig of his Budweiser. He held the empty bottle over his head and hollered, "Hey, hon, how about another round over here. On me."

"You never been to Nam yet, have you, Jerry?" Thomas said, confronting the 25-year-old Gaines. "So you really don't know what I'm talking about when I..."

"What you mean by that crack?" Gaines challenged Thomas.

"Look, I'm 35. Did a few months with the First Marines in Korea when I was 19. Did two 13-month tours in Nam with Third Marines before I became a DI. I saw a lot of kids do things wrong when they hit the shit and I wanted to come back and train them the right way. See if I could save a few."

The waitress brought three more beers. "Keep 'em coming, hon," Gaines said with a wink.

"No, that'll be enough for us after this," Gunny Hill corrected.

Gaines shrugged and returned his attention to Thomas.

"Well, now I've done it," Thomas continued. "I've sent thousands of kids off to war. Probably scores off to their deaths." Thomas paused and tossed the newspaper to Gunny Hill. It was open to the weekly casualty list page. A pencil mark underlined the names of two Marines. Gunny Hill looked at the list and then nodded with a frown.

Thomas peered into Gaines' eyes. "Haven't you ever really liked some of the kids we train? You get to know them pretty good, right?"

"Yeah, but not that good," Gaines answered. "Well, maybe a few. There's been a couple I took a liking to, even in this group. So what?"

"So, what if you knew too many of those guys, the ones that you kinda like would never see stateside again?" Thomas leaned back in his chair. "I've got children nearly their age now."

"You've been a good friend, Jim," Gunny Hill said, tossing the paper back to Thomas. "It won't be the same. I'll sure as hell miss you."

"You're not going to try to talk him out of it?" Gaines cracked. "Some friend."

"Jerry, shut up," Gunny Hill ordered with a glance. "Jim, you and I've done our share, sure. You, even more. But I'm only 30 and I think I've got a few more years in me. But if I can't find a job when I call it quits, I'll be looking you up in Des Moines." He saluted Thomas with a tip of his bottle. "And I know exactly where you're coming from; 2080 is one of the best we've put out. Williams, Sanchez, Brown, Larsen and, of course, our Cajun trio, are gonna make first-rate Marines. I can't stand the thought of losing one of those guys. But I know it's gonna happen—always does."

"Thanks, Gunny. Appreciate you understanding," Thomas said. "Now I gotta get back to the kiddies, I'm on duty and I bet Phil is waitin' on me. Guess I'll tell Mona and the children tomorrow. Y'all were the first to hear it." He slid his chair back and stood.

"Oh, and thanks, Jerry, for the beer. The turds'll thank you, too, 'cause I'm feeling too good to be ornery. I'll sleep good tonight." Thomas picked up his campaign hat and newspaper and walked to the door.

Gaines drained his beer after Thomas left and began to

call for another before remembering Gunny Hill's words. An uneasy hush fell across the table.

"Never been to Nam, eh, Jerry?" Gunny Hill said, peeling away the bottle's damp label. "Don't know what it's really like to be in the shit?"

"No. You know that. But that doesn't mean I can't..."

"No, no, no, don't get me wrong, Jerry. You're a fine Marine and a good DI. You could be a damn fine one if you only knew a little more about what the kids were in for."

Gaines slumped in his chair. "I tried going once, but came down with the damn German measles and they put my orders on indefinite hold," he explained. "They didn't want me infecting a whole damn regiment or something. When they finally did come through, I was already set to graduate from DI school and didn't want to waste all that training, not to mention the misery I went through."

Gunny Hill laughed. He had served two tours in Vietnam and had earned two Bronze Stars for valor in the first. During his second trip, he'd won the Silver Star for destroying an enemy bunker single-handed. Gunny Hill's three Purple Hearts were for scars he never showed.

"This group gets out of here next week and we'll be picking up another batch," the gunny said. "I've requested that you work with me again. You're an ass, Jerry, but you do good work. After this next bunch, I'm taking a little personal leave and goin' down to Houston to visit mom and the family.

"And, I'd like to see you head to the Nam. Do a tour. Mix with those guys, feel the hurt with them. Then come back and train with me some more. You'll be better for it."

"Thanks, Gunny, I think...maybe you're right. I'll give it some thought. I promise. It's just that I just love ridin' these guys, so don't punch my ticket to the Nam just yet."

"Jerry, you've got plenty of the right stuff," Gunny Hill laughed. He stood and donned his hat. "You just don't know it yet. Now go ahead and get that other beer you wanted, this time on me. I'm headin' home for a good night's sleep myself."

"G'night, Gunny."

Gaines stood while his boss departed. Then he again sat, quietly, and listened to more sad songs the jukebox had to offer. He pulled out his wallet and opened it to a photo of his kinfolk back in Alabama. His mom and dad were dead, so was his lone brother. Only his old aunt and uncle remained in Mobile.

He lit another Camel and finished his beer.

CHAPTER 12
Semper Fi
MCRD, San Diego, Calif.
Sept. 14, 1968—6 p.m. local time

The brass belt buckle sparkled under the fluorescent lights. Tuck smiled and gingerly set it aside with a polishing cloth. Sitting cross-legged on the floor near his bunk, he re-examined the spit shine on his black dress shoes. Nothing less than a mirror finish would be acceptable tomorrow—Graduation Day.

He had survived the arduous eight weeks, though it seemed like only last night that he ran his hand over his shaved head and wondered what he had gotten himself into. Tomorrow he would realize his dream and call himself a Marine—not a puke, not a turd, not a titty-baby, not a maggot, not even a recruit, but a Marine. He ran his hand over his bristly scalp, only this time with pride rather than resignation. The cadence of the drums and thoughts of glory returned.

The drill instructors exited their hut with Gunny Hill carrying a stack of papers. "OK maggots, gather around," he hollered. "We've got business. Assume mail-call positions."

The recruits scrambled to the hut and sat on the floor in a semicircle around the trio of DIs. "You ain't Marines just yet," Gunny Hill added, "but I've got promotions and Military Occupation Specialty designations. Most of you are 0300s and headed to war, so listen up."

Gunny Hill handed Thomas a list of eight names printed on a single sheet of paper. "The following recruits will be promoted to Private First Class," Thomas explained. "If your name is called, you will be given single chevrons to sew onto your blouses. PFC Justin Larsen, housemouse; PFC Nelson Brown, another housemouse; PFC Elman Tracy, platoon secretary; PFC Nolan Jackson, highest educational scores; PFC Benjamin Richard, housemouse, second-highest educational scores and top marksman..."

Gaines leaned toward Gunny Hill. "I still say it was the rifle I picked out," he whispered out of the corner of his mouth.

"...PFC Johnny Robert, squad leader and too big for us not to give him a stripe," Thomas quipped. "PFC Moody Chavez, squad leader, PFC Anthony Williams, squad leader and physical training champ. OK, congratulations, now let's move on."

Tuck beamed and turned to shake hands with Johnny. But something was amiss. Donnie-Boy? Why wasn't his name called? Sadness stifling his pride, Tuck watched the life drain from his life-long friend's eyes. "There's got to be a mistake. You're the best of all of us. It ain't right."

"Congratulations, Tuck, you did well," Donnie-Boy replied, his face growing pale with pain, as if his legs had been shot out from under him. "You deserve it. I'll be OK."

"Now let's get to that MOS list." Thomas began rattling off a litany of 70 names. "Larsen Oh-300 infantry...Hebert 0300 infantry...Jackson 0800 artillery...Tracy 2500 communications...Richard 0300 infantry...Robert 0300 infantry...Sanchez 0400 logistics, you're gonna be a truck driver,...Williams 3300 cook, a cook? Our best damn athlete and they're going to make you a cook. Damn.

"Well and I see they're going to send our Cajun trio to the Promised Land. God help the gooks," Thomas concluded with a laugh.

"OK, that's it. When you get to your next segments of training up at Camp Pendleton—ITR and BITS—you'll be training in your specialties, rifleman, mortars, machine guns, etc."

Thomas paused and caught his breath. "Fellas, you've made me proud. You're as good a platoon as I've ever trained. Good luck and God be with you."

Gunny Hill moved to the front and squeezed Thomas' shoulder. "But there's one more matter we have to take care of," he said. "Sgt. Gaines, would you please get the bag out of my locker, please." He motioned Gaines toward his office.

Gaines quickly returned with a thin red and gold garment bag. Gunny Hill took it and held it high. "Private Donald Hebert would you please come forward."

Donnie-Boy frowned and looked at Tuck before approaching Gunny Hill.

"It is my pleasure, Private Hebert, to present you with these Dress Blues as a reward for earning the right to be called Platoon 2080 Honorman." He drew from the bag a navy blue jacket piped in red and a pair of royal blue trousers. "And in my locker is a white dress cover to complete your ensemble, PFC Hebert. Congratulations, son, you've done your platoon and instructors proud. And, now I can tell this to at least one of you—semper fi...Marine."

Gunny Hill shook Donnie-Boy's hand firmly.

"Now get back to work," Gunny Hill ordered the platoon. "And, PFC Hebert, report to my hut in 30 minutes so we can talk Honorman procedures."

"Sir, yes sir," Donnie-Boy replied sharply. The corners of his lips nearly touched his eyes when a once-forbidden grin filled his face.

"I knew something wasn't right. I just knew it," Tuck said. They returned to their bunks. The dreams of that first night's long flight were becoming a reality. What could be better?

"Man, that's somethin', yeah." Johnny said, patting the

new Honorman on the back. "Don't let Tuck mess with those dressy clothes, *non*, he'll just spill somethin' on 'em."

"Thanks, fellas, for a while there I was thinking I'd really blown it," Donnie-Boy said. "My goal was to make PFC. But this is too much. Damn, now this is something to write home about."

•

8 a.m., Sept. 15: Decked out in summer khakis and standing at attention, Tuck felt the platoon ooze with a sense of perfection in formation and function—the embodiment of esprit de corps. The steely faces of the 70 new Marines surrendered not a hint of emotion. They stood for more than the clichéd "lean, mean fighting machines." He and his friends were officially the newest parts of an elite fighting force recognized as the world's best.

Tuck was now in the Corps, and the Corps was in him. That would never change.

"OK, Marines," Gunny Hill hollered. "There's been a delay in the proceedings and you can stand at rest, but keep the chatter down."

"Hey, Donnie-Boy," Tuck hailed from halfway back in the formation. In his Dress Blues and looking like a poster Marine, he turned at the sound of Tuck's voice.

"Great outfit, you look deadly—as in deadly to the girls back home," Tuck said with a grin.

Donnie-Boy returned a respectful smile and a stare. The look was special to Tuck. That "look"—the thin smile, a slight cock of the head and a sideways glance from those gleaming brown eyes—was the same he'd seen during so many special moments. It was the same he had drawn from Donnie-Boy when he had bailed him out on a crucial physics exam their junior year. He had also seen it when Donnie-Boy helped him celebrate his only high school touchdown. And, that look had also come at the end of a mournful week, one he had spent at Donnie-Boy's side following the death of his father.

It was that look—implying respect and thanks—that cemented their friendship.

"Uhhhtennnshun," Gunny Hill blared. "Look proud Platoon 2080."

Donnie-Boy brought the platoon's standard to attention along the right side of his body. The pole's numerous pennants flapped in the breeze. The remainder of the platoon snapped to attention, their M-14s erect by their sides.

"Right shoulderrr...arms." The platoon responded with precision. "Forrrwerd, march."

For the last time, Tuck and 2080 heard the deep voice of Gunny Hill call his singsong cadence. Tuck knew what Gunny Hill was supposed to be saying, but it always came out sounding something like "yo adle rite." The melodic cadence, somehow, not only provided timing but a certain calmness. It could have been the sound of any one of their fathers' voices.

"Look out now, you're bouncing, you're bouncing, Marines," Gunny Hill said. He led his platoon to the reviewing stand for the final ceremony. "Keep it level. Don't make me look bad in front of the brass on the last day. Settle down, focus. *Yo adle rite.*..That's better, that's better, hold it there...*yo adle rite.*"

After listening to a colonel's speech about duty, honor, and Corps, four platoons of proud new Marines, returned their commander's salute.

But when they marched away, Platoon 2080 was granted one last request. As submitted by their Honorman, PFC Hebert, it was a request as traditional as the granting that followed.

They sang while Gunnery Sgt. John Hill watched and listened. He smiled and patted the cigar hidden in the breast pocket of his blouse.

"From the Halls of Montezuma,
To the shores of Tripoli;
We fight our country's battles
In the air, on land and sea;
First to fight for right and freedom
And to keep our honor clean;
We are proud to claim the title of
United States Marine.

But Gunny Hill's smile soon faded. Which ones will never return?

CHAPTER 13

An Unspeakable Act
Village of Cam Lo, R.S.V.N.
Sept. 30, 1968—9 a.m. local time

Pham Van Loi sat in the small canvas chair, taking the weight off his lame left leg, sore from days in the paddies without Trau Gia's help. A pair of Marines had placed the seat next to a green folding table near the back porch of the Pham residence. The family and more than a score of villagers gathered around.

An armed squad of Marines was providing security for the liaison officer from a nearby American base. Standing near his father's side, Trai thought the captain to be apologetic and accommodating. The officer did not concede the Marines had slain Trau Gia, but deplored the soldiers' and convoy drivers' actions.

The death of the water buffalo and the ensuing fuss had reached the upper echelons. The brass, more sensitive about civilian relations since the recent Tet Offensive, agreed the incident was tasteless and barbaric. They also agreed it was paramount to seek a rapid settlement.

The Pham family waited patiently while the young officer calculated the monetary worth of a water buffalo approximately 14 years old. He also factored replacement value, the family's loss of revenue and the embarrassing circumstances surrounding its death. Trai and his family had waited 30 days for the Americans to respond to their request for compensation, another 15 minutes would not matter.

"Mr. Pham, I know this cannot replace your water

buffalo. However, please accept this payment from the United States government as compensation. And, accept as well, my…my…" the officer said, fumbling over his words. "Well, let's just say I'm a farm boy myself, from southern Illinois, I can appreciate what a loss like this can mean. I really am sorry, sir."

Neither Trai nor his father required an interpreter. They had attended the local Catholic schools and understood pedestrian English and French. But they had no idea where Illinois was located.

"Like this war, it is all so unfortunate," Loi said. "Things like this are too often unavoidable. I accept your country's offer and your humble apology."

Trai glowered at the Marines even though he knew $3,000 in American cash was generous. It would purchase not only a young water buffalo, but also the upcoming season's seed and supplies, as well as extras for his mother, Minh, and his sisters, Luu and Linh.

The Marine captain stood and bowed in the direction of Minh, "Good day, ma'am," he said. She nodded with a smile. He then saluted Loi and extended his hand. Loi bowed. When the officer turned to walk back to his jeep, Trai stepped into the Marine's path and brushed his shoulder against the taller man's arm.

"Excuse me, son." The officer stepped around the teen. Trai did not reply.

"Oh, by the way, Mr. Pham," the officer said, stopping to turn and face Loi. "I don't know if it really means anything to you. But that convoy and those soldiers were U.S. Army passing through. They weren't Marines."

A dust cloud wafted across the crowded homestead when the jeep and troop truck sped toward the west. Neighbors rushed to see the money and comment on the proceedings.

Trai stood at the edge of Route 9 and spat on the ground.

MY DYING BREATH

•

"You've hardly said a word since the Americans left this morning," Loi said, washing his hands and face on the back porch. It was nearly 6 p.m. and time for supper. Minh was preparing a family favorite, *Thit bo kho*—a grilled beef jerky dish cooked in soy sauce and served with lemon grass, Chile peppers and French bread.

"I also noticed your attitude and the gesture you made toward the young officer when he left," Loi said. "That was uncalled for and most disrespectful." He toweled his rough hands and then tossed it and the soap to Trai. "Don't ever let me see you act like that again. It's time you start acting like the man you think you are."

Trai caught the soap and rapidly lathered his hands while his father limped toward the kitchen door. "How many more of our family must die at the hands of these Americans before you realize they are not our friends?" he shouted.

"What do you mean how many?" Loi replied, wrinkling his brow.

"You've never told me how my older brothers died," Trai challenged. He pitched the soap cake into the basin and threw the towel to the floor. "I've heard the rumors, and mother has cautioned me more than enough times about the dark in the early morning. Soon I may have to choose to fight. I need to know my enemy, Father."

"It is not the Americans, I assure you," Loi said in a quiet way that underscored an eternal patience with his children. "You are too young and unwise in the ways of the world to judge. But, yes, you are old enough to fight. Though I'd hoped this war might be over by now, and that you'd never have to do so."

"So, what happened?" Trai demanded, slapping his hand on the porch railing.

"So, how did what happen?" Loi snapped at his son, who often tested that eternal patience.

"So, just how did Manh Doan and Trung Tien die? I know they were shot, I do remember that much, I was not that young. But, that is all I know. It was all so confusing," Trai said, his angry tones now more akin to the pleadings of a frustrated teen-ager.

Loi sighed and turned back toward the steps of the porch. He stood tall, arched his back—he would turn 60 this month—and looked west toward a small lake glimmering less than a quarter of a mile away. He shook his head, sighed and then sat upon the top step.

Trai joined his father and sat as close as his young ego allowed. He chose the second step.

"Over there." Loi pointed toward the lake's southern banks like a timid man trying not to conjure up ghosts. "We found them over there. They were dead when we got to them. We never did see who did it. Much like Trau Gia, we just heard the shots in the early morning and found them after the sunrise."

"Doan was older than I am now, but wasn't Tien about my age?" Trai's voice was now like that of an inquisitive toddler. His thirst for the truth was unquenchable.

Loi bowed his head.

"I remember Mama crying, too," Trai recalled, his hand resting upon his father's sandal.

"We all cried. They were so young. Headstrong, like you." Loi smiled. He rubbed Trai's straight black hair. "The soldiers from the north had come into the village for several nights before that morning and had filled the heads of our young men, including Doan's and Tien's, with lies and empty promises.

"They told them of the glory of fighting for Ho Chi Minh and of the sacrifice that had to be made to rejoin our nations. Oh, they were good. They wove inspiring patriotic tales of bravery into a cloak of nationalism. I too, even today, agree with some of the arguments they brought on their recruiting campaigns.

"They told us of the corruption in Saigon and how communism and Ho Chi Minh were going to squash the puppet government. Ha! Young Tien was ready to join the first night. Doan, well, he was more of a farmer and had his doubts. Like me, he saw the might of the Americans and had heard stories of the slaughters of those who went up against that might. Doan also had his eye on a young girl here in the village and was not too anxious to leave."

Trai listened, his head cocked toward his father and his eyes fixed on the small lake. "So, did they join?"

"Like I said, Tien was ready to join the first night," Loi continued. "But Doan's logic swayed Tien over the next few days. The recruiters, a half dozen or so, were upset with Doan. There were arguments, loud ones deep into the evening. Doan's words then began to convince other young men in the village not to follow the recruiters.

"On the last night they were here, the soldiers told your brothers they had to choose by the next day because they would be leaving to join an attack on the Marine base to the south. Doan told them that if they had to have an answer right then, it was 'no' and that went for Tien, too."

Loi's eyes were unfocused and locked in the direction of the lake. "You know how your Mama has always warned you about the morning," he paused and wiped away a quivering tear, "and to stay away from the lake unless you have work there."

"Yes, Father, all the time."

"Doan and Tien loved to swim in the early hours," Loi said, smiling. "It was the only time they had for play before their chores, particularly in the summer. Sometimes they would bring home a fish or two, usually too small to eat. But your mother always made them into a feast.

"The last time we saw them alive was the night before, during an argument with the chief recruiter. My sons refused to join him and he left an angry man, full of threats.

"And, the next morning, his men ambushed my

defenseless sons like animals as they walked like children to the lake for a swim." Tears streamed down Loi's cheeks. Trai leaned over, picked up the hand towel and then handed it to his father. "They cleverly used the black rifles and made it look like...like it was the work of an American patrol."

"But, Father, how do you know it was the recruiters—and not the Americans?"

Loi again sighed and wiped his eyes. "Because if Doan and Tien would not join them, the recruiters could not chance letting them live because they knew about the attack planned on the American base. Now could they?

"That, and the fact that the chief recruiter was Pham Van Bui—my own brother, your uncle," Loi said and then spat on the ground. "And, on the afternoon following their deaths he returned here, to my home, and so much as told me so. Humph, it is only a pity that Bui did not die with his predatory friends.

"You see, Trai, as it turned out, Doan had made the wise decision not to join. The recruiters, and all of the village boys who followed them, were slaughtered two days later when they attacked the Americans. All except, of course, for Bui, who had since returned to the north." Loi paused and coughed to clear his throat. "I guess we would have lost them either way—to Bui's hateful hand or to the ill-fated attack. This damned war."

Both fell silent. Trai slipped his hand into his father's and squeezed.

"But, Father, what if the recruiters return? What then?" Trai asked, searching for guidance.

"No, they don't recruit like that anymore. Now, they just come and, well...take them, any way they can," Loi explained. "But that is enough for now. Let's put our smiles back on, go inside and enjoy your mother's *Thit bo kho*. I know it's your favorite."

With the red sun dipping into its waters, the southern

shore of the lake once more held Loi's gaze. "Damn you, Bui. Damn you."

CHAPTER 14

Baby Pictures
Eunice, La.
Oct. 1, 1968—9 a.m. local time

Despite the steady drizzle pelting the concrete, Curtis trotted gingerly to the mailbox and grabbed a fistful of letters. He shuffled through the stack while walking back into the house and hollering his usual morning announcement, "Two of 'em. They'll be on the kitchen table, Mary."

Curtis fetched his pocketknife and opened Tuck's letter with a quick zip. It was fatter than usual and warranted a smile when he found three snap-shots within. Fumbling through the square photos, he cried a loud "ha." The first was a picture of Tuck and Donnie-Boy standing side by side in their khaki uniforms, arms smartly placed behind trim waists. The second was of Tuck, Donnie-Boy and Johnny posing shirtless with their M-14s propped menacingly on their hips. The third photo was a close-up of Tuck, his cap tilted to show off a proud smile and a confident stare.

Fidgeting, Curtis looked—for the first time in three months—at his son. He put his hand to his mouth. Rubbed the back of his head. Put his fist to his cheek. Again put his hand to his mouth. His eyes watered. He could not stop the tears. Tuck was no longer his boy.

A rain-soaked Dave opened the carport door. "Sure am glad I don't have to mow…Wow, is that Tuck? What'd they do to him? Donnie-Boy? Hell, I'm bigger than Tuck now!"

Dave's exclamation shook Curtis from his melancholy.

He looked at Dave, sized him up, and then nodded with a raised brow. "Yeah, I think you just might be."

"Mama! You've got to come here, quick," Dave shouted. "We got pictures."

"Aaaah, pictures?" Mary screamed with delight from a back room before clamoring over Curtis' back. His ears rang when she again yelled and snapped up the photos. "Oh, my baby. Oh, my baby," she cooed. "Oh, my poor baby. What have they done to him? Don't they ever feed him?"

"They're making a Marine out of him, Mary," Curtis scoffed, discretely regaining composure. "What did you think you'd see?"

"But he looks so tiny with no hair, man," Dave said.

"I've got to call Grace," Mary said, caressing the edges of the photos. "Maybe she's got more from Donnie-Boy. And, you can call Wilfred to see if he's got some."

Mary picked up the handset of the telephone on the kitchen counter and dialed, anxious for the answer. "Grace? Did y'all get...yes, us too," Mary chattered excitedly. "Don't they look great? How many did ya'll get? We got three, and..."

Curtis, meanwhile, dived into Tuck's letter.

Dear family,

Well, when I graduated from boot camp I thought the worst was over. Gunny Hill said the next six or seven weeks wouldn't be much easier and he was right. This ITR stuff is rough. Ever since we got here, they've been running our butts off in the mountains and the mud with full packs and gear. About the only thing better is that we get base liberty and the instructors aren't as mean. We also got an outdoor movie theater, it's like a drive-in but with long benches. I haven't seen anything worth a darn.

Oh, yeah, me and the guys each bought a Kodak camera. Camp Pendleton sure is a big place. It really is pretty and manicured just like the Depot back in San Diego.

Like I said, the training is tough, but different. We still have to do drill, but most of the time we hike the hills to get to classes where they demonstrate weapons like machine guns and artillery. Next week we learn how to throw grenades. Can't wait to see Donnie-Boy throw one.

In two weeks, we move up the road about a mile to another camp to begin BITs (Basic Infantry Training) where we will begin to specialize. Donnie-Boy and me have been designated 0311s, infantry riflemen. Johnny is going into 0330, machine guns. That's right, we're gonna be "grunts." At BITs we'll get M-16s and learn more about combat maneuvers and actual fighting. We'll also be able to call home for the first time. I can't believe there are no phones here. I'll let you know more about that later. Remember me in your prayers—Your loving son, Tuck (Benjamin for Mom)

CHAPTER 15

The Beast
Village of Cam Lo, R.S.V.N.
Oct. 10, 1968—8 a.m. local time

Pham Van Loi stood in the small pen near the porch of his home and, with a stiff brush, stroked dried mud from the broad back of his new water buffalo. It had performed admirably in the knee-deep paddies that morning, but the young bull was not yet what old Trau Gia had been.

Loi's twin daughters, Luu and Linh, eagerly awaited their chance to sit atop the bull. They squatted on the porch steps, giggling and arguing over what they would name it. Scarcely able to walk when their older brothers died five years ago, the twins gleefully accepted the duty and pleasure of naming the young bull.

"He needs a strong name," Luu suggested.

"No, a funny one," Linh insisted.

Loi smiled at their giggles. "We will need a name by sundown; so not too much arguing." He pretended to scold them with a wave of his finger. The girls continued to laugh with dainty hands placed over their mouths.

Loi had sent Trai into the village at daybreak to purchase supplies. The monsoons loomed on the horizon and the muddy roads would make trips into the village for large items difficult. Compensation from the Americans would allow the family to stock up for the rainy months.

Suddenly, from behind Loi came a familiar and unwelcome voice. He no longer heard giggling. The hair stood up on the back of his neck like that of a cat facing an unfamiliar dog.

"So this is the beast you purchased with the cash the Americans were so anxious to part with—to keep you quiet and in your place," Loi heard. It caused his heart to skip. "Once again, you sell out to those despicable capitalists, Loi. I will never understand you."

The words flushed Loi's face red. He stopped stroking the young bull and stared forward, out toward the lake. The day grew darker.

"It would be best if you were gone when I turned around, Bui. You are not welcome here." Loi resumed his strokes, much harder and more vigorous. The bull turned its head and lowed. "Indeed, I am telling you to go away."

"I'm afraid that is not possible. You see, I come for Trai and others," Bui said. He walked toward the porch, leaned over and then ruffled the hair of one of the twins and cooed. "I never could tell you girls apart, which are you? I am your uncle Bui."

Loi teetered when he turned. He seethed, "Luu, Linh, go meet your mother in the house. Now."

The twins hopped up and dashed to the kitchen door, calling ahead, "Mama, mama, there's a mean man here and Daddy's mad."

Loi said nothing but glowered at his brother. Bui, flanked by two armed soldiers, now wore the insignia of full colonel. A new scar slicing across the breadth of his forehead added menace to his otherwise unimposing figure.

Five years younger than Loi, Bui had earned a reputation for cruelty as a child. Loi especially remembered how Bui, who after losing a fight with his older brother as a teen-ager, had cowardly kicked him from behind, causing a severe injury to Loi's left knee.

Their father had later ordered the then 15-year-old Bui

out of the Pham household. Loi also recalled how Bui had spat at his father's feet when he left, vowing vengeance.

Bui never married, but bragged of seducing many women—though most doubted such boasts. The only jobs he ever held focused on his ascending within the ranks of the local resistance, and later, the North Vietnamese Army. He was, however, glib, intelligent and imbued with charisma. A natural guerilla, brilliant organizer and a noted strategist, he was what the NVA wanted—a vicious but gifted leader.

Rumors persisted that Ho Chi Minh had personally promoted him to colonel. It wasn't long before Col. Pham Van Bui became known throughout Quang Tri Province—by both sides.

"What do you mean, you come for Trai?" Loi demanded, brandishing his brush like a saber.

"A fine animal, this one is. You must have gotten a handsome sum for old, uhh, what was it? Oh, yes, Trau Gia," Bui said, guardedly approaching the pen. "But his meat was a little tough, though." Bui turned to share a laugh with his nodding bodyguards.

Loi cocked his head, his face screwing into a question mark.

"Oh, yes, it was us who slaughtered the old brute," Bui said, gesturing with an open hand toward the young bull. "And by the way things turned out, I'd say you're better off for it, too. I know we were. It had been a long march and we were famished. A few buffalo steaks and—well, you didn't really think those trucks could have torn up a water buffalo so soon?"

Loi blinked hard and paused before replying. "Why have you come to recruit Trai? He will not fall for your lies any sooner than did his brothers."

Bui laughed, almost doubling over while taunting his brother.

"Who said we've come here to recruit him, or any of the

boys in this stinking village. No, I said we've come for him, to take him away. If he wants to join us on his own, then so much the better, I will take care of him and perhaps make him my aide. I'll make him like my son. If not, then, he will come anyway...or die by the lake in the morning. Either way you will lose him.

"But fear not, my brother, his uncle will be there to guide him." Bui grinned without smiling. "And there are others up north who know how to convince stubborn young recruits."

"If Trai is all you want, then why do you come here and dishonor me so?" Loi asked.

"Oh, but, I need your help, my big brother, to point him out to me, to call him to his fate," Bui said. "The last time I saw Trai he was but a small boy. I must confess that I could not pick him out of a crowd these days." Bui paused and looked toward the empty porch. "Of course, if you won't help me, then perhaps Minh, or one of your beautiful daughters, could point him out."

Bui was as right as he was cruel. Loi could not stop him from taking Trai. He trembled, his left knee buckled and he slipped to the ground.

"No need to bow before me, Loi," Bui jested, drawing another laugh from his comrades. "It won't do any good." He strutted into the pen and circled Loi to get a better look at the bull. He patted its long, curved horns.

Kneeling with his back to Bui, Loi held quiet his sobs. "I, nor my family, will help you betray my last son."

"Get on your feet, older brother. I have one last thing for you, then I'll be gone."

Loi struggled to stand, raised his chin and turned to face his brother. "I would never bow before you and I hope some day that, if not I, then Trai, will..."

The nine-inch blade of the shiny Bowie knife sank deep into the pit of Loi's stomach. His eyes bulged and his lungs drew air with a rattle. He grunted when Bui forced the blade upward, ripping into his diaphragm. Blood trickled from the corner of his mouth. Bui pulled the blade from Loi's chest. Loi staggered forward and grabbed Bui's collar, he took a final deep breath and spat into Bui's right eye.

Bui grabbed his older brother's shoulder, reared up and then slashed Loi across the throat. Loi gurgled and slid to the ground. He took his final shallow breaths.

"Spit on me, will you?" Bui shouted. He leaped onto Loi's chest to make sure he had breathed his last. "Now, rest easy brother, for your family will be joining you shortly."

Bui motioned the two soldiers into the house. They sprinted to the door, whooping like excited soldiers on leave. A moment later young screams came from the kitchen. A single gunshot rang out. The kitchen door flew open and one of Bui's men staggered onto the porch holding his left shoulder, a patch of red spreading across his arm and chest. Three short bursts of fire erupted from an automatic weapon. No more screams pierced the morning after the second, unsmiling guard emerged from the home.

"See about your comrade, we must go before the neighbors arrive," Bui ordered his lieutenant. "To hell with Loi and his family, and that young Trai as well. But I have to do some thinking here."

Bui entered the home of his older brother. Several minutes later he emerged and walked directly up to the bull. Another shot rang out. The young bull lowed briefly before stumbling forward to its knees, then rolled to the ground near the crumpled body of its master.

•

9 a.m., Cam Lo market: The overcast skies grew darker as the morning wore on. Trai filled his shoulder bags with the various sundries on his mother's shopping list, and then added a loaf of French bread for a special treat. He also

placed—and paid in advance for—orders for the larger items on his father's list. They planned to return to the market with their work cart, pulled by the young bull. Perhaps his mother and sisters would accompany them if the weather abated, he hoped.

"You hurry back, young man," the shopkeeper shouted from the veranda. "You have quite a load to get home before the rains." Trai waved and walked to the shoulder of Route 9, the main east-west highway running through Cam Lo.

A score of eager children crowded the roadside, sitting on the shoulder waiting for the American convoys, which passed almost daily. They often collected treats—mostly unwanted C-rations—thrown by the Marines and soldiers. When the convoys stopped in the village, enterprising youths hawked cold drinks to the Americans, who eagerly paid several U.S. dollars for the icy luxury. The children offered some of their wares to Trai, but he had no time and picked up his pace. Storm clouds were gathering.

Trai hardly noticed the gunshots echoing in the distance. Such sounds were common. It was like that the morning of Trau Gia's death, too. The thought nagged at him. He also remembered his father's account of his brothers' deaths—shots in the distance. What if? No, that couldn't happen again. Or, could it? Still, he felt something was wrong. He again picked up the pace.

Five minutes later Trai neared the outskirts of Cam Lo where the Pham families and their ancestors had lived since colonial times. About a dozen neighbors spoke excitedly. He heard an older child scream, followed by a woman's mournful wail.

Trai's knees nearly buckled and his chest tightened when he realized the crowd had gathered near his home. No, not again, he pleaded. His eyes turned toward the heavens. He dropped his burden and sprinted toward home, where sobbing directed him to the rear of the house.

MY DYING BREATH

Trai pushed his way through the crowd, stopped at the pen and stared at the contorted body of his father, who looked smaller in death. His worst fears lay in two pools of blood—those of his father and the young bull. Nothing could help his disemboweled father. Too shocked to cry out, he frantically sought his mother. She would know what to do; she would say the right things.

Aunt Linh, his mother's sister, met him on the porch with a hug and an anguished mask that left him numb. She buried her sobbing face in Trai's chest, and then fainted.

Another neighbor, a one-armed man who had served in the South Vietnamese army, stepped forward and grabbed Trai. "Please, don't go in. They're all dead."

Trai had to see. He had to know what had happened, and, perhaps, who could do such a thing. He pulled away from the man, entered the kitchen and found his mother. Minh was slumped by the table, her face bloody and unrecognizable. His father's small pistol—once hidden in a place known only to his parents—dangled from the index finger of her right hand. Her bloody left hand seemed to clench the air in defiance. Several shots from close range had sliced off the right side of her head. The twins lay facedown in their mother's lap, their backs and arms soaked with blood. Their bloodstained smocks were pulled above their waists.

Trai fell to his knees. He gasped for air but tears no longer owned a place in his world. Anger and vengeance filled the sudden void. He was alone.

CHAPTER 16

Crossroads
Village of Cam Lo, R.S.V.N.
Oct. 13, 1968—10 a.m. local time

Trai sat on the porch steps. They were the same rough-hewn planks he had so often sat upon with his father to learn the ways of men and the world. Now, they only harbored the splintered images haunting his mind.

Three-day-old bloodstains discolored the ground. The stench of congealed blood persisted inside the home despite scrubbing. It would all soon surrender to the tropical elements, but the sights and smells of that morning would haunt Trai forever.

For days, he had pondered the fate of his family—all victims of the seemingly endless civil war. Now, what of his future? To survive, he would have to leave and change his name. But, go where? North? South? Or, perhaps, another country—if he could get out.

"Father, I am only 16 years old. I don't yet know about these things," Trai whimpered, burying his face in his arms. "What do I do? Where do I go? Where is your wisdom now?" His shoulders heaved. He was surprised to find new tears.

"Well, you won't find it crying on the porch," a familiar voice firmly replied from his right. "Many of us have lost loved ones. My husband and two sons are also gone now. So pick up your head if you are to survive."

Trai looked up, soothed to find Aunt Linh sitting beside him on the top step. He smiled feebly and then leaned his head against her shoulder. It was soft and reassuring.

"That's better," Linh said, stroking his hand. Trai's favorite aunt, she was beautiful—with raven hair, milk-white skin and hazel eyes—and smart, too—an honors graduate from the university in Saigon. Often, when angry with his own mother, he dreamed Linh was his mom.

"I must leave here," Trai whispered hoarsely. He wiped his eyes on his shirtsleeve. "But I don't know where to go, or how, or who I can trust. Can you help me?"

"Yes, I might." Linh rubbed the back of his neck. "But first, don't you want to know who killed your family?"

"It was soldiers, of course. But whose soldiers? I'm not sure. It seems like we're never sure. Like who really killed my brothers? Who killed Trau Gia? I don't know," he rambled.

"What if I could help?" she proposed. "Help you find out who is responsible. Would that help you with where you might go? With what you might do?"

"Maybe, I don't know," he said before pausing to consider the offer. "Yes, yes it would."

"Well then, open your hands as well as your mind," she said, reaching into the pocket of her long white dress. "I was there, in the kitchen, when the men removed the bodies of your family that afternoon. I was also there that night when me and two other women cleaned your home."

"Tell me something I don't know." Trai's anticipation grew when he saw Linh holding an envelope containing several small items. She looked around and lowered her voice to a dramatic whisper. He was amused. There was not another house within a hundred meters.

"This," Linh said. She placed a silvery disc in Trai's palm, "I found clutched in the hand of your poor sister, Luu. It's chocolate."

"I know what it is," he replied, taking the disc. "I've seen many. The Americans throw them to the children when they pass. We've all eaten some. They're good. But my mother would never allow them in our home. She said they were not good for us and would cause cramps and send us to the toilet too often." He smiled and examined the partially unwrapped candy. "Luu was too scared of mother to bring this home, much less out in the open."

"Yes, I know." Linh then pressed several strands of short hair into his palm. "And, this, I found in the left hand of your mother."

Trai examined the hair for several moments. His dark brown eyes widened and his mouth drooped when he realized what he held. "They're blond hairs."

"Yes, indeed," Linh confirmed, folding her arms. "And I don't know any blonds in any Vietnamese army, north or south. And...one of the men found tracks in the yard, tracks made by boots, headed to the west, toward the Marine bases."

Trai now also whispered. "It can't be. Father said they were not our enemy. He said..."

"When sweeping up the porch later, about right here, where I passed out in your arms," Linh said, blushing. She pointed to the spot. "I found dried mud from the bottom of boots, and it led into the kitchen. But what I couldn't figure out was how some of the blood got onto the porch. Your father died out here, Minh and the girls inside. Perhaps your mother's gun wounded one of her attackers. It was fired once."

"Whatever became of it?" he asked. He turned the evidence over in his palm and his mind.

"I was wondering how long it would take," his aunt said, drawing the .25 automatic from another pocket of her *ao dai*. "Here, this, like everything that you see around us, is now yours."

He took it and rubbed its smooth exterior. His father had always cared for the shiny pistol and had allowed him to fire it occasionally. It was still loaded.

"No one saw any soldiers come and go that morning," she

added. "The Marines are good at that. Perhaps it was a small patrol, which stopped and saw a chance for some fun. Maybe they were mad and frustrated, or simply cruel people.

"But it looks to me like they tried to entice the little ones with the candy before having to fight off your mother. She did protect her dignity, if you know what I mean. We checked her body and those of the girls. They'd been molested, but not entered.

"Some of the men figure that while you were off to town, Loi was out in the field training the new bull when he heard the screams and came running. He was probably jumped by others keeping watch outside. That's the only way we can figure it happening."

They sat quietly for several minutes.

"I need to think," Trai began. "I'll decide by tomorrow and let you know. If I decide to leave, I would like for you to take what you want and see to our home. Tonight, however, I will sleep and cry, one last time in my family's house."

"Yes, of course." Linh bid adieu with a kiss to his cheek. "I'll be back tomorrow morning."

Trai had already decided, and sensed Linh knew this as well.

•

8 a.m., Oct. 14: As promised, Aunt Linh returned and found Trai on the back porch packing a small knapsack he would need for his journey. He looked down at his worn sandals, muddied by the early morning drizzle. The monsoon season had arrived.

"Guess I'm going to need better sandals if I am going to get where I think I'm headed," he said, nodding toward the northern hills.

Linh's eyes drifted in the direction of Trai's nod. She smiled. "Then I might be able to help you. First, instead of sandals, take some of the money the Americans paid your family and buy a pair of the boots their soldiers wear. There's a man in Cam Lo that sells them on the sly. He'll charge a steep price, surely, but they'll be worth it."

"Good, I have some money with me but most of it is in my father's lockbox. You know where he kept it, right?"

Linh nodded.

"Take care of it for me and the home as well," Trai said, gesturing as if he were deeding it to his aunt. "And now, how else can you help me?"

She thrust both hands into the deep pockets of her white *ao dai* and stared at the ground. Her black hair flipped under just above her shoulders. "Even though you're young, I'm sure you've heard the talk about me and your Uncle Bui."

Trai cocked his head, smiled and then shrugged. "Only rumors that he had been fond of you since your husband, I mean Uncle Bap, was killed. There was some talk he visited you at night from time to time."

"It wasn't the way people thought," she explained. "This war seems to remove all shame from me and I'm not embarrassed to admit we shared a bed, but it was more than that. We shared a passion about our people and their future—what it would be like without the foreigners. And what it would take to make them leave. But we haven't time for all that now."

Linh pulled a small sheet of paper from her pocket. "Bui trusts me. He gave me this. It's instructions on how to find him whenever I might need to do so. It includes the location of his contact in Dong Ha."

Linh handed him the paper. "Careful, Bui is a vicious man. He once told me how hurt he was when his father threw him out of their home. I like to feel there is still a need of family somewhere in that bitter heart of his. Go, search him out and tell him what has happened here. I think he will help you. And tell him that I send my...my regards."

Trai hugged his aunt. She had been a treasure to him and he would heed her advice.

"One more thing, change your name and do not speak of mine. Let no one know who you are until you find Bui."

"I won't." He flashed a broad grin. "And I've already picked a name, but I won't even tell you what it is."

She returned the smile. "You're learning quickly. Go now. My prayers are with you."

They hugged again.

•

6 p.m., **Village of Dong Ha:** Trai's feet already ached from the tight fit of his new American jungle boots. He put up with the pain because he knew they would comfortably mold to his feet. He also endured the discomfort because the black leather and green nylon boots had cost him 100 American dollars.

The old French-model bus, filled with peasants and noisy livestock, arrived at the large village of Dong Ha. "Ah, here we are," he said. The rickety vehicle slowed to a stop and Trai hopped off. He tipped his broad coulee hat to the driver and waved good-bye to the nameless man he had chatted with during the short trip east along Route 9.

Trai looked around while opening Aunt Linh's directions and protected them from the fine drizzle with his hat. He read them for what seemed like the hundredth time, they were simple enough. With dusk approaching, he hurried off and in less than 20 minutes of navigating the narrow side streets, he found the small market he was looking for. Simple huts tightly surrounded it and blocked the breeze. The market smelled of foul meat, raw fish and chicken droppings. He sniffed, pinched his nose and thanked his father for providing fresh food.

At the far end stood a man who looked elderly—not rendered so by the years, but rather the gnawing of war—

selling withered turnips and over-ripe tomatoes. He was definitely the right man: One leg, one eye, and fire scarred with skin like crinkled leather. He wore simple black pajamas, pinned up to the stump of the missing appendage. Trai approached him, making sure to stay on the vendor's good side so as not to startle him.

Trai bowed. "Sir, I am seeking a man. I hope that you might help me."

"Go away, child, unless you want to buy some vegetables." The man carelessly flicked the ashes of his cigarette toward Trai's feet.

"Sir, I seek the 'Big Blade.' I was told by a woman who knows him that you could help."

The old man, peering at Trai with his one good eye, said nothing for several seconds and then took another drag from his cigarette. The stare was like being ogled by a Cyclops.

"It's nearly dark. Help me close up my cart, then follow me," the old man commanded, as if once a soldier, perhaps an officer.

Gliding along on a single crutch, he led Trai to a house at the corner of the market square. The old man leaned against the wall and pushed the door open with his crutch. He waved him inside. The man appeared to live alone in the two-room shack.

"All I have to offer you to eat are some of my vegetables. They're clean. The meat here is either rancid or of dubious origin. Don't shop in this market," he said with a friendly wink.

"I will remember that, sir," Trai said, looking around the hut. The walls were bare and there was no furniture in the front room, only straw mats on the floor. But it had running water, electricity and what looked to be an indoor toilet. Perhaps there was more to this old man than met the eye.

"You will, huh," the old man laughed and lit up another cigarette. He turned and sat in one of two chairs at a small table in what was the kitchen. He motioned for Trai to sit beside him and reached for the handle of a small refrigerator. He opened it and pulled out two cans of beer. "I am not totally without my comforts, and surprises." A hacking cough interrupted his laugh. "Damn napalm, don't ever breathe in that damn stuff!"

Trai, who'd only twice been allowed to drink rice wine by his mother, accepted the brew. It was American. The label was in a strange writing, though he made it out to read "Schlitz."

"So, you seek the Big Blade, eh?" the old man said, opening Trai's beer with a pointed opener that dangled on a string around his neck. He then opened his beer and took a long pull, followed by a drag from his cigarette.

Trai, too, took a long sip. His eyes watered and he fought off the urge to spit the harsh brew onto his host's table. He swallowed and his soured face confessed to the old man.

"First beer, eh, kid?"

"Yes," Trai admitted, setting the can on the table. "And maybe my last if they all taste like this. I guess it must be, like what I heard my father say, an acquired taste."

"Most assuredly. But once you catch on, well, let's just hope you live so long."

Trai again looked around the room to make sure they were alone. "And, yes, I seek the Big Blade. I have personal reasons to want to meet him."

"I'm sure you do, for you haven't even told me your name."

"And neither have you offered me yours," Trai retorted.

"Bright young man. You just may survive this war after all. But a young one like yourself, who does not say who he is, or what he wants, just does not walk up and meet the Big Blade, just like that. I might be able to help. It takes patience. You can stay here the night if you desire. I'm sure by the morning I'll have something for you."

"That would be most gracious, sir, I accept your offer," Trai said with a bow. "And now, I might try to start acquiring that taste for beer."

Trai's first beer, and one other, soon had him seeking an early retreat to the toilet and then to a straw matt on the den floor. The codger, meanwhile, sat at the table, drank beer and smoked cigarettes into the night. His hacking cough grew annoying.

But sleep came rather quickly and deeply for Trai and without the nightmares that had haunted him the last several nights. But the rest was far too brief.

Startled, Trai awakened to the feel of ropes being looped around his feet and hands. A black hood swallowed his head. He fought briefly before a blow to the back of his neck returned him to dreamland. He did not see the old man's salute of a raised beer and a smile.

•

5 a.m., Oct. 15, hills of the DMZ: When he awoke, Trai was lying on his back in damp grass staring at the silhouette of tall trees. It was still dark, just before dawn he guessed, and he could not make out the new faces kneeling around him. He was no longer bound and quickly tried to sit up.

"Whoa there, young pup, not so fast," advised a hearty Vietnamese voice with a strange French lilt.

"Stand up," another voice commanded. "Let me take a look at you."

He stood, unsteadily at first. He rubbed the back of his throbbing neck.

"Humph, not much to this one," said the second voice, an officer Trai supposed. "You want to join us? You want to fight Americans? Kill Americans? Because if you don't, we have no use for you and you can go back to your mama."

"No sir, I mean yes, sir, I want to kill Americans," he answered. "It is indeed what I want."

"*Mon dieu*, that's all we need, another idealistic young slayer," the first voice added.

"Well, he doesn't look like much of a soldier to me but he does look strong and the old major vouches for his intelligence. Maybe he'll do," the officer said. "But for now, until we can train you, and learn to trust you, you will carry and do what we tell you. Is that understood?"

"Yes, yes sir. It is. I will earn your trust," Trai said, looking around at a dozen or so phantoms standing nearby. A few bowed slightly to welcome him. Most merely walked away.

"And one other thing," the officer added. "We are not Viet Cong, we are North Vietnamese Army raiders and somehow you've merited joining us." He turned to walk away to join the other soldiers but paused and looked back. "Louie, he's yours."

"*Merci beaucoup, fils putain*. Let's go, lad, let's get you fixed up."

Trai smiled. He vowed to learn, and someday the Americans would pay dearly for what they had done to his family.

CHAPTER 17

Long Distance
BITS, Camp Pendleton, Calif.
Oct. 15, 1968—4 p.m. local time

Tuck choked the pistol grip of the short black rifle, snuggled it into his right shoulder and held it as motionless as a mime in Jackson Square. He peered through the sights at the silhouette of a man's torso. From 200 yards, the target appeared large in his eye and vulnerable in his mind.

He squeezed the trigger of the M-16. POP! Its recoil paled before the more powerful M-14. The small but fiendish bullet reached out and placed a hole through the forehead of the "man."

"Very good, PFC Richard, very good," Staff Sgt. Terry Larken said with a distinct Texas drawl. The stocky instructor placed his hand on Tuck's shoulder. "Like the feel, right? Squeeze off a few more. Show us what you can do with your new bitch."

Tuck stepped off the firing line, turned and then grinned at Johnny and Donnie-Boy, who waited their turns. "Guess ol' Tuck's gonna be the fair-haired boy out here, too," Johnny mumbled.

"As long as he's on our side, it's OK with me," Donnie-Boy replied. "Now just you watch."

Donnie-Boy smiled at Tuck and formed a letter "T" like a referee signaling time out. Tuck nodded and stepped back onto the firing line and aimed. POP! POP! POP! POP!...POP! POP! POP! The shots peppered the air when he squeezed off an evenly metered seven-round burst.

Larken, watching the target through binoculars, paused, glanced at Tuck, and then returned his attention to the target. He reached down and picked up a field phone wired to the target area. "Slim, send me the target from No. 10, I've got to see this for myself, over."

Two minutes later, Tuck watched Larken, a Basic Infantry Training rifle range instructor, who had been a sniper with 24 confirmed kills during two tours in Vietnam, look over the target. "You did this on purpose, right? It didn't just happen, did it? I'm kinda hoping it just happened, you know, so I won't have to explain it to the old man. This is gonna be heard all the way to the top out here and he's gonna want to see you."

"I was just trying to show you what I could do," Tuck said. "I'm sure I'll get better."

Larken held up the target and traced the outline of the letter "T" stenciled into the silhouette's forehead. "Son, if you get any better, we'll be sending your ass packing to Da Nang tomorrow."

Tuck had used the first bullet fired as an anchoring point then placed two shots each on either side of the first to form the horizontal bar of the "T." He had then placed three more rounds below the first hole to fill out the vertical leg. The letter "T" fit inside a four-inch circle.

"Hell, I hope they don't make him some sort of sniper," Johnny said. "I'd hate to lose that little security blanket."

"Sniper, never. Tuck's never killed anything but game birds," Donnie-Boy explained. "Give him too much time to think about what he's shooting and he'll freeze up. He's got the ability, but not the heart. I'd like to know how many times he chickened out on squirrel hunts."

•

It was nearly 7 p.m. when Tuck escaped the clutches of the ranking range officer and sprinted to the phone booth across the street from the Catholic chapel, where Donnie-Boy and Johnny waited in line. It was a Tuesday evening and the first time the trio could get together to make short phone calls home.

Donnie-Boy held their places in line while Johnny had gone to the enlisted men's club to buy hamburgers. He joined Donnie-Boy only moments before they saw Tuck sprinting down a gentle hill toward them. "Hurry up Tuck, I've already had to let three or four go ahead of us," Donnie-Boy hollered. "They're only giving us two minutes each."

"Two minutes, that's all," Johnny winced.

"That's all that's fair with the long lines every night," Donnie-Boy explained. He reached inside Johnny's bag for a burger.

"Hey, what you doin'? All I could afford was these three burgers and a malt, man. Get, your hands out, I'm hungry," Johnny snarled at Donnie-Boy, and then turned to Tuck. "And you, you gonna go be a sniper there, Sgt. York?"

"No, I turned them down," Tuck said, watching the man in line before Donnie-Boy enter the booth. "But they said I'll always have that choice."

Johnny broke out into a smile full of burger and shoved the bag against Donnie-Boy's arm. "Here you go. I was just shittin' you," he said, trying to assuage Donnie-Boy's feelings.

"Don't want none of your goddamn burgers. Shove 'em up your big Mamou ass."

"Hell, I'll take it, Johnny," Tuck said. He wedged his hand into the bag and pulled out a soggy cheeseburger that dripped down his wrist. "Damn, just like me and Donnie-Boy like 'em, too. Thanks, Johnny."

"You sure you don't want one?" Johnny said, nudging Donnie-Boy's shoulder and waving the surviving burger under his nose.

"I don't think any frogs peed on 'em," Tuck added with a wink.

Donnie-Boy licked his lips and reached out when the Marine in the phone booth hung up the receiver and yelled, "Next."

Donnie-Boy grabbed the remaining burger and dove into the phone booth.

The Marines had written that they would be calling home soon but could not be specific. So when Grace Hebert's kitchen phone rang after 9 p.m., she had no idea who it might be. "Hello," Grace's singsong telephone voice greeted the caller.

"I have a long distance call for anyone from a Donald Hebert. Will you accept..."

"Yes, yes, of course operator..."

"Hey, Mom, it's me, Donnie, out in California. Can you hear me, Mom?"

"Yes, son, I hear you. I miss you so much, Donnie. Oh, wait just a minute, Mary's here, I need to tell her to hurry home."

"OK, but we have only two minutes each."

"Mary, Mary," Grace hollered toward the den. Mary joined Grace each Tuesday to watch "Peyton Place." It was a weekly ritual.

"What, Grace? Can't it wait until a commercial?"

"No, Donnie's on the phone. You better get home. He says Benjamin's going to be calling shortly."

"Aaaaaaaaagh!" was all Grace heard before the den door slammed.

"Oh, Donnie. There's so much I want to say to you, I don't know where to start. Your step-dad is not home. He's out again. But I'm sure he'll be disappointed."

"That's OK, tell him I...just tell him...whatever. Listen, Mom, we should be home in some two weeks, about Nov. 1. We'll be landing in Baton Rouge at about 6 p.m. your time.

We figured it would save time tonight if I gave you all the particulars. Better come with a big car, us three guys have a lot of gear."

"Uncle Jack already said we could use his station wagon. Oh, Donnie, it's so good to hear your voice. Tell me about..."

•

Wilfred Robert snoozed on the sofa of his den. A copy of the Baton Rouge newspaper's sports section was spread across his bare chest. He'd put in a long day, hauling perhaps one too many freezers into the shop. He had fought off the fatigue to read about LSU's 3-1 Tigers, who were looking to bounce back after a 30-0 loss to Miami. But he had nodded off in the middle of Bud Montet's column. The rhythmic ticking of the anniversary clock on the mantle metered his nap.

The ringing of the kitchen phone clanged like a fire alarm.

"Oh, shit, not another service call," he grunted. "Maybe I ought to just let it ring." It rang three more times. "OK, OK, hold your hosses, I'm comin' damn it."

After the fifth ring Johnny was about to hang up when a grumpy, yet familiar, voice growled on the other end, "Helllloh."

"Daddy, it's me."

"Who?"

"Me, Johnny."

"Joh-Johnny. Johnny, is that you?"

"Yeah, it's me. How are you, Dad?"

"OK, and you?"

"Oh, OK, I guess. Lost a lot of weight. Food ain't worth a shit."

"Yeah, I know."

"I'll be home in a coupla weeks. Maybe we'll go see the Tigers in Baton Rouge?"

"That'd be great, Johnny."

"Listen, Dad, about Nonc Bub. Well, I really am sorry. It hurt and I cried some."

"Me, too, son."

"Well, gotta go now so Tuck can call home."

"OK, Johnny. Uh, Johnny?"

"Yeah, Dad?"

"Uh, I love you, son. You take care, you hear?"

"Uh. Love you too, Dad."

Wilfred hung up the phone, pulled up a chair and wiped away a single tear. Outside of business, he'd never spoken on a telephone for that long.

"Damn, Johnny, you still got a minute and a half to go. Sure you finished?" Tuck asked, moving into the booth.

"Yeah, we was all finished. Couldn't think of nothing else. Daddy never shut up."

•

Curtis and Mary Richard eagerly waited at the kitchen table. It was no accident when Mary snatched up the receiver before Curtis' poorer hearing could detect a note from the first ring.

"Hello, Mom?"

"Tuck, Tuck, is that you?" Mary blurted before noticing Curtis' grin and arched eyebrow. "Oh, uh, Benjamin, it's so good to hear your voice again. Have they been treating you well? You eating better? I have so much to ask you. Let's see…"

"Whoa, Mom. Slow down. I got two minutes, not two seconds."

"Oh, Benjamin. My baby, it's just so good to know you're safe." Mary's tears wet the receiver before Curtis pushed his ear close to hers. "I pray every day for your safety. When are you going to be home, son? Soon, I hope."

"Yeah, we're set to leave here early on Nov. 1. We'll be

getting into Baton Rouge late that night and then you can ask me everything you want. I love you, Mom."

"I love you, too, Benjamin. Here's your father."

"Tuck ol' boy, you sound well," Curtis greeted him.

"Fitter'n I've ever been, that's for sure. Wish I was playing ball again. Dad, this really is a top-notch outfit and I'm going to make you proud. You'll soon realize I made the right decision."

"Tuck, I've known that since I read your first letters," Curtis assured him. "You're going to make a fine Marine. And you've long since made me proud."

"Hey, Dad. I did the 'T' for them this afternoon with an M-16. Just like you taught me with the old .22."

"Get out. You didn't?"

"Oh, yeah, and they were impressed," Tuck added. "I've gotten even better than since when you taught me. They offered to make me a sniper. But I turned 'em down. I want to stay with Donnie-Boy and Johnny."

"Well, you can tell me all about it when you get in. I know your time is getting short, so here's Mom again. Bye, son," Curtis said, handing the phone to Mary.

"Benjamin? How long will y'all be in for?

"Not sure, don't think we'll make Thanksgiving. We'll come back here to Camp Pendleton for about a month of Staging before leaving for Okinawa. About a week after that we'll head to Da Nang. That's what they tell us now."

"That means you'll be in Vietnam about a week into January. That's too soon, too soon."

"I gotta go now, Mom. The next guy is gettin' a little anxious," Tuck said.

A Marine pounded his fist on the door. "Hurry, the hell up, dude. I gotta call my chick," the drunken private threatened. "Get outta there before I mess you up."

Tuck flipped the obnoxious Marine the finger. "Really

gotta go now, Mom. Love you, see you soon." The man reached in the booth and grabbed Tuck's collar.

"Love you too, Tuck. I mean Benjamin. Love you, too." Mary said, slipping the receiver back onto its cradle. Curtis hugged Mary and handed her a tissue.

Johnny, meanwhile, hugged the angry Marine, who suddenly found himself suspended six inches off the ground. "My man ain't finished telling his mom he loves her yet. So just cool down or I'll pop you like a zit."

"OK, man, OK, I got it. Just put me down," the Marine quietly begged.

"Now, apologize to my friend," Johnny said, lowering him.

"Screw you."

"I said, apologize. I haven't been able to tackle anyone in several months now and I'd sure like to slam your black ass to the turf just for the fun of it. Now apologize."

"OK, OK, I'm sorry I interrupted your call, dude. OK?" the Marine said glancing at Tuck, who nodded back. "Now let me go. I gotta make my call."

Donnie-Boy kept close watch on the muscular Marine when Johnny let him go. The man darted into the phone booth and began his call.

"Tuck, we had it under control," Donnie-Boy admonished his friend after they walked away. "You didn't need to flip him off like that. That guy could have put a hurtin' on you. We'll always be at your side, little buddy."

Johnny stopped, turned and then looked one more time toward the booth. He walked over and shoved open the door.

"Yes, operator, Jackson, Danny Jackson. I want to place a long distance call to Tuscaloo…" The Marine paused. He saw Johnny approach. "Hey, what the hell do you want now, big boy. I apologized to the asshole. No, not you operator. What more you want from me?"

"Ain't I ever seen you before? I remember people's eyes. I've seen your eyes before."

"Hey man, you ain't queer or nothing like that, huh? I think I'd remember somebody big and white like you. And, by the way, no way you'd slam me to the turf. I'm too damned fast for your fat ass," he laughed, slammed the door shut and braced it with his foot.

Tuck pulled Johnny from the door of the booth. "Come on, let's go catch a flick before bedtime. You can always crush that guy later."

"I don't wanna crush him. I just wanna know where I've seen those eyes before."

"That's right operator, Tuscaloosa, Alabama. You know, Alabama, where Coach Bryant runs the state..."

CHAPTER 18

A Peacock's Vision
Baton Rouge, Louisiana
Nov. 2, 1968—10 p.m. local time

"Aw, crap. That's about right. We finally get to see an LSU football game again and some frickin' sophomore from Ole Miss kicks our ass. I played freshman ball against that damn Manning kid and I knew he'd be good. But damn, he could've waited a week longer to have a game like this," Johnny lamented, watching the final seconds tick away in LSU's 27-24 loss to the Rebels. It was the second loss for the 5-2 Tigers.

"Heck, I hope we get to see them win one before we have to head back to Pendleton," Tuck added, leaning over to help gather their stadium seats and binoculars.

"Aw, shit," Johnny continued. "We had it won, too. If I had hung around, maybe...naaah, to hell with it."

Wilfred had cajoled a parts supplier into selling him a block of eight tickets to the big football rivalry. Wilfred and Johnny, Tuck, his dad Curtis, and younger brothers Dave and Winston, joined Donnie-Boy and his stepfather John for the outing.

The Marines had arrived home the day before and Tuck's mom had dominated his time. The same held true for Grace with Donnie-Boy. Wilfred had Johnny all to himself. Mary and Grace had, however, surrendered Saturday night to the boys and their Tigers.

"This was great Mr. Robert, I really enjoyed the day," Donnie-Boy said while descending the concrete steps of venerable Tiger Stadium. "But don't take offense if I say I'm ready to get back to Eunice to start checkin' out the chicks and throwing back a few brews."

Many of the fans, mostly older men and women, smiled and nodded at the Marines—decked out in their dress greens. A few wished them luck; a couple even saluted. Longhaired college boys snickered or shook their heads in disgust. A few shot them the peace sign—others, the finger. A few girls tossed a weak smile in their direction. Most, however, ignored them.

"I don't guess it was all that good of an idea to wear uniforms," Tuck commented just before one drunken student cursed them. "Yeah, well fuck you, too, hair-head."

"Don't worry about them, Tuck," Curtis said. "A little beer and a tough loss are their biggest problems tonight, not your uniform."

"No, sir, Mr. Richard. I'm their biggest problem," Johnny said. "I ain't gonna take none of that shit. I've worked too hard to earn this uniform."

"Simmer down T-Johnny. Or else, I'll be your biggest problem," Wilfred interjected. "It's like this all over the country. It ain't personal. It's just this war ain't too popular. I know what it's like. Not much different than when I was back from Korea. They just don't understand."

Winston tugged at Tuck's coat sleeve. "What they mean by baby burners?" he said, looking up with adoring eyes.

Tuck bent over and then swung his seven-year-old brother into his arms, forcing a quick giggle. "I don't understand it either, Win. I don't either." He hoisted the towhead atop his shoulders and carried him to the cars.

•

The two cars lazily turned into the driveway of the Richard home at midnight.

Curtis scooped up sleeping Winston and walked to the

door where Mary and Grace waited. "Great day, great game, but the final score stunk," Curtis said, snatching a welcome-home kiss.

"Yeah, we listened on the radio. That young Manning kid is something, huh." Mary said.

"Yep. We'll get him next year. LSU's young and they'll be loaded," Curtis said. Mary smiled and rolled her eyes.

Reaching the door, Tuck pulled the knot out of his khaki tie and stifled a yawn. Mary gave him a quick hug. "Had fun?"

"Sure did. Johnny's dad not only got us great tickets, but Johnny got us in to meet coach Charlie Mac this afternoon. I thought Dad was gonna bust when they shook hands," Tuck said. "Now, I gotta go change. We're goin' to the Peacock to check things out, and we don't want to look out of place."

"Oh, yeah," Grace said, smiling. She reached up to scrub her palm over Tuck's bristly scalp. "Y'all will really fit in with that crowd."

"Hey, Tuck," Donnie-Boy shouted from the driveway. "Tell my Mom to get on out here so we can go. We'll be back after we change. Johnny's gonna stay over at my house."

•

The Purple Peacock, one of the top nightspots in Acadiana, boasted loud bands, a great dance floor and a big, well-stocked bar. The action and the music inside had reached a crescendo at 1 a.m. when Tuck and his buddies walked up the purple-painted steps. A muscular, tattooed man with a drooping moustache and shoulder-length, gray-streaked blond hair sat on a stool near the door collecting cover charges. Initially insulted when asked for his identification, Tuck proudly produced his Marine ID.

"I expected so. Go ahead, Marines. And *semper fi*, dudes," the fortyish man growled with a wink. He waved the trio through. "Put your money away, fellas, cover charge is on me.

Tell the bartender that Hank said 'good for two.' And let me know if anyone gives y'all shit. You hear?"

"Sure thing, Hank," Tuck said, shaking the man's leathery hand. There was something familiar about him.

"You know that guy, Tuck?" Johnny asked. "He's bad looking—ought to be a DI, yeah."

"Never seen him before tonight," Tuck replied, shrugging his shoulders.

"Nope, me neither," Donnie-Boy said shaking his head. "But I'm gonna find that bartender."

Shaped like a horseshoe, the split-level Purple Peacock's spacious interior faced an elevated stage. There were tables on the upper level and the bar occupied nearly two-thirds of the lower section. Another popular feature was the dance floor, which was fashioned from oak boards purchased from a bankrupt bowling alley. Some of the aiming arrows were still visible.

Donnie-Boy soon found Hank's bartender—a burly, bearded man who approached them with a pronounced limp.

"Hey, Hank sent us," Donnie-Boy hollered over the hard-rock tunes banged out by a group called the Equilateral Fudgesicle. "He said 'good for two.' You the right guy?"

"Yeah, I'm Tom. You say Hank sent you?"

"Yep, he said 'good for two' for me and my buddies here," Donnie-Boy said. "So, how about a couple of beers?"

"Sure, you must be Marines or Hank wouldn't have sent you to me. He don't say that too often. And as for those free beers, well, Hank must like you guys because 'good for two' don't mean two free beers. It means y'all can drink free for two hours," Tom grinned and winked.

"Alllriiight," Johnny exclaimed, reaching for one the cans of Budweiser that Tom slid onto the bar. He turned and handed a beer to Tuck, who was settling into a stool near the end of the bar.

"Me and Hank were grunts back in '65. I just spent a couple of years in the Corps and did one tour in the Nam before catching some of Charlie's trash in my knee and some other places I don't want to talk about," Tom said, raising his voice. "Ol' Hank goes back as far as Korea, even did a coupla years as a DI in San Diego..."

"What I tell you, yeah," Johnny said, nudging Tuck with his elbow.

"...and then he did two tours in that shithole you all are headed to," Tom said with a wink. "Y'all are headed to the Nam, right?"

"Yeah, we're on leave. Just got in yesterday," Donnie-Boy started to explain.

"Yesterday? Damn, that's 'good for three,'" Tom said and winked again. They grinned.

"We head back in a few weeks," Donnie-Boy added, "Go through Staging for a month and then fly out to Okinawa for processing—next stop Da Nang."

"Yeah, I remember the route well," Tom said quietly and with yet another wink. "Look, fellas, y'all have a good time tonight and hold your beer right and I'll keep 'em comin' all night, for you, and for whoever you might meet up with, if you know what I mean."

"Why'd he quit?" Tuck asked, wondering if Tom's wink was just a nervous tick.

"Who?" Tom asked.

"Hank, he can't be all that old."

"Oh. Did you notice the stool he was sittin' on, or was he standing?" Tom asked.

"Sitting on a high stool," Tuck said.

"Well, next time you pass, look for the cane," Tom advised. "A 50-cal took his left leg off just above the knee. Hank was a good Marine, a damn hero, should have gotten the Navy Cross, or maybe even the big one. Never did, but got two Silvers Stars.

"Oh, and don't mess with him, he'll snap you like a twig," Tom added, looking at Tuck and then Johnny. "You, too, big boy."

After three beers and a trip to the men's room, a mild buzz took over Tuck's mind and stride. He landed a friendly punch on Donnie-Boy's left arm. "Let's grab another beer and walk around a bit, see if any of the gang's still around."

"Let's go, little buddy," Donnie-Boy replied. "Want to join us, Johnny?"

"Nah, y'all go, I'll keep Tom company for a while. Holler if y'all find some action."

Tuck and Donnie-Boy walked up to the second level just shy of 2:30 a.m. Meandering through the crowded room, Tuck, unaccustomed to drinking the past months, bumped into a couple of tables and patrons.

"Hey, look out, asshole," a Joe College type slurred when Tuck tilted their table enough to spill a pair of drinks—one on Joe College, who rose shakily to challenge Tuck, and the other on his date, who stepped back into the shadows.

"Oh, shit, man, I'm really sorry," Tuck apologized, dropping to his knees to pick up the spilled glasses. "Let me help you clean this up and then I'll buy you each another drink. OK?"

Tuck felt Joe College grab him by the shoulder and try to lift him. He resisted.

"Hey, I said I was sorry and I'll make it up to you. OK?" Tuck said, slowly raising his head. Instead of looking up at the man, however, his eyes latched onto Joe College's date and followed the elegant legs upward to mid thigh where her miniskirt began. A narrow waist and medium-sized but shapely breasts followed. By the time he reached her face, Tuck and four cans of Budweiser were already in love. Surely, she must be a beauty queen. No wonder Joe College was so smug. Her fragrance filled his nostrils. The winsome brunette with a petite figure had caught his fancy as sure as an LSU touchdown.

"I said, what are you going do about this, asshole," Joe College shouted.

Tuck stared into the young woman's eyes. Darkness hid their color but they most assuredly were as beautiful as the rest of her.

"Hey, asshole, I'm talking to you."

"Yeah, I heard you the first time," Tuck replied calmly, unable to take his eyes off the vision. "I said I would clean up the mess and buy you another drink."

"That's not enough."

"It's not?" Tuck said, refusing to take his eyes off the girl, but not letting Joe College out of his sight.

"No, I want drinks all night, but first I want a piece of you," Joe College shouted again, struggling to remove his sweater.

"Oh, shit. Timmy's mad," one of Joe College's two friends said, moving aside. "There's gonna be trouble. Y'all get back."

Donnie-Boy stood firmly behind Tuck. He glared at the bystanders, daring them to interfere.

"OK, whatever," Tuck said flatly, his eyes still fixed on the girl, who now returned his gaze.

She stepped aside and into the light. Her eyes blazed like that of a cat—they were hazel.

"My name is Tuck, Tuck Richard," he said, extending his hand. She took it and squeezed gently. Tuck's insides quivered. He'd never felt this way. It was something different, special.

"Anna Carlisle, Mr. Richard," she replied. Her voice was melodic. "Now would you please settle this thing with my date so we can get on with our evening, please."

"Oh. Uh. Yeah, sure," Tuck said, reluctantly letting her

hand slide from his. He turned to face Joe College. "Now what was it you wanted of me? A piece of me?"

"That's right, little bald boy."

"Well, then. How about a piece of my fist?" Tuck flicked out a stiff left jab, which caught Joe College across the bridge of the nose. Blood spurted. "Or, maybe..." Tuck spun around. "My elbow...or foot...or my knee."

Four furious blows sent Joe College into a doubled-up knot of pain on the Peacock floor. Tuck turned to Anna, "Your boyfriend, you said? Sorry about that."

"No, I said my date," she corrected. "Anyway, he had it coming. You did all you could. Timmy just gets a bit obnoxious when he's drinking. Poor Timmy, and it's his birthday, too."

Tuck cringed. "You didn't have to tell me that."

Turning to watch Timmy's two friends help him to his feet, Anna stifled a laugh with her fingers pressed to her lips. "You'd better bring him to the car so I can drive him home," she said. "I'm sure Sheriff Tate will be wondering where we are at this hour."

"The sheriff's son?" Tuck groaned. The semiconscious Timmy moaned.

"Yep, but it's OK. I'm sure he won't want to remember this by morning and...well, I'm not going to tell either, silly." Anna said, turning toward the door.

Tuck's eyes followed her every move.

Walking toward the sound of the commotion, Johnny called out, "Anna, come here, *cher.*"

She turned and ran to Johnny, wrapped her arms around his waist and then pecked him on the cheek. She whispered into his ear, laughed and then looked back at Tuck. She wiggled a small finger wave and left.

"Problem here, little buddy?" Johnny asked, pausing to drain his beer. "That was Sheriff Tate's boy, Timmy, they were dragging out wasn't it?"

Donnie-Boy nodded and drained his beer. "Nope, no problem at all. Tuck just kicked the shit out of an asshole that's all. Did it pretty damn efficiently, too. Saw the whole thing. Ol' Gunny Hill would be proud."

"Yeah, there's only one problem," Tuck said, checking to see if he had skinned his knuckles.

"Oh, and what's that?" Donnie-Boy asked.

"How do I get to see her again? And, do I have a chance?"

"Well, she is out of your league," Johnny said, slapping him on the back. "But getting to see her again's no problem. You see, she's my cuzz, little buddy, and she just told me we're invited to her house next weekend for a barbeque. And she wants you two to come along."

"Allllriiight," Tuck whispered, his smile growing into a wide grin.

"Enough of that shit, I've got a hot one lined up for later tonight and the night's gettin' old," Donnie-Boy said, ushering his friends back to the bar. "So let's pay ol' Tom another visit."

Tuck looked back, hoping to catch another glimpse of Anna Carlisle. But she was gone. Instead, he saw Hank sitting on the high stool, his cane leaning up against a nearby door. He was smiling, and giving Tuck the thumbs up. He'd seen it all.

CHAPTER 19

Miss Carlisle
Eunice, Louisiana
Nov. 9, 1968—4 p.m. local time

The short ride north up Highway 13 to the Carlisle residence was sullen. LSU had just dropped a tough 16-7 decision at Alabama and neither Tuck nor Johnny enjoyed losing—particularly to Bama and the Bear.

"Shit, shit and double shit," Johnny said. He banged his left hand on the steering wheel of Wilfred's pickup truck. "Just once, I'd like to beat those assholes. Only time I've seen it was when I was playing freshman ball. We whupped 'em good, yeah. But that didn't mean shit."

"Must have meant something to you, didn't it?" Tuck said. He was jammed in between Johnny and Donnie-Boy. "Well, didn't it?"

"Damn straight it did," Johnny said. He smiled and then reached over and rubbed Tuck's head. "Thanks."

"She got any sisters?" Donnie-Boy asked with a hopeful smile.

"Who? Anna? Yeah, two, but way too young for you hard-leg bastards," Johnny laughed. "But I got a lot of other horny teen-age cousins who'll probably be there. They're pretty damn ugly, though. Not pretty like me, *non*."

Tuck rolled his eyes. "Well, I just hope she remembers me. There was a lot of beer flowing at the Peacock last weekend."

"Oh, I wouldn't worry about that, little buddy. She

called me twice during the week to make sure you'd be comin' today."

Tuck rapped Johnny on the shoulder. "Why you didn't tell me that before?"

"Oww, that hurt" Johnny yelped. "If I had, you'd have been pestering me all week about her. Now wouldn't you?"

"Yeah, you right, but…"

"But nothing. Hurry up and drive," Donnie-Boy interrupted. "I gotta pee."

•

Jess Carlisle, a petroleum engineer who owned an exploration company, and his wife, Marie, lived in a three-story, plantation-style home in the country with their three girls.

Tall, twin white columns—supporting a small but ornate veranda—adorned the front of the white brick home, which was nearly hidden about 100 yards from the west side of Highway 13. A trio of ancient oaks embraced the house in their stout, long limbs, gnarled by storms and the ages. Two of the giant live oaks flanked and shaded either side of the house while a tall red oak towered over from the backyard. They, along with a dozen pines and pecans, instilled a sense of permanence and grace.

"So this is who lives here," Tuck said. Johnny turned into the drive. "I always wondered whose spread this was."

Dozens of dark green azalea bushes, just now setting the buds that promised a trail of lavender in the spring, and mature crepe myrtles, which had only recently dropped their delicate pink blooms, grew like sentinels. They joined to point the way for visitors who traveled the white shell lane that snaked its way through the estate.

Johnny steered the blue truck into a grassy field where a score of cars and pickups crammed their way into a makeshift parking area. A '65 Corvette—a gleaming silver Stingray—

sat beneath a triple carport on the south side of the home. Tuck whistled low and long. "Wow."

Johnny laughed at Tuck's gape. "Told you she's out of your league, dumb ass. Good luck."

Donnie-Boy winked at Tuck and smiled. "Let's go meet the enemy."

A northwest breeze cooled the afternoon and sustained the aroma of barbeque drifting from the backyard. Johnny sniffed the air. "Well, even if you do blow it with Anna, you're still gonna get a good meal, yeah. Ol' Jess sure can barbeque, and he'll let you know it, too."

The trio walked through the carport—Tuck delicately traced his fingers over the smooth top of the 'Vette—and into a huge backyard. Dozens of adults and children, chatting and laughing, milled around. Country and western music blared from a loudspeaker. A balladeer's crooning mixed with the buzzing of countless locusts clinging to branches high atop the trees.

Tuck heard a small group of men cussing about "that damn Bear."

"Well, looky what we got here. The Marines have landed," the burly Jess Carlisle shouted. "Damn, T-Johnny, they've whittled you down a bunch. Haven't they?" He strutted over to the trio with a long fork in one hand and a bottle of Schlitz in the other. A sauce-stained apron surrounded his ample girth. He bear-hugged Johnny. "Damn, it's good to see you again."

"You, too, Uncle Jess. Happy 25th Anniversary."

"Well, thank you, son. Hey, Marie. Look who's here. It's T-Johnny and his Marine buddies," Jess shouted over his shoulder to his wife, who flitted from guest to guest. "Well now, which of you is the one they call Tuck? My Anna's been talking about him all week. Says he beat the crap out of young Mr. Tim Tate. And, I want to shake his hand. That boy, and his daddy, the Sheriff, could both use regular ass-whippings. Ha."

"That would be me, sir," Tuck replied formally, offering his hand.

"You a little shit, ain't you?" Jess said, holding out a thick-fingered hand to shake. He was a head taller than Tuck. "...to be going around kickin' people's ass like that, I mean."

"Well, he kinda asked for it, sir. I just..."

"Yeah, well Tuck goes around kickin' ass a lot," Donnie-Boy interrupted, patting Tuck on the shoulder. "He's one real mean Marine there, Mr. Carlisle." He then pointed to Jess' beer. "You got anymore like that, sir?"

"Oh, hell yes, fellas. We got ice chests full of cold drinks and beer right over there by the big oak," Jess said, pointing to a picnic table. At that moment, Marie arrived.

"Ooo, you look so good, T-Johnny," she squealed, then gave him a hug and a big kiss, which left a bright red lip print on his right cheek. "Look boys, I got to go see about some food in the kitchen and I'll catch y'all a little later," Marie said, turning to trot away. She paused and looked back. "Oh, by the way, which one of you is Tuck?"

The three men looked down at Tuck.

"Oh, you are a cute one, aren't you. I'll see y'all later. Bye, bye."

"Make yourselves at home, fellas," Jess said, pointing toward a pair of large smoking pits filled with chow. "We'll be feeding the little ones first in about 30 minutes, then the grown-ups. Until then, you can snack on some sausage and weenies right over there. T-Johnny, take 'em around and introduce 'em to everybody. By the way, where's ol' Wilfred?"

"He's still back in Eunice visiting Mr. Richard. We watched the Tigers at Tuck's house."

"Yeah, we watched it over here, too. That damn Bama.

Ol' Charlie Mac can't ever seem to beat the Bear...well, hey over there. I'm a comin'," Jess said, walking away after he spotted another group of new arrivals.

Donnie-Boy punched Tuck in the ribs and then pinched his cheek. "You're sooo cuuute...Look, before I get a beer, I just gotta go pee."

"Follow me, I'll show you to the head," Johnny said. "Tuck, you go on and wait for us at the picnic table. And if anybody gives you any shit, just kick their ass."

Johnny and Donnie-Boy walked away howling.

Nodding politely at a few familiar faces he could not pair up with names, Tuck strolled toward the picnic table. He opened the first chest and passed his hand through the icy mixture. It was empty. He stepped toward the next container and leaned over to open the lid when, suddenly, a cold shock stabbed the back of his neck. He rose and turned quickly with a balled fist, ready to retaliate. Instead of finding Donnie-Boy or Johnny, he found himself staring into Anna Carlisle's hazel eyes. Her playful gaze and teasing twist of the hips froze his reflexes.

His heart hadn't leapt in his chest like that since Gunny Hill crashed into his life.

"Looking for one like this?" Anna asked, sipping on a can of beer. Her eyes sparkled. She licked her lips and offered the beer to Tuck. "Take it. There's a lot more where this came from."

"Wh-Where? What you..." Tuck stuttered like a smitten schoolboy. He sighed. "Thanks."

Anna was poured into a pair of denim hip-huggers and her midriff T-shirt revealed a modest amount of tanned tummy. He readily noticed the purple and gold words BAYOU BENGALS, emblazoned across her white T-shirt, pouting up and resting nicely on her breasts.

She giggled softly. "Sit down, silly. I'm sorry I startled

you like that. It's just that I came across T-Johnny and your friend...Donnie-Boy, right?"

He nodded, hanging on her every word.

"And they told me to come surprise you."

"Well, you surely did that, I tell you."

"See anybody you know," she asked, waving her arm around the lawn.

"No, not really. Thought maybe I recognized some..."

"Well then, come on, I'll show you around and introduce you to some of my friends," Anna said, taking his hand. Her warm fingers were moist from the beer can but her firm grasp burned into his heart. "So, what's the first week home been like?"

"Oh, mostly doing the family thing, visiting the grandparents, aunts and uncles, you know. I hung around with a couple of my old school buddies, too."

"I figured that, so I didn't bother to call you," Anna said. They strolled around the base of the magnificent old oak. "I did see you at the A&W in Eunice the other day. But I didn't want to bother you. You looked like you were having so much fun with your buddies and all."

"I wish you would have...bothered me that is. I was wondering if I would ever see you again after that Peacock thing." He looked at Anna and then around the yard. Instead of guiding him through the guests, she had led him to a picnic table yards away from the bustle.

"Sit here," she said, patting the bench next to her. "By me."

Her sweet voice may have lacked the authority of Gunny Hill's orders, but it was just as effective. Tuck sat, but too close to the edge of the seat and slipped off, almost falling to the ground.

"What's your problem, you silly goose? I'm not going to bite," she giggled. "Not yet."

Tuck gasped and nearly spit out his sip of beer. "Why are you doing this?"

"Doing what?" she asked coyly.

"You know. Being...so overly friendly and all," he explained. Crushes had always seemed to be one way for Tuck. "You don't know me. Heck, the only time you saw me, other than at the A&W, was when I was half drunk and beating up your date. And then you invite me over to this big...wonderful barbeque."

"Look, Marine, I'm not easy and I'm not an idiot," she said pointedly. "You saw that 'Vette out there, didn't you?"

Tuck nodded. "It's fine, just like..."

"Well, I picked that car out this summer, not my Daddy. And, I could have had a brand new one—a '69 even. But the '65 is going to be a classic someday. And, you, my silly friend, are a '65, if not a '58. I just know it." She leaned closer to his ear, her warm breath chilling his spine. "The way I see it, Marine, you're not going to be around for very long and I don't have time to waste on being shy. And, I'm not going to let someone else buy this classic until I take it for a test ride."

She softly stroked his hand.

•

Tuck gulped. The knuckles in his right hand were turning white from gripping the armrest of the 'Vette. The barbed-wire fence posts were but a blur when the Corvette sped through the curve at nearly 90 miles per hour. Highway 13 straightened out and Anna shifted the sports car into high gear and prodded the 427 cubic inches of power. His head gave up the battle and he let it settle into the head rest at 115 mph. He closed his eyes. She laughed and floored it. He opened them and gulped again when the needle hit 135 mph. He put his hands over his eyes.

"You big chicken," Anna shouted above the noise, her

shoulder-length hair struggling against the gale rushing through the windows. "I guess you've had enough."

When the Stingray slowed to a modest 75 mph the blood returned to Tuck's brain.

"Big, tough Marine. Baloney," she hollered.

Tuck laughed nervously. "Most planes take off at that speed, Anna."

Dusk had begun painting the afternoon by the time she pulled onto a gravel side road and circled for the trip home. Tawny soybean fields took on the aura of spun gold. Her soft brown hair grew auburn in the bent rays of the setting November sun. Chirping sounds of the night crept forth. A crow landed on a nearby fence post with three strands of straw in its beak. She briefly stared at the black bird.

"But I got to admit, it was a thrill," Tuck said. "I never rode in a Corvette before, it's always been a dream of mine." He paused. "Thanks, I really do appreciate it, and your hospitality. I'm sorry...for my attitude earlier, OK?"

"Listen, Marine...Tuck. I like you. From the first moment I saw you last week I knew you were something special. What? I don't know yet, maybe it's those baby blues. I'm a smart girl and I'll figure it out." She held up her car keys. "Now, you wanna drive?"

"Me?" he said pointing to his heart.

"Who else, silly? Boy, you sure are going to be a tough case."

"You bet," he said, leaning over and playfully kissing her on the cheek. "Mmmwah, thanks." He grabbed the keys and ran around to the driver's side. While slipping over the console Anna heard the startled caw of the crow, which dropped one of its three straws and flapped off into the growing darkness.

Tuck settled into the cockpit of the Corvette and adjusted the seat. He turned the ignition and the car jumped to life with a throaty groan.

"You can do better than that," Anna challenged.

"What you mean? I just turned it on."

She sighed and shook her head. "I mean kiss, silly. You can kiss better than that, can't you?"

"Sure can, Babe, but first I gotta drive." he threw the car into first gear and eased back on the road. Only his wonderment at Anna's behavior competed with the thrill of driving her 'Vette.

"Careful now, she's got some pep."

"Just watch me. Remember, I'm special," he laughed. The car left a smoking trail of rubber through first and second gears. It was her turn to hold on while he piloted her classic.

Anna stared at Tuck, watching him grin and shift through the gears. Testing its nimbleness, he occasionally let out a whoop that gave her an uncommon pleasure. She turned away from him, tears filling her eyes. Was she really falling for him, or merely enjoying giving a Marine what might turn out to be his dying wish? Would this moment ever come again for them both? She was unaccustomed to such feelings. Indeed, he was something special.

•

"What you think of her?" Jess asked, after Tuck and Anna had pulled in the carport. "She's something, ain't she?"

"Yeah, she sure is, Mr. Jess," he replied with a nod, alternately looking at the steering wheel and Anna. "She's something, all right"

"Thanks," he whispered to her. She smiled back with glistening eyes that puzzled him.

"Come on you two. Dinner's ready and Marie wants all of you around before we cut the cake. So hurry on up now."

"You bet, Mr. Jess. We're coming."

Johnny and Donnie-Boy were chowing down on a pile of chicken when Tuck joined them, balancing a heaping plate. "Gotta be better than raw dove," he quipped.

"Bet your ass," Donnie-Boy said with a mouthful. "No feathers either."

Anna arrived, sat and edged close to Tuck. His friends smirked at him. Without looking at their faces, she said, "What was that about a dove? We've got great dove hunting out here. Y'all ought to come hunt some with Daddy before y'all leave."

"Oh, it's a long story," Johnny teased. "But I'm sure he'll be glad to tell you all about it one romantic evening. It'll warm your heart, girl."

"T-Johnny Robert, don't you start with me. You know better."

"Yeah, Johnny, what she really means is shut the hell up," Tuck snapped.

Donnie-Boy laughed quietly and shook his head.

"OK, OK, I'm sorry, little love birds, I mean doves, I mean..." Johnny teased again before a chicken leg slapped his cheek. "Hey!"

"And there's more where that came from, Johnny Robert," she warned, shaking a wing at him. "Come on, Tuck, let's go where we can eat in peace."

"Oooo, oooo, Tuck, let's go where we can eat in peace," Johnny mocked his cousin in a high-pitched voice. The chicken wing whizzed by his ear.

She led Tuck to the same out-of-the-way table they had shared earlier. Again, she sat close to him. "Try the potato salad, it's great. My Aunt Flossie made it."

"Want to see if I can do better?" he said, straddling the bench to face her.

"Hmmm?" she said, biting into a link of sausage. "Do what better?"

"Kiss...silly."

It was her turn to take pause. She slowly turned, stared at him in some disbelief, licked a drop of barbeque sauce from her lips and said sweetly, "Sure."

He leaned over and touched her cheek with the tips of his fingers. He kissed her lips fully, but with the slightest pressure, and held it. The sauce added to the sweetness of the embrace. Pulling away, their lips tugged at one another as if they did not want to surrender the pleasure.

"Wow, I could get used to that," Anna said, softly smiling. She slowly traced a line down his lips with a fingertip. "But, now it's my turn."

Anna clutched the back of Tuck's head and pulled him to her, pushing her lips tightly against his. Before releasing him, however, she allowed her tongue to graze his lips ever so slightly. They parted after a lingering moment but their eyes then joined as promisingly as had their lips. Reality disappeared into the collective hum of the locusts. A perfect world, full of promise, hovered around them.

"Time to cut the cake everybody," Marie yelled. "Y'all come on. Anna, bring your friends over here, too."

"Guess we'd better go, huh?" Tuck said, his gaze locked into Anna's.

"Yeah, we'd better," she sighed and smiled. "But let's not forget where we left off. OK, Marine?"

"Aye, aye, ma'am."

•

It was nearing 2 a.m. when Johnny pulled out of the Carlisle driveway and turned his dad's Ford pickup south on Highway 13 toward Eunice. The crunching sound of the shells gave way to the smooth hum of the blacktop.

Donnie-Boy—filled with his ration of beer for one evening—leaned against the passenger door and tried to nap. Tuck, sitting between his friends, quietly stared ahead. The rocking of the truck swayed him into Johnny's shoulder.

"I'm warnin' you," Johnny said, glancing at Tuck. "She's a good girl, yeah."

"Yeah, real good," he replied, touching his lips.

"No, I really mean it. She's a good girl, so don't you go try messin' with her. Hear?" Johnny emphasized, pausing to allow the thought to sink in. "Look, Anna's real playful like—like a puppy. She's always been like that. Not a teaser, mind you, just real friendly. And she don't go foolin' around, you know. If you try something, it will mess it all up for you....She's a great catch and she really likes you. I can tell."

"When did you get so damn insightful?" Tuck asked, put off by the perceived reprimand.

"I'm not sure what that means, Tuck," he replied. "But she's my cousin and we grew up together. I do know that I know Anna."

"He's right, Tuck. Keep it in your pants, but for a different reason," Donnie-Boy added to the conversation with a raspy whisper. "We'll be gone in a couple of weeks and we don't know if anyone of us is comin' home. I know I wouldn't want to leave anything here that my conscience couldn't handle. Now, y'all shut up so I can get some sleep."

Tuck had found an aspect of life totally new to him. He slid down and rested his head against the back of the seat. He closed his eyes and smiled. Anna's kisses were still with him. Tomorrow could wait—he basked in the wonder of the present.

CHAPTER 20

A Special Gift
Eunice, Louisiana
Nov. 23, 1968—11 p.m. local time

Tuck and Anna lay on the warm hood of her Corvette in the driveway of his father's home, where Tuck had anxiously listened to LSU defeat Tulane 34-10 to finish the regular season 7-3. Tuck, Johnny and Donnie-Boy, however, would be in Okinawa on Dec. 30 when the Tigers played Florida State in the Peach Bowl. Tuck's passion for college football, especially for LSU, was deeply ingrained. But it too was fading among his priorities as the reality of Vietnam drew closer, and as Anna became a part of his life.

It was the trio's last night at home. Tomorrow they would travel to Baton Rouge for the traditional airport send-off. Tuck took a sip from his can of Coca-Cola, stared into the chilly night and silently thanked the darkness that hid the tears in his eyes.

"The past two weeks have me wondering if there was ever a life before you," he said, hoping his quivering voice wouldn't give him away. " Or if there will ever be one again."

"Oh, shut up, silly, and kiss me," Anna ordered. Their kisses had grown deeply passionate, and this one was no less so. The past 12 days had been wonderful. They had spent them like eager ponies romping in a lush meadow, nipping at one another's neck. More than once they reined in their emotions—particularly Tuck, whose sexual fires glowed with the intensity of his newfound confidence. Laughs and kisses filled their hours. No time for pledges of love and thoughts of tomorrow had been allowed—until now.

Tuck rolled onto his back and looked up. "Anna, do you believe in love at first sight?" She did not reply. "I used to think that was just sappy romance stuff for poetry and movies. Now, I'm not sure if there really isn't something to that 'right chemistry' stuff. I mean, like, the first time I saw you that night at the Peacock I felt something different. I can't really explain it. Maybe it's just these stars in my eyes," he said, gesturing upward. "But I knew."

"And you thought I was coming on to you at the barbeque? Just listen to yourself," she said with a soft laugh and a shake of the head. "You're just now beginning to realize what I've known for weeks. You are a classic, Tuck, the real deal. I knew it all along. It just took more time for you to find out for yourself. Too bad it had to wait until the night before you leave."

"That's something else—me leaving tomorrow. It might be better if you stayed home. I don't want you to feel obligated to me or anything while I'm away."

"Oh, sure, now you try to let me off the hook after I've already committed my heart...and let you drive my car."

"Oh, that's another thing. Sure I can't bring this with me to the Nam?" he asked, patting the hood of the Corvette.

"I don't love you that much...yet."

Tuck felt they were at that point, but it was the first time he had heard Anna use the word love in the context of their relationship. Surely, he had never used it before tonight. The realization startled him as much as when she touched the back of his neck with the icy can. He turned, propped his head in his hand and gazed at her, excitement again rising in him.

"What?" she queried with a frustrated sigh.

"You mean, you love...me," Tuck said, covering his

heart with his hand, perhaps fishing for the words he needed to hear.

"Ooooooo, dear God, what do I have to do to make this jarhead understand?" Anna pinched her eyes with her fingers. "Yes, Benjamin, I do love you. What do you think my eyes have been trying to tell you all this time? I've spent nearly every waking moment with you and you've filled my dreams every night." She clasped her hands and brought them to her lips, as if trying to come to grips with something ethereal.

"I am head-over-heels, honest to God, 100 percent in love with you, Tuck. Got it? And it's taking every bit of my will power and Catholic up-bringing not to drag you into my bed tonight and never let you go." Anna's facade had now failed her. A heavy tear streaked down her cheek and onto her elegant neck. "And now...and now that I've found you. I'm afraid that I'm going to lose you without ever having really known you."

His mind reeled and sought the right words. But his desperate heart won out and he whispered. "I love you, Anna. And if I survive..."

Anna stuck out her arm, palm forward like Cupid's traffic cop. "No. Stop right there, Tuck. That's enough for now. That's the world for now." She rolled to her side and curled closer to him like an adoring puppy. "Just hold me, my Marine. Just hold me."

•

Donnie-Boy sat at the kitchen table with his mother and outlined the travel plans for the next several weeks: 30 days in Staging at Camp Pendleton, a long day's flight to Japan and then several days in Okinawa before flying into Da Nang.

"You think he's going to show up," he said, glancing nervously at his watch. "It's still the same, isn't it? Will he ever change, Mom?"

Grace sat quietly, her eyes staring absently into a tepid

cup of coffee. She had grown accustomed to John coming home late. "For years, I believed his stories of overtime and the need for extra money. I wish now that I could still hold onto that trust. But that was lost long ago, just like your dad. As surely as the cancer took Donald, drink will take John."

An only child, Donnie-Boy was 12 when his father died, and 15 when Grace remarried.

"Back then," Grace said with a weak smile, "John was like a shining knight, who had ridden into my life and rescued me from loneliness. Now, all I really have is you... until tomorrow."

She drew from her pocket and caressed a creased and faded photo of five-year-olds Donnie-Boy and Tuck dressed in Indian costumes. They straddled the hips of Donald, a robust half Chittimacha Indian.

"What you got there, Mom?"

"Oh, just a picture I dug out of my dresser today." She tenderly slid the precious photo across the table, taking care not to damage it further.

"I remember this," Donnie-Boy said with a wide smile. "It was for Cub Scouts. Man, look at how small we were, especially Tuck. He's a gem. You ought to see him now. He's so much in love with that Anna Carlisle that he doesn't even know it yet. You just thought he was goofy before. Guess I'll keep an extra eye out on him over there. Lord knows I owe him."

"She a good girl?"

"Good? No. Great. I should be so lucky," Donnie-Boy explained. "And talk about a fit. I bet they'd just about wear the same uniform."

"He really looks up to you, doesn't he? Y'all are closer than brothers."

"Yeah, he thinks I'm this big stud or something. But sometimes I wonder if my courage doesn't come from him; my having to live up to his image of me. I got a feeling though that when it comes time, he'll be stronger than all of us. Like he was for me when Dad died."

Donnie-Boy's fingers slowly tracked the edges of the photo. "You should have seen him in boot camp—a bulldog, he never quit. And talk about a physical change. He was always a little soft, baby fat, you know. Now, you can scrub your clothes on his gut. Strong little sonbitch."

"Donnie?" Grace hesitated to bring up the subject. "Does Tuck know about your...condition? Have you ever told him?"

Donnie-Boy looked away and did not reply. He stood and walked over to his mom and kissed the top of her head.

"What was that for?" she asked, reaching up to hold his hand.

He leaned over her shoulder and hugged her. "For all the times I cussed you. For all the times I didn't listen. For all the times I didn't tell you I loved you when I should have. It's been tough on you, I know, and I appreciate everything you've done for me. You're great, Mom."

He kissed her cheek and his tears wet her hair. "Plus, now we won't have to go through all this again tomorrow at the airport. Right?"

"We'll try not to, now won't we," Grace whispered, clinging tightly to her only child.

Car headlights suddenly lit up the windows in the kitchen. Donnie-Boy turned and brushed aside the drapes and looked out. "Well, what you know. And it ain't even midnight yet."

●

"Here you go, son. I save this for special occasions just like this one," Wilfred said. He turned from the cabinet and pulled the cork on a decanter half filled with Crown Royal whisky.

"By the looks of the bottle, I'd say you've found a lot to

celebrate recently," Johnny laughed and joined Wilfred at the counter. He fetched two small glasses and handed one to his dad.

"Shit, this ain't just any ol' fifth of Crown. My Daddy gave it to me when it was just three fingers over half filled. Said his daddy had gotten it straight from ol' Joe Kennedy, the Joe Kennedy, during his bootleggin' days out of Canada. This shit ain't aged, it's dead."

Wilfred poured just more than a dash of the blended Canadian whisky into Johnny's glass. "Me and ol' Bub drank a couple of splashes after our weddings, and one after you was born. And the last time we had a pull was…was after your mama and aunt was killed. So, you see, it is special stuff."

"What are we toasting tonight? The Tigers' victory? Or, my going away?"

"None of that," Wilfred sniffed. "We're toastin' the fact that we're gonna be toastin' again the day you come walkin' safely back through that front door, back to me. And when that toast comes, it'll be more than just a splash, son. Hell, we just might drain this old heirloom."

The two men tossed back their shots and then burped in unison. They laughed, slapped one another on the back, and hugged. Tears streamed from Wilfred's eyes. "Don't leave me alone in this world. Come back to me. You hear, boy?"

•

Nov. 24, 11 a.m., Ryan Field, Baton Rouge: The tires of the twin-engine jet squealed when they touched down, leaving a brief spurt of bluish-gray smoke to swirl and quickly disappear beneath the threatening skies. Their flight to Los Angeles, via Dallas, would be departing on schedule in 20 minutes. It promised to be as rough as the good-byes.

With the day growing colder outside the terminal, Donnie-Boy huddled and exchanged whispers with Grace and John. Wilfred and Johnny stood by quietly while the

Richard family chattered excitedly about the arrival of the big jet. Tuck held Winston in his arms and pointed into the direction in which the jet would leave. Curtis held tightly to Mary's waist. Dave leaned against his older brother's shoulder and watched the passengers deplane. A truck-pulled cart carrying boarding luggage scooted by. Three olive green sea bags topped the pile.

Tuck kissed Winston's cheek and let him slide to the asphalt. He shook Dave's hand and hugged him. "You the main guy now. Help Dad out, OK?"

"You bet," Dave replied, his eyes moist.

"Mom, Dad, time to go." He opened his arms and drew Mary and Curtis into him. Dave joined in. Winston grabbed him around the waist and began to whimper.

"I can't say don't worry. I know better. Just pray for me. I hope to make you proud."

"Son, you've already done that, many a time," Curtis said, grabbing the back of his neck and squeezing. "Just get your butt back here in one piece, Marine."

"Oh, Benjamin, don't you go do anything foolish," Mary cried. She wrapped her arms around his neck. "I don't want a hero for a son. I just want you back safe. I'll pray for you every day, every hour. And write a lot, OK?"

"I will, Mom. Don't worry."

Donnie-Boy leaned to whisper in Tuck's ear. "Come on, let's go."

Curtis wagged a pointed finger. "Donnie-Boy, you watch out for him, you hear," he said in halting tones before reaching out to squeeze Donnie-Boy's shoulder. "And bring your ass home safe, too...you big lug."

"Don't worry, we will, Mr. Curtis," Johnny interjected. He gently pulled Tuck from Mary's embrace. The Marines did an about face and marched three abreast toward the plane.

"Tuck, Tuck, oh, Tuck, please wait," Tuck heard Anna

cry out and turned. She sprinted to the ramp and wrapped her arms around his waist. "Oh, Tuck." They kissed.

"I thought we agreed you weren't coming today," he said, pushing her to arm's length.

"I wasn't, but after crying all morning, mom and dad said I had best get out here and see you, else I would never forgive myself."

He looked up and saw Jess and Marie Carlisle standing beside his parents near the gate. They waved. "Kick their ass, Tuck," Jess hollered.

Sniffing with a tissue to her nose, Anna rubbed the breast of his green uniform jacket with her palm and then traced her index finger across his rifleman's Expert Medal. "I just realized that I've never seen you in uniform. You look so gallant. Ever the more reason for me not to want to let you go.

"But, I just had to tell you one more time how much I love you. I want you and I want all of you. Come back to me soon," she said, pressing a small gift box into his palm. "Something for you to remember me. Good bye, my Marine." She again kissed him, passionately.

"And you, Donnie-Boy Hebert," Anna said sternly. She turned to him and dug her fingernails into the shoulders of his wool jacket. "You get him back home to me." She reached up, hugged his thick neck and then kissed him quickly but fully on the lips. She spoke so that only Donnie-Boy could hear, "He's in your arms now." He nodded and flashed a smile—the one usually reserved for Tuck.

Tuck watched Anna turn and walk briskly back to her parents' side. He regretted they had never made love as deeply and completely as he desired. Fighting back tears was difficult.

"C'mon, Tuck," Donnie-Boy shouted over the whining engines. "We gotta go."

Tuck spun and ran up the ramp, but before ducking into

the entrance, he turned to his family and gave a thumbs-up sign, hoping to bolster their courage, if not his. Curtis returned the salute.

Settling into his seat next to Donnie-Boy, Tuck looked out the portal and wondered if it might be his last glimpse of family and friends. He saw his brothers leaning against their father's side. Her shoulders heaving, his mom had buried her light brown curls and blue eyes in Curtis' chest. Grace stood close by, dabbing away tears with a white tissue. John absently surveyed the large, surrounding terminal.

He also saw Wilfred and Anna, who seemed to wear a forced smile beneath glistening eyes. She leaned against Jess' burly chest, her lithe frame tenderly swallowed by his massive arms.

The jet turned and taxied down the runway. Tears quietly streamed down Tuck's cheeks.

"What she give you?" Donnie-Boy asked with a nudge. His eyes were also red.

"Huh?"

"What did Anna give you? Other than that big sloppy kiss," he said, also thinking about the kiss Anna had placed on his lips and the words she had whispered.

"Oh, yeah, let's see." Tuck quickly opened the small package and held it up to the light. "Well, I'll be damned."

"Man, my cousin must really love you," Johnny added, leaning over from the row behind. "You're in the big leagues now, yeah."

Tuck held the silver key up to the light. His eyes sparkled. Attached was a small, flat plastic replica of a 1965 Corvette Stingray. A tiny note lay in the box. "Your 'Vette will be here waiting for you. And so will I, silly."

CHAPTER 21

The Prayer
Camp Pendleton, California
Dec. 15, 1968—1 p.m. local time

"Mail call. Come and get 'em assholes," the corporal hollered from the far door of the barracks before laying a large box on a table. "I ain't got time to deliver 'em, come and get 'em."

Tuck hopped from his top bunk. "I'll get 'em. I'm expecting a letter from Anna, anyway," he said to Donnie-Boy and Johnny, who were napping below.

"Go on, lover boy," Donnie-Boy yawned. "Just don't wake me unless there's money."

Tuck dug through the cardboard box and sorted through the letters, mumbling the names as he went. "Tracy, Brown, Muir, Reed, Thibaux, Brown, Thibaux, Reed, Fambrough, Weathers, Hart, ah, here's one for me, Richard and another for Richard. Oh, let's see, another Thibaux. Damn this Thibaux is gettin' a bunch. Hey, maybe we got another coonass in here."

He looked up from the box and shouted. "Yo, is there a Tee-BO in here?"

"*Mais oui*, over here," a squatty Marine yelled from a corner bunk.

"You got plenty mail, come and get it, you dumb Cajun," Tuck again hollered, only this time with friendly Cajun French emphasis.

Thibaux walked over with a quizzed expression. "What'd you call me? A Cajun? What's dat? Whatyoumean?"

"You are from Louisiana, aren't you?"

"*Non*, Maine. And you?"

"Maine! How the hell you got a name like Thibaux up in Yankee land?" Tuck asked.

"From Nova Scotia, actually."

"No shit? They tell me us Cajuns, or should I say Acadians, have roots in Nova Scotia. They told us in history class that they kicked our ass out way back in the 1600s or sometime like that and that some stopped off in Maine, I guess that's you, Thibaux..."

"Name's Chuck, short for Charles. My DI called me Chuck the Canuck."

"Yeah, right, Chuck. I'm Tuck, short for Benjamin." he grinned and offered his hand. Chuck just stared at him. Tuck continued his lecture, "And then a few Acadians stopped around Maryland or somewhere like that, then a bunch more sailed all the way around into the Gulf and stopped around Mobile. But most of 'em came on over to south Louisiana. And that's why I'm here, I mean in Louisiana, I mean, well, you know what I mean. There are two more in here, too."

"OK, that's nice," Thibaux said with an open hand. "Now can I have my letters?"

He handed Thibaux his mail and watched him depart without a thank you. "Acts like a damn Yankee," he muttered and shook his head. "Now, let's see what else we got in here."

Tuck fished out a third letter addressed to him, one for Donnie-Boy and a postcard from Johnny's dad. It was a picture of the family repair shop. On the backside it read:

Dear Johnny,

Like my new card? I'm doing OK. I miss you.—Wilfred.

"No use waking him up for this," Tuck said. He walked back to his bunk and shoved the postcard under snoring Johnny's shoulder. Donnie-Boy's only piece of mail looked like a bill. Tuck effortlessly leaped onto the top bunk.

The trio had been back at Camp Pendleton for three weeks. Less than a week remained of Staging, which concentrated on physical conditioning, survival tactics, prisoner of war code and night maneuvers. There had also been weapons refresher training and after watching Tuck on the rifle range, instructors again made a pitch for him to enter sniper school. He again declined, wanting to remain with his friends, though this time it was tougher.

"Let's see. One from Mark, one from Uncle Joe, and, yesss, here's one from Anna. I'll save this one for last," he promised himself, setting aside the lightly perfumed blue envelope.

The letter from South Korea had arrived on his brother Mark's 23rd birthday. It told of the cold mountains and the heavy snowfall. Because he was bound for Vietnam, there was little chance USAF Capt. Mark Richard would be sent there. Tuck knew of Mark's loneliness. They often wrote one another simply to share what each had learned from home. Mark may not be going to Nam, but he was isolated in those cold mountains for 18 months. "Happy birthday, big brother," he whispered.

He wrinkled his brow at Uncle Joe's letter. "Now what could he be writing to me about. I just saw him the day before we left."

A Louisiana transplant, Joseph Wheats hailed from Philadelphia but had fallen in love with and married Tuck's Aunt Veronica, his mom's sister. Uncle Joe had played minor league ball in the Phillies' organization and was—fitting to both south Louisiana and Philadelphia—a strong Catholic man. Indeed, he'd done the church's bidding by helping produce six fine girls.

Dear Tuck,

I hope this letter finds you in good health and I pray that you will find its contents rewarding and helpful. I have enclosed a prayer to St. Joseph that is said to bring uncanny good fortune and health to those who pray it regularly.

I also pray that it will protect you in Vietnam and bring you home safely to your family. That is all I have to say for now, but believe me, the prayer says more than I could ever write. Take care.—Uncle Joe

He fished the prayer card from the envelope, flipped it over and then examined both sides. A painting of St. Joseph holding the child Jesus graced one side and the words of the prayer were printed on the other.

He read the inscription at the top. "This prayer was found in the 50th year of Our Lord and Savior Jesus Christ. In 1505 it was sent from the Pope to Emperor Charles when he was going into battle. Whoever shall read this prayer or hear it or keep it about themselves, shall never die a sudden death, or be drowned, nor shall poison take effect on them; neither shall they fall into the hands of the enemy, nor shall be burned in any fire or shall be overpowered in battle."

Tuck silently read the prayer: "*O, St. Joseph, whose protection is so great, so strong, so prompt before the throne of God, I place in you all my interests and desires. O, St. Joseph, do assist me by your powerful intercession, and obtain for me from your divine Son all spiritual blessings, through Jesus Christ, our Lord. So that, having engaged here below your heavenly power, I may offer my thanksgiving and homage to the most loving of Fathers.*

O, St. Joseph, I never weary contemplating you, and Jesus asleep in your arms; I dare not approach while He reposes near your heart. Press Him in my name and kiss His fine head for me, and ask Him to return the kiss when I draw my dying breath.

St. Joseph, patron of departing souls, pray for me.

"Return the kiss when I draw my dying breath...wow, pretty powerful stuff," he repeated.

Donnie-Boy awoke. "What's powerful, little buddy?"

"Oh, nothing special; I don't guess. It's just that I got this from Uncle Joe..."

"Joe Wheats? I like that guy. He's cool. Got some nice lookin' daughters, too. What he send you? A Phillies schedule or something?"

"No, just a prayer card."

"A prayer card? What you need a prayer card for?"

"Where we're going, we just may need a lot of 'em." Tuck folded the letter neatly and placed it in his blouse pocket. "And, when I get time later, I'm gonna memorize it. Can't hurt."

Donnie-Boy stood and snatched away Anna's sweet-smelling letter. "Then how about letting me memorize this one."

Tuck snatched it back and held it far away from Donnie-Boy's grasp, but failed to see Johnny awake and standing on the other side of his bunk.

"What's this? Damn, it smells good," Johnny said, grabbing the blue letter. "Oooooo, from my cousin. It must be love."

"Well, I'd love for you to give it back to me…"

"In one piece?" Johnny shot a grin toward Donnie-Boy.

"In one piece. And give me some peace to read it."

"Man, I'd just like a piece of that fine Anna Carlisle," Donnie-Boy teased.

"Aw, fuck y'all, man, give me my letter."

"Fuck y'all? A minute ago you were telling me about memorizing prayers. Man, make up your mind," Donnie-Boy said.

"Go ahead and read it; have your fun," said Tuck, laying back on his bunk with arms folded.

"Yeah, Johnny, go ahead and read it," Donnie-Boy taunted, winking at Johnny.

Johnny turned his back to Tuck and then blew at the side of the envelope, producing a fake ripping sound. "Let's see. 'Dearest Tuck.' Man, she sure makes her Ts look like Fs. I can hardly tell the difference. 'Dearest Tuck, I lay here rubbing my hot palms over my throbbing breasts, while thinking of your swollen..."

"Aw, shit that's enough. Give me that thing back." Tuck leaped out of his bunk like a tiger, tackled Johnny and drove him to the floor. He scooped up the big man with a grunt and trudged to the far door of the barracks. He shoved him out the door, slammed it and turned the lock.

"Whew. Got the letter." Tuck panted. He held it over his head and walked toward his bunk and past Donnie-Boy, who laughed with a fist over his mouth.

Still laughing, Johnny pounded on the door. "Hey, let me back in, it's kinda cold out here."

Donnie-Boy trotted over and unlocked the door.

"Man, that little shit's gettin' strong, yeah. I might have to quit messin' with him."

"Yeah, I noticed." Donnie-Boy flashed a smile in Tuck's direction.

Drained by the rush of adrenaline, Tuck crawled back into his bunk and gently opened the scented, but slightly crumpled blue letter. He smoothed it as if it were fine silk.

Dearest Tuck,

Each time I sit to write you I try to think of some little thing or small moment we shared in the short time we had together. Today I remembered our first kiss, yes, that sweet little thing you planted on my cheek in my 'Vette. That sold me, and the kisses we shared after that sewed up the deal—I was yours.

Lately my friends, and even my parents, have questioned my feelings for you and whether I was being unfair to you, that there was no way I could love you so much so quickly. My friends even tried to get me to date other boys. But I would have no part of it.

I find myself thinking of you daily—almost hourly, if not by the minute. It is hard for me to totally put into words what I feel for you. I am much better with words when I have your face to speak them to. Tuck, I care for you as much as any woman can care for the man she wants to spend the rest of her life with. Yes, Tuck, I do love you. And

I will wait. I only wish I had the type of courage you are showing me, and our country, now.

Hurry back to me, my love. Just saying those words has me emotionally exhausted for this night. I sleep with you in my dreams.—All my love, Anna

He slipped the letter back into its envelope and pressed it against his lips. "*I sleep with you in my dreams.*" No man could ask for more. He pulled out his writing gear and hoped he could be so eloquent in reply.

CHAPTER 22

Christmas Truths
Quang Tri Province, R.S.V.N.
Dec. 24, 1968—10 p.m. local time

No matter how he tried, sleep eluded Doan Tien on the slope of the unyielding ground filled with rocks and curled roots. Years of hard work in the fields had failed to prepare him for this. He was strong, like a feisty young tiger, but carrying ammunition boxes up and down the damp trails of the mountainous DMZ required the strength of a mature bull, like old Trau Gia. The ordeal had exacted a heavy toll on his body.

Doan Tien had not envisioned being used as a pack animal when he joined the North Vietnamese Army. But a teen-aged private with no formal military training deserved little respect, they told him. He would carry ammunition and learn his soldier's trade on the job. That was the agreement he had made with the small platoon of raiders.

The veteran soldiers had nearly laughed him away when he said he lived to slaughter the godless Americans. "Our numbers are half what they used to be because of those pagans and their terrible weapons," the grizzled veteran warned him.

Now, after a month, he still had no rifle. Yet, Doan Tien was armed—with hatred, revenge, and his murdered father's .25 caliber automatic pistol. None of his comrades knew this. Nor did they know his real name—Pham Thuc Trai.

"Doan Tien, I have good news for you, my young donkey," said the weathered one who spoke in a formal manner, as would an educated man, and with a French accent punctuating his Vietnamese. "You graduate tomorrow."

Of dubious ancestral background, his comrades simply called him "Louie." None could tell Doan Tien of Louie's full name but whisperings told of Franco royalty coursing through his oriental veins. The younger troops guessed that Louie, of indeterminable age, must surely be near 50 years. The jagged scar on his right cheek, just below the eye on a leathery face, added to the belief Louie had fought long before all their births. His strength and courage rivaled that of younger men. His mixed Eurasian blood empowered him with the advantage of size. Easily topping six feet, Louie stood as a veritable giant and often treated his superiors like Lilliputians.

Unfortunately, that disdain for authority prevented him from ever ascending above the rank of sergeant. Young officers—who trembled at his sight and the sound of his accent coming up the trail—gravitated to him in tougher times.

Like a Marine DI, one of Louie's main duties was to shepherd young troops and prepare them for battle. Fortunately, for him and Doan Tien, no battles had arisen during the younger man's stay. The past weeks had required only the ferrying of ammunition and supplies across the DMZ in preparation for a rumored assault into the south.

"Tomorrow, I think we'll give you some Christmas presents, eh, a uniform and a rifle. Think you're ready, young Tien?" Louie asked with a squint of his scarred eye. Doan Tien would have thought Louie a pirate in another age.

"Yes, of course yes. Anything to rid myself of these useless burdens."

"Burdens? Yes. Useless? Hardly," Louie scoffed, spreading his flimsy bedding beside Doan Tien's bedroll. "Those supplies you carry are what keeps us going. We're not like the Americans, who have the luxury of helicopters to descend upon them with supplies at anytime."

"Still, it will feel good to know I'm a soldier and not just a mule to you," Doan Tien said. "I'll now carry a rifle instead of supplies."

"A mule? No. I never said that, but a jackass, yes," Louie grunted, settling in for the night. "A rifle you'll carry, yes. But no supplies? *Non*, I don't think you're out of the carrying business yet."

The news lifted Doan Tien's spirits and sleep approached despite the first pattering of a light drizzle. He then recalled something Louie had said— "Christmas" presents. His family, unlike the largely Buddhist population in Quang Tri, had practiced the Catholic faith for decades and Louie's mention of Christmas caught him off guard. Had blind rage and thirst for vengeance caused him to forget God, and the baby Jesus? Or, had he just lost track of time in the eternal sameness of the jungle?

•

6 a.m., Christmas morning: Lt. Dang Van Cam kicked the bottom of Louie's foot, then turned and rolled Doan Tien over onto his side. "Get up you dogs, it's time to move. It doesn't look like this rain's going to let up and we can make good time today marching south. Get up."

Filled with anticipation, Doan Tien leapt to his feet. Louie slowly rolled over and sat up. "To hell, Dang, you kiss-ass, *fils putain.* Don't you ever kick my bad foot again, or I'll shoot you through your good shoulder. Understand?"

"Yeah, yeah old man—old dog, same old bark."

"But bad enough to bite your pecker off, you little ass," Louie warned.

"You think you're so bad, huh?" Dang said. He turned to walk away to wake the remainder of the men. "Well, I've just learned that ol' Col. Pham himself is going to catch up with us soon, and then we'll see who's so bad."

"Ol' Big Blade Bui is coming?" Louie exclaimed, then added a slow whistle. "Damn! We must be headed into some real shit for him to join us."

The exchange grabbed Doan Tien's interest. "Who's coming?"

"Col. Pham Van Bui. That's who," Louie said respectfully. "Probably the best combat officer in this province. I've served with him a couple of times—in fact, he busted me once—he's brilliant. He's probably the only man I know that hates the French and Americans more than I do. Hell, I'll fight for him anytime, anywhere. Even though he's also the meanest and most ruthless *fils putain* I've ever met."

Doan Tien stood quietly, his mind replaying the last conversation he'd had with his father, who believed Uncle Bui had ordered his older brothers' deaths. He doubted his father's story then and clung to his belief the Americans had killed his family. Had not his Aunt Linh's evidence proven his theory? After all, it was why he now allied himself with these men. Well, so be it. Perhaps he would reveal himself as Pham Thuc Trai to his legendary uncle and advance quickly up the ranks. Surely, he would welcome him, he assumed.

True to his word, Louie opened one of the heavy crates that Doan Tien had lugged for the past three days. From it he pulled out a set of khakis. The crate also included a webbed belt with canteen, first-aid kit, and green canvas pouches for Chi-Com grenades, ammo bandoliers, and a tortoise shell-shaped Russian helmet.

The crate did not contain footwear, but Doan Tien didn't care. He clicked the heels of his comfortable American jungle boots. They had saved his feet and ankles on the long treks, but it was taking an eternal vigilance to keep them on his feet. They were the envy of the platoon and he heard rumors of a lottery should an unfortunate fate befall him.

"Merry Christmas, my young friend," Louie said with a smile.

"Thanks. But what of my rifle, my ammunition, my grenades," Doan Tien nettled Louie. He donned his uniform. It fit loosely but the length would do.

"Patience, my young slayer, patience," Louie said. "We don't have boxes of rifles on this trip. But Dang opened a crate yesterday with a big Russian machine gun. The men handling it will pass their weapons down. You will be getting it shortly. The grenades will come later."

"Thanks again, Louie. Pardon my eagerness. It's just that I want to..."

"Yeah, yeah, I know, kill Americans." Louie laughed. "Ah, here comes Dang the Asshole with your rifle now."

Beaming like a groom in a khaki tuxedo, Doan Tien eagerly moved up the trail toward Dang, who was barking orders. "Let's go, we've got a good two-day hike ahead."

Louie feigned a blow to Dang's face when he passed the arrogant officer. Dang flinched and flashed an obscene gesture.

"Here, young man, take this." Dang handed Doan Tien an SKS rifle. "And these clips, too. You'll get more later."

"Thank you, lieutenant, I will take care of them."

"You had better, or Col. Pham will have your ass for lunch," Dang warned, walking away. "Oh, and yes, carry this, too."

Doan Tien looked down—another crate. He groaned while reading the Chinese lettering on the side: MORTAR ROUNDS.

"I told you that you'd be armed and dressed like a soldier. I didn't say you wouldn't be carrying ammunition anymore," Louie laughed before he disappeared down the trail.

Doan Tien's energy ebbed two hours into the grueling trek. The heavy case of mortar rounds, along with the additional weight of his rifle and personal ammunition, bore down even more on his slight shoulders. The morning drizzle lightened when noon approached and the sun emerged from the clouds to add a steamy feel to the air. The added sweat attracted more flies and mosquitoes, as well as the ever-present swarm of gnats.

Dang called a halt for a short period of rest and eating.

Pulling at the sweaty crotch of his stiff khaki trousers chafing his thighs, Doan Tien thought it a good time to learn more about his infamous uncle. He'd also taken a liking to Dang's ability to weave embellished, yet entertaining, tales of combat and glory, though many—including Louie—doubted his veracity.

"Excuse me, sir. If you'll allow me to join you, I'd like to know more about Col. Pham."

"Damn," Dang lamented. He swatted the back of his neck and then looked up at Doan Tien. "Hmm. I guess so. I was hoping to get a little rest…Aahh, sit down and I'll tell you what I know." Dang motioned for his new private to sit. Doan Tien plopped next to him, crossed his legs and then dug into his pack for a ration of rice.

"Don't mind if I sit in, too, eh, Dang?" Louie interrupted. "To make sure you get it right."

"Guess I don't have much choice." Dang glared at Louie then turned his attention to Doan Tien. "So, just what is it you want to know about the colonel?"

"Why is he such a legend? Men praise him and tremble at the same time," Doan Tien said.

Dang cast a wary eye at Louie, who playfully returned an exaggerated scowl. "Because of the battles he's won, of course," Dang began. "He knows Quang Tri Province like it was his back yard. He is the architect of the tunnel complexes in the province," Dang explained with a sweeping gesture of his hand that came down like a pumping fist. "And he knows the feel of these mountains like you know your own dick in your hand in the middle of the night."

Louie laughed at Dang's lame simile.

"For example, this past spring, during Tet, he led an assault on a cannon base not too far from here that was brilliant," Dang continued, nodding vigorously. "He used an old ravine to move in close to their lines unseen. Then he created diversions that confused the stupid Americans. The result was a smashing victory. Many Americans died and their cannons were destroyed. There is even a rumor that the Marines have put a bounty on his head."

Louie nodded, biting into a strip of dried beef. "It's a fact. It was a brilliant maneuver. I was with them. I also know our victory did not last long because of the American jets that chased us off the hill. But the colonel's plan was perfect."

"Yes, I was there, too," Dang boasted, sipping from his canteen. "And I was with him when he left that note that so many young troops just whisper about. I was even the one who got him the paper and pen to write it."

Doan Tien looked to Louie for confirmation. Louie nodded. "It is so."

Doan Tien paused to think and to stir his bowl. "But why is he also known to be so cruel to his men? What has he done to deserve that reputation? Do you have evidence of that also?"

Dang leaned closer to look over the whole of Doan Tien. "A soldier, one as new as yourself, dare not speak to Col. Pham unless he talks to you. I have seen him slice open a man's belly for belching in his presence."

"Now, that's crap, Dang, and you know it," Louie said, laughing loud and long. "You got it all wrong anyway—the man farted, and it was his ass he split open. And you didn't see it happen either, Dang," Louie added and turned to Doan Tien. "That's just a tale, young friend."

"It's not a joke. I've seen him do such things," Dang insisted loudly.

"Yeah, like what?" Louie sneered. "Cutting off little

fingers and dicks for discipline? Now, that I've heard. But only when it involved dereliction in the field."

"I saw him kill his own family." Dang's boast won an eerie silence. "No more than two months ago at that."

Doan Tien's eyes suddenly bulged.

"Well, then tell us about it, big boy," Louie badgered.

Dang reached up with his left hand and gently massaged his right shoulder, like it would hone his memory. "We were on a short mission near Cam Lo when Col. Pham told us he wanted to visit some of his family and take his brother's son back with us. He picked me, and Lt. Ly Nang, to go with him to the outskirts of town where his family lived. When we got there, the old man, Col. Pham's brother I soon learned, was cleaning a young water buffalo and his two cute little girls were sitting on the porch. An old woman was in the house; we could hear her singing."

Doan Tien's body shivered in the noon heat. His stomach churned despite having only eaten two bites of his meal. He quietly wrapped the rice ball in a bit of tin foil and slowly returned it and his bowl to his pack.

Dang continued. "Well, the colonel started arguing with his brother about the kid or something like that, and then maybe the brother spits in the colonel's face or something. We were kind of far away." He paused to unwrap a ball of rice. "Anyway, the colonel takes out that famous big blade of his—did you know he has several of those knives—and guts the old man from dick to tit. And then he waves me and Ly to go into the house and do whatever we wanted with the old lady and kids."

Doan Tien felt like his pounding heart would gush out of his chest. His face flushed with anger, or fear, he could not tell which.

"So I go in first and grab the old lady and tear at her dress, and out pops a titty." Dang shoved a handful of rice into his mouth. "Well, it's kind of worn out and not worth it, know what I mean, so I go to catch one of the little ones. I figure they might be worth one time at least. But the old woman must have heard us coming, because when I reached for the first little girl, she pulls out a pistol and shoots me in the shoulder. Here, see." Dang wiped his hand on his trousers and then pulled down his shirt to reveal a raised red scar. "The ol' bitch."

Doan Tien's coal black eyes glistened. Everything he thought and believed for the past months crashed around him in seconds. Drunk with confusion, his head swam. His hand rubbed at the bulge in his pocket that was his father's pistol.

"Well, I was lucky. The small bullet missed the bone and just tore up some flesh and a vein." He touched his scar. "I tell you, though, I bled like a pig all over that house and porch. After that, Ly goes in and just blows away the woman's head and then shoots the two kids. Heck, we didn't even have time to have our way with 'em."

"That's sick, Dang," Louie said, turning his head to spit. "So then what happened?"

"Not much, really. The colonel sent Ly to take care of me while he went into the house. He said he had 'to do some thinking.' He later said he made it look like the Americans did it. He's always full of tricks like that." Dang shoved another handful of rice into his mouth and spoke without chewing. "He even carries stuff with him. Like the hair from that blond Marine he once scalped. Ly told me later he even saw the colonel pull down the panties of the little girls to make it look like they'd been raped. And he even threw some of that candy on the floor, you know, the kind the Americans eat to make them shit regular. He's one smart bastard.

"Then after all these doings, he added a nice little touch by shooting their water buffalo," Dang concluded with a laugh, rice spewing from his mouth.

"You're a pig, Dang. A sick shit," Louie softly said, shaking his head. "In all my years of soldiering I've never even come close to something so despicable. I've killed scores of enemy, some with these hands, but women and little children, aagh. *Non*."

"I was under orders. Col. Pham would have gutted me, too, if I hadn't done it."

"Yeah, but you enjoyed it, didn't you?" Louie challenged.

"Well, it was sort of a thrill," Dang replied, wiping his hands on his shirt. "Especially doing it with the great Col. Pham himself."

"So what happened to Ly?" Doan Tien summoned the courage to ask. Louie grunted in agreement. "I'd like to hear his version some day."

"Oh, poor Ly. He got burnt to hell in a napalm attack several days later and died. Happened not too far from here." Dang nodded toward the south.

"At least," Doan Tien said absently, "he got what was coming to him."

"What? What you mean by that? Ly was my friend, private," Dang shouted. "He was only doing what the colonel told him to do. I guess you think I should burn too, is that right, private?" Dang pulled his dagger from its sheath and pointed the tip toward Doan Tien.

"No, no sir. Don't get me wrong," Doan Tien said quickly. "It's just that's it's such a horrible story. The way you tell it. It just carries one away. You should be a writer some day."

"The boy didn't mean anything by it," Louie jumped in. "You scared the hell out of him."

"Well, maybe so. You just make sure, private, you don't get in the colonel's way. Or mine."

Doan Tien's stomach churned; his mind swirled. His entire world seemed to turn on end. Were his father's words true? Just who killed his family? Dang's tale seemed too detailed to be a lie and too aligned with the evidence to be false. And Louie did not challenge the story at its end. The planted evidence and her affection for Bui must have fooled Aunt Linh. His father had been right about his brothers. "Forgive me, Father," he crossed himself and prayed quietly.

Doan Tien now needed time to plan Pham Thuc Trai's revenge. Gathering up his gear, he vowed neither Bui nor Dang would see another Christmas. Dang would not die by anyone's hand other than his. And his parents' pistol would not miss the mark a second time. As for dear ol' Uncle Bui—any sort of death would be too easy. And maybe, just maybe, Louie could be of assistance. "Merry Christmas, Trai," he whispered.

PART 2

The Nam

There is an adage shared with newcomers to Vietnam that suggests that if you survive the first four months, then your chances of surviving the tour increase vastly.

CHAPTER 23

A Rude Welcome
Da Nang, R.S.V.N.
Jan. 10, 1969—9 a.m. local time

The flight to Vietnam had been smooth and short compared to the 13-hour trip from California to Kadena AFB in Okinawa. They had spent five tense and tedious days in processing for the last leg of their four-month Leatherneck odyssey. Issuance of camouflaged utilities, jungle boots, and payroll arrangements were part of the final stages. So was the gamma globulin injection, the dreaded "GG" shot that boosted the immune system. No other previous inoculation had inflicted such pain. No amount of processing could prepare Tuck for the horrors ahead.

It had also been the most boring segment of training, which added to the apprehension. Confined to base and not allowed to roam the historic Okinawa countryside, Tuck used the time to write to his family and Anna. The sparks that had first smoldered at the Peacock and then blazed over the weeks on leave now raged. The depth of the emotions were new and he wasn't sure how to handle their intensity. First, there was the matter of this 13-month tour in Vietnam.

Flying over the South China Sea, two giants dozing in the seats of a Boeing 707 again flanked Tuck. He prodded his seatmates. "Fellas, I think we're just about there. You can see the coast now and the plane seems to be doing some weird maneuvers."

"Something evasive," Donnie-Boy guessed. He stifled a yawn. "Probably routine."

"That's real comforting," Johnny added. "And I haven't slept a wink."

"Yeah, you snore wide awake, right?" Tuck joked, shifting in his seat.

"I've been known to," Johnny said without opening his eyes. "No. Actually, I've been sittin' back thinking about the Tigers and what it would've been like if I'd stuck it out with the team. I probably wouldn't be here right now, non."

Donnie-Boy glanced out the left portal. "Looks like we have an escort." A Marine F-4 Phantom jet fighter snuggled up along side the 707.

"Yeah, we must be gettin' real close," Tuck whispered. He craned his neck to get a view of the Phantom. The "Fasten Seat Belt" light flashed but there was no comely stewardess to greet them over the intercom this time.

The plane bucked to the left, in unison with the Phantom, and then descended steeply. Tuck saw Donnie-Boy strangle the armrests, his knuckles getting whiter. Tuck's stomach floated up.

Static squawked from the intercom before the pilot's calm Texas drawl advised, "Please hold on there, Marines, they've had a bit of a ruckus around Da Nang this mornin' and we're gonna come in kinda quick. So sit tight and hustle on off when we stop. We're not gonna be sittin' down there long, just enough to gulp some gas and git. Good luck and semper fi."

"Oh, that's just great. We're gonna die before we even get there," came the ramblings of a Marine seated behind the Cajun trio. "Damn, we're gonna get shot down outta God's blue sky before those gooks even get off a shot at us on the ground."

Johnny's ears pricked up, he'd heard that voice before—not long ago. He lifted himself, turned and saw a muscular black man mumbling a rapid prayer while clutching at a rosary with the cross pressed to his lips.

The man looked up at Johnny. "What the hell you lookin' at white boy?" He cocked his head. "Hey, do I know you from somewhere?" He then pointed his finger. "Ain't you the big bastard who tried to squeeze the shit out of me back in training—at the phone booth."

"Bingo, that's me, shit-ass," Johnny replied, his smile straining to reach ear-to-ear.

"Aw, shit man. It's bad enough I'm about to land in Vietnam under fire and now I find out, if I live, I'm gonna be in the same outfit as L'il Abner. Damn."

"Small world, boy," Johnny said without losing his grin. "Ain't it the shit?"

"Hey, now, who you callin' boy, honky. I may be a shit-ass, but my mama didn't raise no boy. And Coach Bryant sure didn't play no boys. So if…"

"Settle down you two," growled a nearby gunnery sergeant whose facial scars said this wasn't his first tour of duty. "There's enough war at the end of this runway for all of you. You don't need to start a new one."

"Boy," Johnny whispered quickly, then turned and sat down.

"Honky, fat-ass honky," the black Marine shot back.

The Phantom rocketed from the vicinity just before the clumsy 707 made a fast but smooth landing. The airliner barreled to the end of the runway and careened when it turned onto the taxiway. The engines whirred again and quickly shot the aircraft toward the terminal, where it came to a jerky stop, doubling over its passengers. Tuck closed his eyes and sighed quietly.

Air Force flight attendants hurried the Marines off the plane. A ground crew had the cargo hold open and half the sea bags unloaded onto a cart by the time the trio set foot on Vietnam soil.

Tuck sniffed the air—sticky like at home. "Almost feels like home, huh, Donnie-Boy?"

"Yeah, sure does. Smells like rain, too," Donnie-Boy said, looking up at the partly cloudy sky. "But something else. Diesel, jet fuel, I guess. No, something else. Something wrong."

"Must be the Indian in you, 'cause I don't smell nothin' else," Tuck replied.

"Well, I gotta a feeling it's just gonna get hotter, yeah" Johnny added.

"Man, where you guys from, Africa?" the black Marine said.

"No, Louisiana. We have a lot of warm winters," Johnny said with a civil tone before walking away. "I thought you guys had cornered the market on Africa."

"No asshole, we don't, and..."

"Hey, look fellas, we don't need this, OK," Tuck interjected with a hand on Johnny's shoulder. "My name is Benjamin Richard, my friends call me Tuck." He offered his hand. "This is my friend, Donald Hebert; you can call him Donnie-Boy. This big guy here you call L'il Abner is Johnny Robert. We're all from south Louisiana. And you are?"

"Jackson, Danny Jackson from Tuscaloosa, Alabama." He shook hands with Tuck and Donnie-Boy. But Danny pulled his hand away when he turned to Johnny. "You gonna squeeze it, or shake it?"

Johnny flashed another big grin. "Just shake it...if you tell me where we've met before." Hesitantly, they shook firmly. They squeezed. Neither would let go.

"Y'all just can't help y'allselves, now can y'all? Shit," Tuck said. He pried the men loose and forced them toward a formation gathering near the two-story terminal about 50 yards away.

Danny relented and pulled his hand from Johnny's grasp. "Damn, you one strong white boy. Shit! Where'd you get that strong?"

Johnny beamed. "Daddy says it's natural. That and the time I spent at LSU playin' football."

Danny stopped as if tackled and held his hand up to the side of his right ear and snapped his fingers. "Hey, L'il Abner, I think I know where we might..."

THUMP!...THUMP! THUMP!

"Incoming!" shouted the gunnery sergeant. Running, he dragged Tuck by the shirtsleeve and called out, "Follow me, goddammit." The veteran and Tuck scrambled to the safety of a bunker wall surrounding an observation plane.

The Marines darted in different directions. The trio and Danny followed the gunny and hit the ground when the first mortar shells landed less that 100 yards behind them.

WHUMP!...WHUMP! WHUMP!

The mortar had targeted the 707, which was still taking on jet fuel. The first shell hit yards short. The second fell closer. Shrapnel pinged off the fuselage. The third landed beyond the 707.

The gunny looked up and assessed the first salvo. "Oh, shit. They've got her bracketed. I hope those fly-boys know their shit."

Sounds again boomed in the distance like a muffled drum. THUMP...THUMP! THUMP!

The jet engines revved to an ear-piercing whine. The 707 then taxied away from the fuel truck with the ground crew scrambling to pull the hoses from the fuel intakes.

WHUMP! The first round again fell short, but close enough to the tail to send the six-man ground crew sprinting for safety. One man tripped over a hose. Two of his buddies scrambled back to help him up. The 707 gained speed and turned onto the runway with tires screeching and spurting blue smoke.

BLAM! A round exploded near the fuel truck, shattering the air with a thunderous noise. White-hot shrapnel ruptured its tank, sending red metal flying up into a mushrooming fireball. Tuck's face blanched when he saw the three crewmen disappear.

WHUMP! The third round exploded near the 707's outermost starboard engine. Flames shot from the back of the turbine.

Curled into a ball with his hands over his head near the wall, Tuck looked up. His face sagged. The 707 pilot gunned the big jet down the runway. Thick black smoke curled in the plane's wake when it lumbered into the air.

Pieces of the truck raining down upon him, a survivor of the ground crew cried out.

Suddenly, it was quiet and the gunnery sergeant signaled the men to get up. Tuck looked around the airport. Sirens wailed and rescue trucks swarmed toward the wreckage, from which an orange and black plume rose. "This shit happen often? The first day?"

"Yeah, it happens," the gunnery sergeant said. "Not often they go for a freedom bird though. Hell, the gooks probably wanted to hit the damn thing before we got off. Consider yourselves lucky. The first day, shit, the first 10 minutes, and you're already combat veterans."

Tuck watched the smoking 707 turn lazily to the south. "Think he'll make it?"

"Yeah, probably headed to Chu Lai," the gunnery sergeant said. "Not that far as those babies are concerned. Come on, let's go." He waved his arm toward the terminal. "I figure Charlie got what he wanted here today and is hauling ass for the hills."

"This is gonna be one long ass year, yeah" Johnny lamented.

"Got that right, bro." Danny said, his eyes fixed on the smoldering debris. "Got that right."

"Just knew there was something wrong with the air," Donnie-Boy said, staring at the smoldering mass that had been the fuel truck. "Poor guys never had a chance. Probably thought they were safe here in Da Nang. I guess you never know where or when you're safe."

"Well, you always liked to make a grand entrance. So, 'Hello Vietnam,' here's Donnie-Boy," Tuck joked, pulling Donnie-Boy toward the formation. "Let's go get our sea bags before the gooks blow them away, too."

"Yeah, OK, little buddy," Donnie-Boy said. "And look at that, Johnny and his new friend are already gettin' into it again. Let's go."

CHAPTER 24

Alone

Da Nang, R.S.V.N.
Jan. 10, 1969—10 a.m. local time

The Marines jogged toward the barracks with their sea bags slung over their shoulders. Some things never change, Tuck thought, recalling his first night in boot camp. Instead of the gates to the MCRD, they ran through a large oriental-style gate. A sign, painted in red and yellow Marine Corps colors, dangled beneath: "Welcome to Vietnam."

Hundreds of yards of concertina wire, bristling with razor-sharp double barbs, lined the western boundary of the compound. Overlooking the wire and staring across rice paddies and pastureland stood two 20-foot towers 60 yards apart. Two men each manned the sandbagged towers and pointed .50 caliber machine guns across the terrain.

"No, this ain't boot camp," Tuck mumbled. A whiff of diesel exhaust and a low rumble grabbed his attention. A bulldozer was straining to push aside the burnt remains of two wrecked jeeps. Light strands of gray smoke swirled upward. "Must have hit here, too." They slowed to a walk, gawking as if passing a highway accident back home.

"Looks like it," the gunnery sergeant confirmed. "Real recent, too. I'd guess not long before we were dodgin' rounds out on the tarmac."

"OK, you grunts, form up over here," yelled a man, pointing toward a half dozen corporals and sergeants holding clipboards. "Over here. On the double." He urged them on with a wave.

"Gee, no one's really called us grunts before," Donnie-Boy said.

"Well, that's what we are. Even me," the gunnery sergeant smiled with a tilt of his head. "Let me go see what's going on. Seems a bit unusual."

The gunnery sergeant trotted toward an officer who had joined the group. He nodded and shook the officer's hand. They spoke briefly before he put his hands on his hips, dipped his head and then shook it slowly. He traced a circle on the sandy lot with his boot.

"It's lucky we've fallen in with that gunny," Tuck observed. "He saved our butts back at the airport. Anybody catch his name?"

They shook their heads and shrugged.

"He ain't like Gunny Hill, that's for sure," Johnny said. "Not big enough and too white."

"Now, what you mean by that?" Danny challenged, putting his hands on his hips.

"I mean he's smaller than our gunny back in boot camp and a he's white guy, that's all," Johnny explained with an exasperated sigh. "Gee whiz, Danny."

"Just checking," Danny grinned. "Hey, you remembered my name. Not just boy."

"Yeah, and you're supposed to tell me where we met before," Johnny replied. "Remember?"

"That's right. Well, OK, it was..."

"Alright you guys quit your gabbing and gather around. Here's the scoop." The gunnery sergeant had returned. "We're going to form up over here. We won't be staying the night. It seems Charlie's being a pain all over the northern provinces and they want us out of here and into the field ASAP just in case it's another Tet, which means it could get ugly."

Tuck and Donnie-Boy briefly exchanged glances.

"These noncoms have already pulled our orders," the gunnery sergeant added. "Half of us will be headed to the

First Marine Division located right around here. The other half'll be headed up north about another hundred miles to Third Marines in Quang Tri. Wherever you're going, you're going real soon. Pay attention or you'll get left behind and will be in a world of shit with the brass." He pointed toward the assembly area where a dozen or so large troop trucks were parked in a muddy lot. "Now, get over there in company formation. Go on, get."

Tuck then realized, for the first time since boot camp, he might be separated from his friends. The trio had been lucky to have stayed together thus far. He picked up his sea bag and hustled to the assembly area located between two wooden barracks.

The officer, a slender man with dark, sunken eyes, stepped to the front. He did not look the part of a leader but more of a vacant shell crying out for relief. "My name is Capt. Francis Johnson," he began. "Welcome to Vietnam. You men have arrived on a bad day and things are a bit out of sorts. We hear you had it rough at the airport, but that's the nature of this beast. Live with it. You don't have to like it, but you'll learn to live with it, or you'll die."

"Some tact, eh, Johnny," Tuck whispered.

"In a minute I'll turn you over to Sgt. Flowers, who'll pass out orders and tell you which trucks to get on," Johnson continued. "These other men will distribute them, so raise your hand when you hear your name called. As you already know, most of you are infantry, ground-pounders, or grunts, as we like to be called.

"From here you'll head to the respective headquarters of the First or Third Marines. So listen up, good luck, and God bless," Johnson concluded.

"Stand at ease. The smoking lamp is lit," Sgt. Robert Flowers said, stepping to the front. The captain nodded weakly, turned and walked away slowly with his head down. What horrors might he have seen and would never share.

"Before I begin callin' names and assignments, be advised we lost our chief clerk today. He was WIA in one of those jeeps you saw being dozed. Lost along with him were about a dozen sets of orders. So if your name isn't called, it means we don't yet know what to do with you. But, no, it doesn't mean you can go back home," Flowers said, drawing a hearty laugh. "But it does mean you'll be staying overnight until we figure out what to do. Here goes."

"Ames, PFC, First MARDIV," Flowers shouted, handing the folder to an aide.

"Here," the private replied.

"Atkison, PFC, First."

"Here."

"Barnes, corporal, Third."

"Here."

Roll call continued until familiar names rang out.

"Hebert, PFC, Third."

"Here," Donnie-Boy shouted.

A corporal spotted him and hurried with a folder in hand. "Truck No. 4068, get going."

Donnie-Boy sprinted away without a word or a glance.

"Jackson, PFC, Third."

"Here," Danny said. "Guess I'll have to tell you later, Johnny." The corporal directed Danny to truck 4068.

"O'Brien, gunnery sergeant, Third."

"Here," the gunnery sergeant shouted. "Guess I'll be seeing more of you guys soon."

The corporal handed the gunny his orders. "No. 4072, good luck."

"Robert, PFC, Third."

"Here, and that's ROH-bear," Johnny called out. "Hey, Danny, wait just a minute."

The corporal assigned Johnny to truck No. 4072 but Johnny stopped and asked. "Is 4072 going to the same place as 4068?"

"Yeah, why?

"Well, can't I swap with someone?" Johnny asked, adjusting the sea bag on his shoulder.

"Guess so, if you can find somebody to do it," the amiable corporal said. "But don't say anything out loud, OK. The brass thinks these assignments are like written in stone."

"Thanks, man. Hey, Danny, wait up, man, now you're gonna have to tell me."

Tuck laughed at Johnny until he realized the corporal had skipped his name. "Corporal, did you miss Richard, Benjamin, in that stack?"

"Nope the next one coming up is Thibaux, PFC, Third."

"Here," the Yankee/Cajun from Maine hollered, grabbed his packet and then ran to hop onto truck 4072.

"See, I told you, no mistake. We've gone over these orders close. Yours must've been blown up." He patted Tuck on the side of the arm. "Sorry, you'll have to wait till tomorrow."

Watching his friends climb aboard 4068 and shake hands, Tuck felt an overwhelming sense of loss. His moist eyes focused on the big trucks. When roll call ended, 14 men haphazardly stood about. He knew none of them. For the first time since joining the Corps, he felt alone.

Tuck started at the sound of the trucks revving their engines and moving out. Four deuce-and-a-halves passed before he spotted 4068 carrying his friends.

"You've got to be shittin' me, Danny. That's where? I knew it had to be something like that," Johnny shouted before turning toward Tuck. "Hey, Tuck, you ain't gonna believe where we met, *non*. But guess I'll have to tell you later. See ya." Johnny waved good-bye.

Tuck watched his friends slap hands and pat one another on the shoulder. When the trucks passed by, Donnie-Boy turned but said nothing. He only stared with that knowing smile—the look so familiar to Tuck, who returned the stare and nodded. Words needless, their gazes held until the truck rounded a curve a hundred yards away. Tuck was alone.

"OK, fellas. Here's what's gonna happen now," Flowers called out. "Gather 'round."

Flowers, rugged looking with a chipped front tooth, was at least two years older than Tuck. "We'll try in the next 24 hours to recreate your orders from the burnt remains," he explained. "Now, we have the authority to check the headquarters companies in the field and find out who needs replacements. Once we've done this, we can cut new orders right here and ship you out tomorrow morning. That's if all goes right. But remember, this is the military. All we need right now is your name, rank, serial number and MOS."

Tuck reported in and then went inside and waited next to a bunk in the barracks, which was not unlike those in boot camp, except it was wooden and the bunks were singles. He laid his sea bag on the bed and felt the urge. It had been hours since they had left Okinawa. He hustled to the head and enjoyed a long, relieving pee before shuffling over to a bank of lavatories.

Tuck looked into the mirror and noted a small "v" shaped scar above his right eyebrow. "Damn thing made a scar anyway," he muttered, gazing at a face much leaner since boot camp but looking just as helpless. "Well, if this is the only scar I come away with I'll be lucky."

The scar reminded him of Donnie-Boy and Johnny and the way they had helped him on the run that day at the MCRD. He wondered if he'd ever see them again. What would Vietnam be like without them? He pitied the men who came over without friends. He pitied himself.

Tuck returned to his bunk and laid down. He drifted into a shallow, dream-like state that alternated between home and Anna, and the unknown that awaited him. He sensed an unfamiliar darkness in his dream.

After about two hours, he woke to the sound of four men

chattering loudly in a small office 20 feet away. The door was open. Flowers and the friendly corporal chatted, poring over a stack of papers, as his father would do with his mom at tax time. Two other men manned telephones. A minute later Flowers exited the office, bound for the head.

"Mind if I walk around outside a bit?" Tuck asked, intercepting Flowers.

"No not all, but don't wander off beyond the fence," Flowers said, smiling. "Too much shit today, plus you never know when we'll get your orders."

Tuck walked to the far end of the building and peered outside. The late afternoon seemed quiet. He opened the door and stepped into the damp air. Fifty yards to the north was the compound's city-side entrance. Two M-60 machine gun positions flanked the gate. Guards watched the civilians walking or riding bicycles and buses along the road. He heard rock music blaring from the gates. It sounded like the Stones belting out *"...can't get no, satisfaction."*

Across from the gate, a field swept outward from the gun positions for more than 200 yards. Infiltrators would have to navigate rows upon rows of concertina wire and, he presumed, trip flares and land mines. Enemy mortars and rockets, however, could easily clear the killing zone.

BOOM! BOOM! BOOM! BOOM!

Tuck flinched at the sound and sprinted backward into the grasp of Flowers. He nearly fell but the sergeant grabbed the tail of his camouflaged blouse.

"It's OK, Marine, that's outgoing—our stuff, probably 155s. You'll learn the difference soon enough," Flowers advised with a grin. "Had me scared shitless for weeks when I first got here. Didn't sleep much at all."

"How long you been here?"

"Eleven, long-ass months. Fifty-nine days and a wake-up and I'm outta here. Gonna go home to the World and mama-san."

"What's a wake-up?"

"You don't count your last morning," Flowers explained. "You just subtract one and call it a wake-up. Just a little grunt lingo, that's all. Like the sounds of the big guns, you'll learn the language soon enough." Making sure to turn his back and cup his hands, he lit up and took a drag on a cigarette pulled from a narrow four-pack of Winstons. "Want one?"

"Nah, don't smoke. Never have."

Flowers turned and sat on a short sandbag wall surrounding a fighting hole. "You might...before it's all over." He exhaled with a pleasurable smile.

"So, that means I have like 394 days and a wake up, right?"

"Yeah, I guess that's about it," Flowers laughed. "But I don't think I'd start counting just yet. Kind of depressing, know what I mean."

Tuck bowed his head. "You been doing this work your whole tour?"

"Oh, shit no. I was with mortars for the first nine months—out in the boonies with the rest of the grunts. But I wrecked my knee sliding down a hill in the bush one day, and, well, three weeks of rehab time and then they sent me here. Couldn't hump no more."

"Yo, sarge, we've got something coming in from Third MARDIV you need to look at," the friendly corporal hollered from the doorway.

"OK, I'm coming," he shouted back over his shoulder. He looked at Tuck and stared with a serious gaze. "Don't be out here too much longer. You never know what's going to happen once it gets dark. Time shifts, focus blurs...in the darkness. OK?" Flowers put out his cigarette with the toe of his worn jungle boot and limped up the short wooden steps of the barracks.

Tuck started to follow but paused to sit on the bottom step. Three more friendly boomers rocketed out from a nearby firebase. "Thirteen months, 395 more days. More than a whole year before I see the family and Anna. Hell, I'll be 20 before I get home. Has this all been a mistake or what? Damn," Tuck whispered, his head bowed and eyes closed. He ran his hand through the fresh haircut he'd received the day before. "Tuck, what have you gotten yourself into this time?"

He also wondered what Donnie-Boy was doing and what Danny was telling Johnny. He sat until darkness surrounded him, then he returned to the barracks. Passing the knot of noncoms, Tuck noted a foreboding in the faces of Flowers and the corporal.

"You still want to go? Are you ready? Ready, for what you might find?" Flowers asked.

Tuck shrugged. "What do you mean? Ready? What I'll find?...Sure I am."

Flowers paused and looked to the corporal at the typewriter for assistance. "Quang Tri just called. They've got trouble," the corporal said. "Today's convoy hit a couple of tank mines going up Highway 1 and took *beaucoup* casualties. Four dead, six wounded we're being told."

Tuck's heart leapt in his chest. "Any idea who..."

"No," the corporal said. "But a couple of the truck drivers that were in the convoy will be back later tonight. Maybe they'll know. In the meantime, Third MARDIV wants at least a half dozen replacements first thing in the morning."

"Yes. Yes I'll go," Tuck said hesitantly. He realized what he might find in Quang Tri could present a nightmarish start to his tour.

Flowers put his arm around Tuck's shoulder and took him aside. "Look, Richard..."

"It's pronounced REE-shard, not Richard."

"Whatever. I also got a request from First Marines. If you want that, I can go that route, too. I know you came in with a group of other guys and you all looked pretty tight. So, if…"

"No, sarge, I'd like Third if you'll do it."

"OK, you got it. Now go on over to your bunk and I'll call you when those drivers get here."

An hour turned into two while Tuck tried fitfully to catch another nap. At 10 p.m., Flowers called out to him, only seconds after he heard the slamming of the barracks door. Flowers beckoned with a wave. "Hey, Richard, they're back." He then turned toward the opposite end of the barracks. "Yo, Sammy, Big Bop, come on over here."

Tuck hurriedly joined the group gathering around a coffee urn.

"Hey, Sammy, I heard you had some trouble up Quang Tri way today," Flowers began.

"Yeah, man. We hit some damn mines," Sammy said. "Blew one of our trucks all to hell, wrecked two others. Can't trust the goddamned Army for shit. They were supposed to have cleared that road yesterday. Found out though, they thought it was supposed to be tomorrow."

"Bad luck, dude. Want some coffee?" the corporal offered.

"Nah, man. I got to get some sleep," Sammy said. "They want me back up there early tomorrow with more FNGs."

Big Bop held out his hand. "I'll take a cup."

The corporal turned and grabbed the coffee pot. Slopping into the cup, the thick brew looked like used lubricating oil.

"By the way fellas," Flowers said. "What happened up there? Any idea on the KIAs?"

"You tell 'em Big Bop," Sammy said, waving off the group. "I'm headed to the rack."

Big Bop, a corporal as tall as Johnny but as lean as a distance runner, took another long pull on the cup, gulped and then held it out for another shot. "Happened only a couple of miles south of Quang Tri. One of our lead trucks hit a tank mine, flipped the sucker 10 feet in the air. The trailing deuce caught part of the wreck, and the truck behind it rear-ended the whole mess.

"I was two behind the rear-ender and saw the whole thing—blew one poor colored dude in half. Hell, we lost a gunny, too. And two other FNGs. Took an hour to secure everything and get the rest of the route swept enough for us to go on," Big Bop explained.

Tuck swallowed hard. "Any names, IDs at all?

"No names I caught for sure, except heard one was a gunny and I heard a French sounding name, too. Then there was the black dude and some other big guy, but he was so messed up, nobody knew who he was yet," Big Bop continued. "Well at least those FNGs didn't have to suffer a whole year in this shit hole before buyin' it. Huh? Guess if you're gonna get it; just as soon get it early. Right, Flowers?"

Tuck watched Flowers nod slowly, as if recalling some sad event.

Big Bop put his cup down. "Now, I'm goin' take a shower, but that ain't no invitation."

Flowers waited until the group broke up, and then called Tuck to his side. "Sure about it? Still want to go up there?"

Tuck's face was ashen. "More than ever, sarge. Got to know. If I went to the First, well it might be weeks or a month before I'd find out for sure. Find out if it was my friends, find out if it was…Donnie-Boy."

"OK, Richard, here's your orders," he shoved a folder under Tuck's arm. "I figured you wouldn't change your mind. Don't lose 'em and be ready for 6 a.m."

"Thanks, sarge. And if I don't get to talk to you again, good luck when you get back to the World." He thumbed through the folder then asked, "By the way, sarge, what's a FNG anyway?"

Flowers smiled and pointed back. "Somebody just like you, a Fuckin' New Guy."

CHAPTER 25

The Reunion
Quang Tri Province, R.S.V.N.
Jan. 11, 1969—9 a.m. local time

After two hours aboard the swaying truck, Tuck's head nodded under a brilliant morning sun like an angler's cork on a rippling pond. Motoring along the coastal terrain up Highway 1, Tuck, when he wasn't dozing, gazed at the passing scenery. Resembling the Acadiana prairie of south Louisiana, eastern Quang Tri Province resembled a patchwork of green pastures and glistening rice fields, stitched together by levees and small irrigation canals.

The familiar green and yellow John Deere tractors and combines were missing, of course. In their stead, gray-black water buffaloes—often with smiling children aboard—supplied the power needed to plow the fields and haul the harvest to market.

Four versatile deuce-and-a-halves—M-35s by designation but also known as "six-bys"—comprised the small convoy. One truck transported Tuck and five other FNGs. Two more M-35s brimmed with supplies while the lead truck brandished a Quad-50—four .50-caliber machine guns mounted and linked to fire in unison. After specialized repairs in Da Nang, the Quad-50 was heading back to the Rockpile, about 35 miles past Quang Tri along Route 9.

Cpl. Sammy Kathee slowed the 10-wheel vehicle to a stop when it neared the site of yesterday's fatal mine blast. The truck lurched forward and Tuck braced himself on the wooden seat. He craned his neck to see where crews had cleared the wreckage. Two fresh asphalt patches covered up large craters in the center of the road, but debris still lined the narrow shoulders. Dark stains in the soil revealed what might be dried blood—maybe that of his friends. Ahead, he saw a crew of Marine engineers meticulously sweeping the road for mines.

"We're gonna be here a while. Y'all might want to grab a nap. I am," Sammy advised, pulling down the brim of his cap and slumping into his seat. "That Quad-50 is gonna watch over us. So go ahead and kick back."

Tuck heard the receivers on the Quad-50 cock and clang home. Whirring like his mom's mixer, the motor-driven pivot made a 360-degree sweep of the area.

Deep sleep finally captured Tuck and he again dreamed of family and Anna. He could see their faces and feel their embraces, but they would not speak to him. He frowned in his sleep.

Sammy fired up the truck's diesel engine and its sweet fumes filled the air. The rumbling awoke Tuck. "How can they speak to me?" he said, opening his eyes. "They don't know my address. I gotta remember to fire off a letter soon."

"What was that, Marine?" Sammy shouted above the rumbling.

"Oh, nothing. Don't worry. I just mumble to myself sometimes."

"Yeah, lot of that in the Nam." The convoy lurched ahead and charged past the engineers. "Next stop Quang Tri," Sammy yelled.

•

Third Marine Division headquarters at Quang Tri covered a largely flat area that gave way to a slight roll—almost hills to a flat-lander like Tuck. Small trees dotted the compound that the grunts called the "rear." But he saw mostly wood-framed tents and plywood hooches. Tattered volleyball nets and tilted basketball goals awaited men in search of diversion.

Sammy brought the truck to a squeaking halt near the front of a plywood building and a waiting corporal with a clipboard. "Here's where you FNGs get off. Nice hauling your grunt asses up here, now get the hell out," Sammy shouted with a smile and a wave. "And good luck."

"Thanks for the ride," Tuck replied, hopping off and sliding his sea bag behind him. The ground was hardpan and dusty, wanting of the afternoon rains that were sure to come. "And good luck to you, too. Watch out for those mines, hear."

"Hey, Marine, watch your ass. OK?" Sammy said, pointing to a group of four tents less than 50 yards away. "Go look for your buddies over there first." Tuck nodded.

Four-foot high walls of sandbags surrounded a 20-foot by 50-foot building standing behind the corporal. Strategically placed sandbags helped secure its tin roof. A sign hung just above the entrance. Cut from a wooden plank and painted red were the letters: "KILO CO. 3/9."

The corporal looked at his watch three times. He rocked back and forth on his heels. "Hurry up. I gotta get you checked in and get you to your outfits ASAP. When I call your name, come up here and give me your orders." Though the six Marines stood less than 10 feet away, the corporal called roll, shouting even louder. Tuck thought him to be unfriendly.

Richard was the last name called.

"Here." Tuck handed over his folder. "It's pronounced REE-shard."

"Whatever. Follow me." The corporal conducted a brief tour—company headquarters, mess tent, supply, armory, and infirmary. All were of the same cookie-cutter design.

The unfriendly corporal began his indoctrination when they returned to the Kilo 3/9 hut. "Tomorrow you'll be shipping out for Vandegrift Combat Base, about 40 miles from here. Most grunts just call it Stud. It is a staging area for Ninth Marines and other regiments. It is where you will be quartered between operations—better known as ops—and patrols. It is somewhat safe but it is also considered the bush and hostile.

"That is also where you will be assigned to a more specific unit. For now, all you need to know is that you have been assigned to Kilo Company of the Third Battalion of the Ninth Marine Regiment of the Third Marine Division. In short, you will refer to your unit as Kilo 3/9, Third MARDIV." He jerked his thumb over his shoulder to the wooden sign. "This hut behind me, obviously, is our home office.

"Take your gear over to one of those four tents and find a bunk. The noncom in charge over there will help you find chow, store your sea bags, pick up what gear you need and get you a weapon. That's all...Oh, and good luck and God Bless," he concluded in a friendlier tone.

Tuck figured everyone puts on an act in the Nam before they reveal their human side. He tossed his sea bag over his shoulder and marched to the nearest tent. The sides of the four canvas tents were rolled up high for lighting and cooling. He looked inside. Each tent held about a dozen cots. A three-foot high wall of sandbags and narrow slit trenches surrounded each tent.

Tuck strolled through the first tent but did not recognize any faces and moved on. The same held true for the second tent, where a gaunt corporal said some troops had already trucked out to Stud. He thanked the man, hoisted his sea bag and moved on to the third tent.

"What you mean? You big dumb honky, Bama'll whip yo Tiger ass any time, anywhere. And you can take that to the bank."

"Yeah, well we'll see next season when they play in Tiger Stadium. Then we'll see."

Tuck's heart skipped a beat. He knew those voices, those accents, and surely the topic.

"Johnny, Danny," Tuck screamed and then leaped into the tent with open arms.

"Well shit, look what the wind blew in. Another Cajun asshole, that's all we needed." Danny grinned, standing to greet him. But Johnny shoved Danny aside and squeezed Tuck.

"Oh, man, I thought I'd never see your little ass again. Man, I was worried about you, all alone back there...Hey, what unit did you get?" Johnny asked.

"Kilo 3/9." he said, still trying to catch his breath.

"Same here, little brother," Danny laughed, slapping Tuck's palm then Johnny's.

"We heard back in Da Nang about the convoy and I thought...well, they said there were four killed, including a gunny, a black man and two others, one with a French-sounding name, too. So you can imagine what I thought when they..." Tuck paused and looked around. Where was Donnie-Boy? Panic gripped him. "Donnie-Boy? Where is he? Was he..."

"Calm down, calm down, man, Donnie-Boy's just fine. He's over at the infirmary getting his bandage rewrapped, that's all."

"Bandage?" he exclaimed.

"Oh, it's not that bad," Danny explained. "He just cut up his arm and got it burned a little bit helping drag some wounded guys out of a truck. Hell, they'll probably give him a medal or something...that damn truck was still on fire. He should be back any minute."

Tuck sighed and plopped down onto an empty cot. He wouldn't be relieved until he saw Donnie-Boy. "This one taken?"

"Nope, I was saving that one for you, just in case," Donnie-Boy said, walking up from behind and playfully knocking Tuck's cover to the floor.

Tuck turned and hugged Donnie-Boy, who yelped, "yie, yie," and jumped back.

He looked at the white bandage wrapping Donnie-Boy's left forearm. "Sorry man, it's just that I thought y'all were...you know."

"Yeah, I know. We thought about you, too. We figured if word got back to Da Nang, you'd be worried shitless," Donnie-Boy said.

"Well, it did and I was...so what happened?"

Danny started. "Man, the truck in front of us, 4072, hit a damn mine, maybe two. And that was the truck they wanted me to ride in. Hell, it darn near landed right on top of us, and then the truck behind us rear-ended our ass. Heck, that threw Johnny and me right out. But we was OK."

"I jumped out and ran over to where it landed," Donnie-Boy added somberly. "I saw this colored dude pinned underneath and hollering and all. I tried to pull him out. But when I yanked, only the top half came out. He got real quiet...just before he died.

"Then I saw the gunny, the one we flew in with. He was yelling, and all on fire and part of his left hand was gone. Man, it was gross. I got him out but my arm got stuck in some twisted up metal that was real hot," Donnie-Boy said, his voice almost a whisper. "He died about an hour later right there on the side of the road. He'd told us this was going to be his third tour."

"What about the French guy? They said one of the dead guys had a French-sounding name."

"Oh, yeah," Johnny said. "That was the guy from Maine, you know, Thibaux. They found him under the truck after they pulled it off the road. He was smashed up pretty bad."

"So, who was the fourth guy?"

"The driver. Got thrown clear but broke his neck when he hit the ground," Johnny said.

The four sat quietly for nearly a minute. Tuck said a silent prayer, his newly memorized prayer to St. Joseph. He had met Thibaux the same day he'd received the prayer from Uncle Joe.

"So what have I missed here in the rear?" Tuck finally asked.

"Not much. We got in real late last night," Danny said. "Hell, they got us up early this morning for a five-mile run. Can you imagine? Said they want to get us in shape for the bush."

"Been sittin' here ever since. They tell us we're gonna get our gear this afternoon and maybe stand lines tomorrow night," Donnie-Boy added. "Or maybe tonight."

A Marine, who looked as if he knew something sinister, half smiled. He puffed on his cigarette and sauntered over. He had the same distant look about him that Tuck had seen in the face of Capt. Johnson in Da Nang.

"Y'all don't know shit yet, and won't for a long time. I've been listening to you dudes and been wondering how long you've been in the Nam...a day. Maybe?" The slender grunt with a tousle of blond hair laughed—a haunting laugh. "Bunch of damn newbies. You don't have a clue, now do you?"

"Clue about what?" Tuck asked, almost cringing.

"The Nam. What this shithole really is. Well, I'll tell you. It's a man-eater. A goddamn tiger that will paw and play with you and have you screaming with insanity before it eats you up."

"That sounds crazy, man," Danny said, brushing him off with a wave.

"Damn straight it's crazy. You know why? Because I'm insane. And the goddamn tiger's about to eat me," he said with wide eyes and another loud laugh.

Disgusted, Donnie-Boy got up to walk away. "You ain't crazy, just stoned."

"Hey, newbie, you don't believe me? Maybe I am stoned. What of it, dude? But what I say is straight. I shit you not. You dudes had best just listen, learn and pray."

The four stared at one another and laughed softly while the giddy Marine walked away.

Another voice from behind quieted their snickering. "Don't pay no mind to Lance Cpl. Bryant. He's just back from Bangkok, R&R you dig, and probably ain't come down yet. He's cool, you'll get to like him. He's one of them California dudes," said a stout black corporal, who had walked onto the scene. "But when we're in the bush, listen to what Jimmy B. says. He's a good Marine, a fire-team leader. Been here about seven months, just like me.

"My name is Cpl. Charles Booker, from Memphis," he said extending his arm to shake hands with each of them. "You can call me Chuck as long as you listen to and do what I tell you to do. I'm a squad leader where you guys are headed to, so they put me in charge of this tent. I suppose I'm to nursemaid you guys until we get to Stud."

"So what are you doing here in the rear?" Tuck asked.

"Like Jimmy B., I'm just back from R&R. That's 'rest and recuperation' in case you don't know. I went to Australia," he said with a sly grin. "Just had to see some round-eyed women again—and found *beaucoup* of them, too."

Chuck slapped Danny's palm. "Where you from, brother?"

"Alabama, around Tuscaloosa. My friends here are from Louisiana."

Chuck smiled. "So y'all already used to the heat, right?"

The men nodded. Tuck in particular had learned to work in the heat in his uncle's rice fields.

"I'm sure y'all are. That's a plus. Some of them Yankees just about die out here the first month or so. But believe me, in another six weeks the cooker's gonna turn on and this place will be a furnace, especially in the elephant grass."

"The elephant grass?" Danny scrunched his brow. "What's that?"

"You'll see soon enough, lots of it where we hump. Ten-foot high, saw-tooth grass; looms over you like an oven and slices you to ribbons."

"I thought we were going to be sloshing through the rice paddies?" Tuck added, almost disappointed. He'd practiced walking the levees during the summer before boot camp.

"Not much of that where we patrol. That's First Marines' headache. Us? We got mountains and elephant grass. You'll see. Get ready to hump. We the Mountain Marines," Cpl. Booker said, turning to walk away. "Oh, and form up here in about an hour. We're goin' to turn in your bags and pick up your gear. We got to stand lines tonight."

They lined up at mid afternoon outside the cookie-cutter supply building and waited. A worker issued each grunt a field pack, helmet with new camouflaged cover, webbed belt, four canteens, flak jacket, an M-16, two grenades and two bandoliers of ammunition. Sundries such as letter-writing gear, first-aid pack, one box of C-rations and a plastic bottle of mosquito repellant or "bug dope" filled their packs. A poncho, a camouflaged nylon poncho liner called a "Snoopy blanket" and an inflatable mattress, lustily called a "rubber bitch" were also issued.

The newbies tagged and padlocked their sea bags and turned them over to the supply crew. "Chickenshit supply pogues. They'll probably rob you blind," Chuck said, leaving the supply area. "When I came back here to go on R&R I found all of my personal shit had been gone through and a bunch of civvies gone. You'd think they'd have more respect for grunts in the bush. But no, they're just a bunch of queers in the rear with the gear."

Tuck examined his M-16, aiming its sights at the cloudy

sky. He then pushed in the takedown pin and raised the upper receiver group to check the smoothness of the action.

"You know something about the M-16, private?" Chuck asked. "Know how to shoot it?"

"Yep, sure do." Tuck said.

"Yeah, he knows how to shoot it damn good, too," Johnny added.

"Know how to shoot it at, and kill, a man?" Chuck challenged.

"No, corporal," Tuck replied, turning to look at Chuck. "I'm hoping you'll teach me that."

"Good answer. You can call me Chuck."

With the sun drooping in the west, Chuck led them back to the tent. He kicked the foot of a sleeping Jimmy B., who snorted and then rolled over. "What the hell you want, Chuck?"

"You've slept it off enough. Get ready, you're coming out with us to stand lines."

"Aw, shit man. That's your job, nursing those newbies. Not mine."

"Is tonight," Chuck ordered. "I got to man two holes and I can't fill 'em all with FNGs. Gonna put four in each bunker. I need you to shepherd one hole and teach 'em a few things."

"Aw, shit."

"Come on, we were new once—scared shitless and just as green."

"Oh, all right I'm coming," Jimmy B. sighed. "Let me get my gear, if I can find it."

After about a 200-yard walk to the perimeter, Chuck deposited Tuck, Donnie-Boy, Johnny and Danny at the first bunker. He then accompanied Jimmy B. to the next site about 50 yards away. He returned 15 minutes later and reminded the newbies of what they had learned in training about covering fields of fire. He also had them examine the terrain in front of the bunker before it got dark. The area had been bulldozed and little lay between the bunker and the tree line several hundred yards away.

The bunker was dug into the ground about two feet deep, thus the surrounding four-foot sandbag walls allowed most men to walk upright inside—except for Johnny and Donnie-Boy. Danny's head just barely brushed the six-foot ceiling. Tuck could have done jumping jacks.

Corrugated metal planks served as a ceiling. Sandbags created a protective roof while steel construction stakes driven into the ground inside and outside the bunker provided stability. A long and narrow, forward-facing window slit provided a secure firing position.

"Take a good look at this bunker, you won't see many this nice out at Stud, and surely none in the bush," Chuck explained. He showed each man his position.

As the evening set in, the newbies told Chuck of the mortar attack at the airport and of the truck mines. "Damn, maybe I ought to cut you guys a little slack," he replied. "You've seen as much shit in a day and a half as I did the first month I was here."

The Marines sat quietly for several minutes before Tuck started slowly. "OK. Now, you two. Johnny and Danny, what's the big secret? We've got the time now, so tell us."

"What secret? What you mean, Tuck?" Johnny replied.

"I think I know what he means," Danny added.

"You know, just where did you two guys meet before?" Tuck urged. "Please, tell us."

"Oh, that," Johnny said with a wide grin. "Well, I tell you…"

"No, man, you gonna get it all wrong," Danny said. "You know you just gonna lie, lie, lie."

"Screw you, boy, I ain't gonna lie. You just can't…"

"Hey, what's this boy shit, I thought we had that cleared up, honky," Danny chided.

"Yeah, you right. Sorry. As I was saying, me and my new jigaboo friend here…"

"Aw shit, man. Tuck, you got a cure for this big asshole here?" Danny begged. Tuck shook his head. Chuck laughed heartily.

Donnie-Boy laughed. "This is gonna be good."

"OK, OK, my Afro-American friend. I am sorry, yeah. Truly sorry…kinda," Johnny joked.

"Please, just tell the story, asshole, I'll jump in when you start lying," Danny assured.

"Well, remember when I told y'all back in New Orleans how I got my scar, eh?" Johnny began. Tuck and Donnie-Boy nodded. Chuck waited. Danny impatiently rolled his eyes.

Johnny looked at Chuck and pulled his camouflaged blouse down over his shoulder to reveal a long surgical scar. "I got it while playing freshman football at LSU. I separated it while tackling a halfback from Alabama. Well, ladies and gentlemen, you're looking at that Alabama halfback right here," Johnny said, grabbing Danny on the back of the neck with his large paw.

"And just how in the hell did that happen?" Tuck asked. "Come on, details."

Danny jumped in and quickly began to explain. "I had already scored two touchdowns on those lame ass Tigers and was about to go for a third TD on the second-half kickoff…"

"And just remember who was leading at halftime, asshole, LSU 24-14. We was kicking your Bama ASS," Johnny interrupted with a shout.

"OK, fellas, keep it down a little," Chuck warned. Tuck cringed and looked toward the slit.

"Like hell, it was only 17-14, you see how you lie. Anyhow, it was the second-half kickoff and the ball was comin' a flippin' on down to me at about the two," Danny continued. "I had already returned one kickoff about 50 yards and I knew where it was I wanted to go. I took the ball and started to my left before making a sharp cut at the 20 and sprinted to the right sideline where we had a wall set up..."

"Some blockin' wall, I blew the sucker down..."

"As I was saying, I got behind that wall and by the time I reached the 50, I was headed for pay dirt when..."

"When I busted through and knocked your ass two yards into the sidelines..."

"Not before I drove my strong-ass knee through your weak-ass shoulder. You curled up like a baby on the sidelines and damn near started crying, holding your shoulder and rolling around like a big ol' pig."

"Yeah, and tell 'em what YOU were doing at the same time, huh, big boy?"

"You tell 'em, I don't want to talk about that," Danny said quietly.

"Danny, here, was holding his knee, tears in his eyes. He looked right at me, just stared at me, helmet to helmet, eyeball to eyeball." Johnny related, the tone of his voice turning serious, as if lost in that moment. "I knew I'd never forget those eyes."

"Anyway, Coach Paul Bryant, he's what you unwashed call The Bear," Danny added, "said I could've been an All-American at Alabama the next year. He'd never had a colored boy play for him before and I was going to be his first. Said I was good enough to play right then. He really cared about me. Didn't never have a family care like he did. Felt like I let him down.

"Well, I tore it up, and surgery ended that dream. Never told you about that part, Johnny. Didn't want you to know you'd hurt me worse than I'd hurt you." Danny pulled up his trousers to reveal a long vertical scar running over his left knee. "The whole knee is shot to hell, for playing ball that is. But I can still run. Fast."

"I didn't know, man. I didn't know," Johnny said. "I thought you just sprained it or something and then flunked out of school. But I know how you feel, I thought I had a chance to be something special myself. Instead, here we are, all sewed up and in the Nam."

"So! Who won?" Tuck nearly shouted. "The game?"

"Hell, I don't remember," Johnny replied.

"Me, neither," Danny added. They both laughed. "We were too busy hurting."

"OK, enough with the memories tonight," Chuck said with a smile and a clap. "Let's get a little serious about what we need to do out here."

Johnny and Danny stood and embraced as brothers. They weren't laughing now.

Tuck looked out over the field, he couldn't make out any of the landmarks he'd spotted during the daylight. "Chuck, how do you see in this? I mean it's really dark out there." The darkness had left him with a feeling of uncertainty. How was he going to learn all of this?

"If you don't have some moon glow, or a Starlight scope, then you just have to concentrate and try to pick up movement. You have to rely on your hearing a lot, twigs snapping, and shit banging together, like canteens. Get used to it, you're gonna be going out on a lot of LPs…"

"LPs?"

"Listening posts…and night ambushes," Chuck explained. He took a sip from his canteen and began teaching them how to set up a fire-team watch rotation. Usually beginning around 10 p.m., the watch ran in two-hour increments until 6 a.m.—if the team was lucky to have four men. Otherwise, night watch in the bush was a long ordeal.

BOOM! BOOM! BOOM!…BOOM! BOOM!

The newbies jumped. "That's outgoing. Big stuff," Chuck said. "Hard to tell the difference at first, but you'll learn. Mostly the gooks use mortars and that'll sound like a low thumping in the distance. But, if they're using rockets, then there'll be a hissing sound. If you hear a long hiss, chances are it's gonna land a long ways away. A short hiss means it's gonna be close. If it's rockets and you hardly hear a hiss, then just kiss your ass good bye.

"But, for now, just watch the short-timers and veterans, if they run, you run," Chuck said chuckling. "If you see me duck, you be damn sure to duck."

A low rumbling in the distance confirmed the impacts of the outgoing salvo. "Now, that's music," Chuck added.

Tuck pulled first watch and peered into a darkness made even blacker by a thin cloud cover. Donnie-Boy, Johnny and Danny each crouched in a corner of the bunker and pretended to sleep. Chuck, evidenced by his snoring, slept.

On at least three occasions, Tuck thought he had seen movement or heard something unusual. After waking Chuck twice, he fought the urge to wake him a third time. It was going to be a long year. Would he ever learn all there was to learn just to stay alive?

The night was long, but uneventful, except for shortly after midnight. Chuck awoke to the scent of marijuana smoke wafting over from the adjacent bunker. "That damn Jimmy B. I'm goin' chew some ass," he growled. He left the bunker hollering. "You dumb shit, what have I told you about..."

Several minutes later he returned grumbling and threw his helmet into the corner. "You guys remember this and remember it well. You don't smoke no damn dope when you're on watch. What you do on your free time is something else, but I ain't gonna get zapped because some bastard was too stoned to stay awake. Else I will drill your ass myself. I shit you not."

The remainder of the night passed quietly.

•

Jan. 12, 7 a.m.: Their first night on watch ended shortly after dawn. A light rain trickled from the low clouds. The weary newbies found a truck convoy forming near the tent area when they returned. The unfriendly corporal, with his omnipresent clipboard, summoned Chuck to a meeting at company headquarters, leaving the four new grunts to themselves.

"Let's get some breakfast. Ol' Wilfred's son here is gettin' mighty hungry," Johnny said, rubbing his stomach.

"Yeah, man, let's go," Danny agreed.

An hour later, with stomachs full of powdered eggs, soggy bacon and weak Kool-Aid, the group returned to find Chuck packing up. "We'll be moving out for Stud at about 1500," he said. "I'd hoped for another day of rest. Shit, probably means we're goin' back to the A Shau."

"What's the A Shau? Somewhere bad?" Johnny asked.

"Yeah, somewhere bad, somewhere real damn bad. It's a valley way south of Stud. Full of gooks. Full of 'em. When we left for R&R, 3/9 and a bunch of others were just starting a big op down there, Operation Dewey Canyon. Hittin' the shit on a regular basis. Bunch of KIAs. I was wishing it might be over and we'd be able to stay at Stud for a while. Don't look like it now."

"Did I hear you right? Did you use the word A Shau?" Jimmy B. cried out from his nearby cot, incredulity in his voice.

"Yep, looks like we're going back in there," Chuck replied.

"Oh, shit. I think I'm gonna blow off a toe," Jimmy B. said, pulling on his jungle boots. "Hell, man. I already got hit once in the A Shau. My leg's just gettin' right again. Anything you can do, Chuck?"

"Yeah, give you an extra frag and another bandolier."

"Aw, shit man. Shit, shit, shit."

It was raining harder but the sky showed promise of clearing when Chuck gathered the newbies around. "It's been a little hot in this area lately and I want y'all to keep an eye out. Be ready to dismount and deploy on my command. Oh, and after you mount up, lock and load but be damn sure to safe your weapons. We'll all be together, the 10 of us in one truck. And in spite of what Jimmy B. here says, I don't want to lose a toe."

"Blow mine off, assholes," Jimmy B. whined. "I just don't wanna go back to the goddamn A Shau."

The Kilo 3/9 Marines gathered up their gear and mounted the deuce-and-a-halves. The convoy roared when its huge engines sputtered to life with the intoxicating smell of diesel fumes filling the air. Donnie-Boy helped Tuck aboard. They sat next to Chuck and Jimmy B. while Johnny and Danny sat across the way with the other newbies.

The trucks leaped forward and the 20-vehicle convoy rolled out of Quang Tri at 3 p.m.

The rain stopped, and the sun came out.

CHAPTER 26

Louie's Secret
Quang Tri Province, R.S.V.N.
Jan. 12, 1969—9 a.m. local time

Doan Tien, as Trai now called himself, craned his neck through the brush to snatch a distant glimpse of home. The NVA outfit he now reluctantly called family lay behind a mass of bushes on the down slope of a small hill about a mile north of Route 9 and just above the banks of Song Cam Lo (Cam Lo River). It hoped to spring an ambush on any column of American trucks that might rumble through that day and before teaming up with the notorious Col. Pham that night.

Doan Tien had wrestled with his conscience, his mind, and his very soul over the past three weeks, trying to sort out feelings, and plans. His view of the Americans and the North Vietnamese Army had taken a radical turn. Since learning the truth about the death of his family, he no longer saw Americans as devils. They were responsible for neither their deaths nor Trau Gia, and had indeed acted honorably just as his father preached. He was sure of that now.

Why had he not listened to his father? Would he not be in this situation now if he had listened? How would he act when ordered to fire upon American soldiers? How and when would he exact his revenge on Col. Pham and his accomplice, Lt. Dang? Could he do it without Louie? These questions tortured him daily. But for now, he wanted one more glimpse of home.

Louie peered through binoculars toward the road. "You've been fortunate, young slayer, not to have been thrust into battle too soon. But today, I think, will come your first taste, *non?*"

Doan Tien, silent and intent, did not reply.

"What's with you lately? When you first arrived, all you'd talk about was killing Americans. Now you hardly talk at all." Louie lowered the binoculars and nudged Doan Tien with his elbow. "It's me, Louie, I've heard it all. You can't surprise me. Talk to me. What is the matter?"

Like an insolent beggar, Doan Tien held out his hand without looking at Louie. "May I borrow your binoculars?"

"Aagh, kids," Louie fumed like a frustrated father. "Here." He shoved the Russian-made binoculars into the teen's hands.

Doan Tien brought the heavy field glasses to his forehead and adjusted the focus. He looked south and found the road leading through Cam Lo, then tracked to his right, west along Route 9 about one mile until he spotted a loose clutch of huts. There it was, Thon Tan Dinh, the home of his Aunt Linh and other relatives. His home lay a hundred meters farther west. The small lake, which harbored so much of his family's joy and sadness, glistened nearby like a silver coin in the morning sun. Tears blurred his focus.

"See what you wanted to see?" Dang asked, surprising Doan Tien on his right. "Not much down there, now is there? Did you see those houses just west of the village?"

"Yes, sir."

"That's where we're going to hit the convoy, right outside of Thon Tan Dinh."

"But there's a lot of civilians around there. Wouldn't it be better if we waited until the Americans were further down the road? We'd get a clearer shot," Doan Tien observed.

"Aaagh! Let the Americans worry about not hitting peasants. That's not our worry, and it surely isn't Col. Pham's worry. Heck, that's about right where we slaughtered his family that I told you about. You think he'd worry about other peasants? No, we'll hit them there, the Americans will let their guard down after they come through the village."

"That's what I love about you, Dang, you're so damn professional," Louie spat. "Asshole."

"Watch it old man, or I'll report you to the colonel. I have connections with him, remember?" Dang boasted.

"Aaagh. So just how are we going to do this?" Louie asked, turning his mind to business.

Dang brought up his binoculars and studied the area. "The American Marines often bring in their new troops late in the day from their base in Quang Tri. Our contacts say there may be such a convoy today. Green troops are easily confused." He lowered his binoculars and smiled. "We are well-armed and rested. Our 15 men should easily take out twice that many."

"Yeah, right. Funny how it hardly ever works out that way, *non*?" Louie teased Dang.

"I said watch your tongue, you old half-breed," Dang said, nodding for Louie to again look through his binoculars. Dang pointed to an outcropping of boulders about 100 yards from the road. "We'll use the rest of the morning to cross the river and then set up in those rocks."

Louie grunted his approval.

"We'll hit them hard with two RPG teams and the Russian .51. Louie, you and young Tien pick off whatever troops try to maneuver against us. This will be a quick hit and run. No more than a minute or so then we scramble back here, and get back into the tunnels," Dang added.

"Yeah, and let's hope there aren't any eyes in the air," Louie offered. "We're close to the cannon base they call the Rockpile. If they get those big guns spotted on us, well, you may not get your chance to report me to Col. Pham."

Dang waved off Louie's final insult and crawled further down the line to advise others.

Louie rose to a stoop and motioned Doan Tien to follow

him down the hill. After an hour of tedious movement and an exposed fording of Song Cam Lo, the unit stopped for rest.

"Louie?" Doan Tien called out.

"Ah, he speaks again."

Doan Tien scooted closer to Louie so that he could whisper. He found security in lying next to Louie. He sipped from his canteen. "What will it be like? My first battle? To kill a man?"

Louie smiled and shook his head, and then pushed Doan Tien's helmet over his eyes. "It differs from man to man, I suppose." His smile disappeared. "As it was for me, and for those who will admit it, I imagine it will be the most frightening thing of your life. Don't be ashamed to be afraid. And don't be afraid to run if you have no other chance for survival.

"I've been fighting this war for more than 20 years and haven't survived by being stupid. Live," he stressed, bobbing his head. "Live to fight another day."

"Why?"

"Why what? You don't want to live?" Louie asked, unsure of Doan Tien's question. "If not, then get away from me."

"Yes, I want to live. But why have you fought for 20 years?" Tien whispered like a child in awe. "You could have quit long ago and gone home. No one would have thought dishonorably."

"Must you really know?"

"You've told me much about yourself over the weeks. But never why you fight on."

For decades, Louie's secrets had been kept safe within. But he was growing weary of suffering them alone. He poured water into his palm and wiped his face, which bristled with a two-day stubble of salt and pepper whiskers. His French heritage had willed him a much heavier beard than most Vietnamese. Only his gray-streaked black hair, which he wore closely cropped, and mildly slanted eyes attested to his Vietnamese heritage.

"Long ago, back in the '20s, when the French colonials were here, my mother became infatuated with a young Legionnaire. She satisfied his every desire with the promise he'd take her back to his home in Europe, a magical sounding place called Alsace-Lorraine.

"He was a handsome lad, much like me," he added with a grin and with two fingers hiding the scar on his cheek.

Doan Tien stifled a laugh. Louie could be such a clown.

"But, when she became pregnant with me, well, let's just say he disappeared, never to be seen again," Louie continued with a twirl of his hand. "All she knew was that his name was Louis, ha, and that he boasted of traces of aristocracy."

"That's not fair, Louie. But, it's a familiar tale. Is your bitterness that deep?"

"Oh, but there's more. Much more, my young friend." Louie took a long swig from his canteen. He rinsed and spat, rolling over a centipede crawling near his boot.

Propped up on an elbow, Doan Tien gazed at Louie. "Tell me," he prodded. If only for a while, he was a child again, listening to a tale on the porch of his father's home.

"Nosy little bastard, aren't you?" Louie found an unfamiliar comfort in the boy.

"Yes. I am. Tell me something—secret," Doan Tien teased. "And I'll tell you one, too."

Intrigued, Louie lifted an eyebrow and stared into Doan Tien's eyes.

"I'll tell you what no other man knows. I had a sister, two years younger. She, too, was part French by yet another soldier. She was quite beautiful. They called her exotic. And the men swooned over her.

"When the French became our enemy in the '50s, their troops were all over Indochina. And as my mother did, my sister, too, fell for a young French soldier. This soldier also promised to take her back to France if she satisfied him. Of course, my mother tried to tell her different, but Linh was in love."

"I have an aunt named Linh. She, too, is beautiful, with big…"

"Hey, whose story is this? Mine, *non?*"

"Yes, go ahead," Doan Tien said excitedly. "Hurry, I think we are about to move out."

"Well, as you can imagine things did not work out," Louie continued. "Like our mother, Linh, too, became pregnant. And when Linh threatened to report the young man to his commanding officer, he beat her severely. She lost the baby.

"My mother then got involved and, well, it got worse when she too went to the man's headquarters to protest. There, the young soldier again beat them both, even while his comrades and a senior officer watched, and probably laughed. It got out of hand. One thing led to another. My mother grabbed for the young man's pistol. Things happened." He paused to clear a halting throat. "They both died; their bodies burned and buried to hide the evidence, I later learned."

"But, but where were you? Could you not help them?"

"Me? Humph. I was in France. My mother may have been a whore, but she was a frugal one, and had saved up enough for me to go."

"What were you doing there?"

"What else? Looking for my father—and getting a proper education from the people who were slaughtering my family. But there were witnesses, locals, mind you. They held an inquiry, but it did no good. They just sent the young soldier and officer back home."

Louie paused to summon the courage to continue the story he had often played over and again in his mind, but had never before spoken aloud.

"When I learned what had happened, I returned

home," Louie said. "I started drinking, at first to calm myself, or maybe to summon up the courage to act. I'm not sure anymore. I went berserk and stormed into the French headquarters, and shot four officers to death. One each for my mother, Linh and her unborn child—and one, I suppose, for myself...Well, I made good my escape, and hid myself by joining the northern resistance. Little has changed since."

Doan Tien waited. "But why, now that the French are gone, do you still fight?"

"Because, my young friend, I am what you want to be—a slayer. I know nothing else, and I am good at it," Louie replied, gathering up his gear.

"'It is well that war is so terrible—for we would grow too fond of it,'" Trai recited, pausing to prepare to move out. "Just something I remember from a history class."

"Robert E. Lee, a general in the southern resistance during the Americans' civil war, *non*," Louie replied, much to Doan Tien's surprise. "I studied military history in France. Now, let's go. You can tell me your secret another day. It's time to get a little closer so you, too, can wet your feet in blood. And see if you shall grow fond of it."

Yes, Louie would understand. He could help.

CHAPTER 27

A Dang Ambush
Quang Tri Province, R.S.V.N.
Jan. 12, 1969—4 p.m. local time

The 20-truck convoy churned up dust while it bucked along Route 9 toward Vandegrift Combat Base. "Hey, Chuck?" Tuck yelled above the roar of the diesel engines.

"Yeah, what is it?"

"What's Vandegrift anyway? I mean, what's it like?" Tuck yelled again.

Chuck thought for a moment, then turned to Tuck and smiled. "Kind of like the rear, but the gooks mess with you more. You know, mortars and rockets, and shit; sometimes a line probe. Stud, that's what we call it, is our combat base, a big-ass spread. Kind of like Khe Sanh was before they abandoned it last summer. You know about the siege. Right?"

"Yeah, watched a bunch of it on TV back home last spring," Tuck replied. "A schoolmate of mine, Donald Etienne, died there. I went to his funeral and all, it was sad. The whole town was upset. It was kind of what got me thinking about joining up. Good guy, Donald was, you would've liked him."

Chuck grabbed Tuck's shoulder for support and lit a cigarette. "Lot of good guys died out there," he shouted, waving away the dusty air. "I got here just a few months after they abandoned it. Stud is a big time operation, too, takes up the whole valley; *beaucoup* Marines there."

"Where's the A Shau?" Danny joined in.

Jimmy B. cringed. "Aw, shit, man, don't use that word."

"Like I said before," Chuck continued. "The A Shau's a bad place. About 30 or so miles south of Stud, down in Thua Thien Province but still in the I Corps. Everybody works out in there, First and Third of our guys, the Army's 101st Airborne, Air Cav, Americal. You name it. Just about everybody has an A Shau horror story. They say that's Charlie's main entrance into the Nam from the Ho Chi Minh trail." He paused when the truck swerved to miss a large pothole. "Last year they used it to feed Tet on down around Hue," he added. "Some really bad shit happening there most of the time. Right now 3/9's down there trying to interdict more shipments. Seems like somebody's always fightin' in the A Shau."

Donnie-Boy then quizzed Chuck. "Think we'll be going there?"

"Aw shit, yeah," Jimmy B. cried, bowing his head and covering his helmet with his hand.

"Shut up, Jimmy B., you don't know that for a fact," Chuck ordered. He saw Tuck's eyes grow distant. "Jimmy B. lost two good friends in there a few weeks ago and he took some shrapnel in his leg. As you can tell, he ain't fond of the A Shau."

"So, that means it's pretty quiet up here, then. Right?" Johnny asked hopefully. "I mean if the NVA likes the A Shau so much, then it ought to be calm up here. Right?"

"Yeah, right," Chuck grinned. "When those TV people talk about the northern part of the Nam and the I Corps, they talk about Da Nang. Mutha fucka, you about a hundred miles north of Da Nang right now." Chuck then pointed to the hills to the north. "Be advised, big newbie, that you ain't but a half dozen miles from the Z, the DMZ that is. You know, Uncle Ho's front yard?

"Now, how would you feel if the enemy camped out in

your front yard? Think about it. Plus, Stud is only about 12 miles from Khe Sanh, and Charlie shelled that place for more than two months straight. Think about that, too.

"No, fellas, this ain't no quiet place. Ain't no such thing in the Nam," Chuck concluded his lecture. "I shit you not."

•

Lt. Dang positioned his 15-man platoon along a line parallel to and about 100 yards north of Route 9. Only open pasture and rock outcroppings stood between them and the road. Doan Tien and Louie anchored the western end of the line.

Rising dust and a rumbling from the east signaled a convoy's approach.

•

"Hey, looks like a village ahead. Lots of people on the road, too," Danny called out at about 5 p.m. after two hours in the truck, located roughly in the center of the convoy.

"Must be Cam Lo," Chuck shouted. "Watch out for the kids on the side. They'll be begging for food and treats. Whatever you do, don't throw between the trucks." His shout came too late.

"Here you little gook shits, eat this, Charlie-san," Jimmy B. howled after throwing a chocolate disk into the middle of the road. A skinny boy darted out, snatched up the candy and then sped unscathed to the other side.

"Fast little turds, aren't they?" Jimmy B. laughed and clapped like he was watching a minstrel show. "Hey, Johnny, give me some candy, man. Let's see if the next one's that fast."

Tuck stared at Jimmy B., wondering if he'd be so jaded in six months' time.

"Damn it, Jimmy B.," Chuck hollered. "How many

times am I going to have to tell you, man? These are people, not dogs."

"Aw, shit, Chuck. These kids'll be shootin' at Marines in two years time. Maybe we can flatten a few and save Uncle Sam some Purple Hearts." Jimmy B. continued to laugh.

•

"Remember, fire on the two lead trucks first," Dang ordered his RPG crews. "Then go after a middle truck and one in the rear so we can hem them in. After that, withdraw to the river."

Dang moved to the machine gunners and ordered them to rake the column from front to back, and to the front again. He then scurried to the end of the line. "Louie, you know what to do. Take care of this one," he said, nodding toward Doan Tien. "Remember, wounding them is as good as killing them."

Louie didn't have a comeback for Dang this time. He turned to Doan Tien and smiled with a nod. "Dang may be an asshole, but he knows his tactics. If he follows them."

Doan Tien's mind swam. He fretted over killing Americans, now innocent Americans in his mind. His father had been right: The Americans had always been friends to his family. Could he kill an American? What would he do?

•

Though fewer now, children lined the road and stood on the two-foot high levee of a wide, shallow ditch that ran along the northern side of Route 9.

"That was Cam Lo," Chuck advised. "Next stop, the Rockpile."

"And just what is the Rockpile?" Tuck shouted. He couldn't learn enough about this strange land that he'd been indentured to serve for the next 13 months.

"What you think I am, a tour guide? You'll see when we

get there." Chuck looked around and saw genuine interest in the eyes of his newbies. "Aaah, it's just another firebase, but a big one. There's some really steep hills there that look just like, well, big rock piles sticking out of the ground, kind of like those little ones over there in that pasture. It's a cool sight, though. So is the Witch's Tit. And the Tit's just another real pointed hill that look's like a..."

SSSSS, BOOM!...SSSSS, BOOM!

The deuce-and-a-half skidded to a halt. Two rocket-propelled grenades slammed into the sides of the convoy's lead trucks—one a Quad 50, the other a supply truck. Black smoke instantly billowed when diesel fuel ignited with a muffled bang. Nearby Marines shouted and children screamed in the distance.

Thunderous explosions and cracking noises like that of a hard rain followed. A large-caliber automatic weapon stammered out lead in a slow but steady hail. Greenish white tracers flitted above like angry fireflies. In a flash, the side of their truck erupted in a spray of sparks and shrapnel when .51 caliber bullets—nearly three inches long and a half-inch wide—tore through the cab and troop area. One of the newbies yelled when a round slammed through his knee, ripping it away from his leg.

"Get off the truck," Chuck yelled, shoving Tuck out of the back gate behind a scrambling Jimmy B. "Get the hell out of here." Donnie-Boy leaped over the side and returned fire. Tuck saw Danny pulling Johnny, who grabbed at his bloody shoulder.

"Get down there," Chuck again ordered. He grabbed Tuck by the back of the neck and shoved him toward the shallow ditch between the convoy and the rocks from where the fire was coming. "Get in that ditch and get some fire on those rocks. Get something out there."

SSSSS-BOOM!

The troop truck that had been following them erupted

in smoke and sparks. Diesel fuel ignited and flames engulfed several Marines. Tuck heard a terrible wail but couldn't force himself to turn and look. His hands trembled but he flicked his rifle's safety to semiautomatic and looked for targets. His body cringed at the symphony of noise and his first shots flew errantly from the muzzle. He had never felt such fear; never imagined fear could feel like this. All his entrails seemed to shiver. Nothing, no one, could have prepared him for this. *"O, St. Joseph whose protection is so great, so strong, so prompt before the throne of God..."*

Tuck felt something warm and wet below him. He rolled over and stared, his muscles contorting his face into a shape he'd never felt. It was a Vietnamese child, a boy no older than his brother Winston. The boy's eyes were wide open and as blank as a rubber doll's. A .51 caliber round had punched a hole as large as a lemon through his thin chest. Tuck had never imagined that his first glimpse of death in Vietnam would be that of a child.

"...I place in you all my interests and desires."

He tore himself from the horror and rolled twice before rising to see what was happening. A big, bloody mitt slammed him against the turf. "Stay down, little buddy. They got us pinned down, man," Johnny shouted.

"You two, get over here," Chuck hollered and then pointed toward the rocks. "Quick, give me some fire over here on the flank. We need to know how many there are out there."

They crawled like frightened puppies toward Chuck. Tuck, however, couldn't find his best friend. He popped his head up and shouted, "Donnie-Boy?" Tracers dug into the turf within two feet of his helmet. Red dirt sprayed his face. Damn it, where was Donnie-Boy?

•

"We've got them pinned and they don't know where we

are," Dang shouted, pumping his fist in triumph. "I knew these green troops would be confused. Give me another three or four rounds in the center of the convoy," he urged his RPG crews before turning to shout to his machine gunners. "Tear up the supply trucks. Keep pouring it on."

Louie sprayed the scrambling troops with AK-47 rifle fire, knocking down at least two Marines. Doan Tien used his SKS to pump round after round into the engine block of a burning truck. Once he fired in the Marines' direction, but safely over their heads.

•

The fusillade temporarily shifted, allowing Chuck time to plan a counterattack. He surveyed the area. "Who's that off to the right?" He pointed to a Marine with a bandaged arm sprinting toward a large rock about 70 yards from where the RPGs blazed.

"That's Donnie-Boy," Danny shouted. "What the hell is he doing?

"He's got the right idea," Chuck hollered. "We've got to knock out those RPGs and that machine gun. Tuck, you and Danny get back over to the right behind your buddy and cover whatever he's got in mind."

Emboldened by the shift in fire, Tuck and Danny scurried toward Donnie-Boy. Running in the open, they presented new targets. The fire traversed in their direction, red spurts of dirt followed their heels. They dove behind a low rock several yards short of Donnie-Boy. Chuck joined them.

"I just sent Johnny to the left with Jimmy B. to get their attention over there," Chuck said, pausing when he saw Donnie-Boy swing into action. "Hey, what the hell's he gonna do?"

Donnie-Boy pulled the pin on a grenade and prepared to throw toward the rocks hiding the RPGs. He peeked over the protection of a boulder. Once, twice, three times he peeked.

"He can't expect to throw a frag that far," Chuck said, wiping a trickle of blood from his left hand. "Nobody can do that. We need a blooper."

"You just watch. He wasn't our star center fielder for nothing," Tuck answered, silently praying, *O, St. Joseph do assist Donnie-Boy through your powerful intercession...*

Donnie-Boy stood and peeked a fourth time, and then threw a strike that hit home. The grenade exploded in a dark gray cloud of smoke and dust. An RPG launcher and the arm that aimed it flipped into the air and landed amid the rocks. He had a second grenade in flight before the victim's cry echoed across the field. It, too, found its mark and two more enemy soldiers spun and fell from behind the cover. Another soldier retreated up the slope empty handed.

"Take him," Chuck ordered Tuck, who paused before bringing his M-16 to bear. Tuck judged the fleeing man to be little more than 100 yards away. "Take him, I said, now."

Tuck froze. The man was unarmed; scared, just like he was, and not a threat. Once again, the illusion of glory faded. Only fear and confusion dwelled in him.

"Shoot, damn it. Awww, shit." Chuck sprung up and fired four quick shots. The fleeing soldier fell in a heap. Chuck then dropped to his knee, grabbed Tuck by the collar and pulled him to his face. "You wanted me to teach you how to use that weapon, how to kill a man? That's how you do it. Now look over there. Look at those dead Marines burning in that truck. What kind of a chance did that little son of a bitch give them? Huh?"

Charred, unrecognizable bodies dangled over the sides of the truck. Tuck thought he saw the arm of one doomed Marine weakly slap at the flames consuming him. In the sea of his emotions a storm raged. Anger swelled and quickly drowned his doubt. His trembling subsided when the Corps' training took over.

"Now get going, this firefight is far from over," Chuck

ordered. He slapped a fresh magazine into his M-16. "Go on. All of you, get over to the left and help those guys."

Danny sprinted away. Renewed fire erupted around them. Tuck looked back for Donnie-Boy and saw his best friend galloping back from the center field rocks and bearing down on his position. Red clay sprouted behind Donnie-Boy's heels and he dove to the ground.

"I said get going," Chuck hollered. He shoved Tuck and a breathless Donnie-Boy in the direction of the other grunts, who were drawing fire from the enemy's .51 caliber.

They plopped into the bottom of the ditch by Jimmy B.'s side. "We got the gun spotted, but we can't hit it," Jimmy B. explained. "It's too far and in tight with those rocks. Our shots just ricochet off. If we could only get a couple of rounds in there, we might slow it down enough to flank 'em...By the way, who threw those frags? That was cool."

"He did." Chuck pointed to Donnie-Boy with his thumb.

"You comin' with me to the A Shau, dude," Jimmy B. smiled. "I shit you not."

Another slow, stammering burst of fire from the .51 caliber interrupted the interlude.

Donnie-Boy looked at Tuck and nodded with that knowing smile. "Think you can do it, little brother. It's no tougher than shooting a T, you know what I mean."

Tuck nodded and crawled another five yards to his left. He shifted into a more comfortable prone position, promising himself not to freeze up again and to focus. It was a chance for redemption he could not pass up.

"Somethin' I need to know here?" Chuck asked with a quizzical look on his dirty face.

"Just watch," Donnie-Boy said, and then hollered. "I'll spot you."

Tuck nodded and adjusted his rifle's sights. "OK, Jimmy B., where you want it?"

"Hell, I don't know, just stop 'em long enough to give us a chance."

"Give me a minute before y'all do anything." Tuck again shifted his position slightly. "They've got that thing in there tight but I can make out a piece of a uniform. There's about an inch or two of an opening. But I'm gonna need a reference."

Jimmy B. stood up and flipped the enemy the finger. "I'm over here you assholes." He dropped back to the ground like a stone. The Russian machine gun erupted, again spitting out fierce green tracers.

"Got it," Tuck advised. He squeezed off a round. POP! The stream of tracers died instantly.

POP! POP! The barrel of the .51 caliber shifted and aimlessly fired a burst into the sky.

POP! A low scream emanated from the rocks. Two men stood and fled up the slope, but this time he was ready. POP! POP! Both men fell lifeless. Tuck felt no remorse.

"You learn quick," Chuck said, whistling softly.

"Well, shit, you're coming to the valley with me, too," Jimmy B. said, gawking.

•

Dang cursed after two men dropped. "Damn, this is not going well."

"No shit, *fils putain*," Louie shouted, slapping Dang on the back of the head. "You said hit and run. But, no, you had to get greedy. Try to take a whole convoy out with 15 men. You knew this could happen. Now let's get the hell out of here while we got our own balls."

Dang started to shout back but stopped. His plan had backfired. Eleven of his 15 men were dead. "Very well, you get the boy, I'll get Nguyen Ly."

Louie grabbed Doan Tien—still busy keeping the Marines safely pinned down—by the collar. "Let's go, little slayer. We've done enough for today. Now, let us run, and live."

•

"Look, Chuck, there's four more running up the slope," Jimmy B. cried out.

Chuck grinned. "Yeah, we got 'em back good. Save your ammo, they're out of range. We'll let the artillery boys take care of 'em. Get me a radio and I'll get with the Rockpile."

POP! POP!

Chuck spun around at the sound of the M-16 and saw Tuck standing tall and preparing to sight in again. POP! Chuck wheeled around again and saw one of the four fleeing men's head explode in a burst of red. Another lay flat on his back.

•

"Aiiyee," Dang cried, spinning to the ground, his shoulder hanging limp. A near headless Nguyen lay beside him.

"Shoot back, cover me," Louie shouted at Doan Tien. He reached down and hoisted Dang onto his shoulders. "Shoot, now, frighten them at least."

Doan Tien raised Dang's AK-47 to his shoulder, pointed the automatic rifle at the Marines, closed his eyes and then fired a long burst. A Marine fell to the ground.

"Good work, young slayer. Now let's get the hell out of here. We live to fight another day."

They safely ran through the jungle grass and to the dense forest beyond. First, Doan Tien looked back one last time. Hoping his final shot was again a wayward one.

•

Lying on the ground, Tuck grimaced and writhed from the fire burning in his left thigh. He fought back the urge to cry. Chuck applied a field bandage to the flesh wound. Donnie-Boy knelt by his side.

"Good shooting there, Tuck. But maybe we oughta call you 'Duck' until you learn how to do just that," Chuck laughed. "You'll be OK. After a trip up to Charlie Med and some light duty, you'll be as good as new. Too bad it ain't enough to send you back to the World, or to the ship." Chuck sighed, then looked back over his shoulder toward the burning trucks where at least six Marines died. "At least you ain't like those poor dudes."

Several seriously wounded Marines lay on the roadside. The convoy's lone corpsman and volunteers attended to their injuries. Wailing Vietnamese women gathered around another half dozen shattered bodies of small children.

Two of the dead grunts were FNGs under Chuck's charge. It had taken less than 15 minutes of the third day to end their tour in the Nam. Lying beside them were the remains of two truck drivers—a wiry black man named Sammy, and a tall white guy most just called Big Bop.

CHAPTER 28

Revenge Denied
Quang Tri Province, R.S.V.N.
Jan. 12, 1969—6:30 p.m. local time

Watching the old veteran flee through the elephant grass with Dang draped over his shoulder, Doan Tien vowed to never again complain to Louie about his burdens. "Please Louie, let's stop. We're far from the fighting…and you need your rest," he said, puffing and trying to keep up. "At least let me help you with Dang."

Louie ran another 200 yards before stopping at a thicket of white-barked saplings and banana trees. He scouted the jungle's edge, grunted his approval and then dropped Dang, who hit the ground with a thud and moaned.

"At least we know the *fils putain* is still alive," Louie spat. He placed his hands on his knees and panted. "I want him alive so I'll have something to hold over his arrogant head."

Staring at one of his family's murderers, Doan Tien thought otherwise.

"You, stay here," Louie said, looking up at the jungle canopy. "I'm going check to make sure there's no American patrols around. This is where we're supposed to meet Col. Pham."

Doan Tien now realized Louie knew much more about planning than he allowed. "So that's why you pushed on."

"Yeah, so watch Dang. I'll be back in a few minutes." Louie nodded, took a deep breath and swiped his brow. He rose and then disappeared into the jungle.

Doan Tien stood and walked to where Dang lay. He stared at the man through Trai's eyes—the same eyes that saw his father's bowels spilled into the dirt; the same eyes that had witnessed the aftermath of the slaughter of his mother and sisters.

"Perhaps now is the time for revenge," he whispered, kneeling beside Dang's head. "I could just strangle you and tell Louie that you merely died from your wounds. Or, perhaps I could bash in your head with my parents' pistol. Or, I could simply awaken you, introduce myself, and shoot you between the eyes and not care what Louie thought. He would understand."

Savoring each second, he stood and slowly drew the .25 caliber pistol from his pocket. He stepped on Dang's wounded shoulder and aimed. Dang groaned and slightly raised his head.

He cocked the pistol and spat in the doomed man's face. "This is for my..."

"Halt, soldier!" commanded a Vietnamese voice from behind. "Halt right there!"

Doan Tien spun and brought the pistol to bear on the silhouette of a slight man emerging from the gathering mist. It was not Louie.

He aimed at the man's chest, keeping his foot on Dang—now semiconscious but helpless.

The man stepped from the shadows and motioned slowly with outstretched arms. "Whoa, now soldier. Just calm down, now. Lower your weapon."

"Don't shoot, Doan Tien," Louie's voice suddenly rang out from the opposite direction. "That's Col. Pham."

"That's right, young man, I'm Col. Pham and I'm ordering you to put that weapon down. OK?" Pham's voice grew more fatherly than commanding. "Whatever this man here has done, we'll take care of it."

Doan Tien blinked hard twice, and then dropped the

pistol to his side. He nodded, uncocked the weapon, engaged the safety and put it back in his pocket—and began to think.

Louie reached Doan Tien's side before Pham and his bodyguards. "What's going on here, Doan Tien?" Louie whispered into his ear. "Watch what you say."

Doan Tien stood his ground and pressed harder on Dang's shoulder. Dang lowed like a wounded water buffalo.

"I am sorry, Col. Pham," Doan Tien said, pointing at Dang. "But this man here led us into a slaughter this afternoon before himself being wounded. When he awoke he thought I was the only other survivor because Louie had left to scout the area..."

"Ah, yes, Louie," Pham interrupted. "I thought I recognized that old half-breed voice."

Louie nodded respectfully.

"Go on, son."

"He said he wouldn't let any boy live to ruin his career, and was reaching for his pistol to do me in when I stepped on his shoulder and pulled my own pistol. That's when you arrived, sir." Doan Tien ceremoniously bowed his head and awaited the colonel's judgment.

Pham stepped closer. "Is this right, Louie? We heard the fighting. How did it go?"

"At first, it went well. But Dang insisted on pursuing the fight even though the Americans were gaining the advantage. Twelve of our 15 men died because of his arrogance," Louie explained, turning his head to spit in Dang's direction.

"Hmm. I see," Pham said, rubbing his chin. "Dang, you awake?"

Doan Tien pressed harder with his boot. Dang opened his eyes and slowly nodded.

"Do you hear what these men are saying?"

Dang looked up at Louie and then Doan Tien. He slowly shook his head.

"Well, it wouldn't make any difference even if you had," Pham said. He walked over to Dang and motioned Doan Tien aside. He bent over, grabbed Dang by the hair, and then pulled out his big knife. The Big Blade slit Dang's throat from ear to ear. Dang's eyes bulged. He gurgled and died with a stare fixed on Doan Tien's satisfied smirk.

Pham stood and said loudly. "Let this be a lesson. I will not tolerate stupidity in my command. Especially stupidity that costs lives."

And no more witnesses to your crimes, Uncle Bui, Trai thought. He watched with pleasure when the nerves in Dang's foot shuddered one last time.

Pham turned to Doan Tien and raised his knife to the level of the young soldier's face. He slowly twirled the blade so Doan Tien could see the blood dripping from its razor-sharp edge. Doan Tien's eyes grew as wide as rice cakes. Pham laughed and wiped the blood onto the khaki cloth of Doan Tien's shoulder. Pham's demeanor suddenly turned serious. "Let this be a reminder, young man, that I dispense justice and punishment in this army. Not you."

"Yes, yes sir, colonel," he replied with a crisp nod.

"What's your name? You look familiar. Have I seen you before?" Pham sheathed his knife and summoned for water to wash his hands. "And get this carcass out of my sight...Well, what is it? Where are you from?"

"Doan Tien, sir. I come from Dong Ha. My family was killed in a bombing raid."

"No kin near Cam Lo, eh?"

"No. No sir. None that I am aware of," Doan Tien lied, noting how much his sadistic uncle resembled and sounded like his father.

"Well, you have courage for such a young soldier. Kill any Americans today?"

"I don't..."

"Yes he did, my colonel. Indeed, he killed a Marine

just as we escaped," Louie said, stepping in to prevent him from getting further involved. "Begging the colonel's pardon, sir, but we must see to Dang's body and find more ammunition."

"Of course. Go. But I'm going to keep my eye on you, young man," Pham cautioned.

Dozens more NVA soldiers suddenly poured out of the darkness. Louie, Doan Tien and Pham's two aides stripped Dang's body and then buried him in a shallow grave. None said words, nor offered prayers.

"Ah, here they are now," Pham said, motioning for Louie to join him. "You and your young friend will join with me now. I have nearly a battalion of 300 soldiers arriving and we're going to meet with two more battalions tomorrow."

"What are you going to do with so many men?" Louie asked.

Grinning like someone bursting to divulge a secret, Pham took Louie aside. Doan Tien watched them walk away. A moment of jealousy gripped him before he remembered what his uncle had done. He trailed them in the shadows and just within earshot.

"In the next weeks, our army is going to make a new big push through Laos and into the A Shau," the colonel explained. "Until then, it will be our job to pester these Marines and make sure they stay put in Quang Tri and not reinforce their Army friends to the south."

Pham strutted with his arm around Louie's shoulder. "I am going to have to rely heavily on veterans like you, and brave young fools like your little friend there. Stand by me and you will be richly rewarded. I am going to need a new lieutenant now."

"You mean if we survive, of course," Louie replied.

"Oh, as always, but of course."

Doan Tien watched the two men laugh. Getting Lt.

Louie to help carry out his revenge might now be more difficult. And what if he had to go it alone, then what?

CHAPTER 29

Stud
Vandegrift Combat Base, R.S.V.N.
Jan. 13, 1969—12:30 a.m. local time

The convoy's 16 surviving trucks bypassed the Rockpile and limped into Stud at midnight in a misting rain. The uncovered troop truck lurched to a stop and roused the napping Marines. Tuck yelped—his stiff thigh burned with every move—and opened his eyes. Heavy clouds pitched him into a darkness he hadn't imagined. Nothing, save for the ghostly shadows of his friends, the idling engine and the smell of diesel exhaust, was familiar. The confusion reminded him of his first lost, and perplexing, night in boot camp.

"Welcome to Stud, newbies," Jimmy B. said with an exaggerated cheer.

"Oh, yeah, where is it?" Tuck's laugh cracked with anxiety.

"You're in the middle of it. And it won't look much better in the daylight, believe me," Chuck reassured him with a hand on his shoulder when they dismounted.

Using flashlights with red lenses that dimmed the glare, Chuck and Jimmy B. guided the newbies to an area where the fuzzy outline of tents took form. Soon they stood in the center of a large tent similar to the one back in Quang Tri. "Y'all crash here. No cots. Just throw your Snoopy blankets down and get whatever sleep you can," Chuck advised.

They followed his advice, and despite their collective apprehension and confusion, sleep came quickly for the newbies—except for two. Donnie-Boy reached out and gently squeezed Tuck's forearm. "You OK, little brother?" he whispered. "That leg has got to hurt."

"Yeah, you bet it hurts. But I'll be OK. The bleeding's stopped. I'll get it seen to in the morning...Oh, and uh, nice throw this afternoon."

"What? Oh, yeah. Ha. Thanks...Nice shooting, too."

"Think it's going to be like this all the time," Tuck asked. "I mean, like how many guys see this much action in the first few days."

"I dunno. Hope it's just bad luck." Donnie-Boy replied, stifling a yawn. "It's gotta calm down sometime."

"Yeah, hope so...before we get zapped," Tuck laughed. "G'night, man."

"G'night, little brother."

•

The 600-meter peaks of the Nui Ba Ho mountain range that bordered the valley still shaded Vandegrift at 0630. The overcast had broken, allowing the rising sun's corona to crown the eastern zenith with a pinkish glow. Morning's fresh smell slid into Stud with the dew. Fifteen minutes later sunlight crept across the valley and the newbies rose to survey their surroundings.

Tuck stood and stroked his burning thigh. It had bled again during the night and a red patch surrounded the rip in his trousers, also muddied by his crawl through the ditch.

"Damn, Tuck, you look like you've already been here six months," Jimmy B. said with a snort and hacking cough that choked off an early morning laugh. He lit up a smoke and then turned to Johnny, still asleep. "And you too, big boy," he said, slapping Johnny on the shoulder.

"Aiiiiyyyeee," Johnny cried out, bolting upright and panting, not moving his shoulder. He whimpered softly and then cursed under his breath.

"OK, let's see what we got goin' on here," Chuck said,

kneeling to examine Tuck's leg. He grunted a motherly, "Umm, hmm."

Chuck then turned and coaxed Johnny, with Danny's help, to remove his T-shirt. "Damn, man. You said you was OK last night," he chided Johnny while examining three raised, red-ringed pustules the size of marbles. They straddled both sides of a long scar left by a surgeon's knife and college football. "You've got shrapnel in there that needs to come out," Chuck observed. "You don't hide shit like this in the bush. It don't take no time for infection to set in. Jungle rot and the creeping crud is everywhere. You and Tuck need to di-di on up to Charlie Med, ASAP. Y'all are no good to us like this.

"Anybody else hurt I need to know about?" Chuck shouted.

"My shoulder's a little sore," Donnie-Boy joked, slowly wind milling his right arm.

"Hell, I guess so. Nice throw." Chuck grinned. "Jimmy B., take these guys to Charlie Med."

"Oh, hell yes," Jimmy B. eagerly replied. "Chow's a lot better around there."

"As for the rest of you, let's go find us some chow," Chuck called out.

Sunlight filled the valley while they walked toward Charlie Med, a field hospital located near the southwest corner of Stud atop a 30-foot high plateau. Stud was nestled in a valley that ran north and south for three miles and for two miles east to west. Nui Ba Ho bordered it on the east, and 200-meter high Signal Hill rose to the west just outside the perimeter of Stud. Tuck squinted and looked up to the top of the grass-covered hill. He could make out antennae and bunkers.

"Route 9 enters and exits Stud from the north and south. The Rockpile is only a few miles to the north and you can see it on a clear day," Jimmy B. explained, pointing toward the north.

Tuck's leg ached again, and he asked Jimmy B. to slow the pace.

"Sure thing, maybe we can flag down a mule or something," Jimmy B. said before continuing his tour. "Firebase Calu and a small Montagnard village are immediately to our south. Khe Sanh is about 12 miles or so that way to the southwest near Laos."

A long landing strip made of metal planks was the most prominent man-made feature of Stud. Dozens of helicopters—mostly twin-bladed CH-46 Sea Knights, CH-47 Chinooks and CH-53 Sea Stallions—buzzed the area. Army UH-1 Hueys also darted about. Tuck spotted a gangly crane helicopter lifting a load of supplies like a praying mantis escaping with its dinner.

"I imagine the strip could handle C-130 cargo planes but I've never seen one. For sure it can't handle jets," Jimmy B. said. "The fast-movers come from Dong Ha, Quang Tri, Da Nang or a carrier in the Gulf."

Patience rewarded the trio when a mule came puttering along. A small vehicle with a wooden platform, seat and steering wheel was all there was to a mule. The sturdy four-wheel drive mule mainly ferried light supplies, ran errands, and delivered hot food to the units providing perimeter security. Heavy weapons could also be mounted on the platform.

Jimmy B. flagged down the driver. "Headed up to Charlie Med. Can we hitch a ride?"

"Sure, just goin' up there myself to get supplies. Hop on, *cher*," the rugged-looking driver said with a rich Cajun accent. Tuck and Johnny looked at one another and smiled.

"*Mais*, where you from, *cher*?" Tuck asked, adding a little drip to his light Cajun accent to make sure the mule driver caught it. He hoped it wasn't another Maine Marine.

"Golden Meadow, down near the Gulf. You know, on the way to Grand Isle," the man turned and said with an alligator grin. "They call me Swamp Rat out here. Rat will do just fine."

"Golden Meadow? I got a speeding ticket there one time," Johnny said with some effort.

"Everybody has," Rat laughed. "Biggest damn speedtrap south of Port Barre."

Tuck extended his hand. "Glad to meet you, Rat. I'm from Eunice. You can call me Tuck. This is Johnny, he's from Mamou."

"No shit, both of you from back home?" Rat said, almost losing control of the mule. He turned for a closer look at the Cajun pair. "Damn, this place is gettin' overrun with Cajuns."

"Yep, you got it right, Rat."

"Yeah, Eunice. I know where that is," replied the burly Marine whose mustard colored hair flipped up from beneath his cover. "Played some baseball against y'all a few years ago in the playoffs. Never been to Mamou, though."

"Ain't missed much," Johnny mumbled.

"What y'all going up there for?" Rat said, nodding toward Charlie Med.

Tuck rattled off the events of the previous three days.

"Heck, I've been here nearly four months and been standin' lines at Stud and up on Signal Hill just about the whole time. Our squad's had a lot of incoming and probes, but we haven't seen as much shit as you have in three days. Don't know whether to be jealous or thankful," Rat said with a wink as they neared Charlie Med. "I can hang out an hour or so up here if y'all want a ride back. And if y'all ever need a ride, Tuck, just holler. I seem to be everyone's favorite chauffeur these days, even up as high as the colonel. You know he's from Louisiana, too."

•

Navy Lt. Jimmy DeSchott, M.D., leaned against a sandbagged wall surrounding Charlie Med. Sweat and blood soiled his green scrubs. He puffed on a cigarette as if it would be his last and stared over the expanse of Stud. His mind was clearer now. Vietnam's air was refreshing.

He looked up at the sound of a sputtering engine. He smiled and ground his cigarette butt into the red clay.

"Hey, Rat. Figured you'd be up this way today. Nurse Bitch has some supplies boxed up for you," DeSchott said, welcoming them with a smooth Southern drawl. He had been in-country three months, serving the beginning of a four-year commitment to the Navy, which had put him through the University of North Carolina Medical School. He had completed his residency in a surgical trauma unit in Raleigh, but nothing had prepped him for what he had found in the Nam.

"Got some more work for you, Doc Shot, two newbies from yesterday's convoy," Swamp Rat hollered before killing the engine.

"Figured as much. Just took the leg off a poor kid that got caught up in that shit."

"Don't think they're too bad, just a couple of my homeboys with some dinks, a shoulder and a leg," Rat said. "Smells like infections, though. Need to be cleaned out and rewrapped."

"Thank you for that diagnosis there, Dr. Rat, but I think I'll have a look at 'em just the same." DeSchott beamed—most everyone liked Swamp Rat.

Jimmy B. helped Tuck and Johnny dismount and they walked toward the surgeon.

"Let's see here, y'all seem to be doing OK, just like Dr. Rat called it." DeSchott gently tugged at Johnny's soaked blouse. He hissed when the matted material pulled away from the wound. It smelled of day-old chicken fat in a garbage can—not yet rotted but foul.

DeSchott turned and noticed a grim-faced Vietnamese nurse standing close by with a large box stamped "Supplies, Medical." She had joined them with a stealthy silence.

"Don't look too bad," the doctor mumbled, "but you've still got some shrapnel in there and the rot's setting in. Go with Nurse Bitch...err, Nurse Binh, and she'll get you cleaned up."

Nurse Binh glowered at them, and then guided Johnny toward the entrance.

The doctor turned to Tuck. "How about you, fella? Leg wound, huh? Don't imagine it's as bad as the last kid I just finished cutting on. Let's see." Using both hands, he tugged at the ragged hole in the trouser leg to split them open. "Don't worry, we got plenty more of these."

"Ouch!" Tuck winced. "It's a bit stiff and sore, doc." It reminded him of the scar on his dad's leg, but not nearly as severe. But the wound would add to their bond.

"Don't look too bad, just a flesh wound, but it's significant," DeSchott said. "I can clean it up and stitch it, but I'll tell you right now you're going to have a pretty nasty scar. Of course, it's not bad enough to send you home or to the ship. But, I'll give you and your buddy a few days light duty and some pain medicine."

"That's OK, just glad I got through that thing alright." Tuck said, pointing toward the surgeon's bloody gown. "I've still got my leg."

The surgeon put his hand on his shoulder and guided him to the door.

"Hey, Doc Shot, what about me?" Jimmy B. hollered, feigning a grimace.

"What's the matter with you, Marine?"

"Oh, uh, concussion I think. Hit my head. Could use a shot of some pain medicine, you know," Jimmy B. said with a hopeful smile. "Or, a few pills."

"Yeah, right," DeSchott retorted. "Rat, get this guy to

help you carry the supplies down the hill. And don't let him dig in the box, OK."

"Aaah, shit," Jimmy B. exclaimed. "Let's go find some hot chow, Rat."

"Doc Shot, huh? Bet you get a lot of ribbing with a name like DeSchott," Tuck asked.

"You bet. In fact, they told me I could never be a pediatrician. The kids would never trust me," he said laughing at the irony. "But it would be a good Mafia name though...Jimmy 'The Shot'."

Tuck laughed. It was good medicine.

CHAPTER 30

Snow and Europe
Eunice, La.
Feb. 1, 1969—10 a.m. local time

After three weeks, letters arrived in bundles. It was bittersweet times in the Richard, Hebert and Robert homes when they read about their sons' harrowing arrival in Vietnam. But only Tuck detailed those early experiences, and his and Johnny's hospital visit.

Mary Richard and Grace Hebert soaked one another's silk blouses with mothers' tears when they shared shoulders and exchanged letters. It was Curtis Richard and Wilfred Robert, however, who grew closest through Tuck and Johnny's shared ordeal.

On a cold Saturday morning under threatening skies, Mary sat at the kitchen table and wept quietly. For the third straight day she read from Benjamin's letters, tracing her fingers over his signature. Sleepless nights had colored dark circles beneath her once bright and blue eyes.

...I would be lying if I said it was only a scratch. It was too wide for stitches to close neatly and will leave an ugly scar. But then again, it is nothing to be concerned about, as I have returned to my squad after only a few days of light duty. Indeed, it is the wound that has provided me with the time to write this series of letters...

...Johnny's shoulder wound was also minor and he is back with us. Please call Mr. Wilfred and reassure him, as I am sure Johnny's letters have not been so detailed...

...Donnie-Boy has not yet been wounded but he's so reckless, or is it brave, that I'm sure it is only a matter of time. Donnie-Boy

has already been recommended for two commendations, one for pulling some wounded men from a burning truck and another for helping turn a firefight we were losing into a rout of the enemy. He's good to have around...

...We will learn of our permanent assignments in the next few days when our main unit comes back from Operation Dewey Canyon in the A Shau Valley. It turns out that activity has increased in our area and they need more men to stand lines around Stud and that's what we have been doing for the past week or so. Two of my new friends, Chuck and Jimmy B., are excited about standing lines despite the daily mortar fire we've been taking. They say it's still a lot better than being in the boonies. They tell us not to get impatient...

...Please ask my friends to pray for us and tell Anna that I will be writing her soon. Also, go ahead and let her read these letters so that I won't have to repeat myself too much. I don't mind telling you I've fallen in love with her and would like for you to get to know her better...

...Tell Uncle Joe thanks for the prayer to St. Joseph. It's getting a workout...

"Babe," Curtis shouted from his office. "I'm gonna ride up to Mamou and see how Wilfred's doing, OK?"

Mary sniffed, then mumbled, "OK."

"He's going to be alright," he reassured her, standing at her side. "They've trained him well, and he's a smart kid. He won't do anything foolish." He leaned and slipped his arms around her waist. He kissed her lightly on the side of the neck. "So, why don't you try to take a nap after lunch?"

"OK, I'll try, but..."

"But what, Babe?" Curtis asked. He stood and reached for his leather jacket on the old coat rack that leaned to the right. It was drizzling and the weatherman predicted a wet weekend in the upper 30s. The nagging pain in his left thigh agreed with the forecast.

"Do you sleep at night? I hear you breathing deep, but not snoring like you used to."

Curtis paused when he reached the door, turned, and then returned to his wife's side. He placed his hands on her shoulders and gently massaged her neck. "No, not much, Babe. I just do my darndest not to disturb you, that's all. I hear your crying...sleep will eventually come. That's why I want you to take a nap."

Mary pressed a page from Tuck's letters to her breast with one hand and grabbed Curtis' jacketed arm with the other. "I think it's time we just give him up to the Lord and let Him take care of it. I can't go a year like this. It's just too painful."

"I know, Babe, I know. I gave him up to God a long time ago. Just like my mom did with me back in '43."

"You didn't tell me."

"We have to deal with it in different ways," he said, kissing the top of her head. "Love you."

"Love you, too." Mary smiled and returned to the letters.

"And now, I have to go help Wilfred deal with it some. See you later."

•

A dusting of snow, a rare event for much of south Louisiana, added several minutes to the 10-mile drive up Highway 13. The flakes mostly melted when they hit the roadway, but when Curtis arrived at Wilfred's house, he saw a white crust accumulating on car tops and the brown grass lawns. "Hmm, may stick after all," he said to himself when he reached the horseshoe drive. He thought about how Dave and Winston would be excited and what Tuck would give to have the cold stuff right now. Mark would give anything for a mild Louisiana winter.

SPLAT!

A snowball showered the windshield with slush before the Chevy rolled to a stop. Two small boys giggled and ran through a row of snow-covered azaleas and on to the safety of the house next door. Curtis grinned and stepped out of the car, cautious not to slip on the icy lawn.

The screen door at the entrance of the white house swung to life. Wilfred propped it open with his boot and beckoned Curtis to join him. "Cold as shit out here and looks like the snow just might stick," he said, blowing into his hands. "So get your ass in here and get warm."

"Enough to freeze your pecker off if you pee too long outside," Curtis said, briefly remembering about how this frigid arrival differed from their sweltering meeting back in August.

"Yeah, I remember what they used to say in Korea, 'don't eat the yellow snow.'" Wilfred reached out to shake Curtis' hand.

"Yep, said that back in England, too."

"Watch out now, the porch is getting kinda slippery."

Wilfred disappeared into the kitchen to fetch coffee. Curtis stopped in the den and settled into a wooden rocker he had grown fond of during his regular visits. Wilfred's coffee wasn't the best, but Mello Joy was Curtis' favorite blend and he was getting used to it. Besides, the company was great.

Wilfred returned holding two cups of his steaming brew.

"Any more news from…"

"Any more news from…" they asked in unison, then laughed.

"You're my guest, go first," Wilfred said.

"Yeah, Tuck likes to write letters. He lays it all out in detail. Wish he'd hold back sometimes. It's really gettin' to Mary."

"Can imagine. My problem's just the opposite. It's tough tryin' to get anything out of Johnny's letters."

Curtis blew into his cup before taking a sip. Nodding, he reached into his pocket. "That's why I brought these. Had to steal 'em away while Mary wasn't looking." He tossed three letters onto the coffee table.

Wilfred reached over from his recliner and snatched them up. "Thanks, I'll bring 'em back to you tomorrow, if that's OK?"

"Sure, no rush. Mary's probably got 'em memorized." Curtis paused to take another sip. "By the way, he also mentions that niece of yours, Anna Carlisle. It looks like there's something serious brewing. They were gettin' to be quite an item while he was on leave. And you saw 'em at the airport, you'd swear it was 'Casablanca' or something."

"Oh, yeah, sweet girl. She's been coming by the shop regular ever since the boys left, asking about Johnny and whatever she can get out of me about Tuck. She'd be a great catch."

"Mind if I use your bathroom a minute," Curtis said, rising gingerly. "Or, do I have to go outside and make some yellow snow?"

"Aw shit, Curtis, you don't have to ask around here. My pisser is your pisser. Go ahead." Wilfred quickly opened and read Tuck's letter detailing his and Johnny's trip to Charlie Med. A minute later Curtis limped back to the rocker, sat, and rubbed his left thigh.

"Johnny never told me that his shoulder scratch—as he put it—got infected and put him in a field hospital overnight. Glad to see Tuck's leg is better, too." Wilfred watched Curtis reach down and massage his thigh. "How about yours? I see you're limping around pretty bad today."

"Aw, yeah, the cold I imagine. When the weather turns likes this it gets worse."

"You never really told me about your leg. All you ever said was it happened in a B-17 over Germany." Wilfred slurped at his coffee. "Saw a little combat in Korea myself. Served most of my time in artillery. I think I know a bit what you went through. But I never got hit."

"A little combat!" Curtis scoffed. "Wilfred, a little combat is too much combat, my friend. And you don't have to get hit to know what war's about." He stood up and walked to the window to peek out at the snow.

"How about another cup of coffee?" Wilfred asked, joining his new friend at the window.

"Sure, that'd be nice."

Wilfred returned shortly with a fresh cup and saw Curtis staring out at the gray sky.

Curtis took the cup and gently stirred the coffee. "It was also in February…1943. A cold day, much colder than today." He took a sip, smiled, and toasted his host with an approving nod. It was one of Wilfred's better batches. "You sure you want to know all about…"

"Yeah, man. You just go on and tell it like you want to. Just me and you here."

Curtis wondered just who was helping who today. During most visits they talked about high school and college football. They were excited about the Saints, the new pro team in New Orleans. Sometimes they sat and watched a ball game on TV. Other times they simply sat and napped. But occasionally Curtis had brought Wilfred to tears when he asked him to speak of his recently deceased brother and wife, who had died tragically years ago.

Curtis returned to his favorite chair, sat back, and rocked slowly. "Like I said, it was February 1943 and we were en route to western Germany. Kassel, I think it was. We were gonna bomb some aircraft factory. When we climbed to better than 10,000 feet, the pilot ordered us to go on oxygen. I was the top turret gunner and engineer, I was to keep an eye on how the engines were running and all, and then protect our scalp when the fighters arrived.

"After a few hours, we reached the frontier of Germany and the krauts came up after us. Mostly ME-109s and Focke-Wulfs. Then the flak got heavy, and then even heavier, like the snow outside. Sometimes it got so thick, you'd swear you could walk across those puffs of smoke. A few pieces of shrapnel rattled our skin a coupla times—no real damage, no one got hit.

"Then the captain called out 'bandits at 10 o'clock' and I wheeled around and caught a Messerschmitt in the sights of my twin .50 cals and ripped off no more than 10 rounds. And I'll be damned if that 109 don't ball up and blow apart just a hundred yards from us. It was my first kill, lucky shot really. Heck, it was just my third mission. The first two missions were easy, 'milk runs' we called them, and I had only fired on one plane before then. I didn't give much thought to it back then...to the pilot I'd just nailed. He couldn't have gotten out quick enough. Thought about him a lot over the years though." Curtis paused for a sip.

"The fighters were like flies and the flak was still coming up despite their planes being in the area. They didn't want us to get to that factory. But, we did, despite their best efforts. We bombed the shit out of 'em," Curtis said with a smile. "The bombardier let out a whoop when the bombs hit, claiming 90 percent on target. We could also feel the air buck up when the heat and concussion reached us from the planes that were bombing up ahead.

"Then, finally, captain said we were headed home—a long four-hour flight. Well, when we headed out of Germany, there they were, waiting for us again. More planes than you could count. No flak this time. But it was like black birds on a cold day. They were all over us. One plane came right at us, head on. The nose gunner and me lit him up at the same time and I watched him spin in for a long time before his chute opened. Kind of upset me, back then, that he got out. Now I hope he's an old man in Berlin telling his kids how he got shot down one cold day.

"All of a sudden the plane jerked and bucked again when the bullets peppered our ship..."

"What was her name, again?" Wilfred interrupted. "The ship, I mean."

"Oh, uh, the captain named her *Belle Ami*—'beautiful friend,' after his dog."

"Sorry, go on, Curtis."

"Then I heard our two waist gunners cry out. I wanted to help 'em, but the fighters were all over us. Turns out both of 'em just had minor wounds and continued to shoot. What we didn't know was our tail gunner, a young Texas kid, from near Humble I think, had been blown apart.

"I got a third 109 about five minutes later when it passed by. I must have caught it in a fuel tank because the right wing just blew away and it spun away wildly." Curtis gestured, spinning his fingers toward the floor. "Never saw a chute. I may have gotten a fourth one, too, and helped out on a fifth, but never got confirmation. If I would have, you'd be having coffee with an ace. I'll never really know. Guess it's best that way.

"Action was getting lighter and we continued on toward England. Then our air cover showed up and the kraut fighters started pulling back. I was running low on oxygen by then. Damn near hyperventilating the whole time, you know. I reached down for a new bottle but got caught up in my jacket and gear, so I had to hop down to the corridor to pick up the cylinder. And while I was crawling back up to my perch, that's when he hit us."

"Who hit y'all, Curtis?" Wilfred asked, draining his cup with a loud slurp.

"A stray, I guess. The last man out, maybe, who knows. Anyway, a 109 came up behind us and opened up with one, hellishly long burst of 20-millimeter fire. Damn near took *Belle Ami* apart. He could've if he had stayed on us longer. But air cover chased him off.

"Still, that long burst killed one of our waist gunners,

our navigator and co-pilot...and took one inch out of my left leg that was still dangling during my ascent."

Curtis paused to take his last sip of coffee.

"At first it felt like a baseball bat had hit my leg, then it burned like a thousand fire ant bites. After that, it got numb and I got weak. The slug had shattered my thighbone and the artery. I was losing blood so fast there was little they could do. Then Benjamin Jenson, a waist gunner, tall guy from California with long fingers, stuck his thumb and forefinger into my leg—that's how big the hole was—and pinched the artery...Any idea what it's like to watch someone stick their fingers in your leg and save your life?"

Wilfred slowly shook his head.

"Well, ol' Ben did it for me. Thankfully, my leg was numb—enough nerves had been blown out of there as well. Then, somewhere near England I passed out, lost so much blood they had just given up on me—except for Ben. They put me on the wing after we landed and tended to the other wounded first. They figured I was a goner. But there was Ben, still pinching that artery. He saved my life..."

"I spent nine months on my back in a body cast. But I made it, thanks to Mr. Benjamin Jenson." Curtis fell into a silence, akin to a trance.

"What happened to him?"

"Hmm, what?"

"What happened to Jenson? You ever look him up after the war?"

"No...the *Belle Ami* was shot down on its next mission several days later. She littered the fields of Germany and all hands were lost, including Ben. They never found his body. And they gave me a medal for shooting down all those planes. Ol' Ben never even got a funeral." He turned and stared at Wilfred. "But, now, you know where Tuck got his 'real' first name."

"Shit, Curtis. I can't imagine our boys having to go through something like that."

"They have already, Wilfred. They have already. And I'm afraid my one-day nightmare over Germany will pale before what they will have to suffer through."

The two men rocked, and thought. Little more was said.

CHAPTER 31

The Locusts Return
Vandegrift Combat Base, R.S.V.N.
Feb. 10, 1969—5 p.m. local time

They swooped unannounced from the southern sky, emerging through the overcast like a plague of twin-bladed locusts. The powerful CH-46 Sea Knights and their precious cargo within circled Stud, seeking a place to light. Third Battalion of the Ninth Marines was coming home.

Standing beside his bunker along the western perimeter of Stud, Johnny looked up and pointed toward a score of helicopters. "Look at that. Now ain't that a sight." He called out to his napping friend. "Tuck, wake up, man. You gotta see this."

"Our brothers are comin' home," Chuck added reverently. "I'll be introducing you to the guys by supper. Can't wait to see 'em, especially ol' Sgt. Cosmo and Ike."

Tuck sat up on his rubber bitch and watched the swarm circle overhead and flare their noses for a final approach to the metal landing strip a half-mile away.

Compared to their first days in country, the past weeks had been uneventful. Sporadic enemy contact had been limited to daily harassment fire from mortars and rockets. Nightly line probes were becoming regular. Chuck's squad had suffered no casualties and Tuck's leg wound was nearly healed.

The Cajuns saw Swamp Rat on a daily basis when he delivered hot chow on his mule, which he called Skeeter. They enjoyed his company and laughed at his humorous tales of home. They also enjoyed the extra slices of bacon Rat sneaked to them each morning. Even Danny was warming up to Rat. But next to Johnny—his football soul mate—Danny had become a close friend and protégé of Chuck.

The boredom of standing lines provided time to adjust to the fickle weather—alternately depressing rain and oppressive heat. It also gave Tuck and his friends a chance to learn grunt customs and lingo, a chore Chuck and Jimmy B. relished.

The colored guys were called "bloods" by all, or "brothers" within their own ethnic circle. A ritualistic handshake—akin to a secret fraternity—requiring the knocking of fists, and/or slapping palms, together in a pattern served as their greeting and sign of racial recognition. Once friendship and trust were established, however, the largely Afro-American ritual was extended to whites, or "chucks," as well.

The term "chucks" both amused and perplexed Chuck, who was a handsome and stoutly built man with light brown skin and green eyes. He often joked about his ancestry and how, "This ol' Chuck here probably got some 'chuck' in his blood somewhere down the line." To which he would quickly add, "But it don't mean nothin' as long as my ass don't become ground chuck before I get out of the Nam."

They also learned about chores—like burning the "shitters," filling sandbags, and digging and constructing bunkers. An outhouse at Stud consisted of little more than a 4-by-4 wooden hooch standing about seven feet, complete with a hole in a piece of plywood over which to sit. Some fancy ones boasted a real toilet seat. Grunts provided their own toilet paper, which could be obtained from the assortment pack in any box of C-rations...or a well-read letter from home.

The "shitter" sometimes, but rarely, had a door for privacy, the logic being a grunt might have to make a quick exit. It also had a hinged door on the backside from where a cut-down 55-gallon drum could be inserted. This so-called septic tank needed emptying on a regular basis. The unlucky grunt chosen for the duty would stir diesel fuel into the grimy, maggot-infested mess and then ignite the flammable concoction. It produced an odd but beautiful curling plume.

Tuck once told his dad in a letter. *"The hardest part about burning the "shitters" is pulling the tanks out from beneath the hooch. Shit is heavy. It stinks. And it splashes. Strangely enough, Johnny seems to enjoy burning the shitters. He often volunteers for the job. But no one has ever figured out why, and he's never offered an explanation. And I ain't gonna ask."*

No one volunteered to fill sandbags. But Tuck could see why they did it so often. Sandbags were everywhere—around anything that had a wall or a hole in the ground, on rooftops, beside signs, even on jeep bumpers. They were inert, just laid there and did nothing, yet were indispensable for protection and defense.

Marines learned in training that they would have to dig "fighting holes"—only the Army and civilians called them "foxholes." But they had no idea how many. Blisters were the order of the day. Tuck figured they were called grunts because that's the noise they made while digging yet another hole.

Whenever an impatient FNG expressed a desire to go out into the boonies, Jimmy B. was there to tell horror stories about the A Shau. "Just be glad, dudes, that they didn't send us to the A Shau to meet 3/9. And pray they don't ever send us back. Be patient to die." He added there were plenty of enemy soldiers just outside the perimeter and within eyesight of Stud to keep a whole regiment of Marines busy if, and when, Ho Chi Minh chose to give the word.

But, now, 3/9 was returning. What did that signal for the future? Tuck wondered. It was obvious that standing lines was only temporary. The only reason they had not been choppered to the A Shau was because of increased activity around Stud.

Chuck searched the lines for Jimmy B. and then called out, "They back, man. Let's sky on down to check 'em out."

Jimmy B. simply smiled and waved weakly.

Chuck shook his head. "Stoned again," he whispered, then again shouted. "Come on, man."

"Naw, you go ahead. I'll wait until they call us in later. Nobody I gotta see just yet," replied Jimmy B., whose two closest friends had died within arm's reach. They would not be among the stream of grunts hustling off the back ramps of the choppers.

Chuck nodded. "Suit yourself. It's pretty quiet now anyway. I'll take the new kids down with me to meet the outfit. OK?"

"Sure, there's enough other guys around here if I need help...but, don't be too long. OK?"

"Just enough time to find out what's goin' down." Chuck led the Cajun trio and Danny down the shallow western slope. Kilo 3/9 would be bedding down in the tent area.

•

"Chuck," a man cried out when they approached. "Chuck, over here you skatin' sonbitch. Get your ass over here, dude."

"Who's that?" Tuck said, pointing toward a trim blond shedding his gear.

Ignoring him, Chuck laughed and shouted back. "Ike, you dog. You made it back. Man, are you a sight for sore eyes."

The two grunts clasped palms and hugged. "Stink pretty bad, too," Chuck added, before turning to Tuck. "This here is Cpl. Ike Likens—the second-best squad leader in second platoon. And the only white boy with a pecker bigger'n mine."

"And don't you forget it. By the way, talkin' about peckers, how was R&R? Or should I say, the poontang?"

"Beaucoup, my man, beaucoup." They laughed and hugged again.

"I knew you'd like Sydney and those round eyes. Did you look up Sally at the Majestic?"

"Yep, and she was there, and remembered you. That is till I made her forget all about you."

"You dirty dog, give me all the details so we can compare notes," Ike laughed.

"Sure, but let's get ol' Cosmo over here," Chuck said, turning to look about the tent. "So I don't have to repeat myself."

Ike's smile disappeared. He hung his head and shuffled his feet. "Uh, sarge didn't make it."

Danny placed his hand on Chuck's shoulder from behind and Tuck drew closer to his right side. Chuck shrugged them away. "How'd it happen?"

"Rotten luck, really. Him and Scotty bought it at the same time."

"Not Scotty, too. Shit. Hell, we all came in together. That just leaves me and you from the original gang," Chuck lamented. Ike nodded.

Tuck, Donnie-Boy, Johnny and Danny traded glances, then looked down. Which one of them might...?

"Hell, since you and Jimmy B. left for R&R, the A Shau's been pretty quiet," Ike said. "Except for...By the way, where is Jimmy B.? That ol' dope head, he is OK, right?"

Chuck placed his hands on his hips and looked around the tent, searching for familiar faces. Twice he stopped to wave at fellow grunts. "Yeah, we've been on lines the past few weeks and he wasn't ready to come down just yet, you know, Lee and Dave...well, you know."

"Yeah, sure do. They were a coupla good grunts, too," Ike said quietly.

"So what went down with Cosmo and Scotty," Chuck asked again.

Ike reached up and rubbed his matted hair. "One night about two weeks ago the gooks hit us with some incoming, more of that harassment shit. And I'll be damned if a mortar round don't land smack dab in the middle of Cosmo and Scotty's hole. Both went pretty quick, Cosmo instantly, gutted him. Scotty lived about half an hour even though his legs and half his ass was gone. Doc couldn't do nothing."

Ike searched his pockets for a cigarette. Chuck offered him a four-pack of Winstons. "Thanks." Ike lit one up, noticed the newbies for the first time, and nodded.

Chuck swiped his glistening eyes and looked away. "Anyone else?"

"No. Not even any wounded. Few heat casualties humpin' the hills though. But we ain't fired a shot in, oh, two...three weeks. The brass is scared shitless. Too quiet they say. Think something big's gonna happen soon, and it's probably gonna happen up here. That's why they left you here and brought us back a couple of weeks early." Ike paused to take a deep drag on his cigarette. He exhaled slowly, glancing again at the new grunts.

"Skipper says we're gonna be gettin' a new platoon sergeant soon to replace Cosmo," Ike added. "But you're gonna need a fire team leader when we put your squad back together. We're gonna need a gunner and assist, too. Paul and Jay are rotating next week," Ike said, laughing nervously as he sized up the newbies. "Good thing they pulled us back in, we're runnin' out of guys. Any of your FNGs worth a shit?"

Chuck's face lit up. "Yep. Pretty damn good."

"You say that like they got some experience," Ike said with a quizzed expression.

Chuck put his arm around Ike's shoulder and turned him toward the entrance of the tent. "Ike, ol' buddy. Let's see if I can find you a not-so-warm beer and I'll tell you all about 'em."

The two corporals exited the tent, leaving the four

newbies in the middle of a group of strangers. With their chaperone out searching for beer, they returned to the lines.

•

Chuck and Ike walked up the dirt trail an hour later laughing and joking. Tuck thought how it was odd that, in the Nam, memories of the dead could be so quickly buried in the survivors' minds. Thoughts of personal loss resided there surely, surfacing occasionally, but never dominating the present. It must have something to do with one's own mortality.

"OK, guys. We just met with the skipper, and here's what's shakin' and what's gonna happen," Chuck said, signaling for them to gather around. "First, Donnie-Boy, papers have come through and you've been promoted to lance corporal, effective immediately. You'll be taking over one of my fire teams. I'm putting Tuck and two veterans in it, so you're gonna have to earn their respect real quick. Now, I've filled in Ike here on what you've already been through, and he doesn't think there'll be a problem."

"No, not at all," Ike joined in. "The skipper also said he's sending off recommendations for both the Bronze Star and Navy Com on your behalf, Hebert. He wants to meet you personally in the morning." Ike reached out and shook Donnie-Boy's hand.

His friends patted him on the back and jabbed him in the ribs. Donnie-Boy blushed.

"OK, enough now. Listen up," Ike continued. "PFC Robert..."

"It's said like ROH-bear," Johnny corrected.

"Yeah, and Hebert is AY-bear and Richard is REE-shard," Donnie-Boy corrected. "It makes a difference to us, Ike."

"OK, sure fellas, ROH-bear, how much M-60 training did you get back in the world?"

"The basic stuff, my MOS is 0330 and I caught on pretty fast and like that gun a lot. And I can handle the big sucker easy, too, yeah."

Ike grinned at Johnny's thick accent. "Good, that's what I was thinking, because you're gonna be training on the 60 this week with two of my short-timers. And Jackson, you're gonna be the A-gunner, his assist. You'll hump a lot of ammo and help with the gun. You'll also get a lot of training on the trigger," Ike explained. "Y'all will be attached to Chuck's squad, too."

The four grunts exchanged grins. "Still together, just amazing," Danny said.

Darkness was settling in when Chuck and Ike began walking back toward the tents. Chuck stopped after a few steps and turned. "By the way fellas. Two more days on the lines while the guys down there get some rest and then we're goin' on a short operation. We'll be sweeping near the Rockpile, not far from where we got ambushed. Charlie's been gettin' a bit too active in this area." The two corporals turned and walked away.

"Well, well, well. Lance Corporal Donnie-Boy Hebert. What do y'all think about that?" Tuck laughed in a mocking voice.

"That's right sonbitch, you got to listen to me now," Donnie-Boy shot back. "And my first order is for you to bite my ass."

Tuck tackled Donnie-Boy and dragged him to the ground. They rolled in the dirt like schoolboys until Tuck pinned his friend on his stomach. He opened his mouth wide and bit him on the buttocks and growled. Donnie-Boy yelped. "What the hell you doing?"

"Any more orders, smart ass?"

Donnie-Boy sat up, shook his head and flashed that knowing grin. "At least I know you'll obey my orders."

Tuck rose to his knees and looked up at the sky. It was

nearly pitch black and the night was spreading its carpet of glitter. "Two days, Donnie-Boy, two days. And we'll be out there, tempting the darkness. Two days."

CHAPTER 32

Trai's Confession
Quang Tri Province, R.S.V.N.
Feb. 11, 1969—11:45 p.m. local time

Col. Pham drove his troops mercilessly and when they complained, he raged to the point where even Louie flinched. Men whispered about Pham shooting, or worse yet, gutting those who thought to go over his head. They feared him more than they did the Americans. Yet, they trusted Pham. Moreover, they fought for him. Pham's superiors ignored his callousness because of his enormous field success.

Doan Tien often thought of desertion, but each time he considered surrendering and becoming a "chieu hoi," he remembered unfinished business. Revenge came first, he vowed. So far, when confronting the Americans, he fired safely over their heads. He learned to set harmless booby traps and cleverly explained his deficiencies sprung from his youth and lack of formal training. Still, he dreaded the thought of having to kill an American to save his own life.

He lay next to Louie along a stream often patrolled by Americans. But the ambush had yielded nothing. He could not recall a moonless night so dark. Heavy clouds and the jungle canopy cast a gloom so thick he could scarcely see the end of his gun barrel. He yawned.

Louie nudged him in the ribs with a sharp prod of his fingers. "Hey, my little slayer. It's time you tell me that secret you've been hiding. This ambush is no good, and it's just going to cost us sleep. So you might as well confess—a tale of some young conquest, I hope, hmm?"

Doan Tien's exhausted mind swam. Could he trust Louie, now that Pham had promoted him to lieutenant and confidant? Would Louie merely laugh? Or, would he turn him over to Pham when he learned the secret? Even if Louie would turn him in, he could reveal himself as Trai and pray upon his uncle's mercy. Mercy? The man knew no mercy. Still, Louie, if anything, was just and knew the pain of a slaughtered family.

"Come, little one, tell me. Didn't I share with you the secrets of my family, my past? Can your secret be so grave?"

Doan Tien closed his eyes and prayed a quick Catholic prayer, the best he could remember of the Hail Mary from his childhood classes.

"Well? I'm waiting," Louie insisted.

He gambled on the haunted man's sense of justice. "Louie, remember how you felt when your mother and sister were murdered by the French? And how you came to hate the very people from whom you came? So much so that you wouldn't stop until you tasted revenge?"

"Yes. Yes of course I do. One neither forgets such horror, nor forgives, as far as I am concerned. Drunk or not, I did what I thought I had to do."

Doan Tien whispered deliberately, making sure there would be no misinterpretation. "Then you might, you must, understand the secret I harbor in my heart. I, too, have a hatred so intense that I'm willing to seek a terrible revenge."

Louie rubbed his eyes with his fists and licked his lips as if it would prepare him. "I don't know if I like where this is headed, but I don't think I'd be able to sleep another minute if I didn't learn more," he whispered. "Tell me more, now."

Fortunately, they lay at the end of the ambush line and several yards from the nearest position. He slid closer to Louie's side, touching shoulders with the larger man.

"First, let me confess to you, and only to you, that Doan

Tien is not my real name. It is the names of my dead brothers. I use it to honor them and so that I can carry out the task I'm destined to perform. My real name is Pham Thuc Trai and I'm from Cam Lo, not Dong Ha."

"Trai, huh? Well, if you don't mind, I'll just keep calling you Doan Tien. OK?"

"Please, that is how I wish you'd call me. Several weeks ago we listened to that damned Lt. Dang tell us how he and his friend, Ly, along with Col. Pham, butchered a family in Cam Lo."

Doan Tien fought back tears.

"That was my father, whom Col. Pham gutted, my mother and sisters that Dang and Ly shot to death. Louie, that damn Col. Pham is my Uncle Bui. He slaughtered his own family, my family—while looking for me. He also had my two older brothers, Doan and Tien, murdered long ago because they would not follow him. I fear he might kill me, too, if he knew who I am."

"*Mon Dieu*, I should have known by the way you acted when Dang told that story."

"Until then, I thought their deaths came at the hands of the Americans and that's why..."

"And that is why you joined us and was at first so anxious to kill Americans." Louie nodded in the dark, putting the puzzle pieces together. "It probably also explains why you suddenly became such a terrible shot."

"Yes, it does." Doan Tien managed a quiet laugh through his tears. "But I was ready to put a hole through Dang's head when you and Pham arrived. Another few seconds and I would've had part of my revenge. Oddly, my uncle did my bidding when he slit Dang's throat. I enjoyed watching his life gurgle away, but not as much as if I'd been the one to slice his neck open."

"Damn, you are a slayer at heart. Remind me not to piss you off," Louie swore. "But now, I'm afraid to ask what more is in your heart—and of your plans. I doubt if you're satisfied with the way things are now."

"No, of course not. It won't end until Col. Pham, my loving Uncle Bui, is lying on his back staring at the sky with fixed, unblinking eyes. Then, and only then, will I find peace."

"And what role do you have planned for me?" Louie said, pointing toward himself.

"What? What do you mean role for you?"

"I'm no idiot, boy," Louie snapped. "I know you will need help to pull off something like this. That is unless you're willing to give your own life in return. And I don't think you're ready for that. Hell, I wasn't and didn't."

"There was a time earlier when I was going to seek your help," Doan Tien said. "But once I saw that you were taken into his confidence and promoted, I thought you would not want to be part of my revenge and might even stop me, or maybe even kill me yourself. That is why I have been so hesitant to share all this with you."

Louie removed his helmet and rubbed his head vigorously. "Damn it, Doan Tien, Trai, or whoever you are. Col. Pham has helped me, yes, but he is a pig and I owe him no allegiance. I figure the promotion and confidence has been owed to me for a long time by more than just your uncle. I have been using him as much as he's been using me. I've been in this war so long, it would not disturb me in the least to see your uncle lying on his back, as you say, staring up at the sky with fixed, unblinking eyes."

"Then you will help," a suddenly excited Doan Tien blurted out.

"Shhhh. I didn't say that." Louie gave caution with a raised finger to Doan Tien's lips. "I won't stop you in your quest for vengeance. I'll even cheer you on. I know the burning in your heart. I've felt it. But, help you? I don't know. That is something I'll have to think about. But for now, let's sleep on it. This ambush is a washout."

Doan Tien smiled and closed his eyes. He could sleep as Trai tonight.

CHAPTER 33

The Listening Post
Near the Rockpile, R.S.V.N.
Feb. 23, 1969—6 p.m. local time

A triple canopy of trees covered the peaks of the rain forests in the mountainous northern regions of South Vietnam. Ancient teaks and ebony pushed their way skyward to form the highest level. Rare species of oak and other hardwoods meshed to make up the second tier. Hardy smaller trees survived at the bottom to form a thorny thicket. Bamboo groves and the ubiquitous banana trees sprouted wildly to give the landscape a traditional jungle look.

In a twilight created by the setting sun and jungle canopy, Tuck sat cross-legged, leaning against the twisted base of a massive hardwood tree. Narrow sunbeams sliced through the branches like small searchlights and fell in oblong circles upon his trousers.

He did not recognize the species, but the tree was old. Its roots were knuckled and tall—and they were irritating Tuck's butt. The back of his trousers were ripped from left hip to knee. Starting as a little tear, when they had caught on one of the long thorns that every tree seemed to sprout, it had grown into a long rip. If not for Donnie-Boy finding a safety pin, the situation would have been even more embarrassing—grunts wore no shorts. And after six weeks, his olive drab T-shirt was so sweat-soaked that each night it dried as stiff as if it was starched.

Tuck fished through his rucksack and pulled out a leaky ballpoint pen and a worn writing pad wrapped in a plastic bag. Humping had ended for the day and after a short break, Kilo Company would set up a perimeter around the top of Dong Ke Soc, a hill 660 meters high.

Just enough time and light remained to begin a letter to Anna. An inspired Tuck wanted to tell her about the day's torturous climb up steep Dong Ke Soc and of its gorgeous view. The hill overlooked the western fringe of the Rockpile and when the canopy permitted, he could see into the DMZ some four miles to the north. A picturesque river snaked and shimmered its way along the hill's steep southern slope.

Operation Cameron Falls, its start delayed by nearly two weeks, was 11 days old. The mission of the company-sized operation—to sweep and clear the areas to the east and then to the west of the Rockpile—had been poorly defined and, thus far, without contact.

Tuck knew it was a Sunday because the platoon's Navy corpsman had passed out big malaria pills that morning. Scuttlebutt said they'd be extracted and choppered back to Stud the next day. Field rumors, however, always said an op was ending the next day. Nonetheless, the operation had taught him and the newbies how to live, and survive, in the bush. Water was used for drinking, not bathing. Toothbrushes were for cleaning M-16s, not brushing your teeth. Strange, but no one really stunk or had bad breath. Or did they all stink and breathe the tiger mouth, and he was just getting used to it? He was becoming an old salt.

And grunt jargon was getting easier to master. If you did not understand the terms in a certain question, just shrug and add, "fuckin'ay" to the reply. It all made sense somehow. He smiled at the thought and looked around their position, observing the weary grunts. Most, like him, merely sat and tried to recoup their strength. A few rummaged through their gear looking for a snack. Even fewer began to dig in for the night.

It surprised him that a grunt in the bush had little

contact with anyone outside of his squad. Forget about conversing with anyone outside of second platoon. Second squad was a close-knit clan, mothered by its leader, Chuck, and his fire-team honchos Donnie-Boy and Jimmy B.

Second squad, or Kilo 2 Bravo, should ideally have included 13 men—Chuck and three full fire teams of four men each. But attrition had whittled it to only 10 grunts, including Chuck and the attached machine gun team of Johnny and Danny.

First and third squads suffered similar shortages. Ike's first squad was down to eight men, including him. He was also splitting platoon sergeant duties with Chuck. A veteran lance corporal headed up third squad, which boasted 11 men.

The "skipper," Second Lt. Hank Smith, commanded second platoon. Maybe 24 years old—he looked 16—Lt. Smith was a college graduate with a degree in economics and often used terms like "the bottom line." Tuck thought him to be aloof and indecisive. Most credited Sgt. Cosmo Brown, before his death, with keeping Lt. Smith alive through the first five months of the moon-faced officer's tour. Chuck and Ike often argued, and laughed, over whether it would be beneficial to continue to shelter the platoon commander.

"The skipper knows that his personal success is tied to the platoon," Chuck once explained to Tuck. "He views our promotions and decorations as his assets. Now, he ain't gonna give you something you don't merit, but Lt. Smith will make it a point to quickly process and push through honors."

He also watched Donnie-Boy, already a recipient of the skipper's expedience, grow under Chuck's tutelage. He had difficulty, however, in winning over the respect of veterans Ron Bremmer and Jason Green, who had been in country for more than five months. They were neither good nor bad Marines. Both had seen combat, but hadn't distinguished themselves.

Bremmer, a tall gangly slob from Baltimore, displayed an attitude befitting the wealth of his upscale, colonial family tree. "That dimwit was still trying to figure out how he wound up a Marine after only visiting an Air Force recruiter," Ike laughed, repeating his favorite Bremmer tale. "He suspected his daddy had something to do with it. The idiot didn't even realize he was in the Corps until his bus turned into the gates of Parris Island."

Jason, a burly black man, was a brute and a bully from the streets of inner Detroit. He wore his prejudice on his sleeve and had "little use for these white boys from Louisiana," he told Chuck. Tuck thought that Jason took small pleasures in taunting him.

But Jason had nothing on Donnie-Boy physically, and Ron was an idiot, so Donnie-Boy heard little complaining from the pair. "It's just that they hesitate at and distrust my every order," he told Tuck. "They hate the idea of having to listen to a newbie."

Jimmy B.'s fire team included a laid-back trio of veterans—Kenny Charles from Chicago, Steve Rodriguez from Houston and Paul Parker of Corvallis. Kenny was dead on with an M-79 grenade launcher. Paul towered over everyone except Johnny and could hump all day long.

"Rodeo" Steve, the consummate cowboy or *caballero* as he called himself, and "Tall" Paul had a little less than two months to go in the Nam. No one blamed them for their superstitions and obsessions associated with being short-timers. Chuck and Ike catered to them when possible.

Tuck stared at the reddening remains of the setting sun, which seemed to weave its way through the branches. He wondered what his mom was cooking for breakfast, for home trailed the Nam by 13 hours. He could smell the bacon and taste the sweetness of the French toast sizzling in the pan. He daydreamed of what Anna might look like in the morning.

Surely there could be nothing ordinary about her. But if he was going to write her, he need hurry.

Dear Anna,

It's been about six weeks now and we still haven't had any direct contact with the gooks since those first horrible days. We're about to wrap up our first operation in the bush without any action. All we do from sunup to sundown is hump. I wish it meant what it sounds like. Ha, ha. But it only means that we put on our 75 pounds of gear and hump up and down the hills.

Every hill is steep, going up and going down, and every tree seems to have a thorn on it. Between the trees and the razor-like elephant grass, I have too many festering sores to admit. It's strange though, there is a sort of peace in humping. It's not a hard concept, you just put one foot in front of another and pull yourself up the hill any way you can. But there is more to it than that. It is a challenge and every step taken is like a small battle won. Not much is said, it's each man's personal struggle, often done in solitude. When we stop, everyone tries to take a quick nap. But at the end of the day, when we get where we're going, there's a certain exhilaration, or sense of accomplishment. But when I get home, please don't ask me to take you hiking, because...

"Hey, Richard. Get up off your ass and come dig this hole over here. Chuck wants us dug-in at least three feet tonight and I've already dug the first...," Jason shouted, pausing to look down into the hole with a grin, "first six inches."

"Yeah, in just a bit. I want to get a little further on this letter before we start," Tuck replied absently. "And, like I've said before, it's REE-shard."

"Shit on that, newbie, come dig your share. You can write the bitch tomorrow when we get back to Stud. Or, maybe, I'll finish the letter myself, if you know what I mean," Jason taunted.

Tuck looked up from the page and glared at Jason. He said nothing but Jason read the look and backed off. The feelings evoked by the challenge surprised him. He knew he loved Anna, but the urge to protect her—even if only the thought of her—like a man would his wife, was new. He almost felt like thanking Jason. But he wasn't about to give the bully such satisfaction.

Tuck closed the pad, returned it to the plastic bag and slowly shoved it into his rucksack. "OK, big boy, I'm coming, but you're gonna dig more than six inches."

"Yeah, yeah. But just keep in mind I already busted it through the roots and all." Jason shoved the entrenching tool into Tuck's arms. "And don't forget where you got that e-tool."

"Don't worry, there's no black market for e-tools that I know of, shit-for-brains."

The much-larger Marine stepped forward. "Hey, man, don't be startin' no shit with me or I'll crack your honky ass wide open."

Tuck threw the e-tool into the hole and stood his ground with balled fists like a linebacker waiting for a fullback to come crashing through the line. "Well, maybe its time we settled this shit once and for all."

"Why you little honky shit, I'll..."

Jason cocked his right arm but suddenly fell onto his back, staring up at a slab of marble that was Johnny Robert. Donnie-Boy deftly pulled Tuck away and held him back by the collar of his flak jacket.

"It is best everyone just chill most ricky-tick and learn to get along," growled Chuck, who stood next to Johnny. "Particularly tonight, since both of you are goin' out on an LP. Got it?"

Chuck walked over to Jason and helped him up. He turned and ordered Tuck to shake hands. They glared at one another like prizefighters at a weigh-in. Jason put his hands behind his back.

"Look fellas. I know there's different worlds colliding here. But, damn it, we all have the same goal—to get out of this place alive. And that ain't gonna happen if the likes of you two continue to feud," Chuck warned. "Now, Jason, cut out the picking, I mean it, man. And, Tuck, quit egging him on. This will cease right now, or I'm gonna take action. I shit you not."

Tuck and Jason begrudgingly shook hands, and then wiped them on their trousers.

"Now, like I said, the skipper wants a four-man listening post a hundred yards to the east and down the finger of this hill about here," Chuck said, pointing in the direction of the thicket. "First platoon will be sending an LP down the west slope."

Chuck motioned Donnie-Boy nearer and pulled a green and brown topographical map from his right thigh pocket. He pointed to the closely spaced brown contour lines. "It's a pretty steep slope, just like this afternoon. If y'all hit the shit, gettin' back up here will be a bitch and will take time. So if you get any movement out there, don't wait for contact. Radio us real quick and get up the hill. You're not an ambush, you're an LP, so don't initiate anything except in self-defense. Understand?"

Donnie-Boy nodded nervously. "Yeah, I got it. Who's going?"

"Just your team—you, Jason, Ron and Tuck," Chuck explained. "Ron will take point. Jason will handle the radio. They know what to do. Fightin' gear only. Johnny and Danny will cover your return route."

Twenty minutes later, it was drizzling when Donnie-Boy led his team down the steep finger of the hill. Tuck mumbled, *"O, St. Joseph…"*

Donnie-Boy paced off the distance. At 90 yards he located a defensible position behind a large tree that had fallen into thick fern. The horizontal trunk provided a three-foot high wall. "Tuck, take the right flank. Ron you take the left. Jason you set up between Ron and me in the middle. Stay within arm's reach. Tuck, try not to fidget too much."

"You bet," Tuck said, feeling Donnie-Boy's smile in the darkness.

Listening posts tested a Marine's mettle. They lacked the safety of numbers and firepower that ambushes provided. LPs demanded discipline, quiet and rapt attention. Exposed and unaware of what to expect, Ike told Tuck that being on an LP was like combining the proverbial dreams of sitting naked in a classroom and not knowing you had an exam to take.

The team stood vigil together until about 10 p.m. when Jason took first watch with the heavy PRC-25 radio—the grunts called it a "prick." Every 15 minutes a Kilo 2 radioman polled the LP by keying his handset once, producing a low hissing squelch. The LP radio operator replied with a double-key squelch signaling all was clear. Security procedure often reversed the number of key presses. Voice contact was reserved for urgent matters.

It was 2 a.m. when Ron, who had taken over from Jason at midnight, reported "all quiet" to Tuck, who rubbed his eyes, yawned and then deeply sniffed the air. The drizzle had stopped and the scent of damp fern was heavy, like in the Atchafalaya Basin back home. It reminded him of the first time his dad took him and Mark squirrel hunting. "Home," he whispered.

"HISSS." Tuck keyed his handset twice— "HISSS, HISSS."

At 3:15 a.m., according to the glowing dial of his watch, Tuck tugged at Donnie-Boy's sleeve. He placed his shaky finger on Donnie-Boy's lips and then pointed toward a broken tree about 30 yards away. He was unsure of the sounds, but he sensed movement in the underbrush.

Donnie-Boy turned toward Ron and Jason, both were asleep—thankfully, neither snored. He let them be and then leaned his head toward Tuck. "What is it?"

"Think I heard clanking, like canteens bumping—and cracks, kinda like twigs breaking," he whispered directly into

Donnie-Boy's right ear. They rose slightly, just enough to see over the top of their log. An eerie ground fog had snaked in and swallowed the surrounding fern.

The clanking returned, noticeably closer.

"I hear it," Donnie-Boy turned and breathed into Tuck's ear. He pointed with his hand and finger pulled in close to his shoulder. "There. I make it about 20 yards."

"That's it. That's what I heard."

"Damn, they're awfully close," Donnie-Boy sighed.

Tuck's eyes bulged when they tried to penetrate the darkness. His mind spun while he tried to sort out the intensity and direction of the sounds. The uncontrollable, inner trembling returned. His fingers sought out and quietly slid the safety of his M-16 to "semi." His heart prayed, *O, St. Joseph whose protection is so prompt before the throne of God...*

"Look there." Donnie-Boy stabbed at the fog toward three gray silhouettes moving slowly from left to right. He judged that they would be on top of them within seconds. "No time to phone home."

"There's only three of them," Tuck whispered anxiously, his voice cracking. "Probably wire probes. Looks like one's got an RPG, too. What you think?"

"Yeah," Donnie-Boy whispered back. "No, time to wake those two. We can take 'em."

"We gonna fire or haul ass?" Tuck asked, remembering their orders. "There might be more."

"Forget that shit, little brother," Donnie-Boy ordered. "You get the middle guy and the gook to the right. I'll get the one on the left with the RPG and watch to see if there's anymore....Oh, shit, they're right there, let's do it..."

"O, St. Joseph do assist me..." Tuck grunted. He popped up from behind the log and ripped off four shots. Two helmets flipped into the air and the bloody heads that had filled them followed their bodies to the ground. He dropped and rolled to his left for another vantage point.

A burst of automatic fire from Donnie-Boy's M-16 spun the other NVA soldier to his knees, but not before the man wildly fired his rocket propelled grenade. The RPG slammed harmlessly into the turf in front of him with a loud boom. Shrapnel sprayed the fallen log, sparing the Marines. A second burst from Donnie-Boy's rifle ended the man's life.

"What the hell?" Jason shouted. He scrambled for his weapon, where he found a dead enemy soldier laying less than 10 yards away. He looked up. Tuck stood over him, a smoking M-16 still drawn to his shoulder.

"Geez shit," Ron cried out, slapping at the ground for his rifle.

The skipper's voice screamed over the radio. "Lima Papa 1, Lima Papa 1, this is Kilo 2 Six, What in the hell is going on? Give us a sit rep, now. I say again, give us a sit rep. Over."

Donnie-Boy grabbed the handset. "Kilo 2 Six, this is Lima Papa 1. We've got three enemy KIA down here, sir. Request you advise and send some backup. Over."

"Lima Papa 1, are you sure of number of KIA? Any other movement, I say again, any other movement? Over."

"No, sir, not at this time. But we'd like backup before sweeping the area for bodies. It's just too dark to tell right now. Over."

"That's a negative, Lima Papa 1. Too dangerous, we'll sweep later. Get your team back up here on the double and watch your six. Over."

"Will do, and don't shoot our ass on the way back up. Lima Papa 1, out."

They stood and swept the area with their eyes and M-16s at the ready. The smell of gunpowder and fresh blood mixed with the misty smell of greenery. Donnie-Boy mentally marked the spot and signaled for Tuck to take the point.

Thick, red mud bogged their boots and progress was slow. Only 15 yards up the hill, Ron cried out "ChiCom!"

His world exploded and his voice turned into a trembling shriek. The grenade severed Ron's right leg below the knee and somersaulted him onto his shoulder.

"There must still be some gooks down there," Tuck shouted. There was no reason to whisper. "We didn't get 'em all."

"No shit, Sherlock," Donnie-Boy hollered. "Jason, get him back to the perimeter, on the double. Me and Tuck will stay here and cover y'all."

The slender Ron let out a weak groan when Jason slung him over his shoulder. Jason turned and leaned toward Tuck, their noses nearly touching. "Don't leave my ass uncovered. You hear?"

"Just go, nobody's gonna get to you. That I promise," Tuck said with a grin. "But I might kick your big black ass if you don't get going." Jason returned the smile, swung the radio toward Donnie-Boy and began his ascent—slipping slightly on his second step.

Donnie-Boy knelt and pulled Tuck beside him. "Let's not give the gooks a good target."

"So, what we're gonna do?"

"We'll wait until Jason gets well up the hill before we do anything, that's for sure. I've got the prick and we'll do what we came down here to do…listen. There just might be more than one gook down there and we've got to know before we get out of here."

"But the skipper told us to get back up there, now. We're not an ambush, remember?"

"Yeah, but that was before they blew ol' Ron damn near in half. And I suspect the skipper's gonna be calling any second for a situation report."

The PRC-25 hissed to life on cue. "Lima Papa 1, this Kilo 2 Six, is that your team nearing the lines at this time? Over."

"What I tell you?" Donnie-Boy said with an unseen

wink. He replied quietly. "Roger that Kilo 2 Six, that's Green coming in carrying Bremmer, he's going to need medical attention ASAP, get the doc ready."

"What is your sit rep? Are you following? Over."

"Negative, me and one are remaining to cover their retreat. We'll try to ascertain how many more November Victor there might be out here."

"I'm giving you 10 mikes, that is all. Then get your asses up here. Over."

"That's a big roger. Lima Papa 1, out."

Tuck and Donnie-Boy crouched side-by-side about 20 yards up the trail from the fallen tree that had earlier been their roost. They lay in wait for five minutes before shuffling sounds crept from the fog.

"You hear that?" Donnie-Boy whispered hoarsely.

"Yeah. Just on the other side of our log," Tuck replied. The trembling that had subsided was now back as strong as before. Dread again filled the darkness but Donnie-Boy was at his side. Out of the corner of his eye, he spotted a flickering spark against the black overhead. It looked like a tossed firecracker, flipping and fizzing. The sparkling light landed five yards in front of them. A loud wham rang their ears when the ChiCom grenade exploded with a flash and short-lived sparks. He saw two more flickers descending. Each landed short and to the left, exploding harmlessly. Two more landed to the right—again short.

"They're trying to bracket us, let's get up the hill," Donnie-Boy shouted. It was no time for stealth. The loud rustling in the jungle grew busier.

"There's more than one of them out there," Tuck yelled. "We must have knocked off a point team or something. That's reinforcements, warn the guys. I'll keep you covered."

Noises became thin gray shadows, new targets. No longer trembling, Tuck slid a magazine into his M-16, rose to one knee and then squeezed off two shots, then a three-shot burst. One shadow fell hard, silent. Another screamed and fell on his back, thrashing in the fern.

"Kilo 2 Six, Kilo 2 Six, we have beaucoup movement. We think reinforcements. Get the perimeter ready for fireworks. We're comin' in."

"Roger, Lima Papa 1, we'll check fire until you're in safe. Over."

"That would be awfully sweet. And, now, I'm gonna ditch this heavy prick. See you up the hill," Donnie-Boy said. He threw the radio to the ground and fired two bullets into its side. "Let's go, little brother, the rifle range is closed."

"You bet." Tuck flipped his M-16 to auto and emptied the magazine in the area of the shadows. He slapped in another full mag. "I'm right behind you. Don't wait for me." He struggled through the damp underbrush. Slipping twice, he lagged 20 yards behind Donnie-Boy, who sprinted up the hill with a graceful gait.

After another minute, Donnie-Boy stopped and looked back. He saw Tuck fighting the muck. An NVA soldier was sprinting up the hill and closing to within 15 yards of his friend. Donnie-Boy dropped to a knee, aimed and fired.

The shots surprised Tuck; he slowed and looked back at the soldier, curled up in a ball of pain. He swung his rifle around and shot from the hip. The rounds slammed into the man's back.

"Let's go, let's go," Donnie-Boy called out. "Only a few yards left. I can see the lines now."

Donnie-Boy ran and waved his arms to alert the perimeter. He stumbled the last few steps and collapsed into Chuck's arms.

"Where's Tuck?" Chuck shouted.

"Down there," Donnie-Boy said, gasping. "Maybe 30-40 yards."

Johnny and Danny glanced at one another and nodded. They stood and sprinted down the hill, sliding part of the way.

Nearly 40 yards from the lines they found Tuck, exhausted and crawling, his rifle still gripped in his right hand. They scooped him up under his armpits and turned for the lines. "Haven't we danced this dance before," Johnny laughed amid a heavy pant. Danny flinched when his elbow rubbed against the searing barrel of Tuck's M-16.

In seconds they were back within the safety of the lines. The two machine gunners dropped Tuck unceremoniously and hustled back to their position, waiting for the assault.

Ike helped Chuck lift Tuck and Donnie-Boy to their feet, guided them to the skipper's position and gave them full canteens of water.

"What about Ron? He gonna be OK?" Donnie-Boy asked between gulps. "It looked real bad. But couldn't really tell in the dark."

"And Jason?" Tuck added, pouring water over his face and the back of his neck.

"Jason's gonna be OK, just worn out like you two. But, Ron didn't make it," Ike said softly. "He just lost too much blood. Not much doc could do."

"Damn, from losing his leg," Tuck wondered aloud. He'd heard tales of men losing both legs, only to fight on and survive.

"Heck, no, ripped his gut and took both his nuts off too. He went shocky on us," Chuck added. "Guess y'all couldn't tell in the dark and shit."

Tuck and Donnie-Boy said nothing but exchanged glances. It was 4 a.m., barely 30 minutes had passed since the first shots. Chuck ordered the two to rest, if they could. Sleep came quickly.

•

"So, we screwed up, right?" Donnie-Boy asked well after sunrise, still trying to shake off a deep sleep. "We weren't supposed to be an ambush and we got a man killed."

"Not hardly, Marine," the skipper said, making notes on a clipboard full of forms. Paperwork went on in the field as well. "We put LPs out last night because intel said there was a large NVA troop movement in this area. You four guys just happen to get in the way of what was probably a whole company of gooks making their way up the slope."

Chuck added, "There's no telling how many of our guys would've got it if you hadn't fouled up their plans. You took away their surprise and they apparently abandoned the assault."

"While we were letting you two get a little beauty sleep this morning, we swept the area," the skipper said. "The guys are still down there. Green led 'em back down. He's the one who insisted we let you get some more sleep. And they radioed up just a few minutes ago, said they've found at least six bodies and beaucoup tracks leading both up and back down the hill.

"I almost hate to say this Hebert, but it looks like I'm going to have to put you up for another medal," the skipper announced. "Oh, by the way, congratulations Hebert, both your Bronze and Navy Com were approved. They'll look real nice next to the second Bronze I'm putting you up for now.

"There'll probably be a Bronze in it for you, too," the skipper added, pointing to Tuck. "And I'm putting you up for lance, as well. We're gonna need more leaders like you, plus we're running out of guys."

"Heck, lieutenant, right now I'd just be happy with a new pair of pants." Tuck turned so that Lt. Smith could see the long rip.

The skipper nodded. "Sure thing. Now, the two of you get the hell out of here. I've got some new reports to file with the company boss."

"Sir, one other thing," Donnie-Boy asked. "What are our orders for today?"

The skipper looked up from his clipboard. "Didn't you

hear yesterday's scuttlebutt? They're coming to get us. The op's over. We're going back to Stud within the hour."

Donnie-Boy turned to Tuck and they slapped palms. "Well, what you know, little brother. We're in for a break."

"Yesss," Tuck replied, before catching a glimpse of a body bag being carried to a hastily prepared LZ. The op hadn't ended soon enough for Ron Bremmer.

CHAPTER 34

Revelations
Signal Hill, R.S.V.N.
March 18, 1969—3 p.m. local time

Dear Anna,

Happy birthday to me, I'm 19 today. And yes, these days I do feel different. No, not older or anything like that. But since I got here, I seem to look at each day differently. I appreciate things more, like packages from home and letters from you, a full canteen of CLEAN water, good buddies, the joy of opening a C-rations box and not finding ham and lima beans again. Ha, ha.

I've also seemed to have grown more introspective. It surprises me at times. Thoughts and feelings about life I never knew existed are now commonplace, and more easily understood.

I also look forward to things more, like sleep, R&R and above all…turning 20. Ha, ha. And of course, seeing you again. Though I have known you for only a relatively short time, I long to share the remainder of my life with you. I hope you still feel the same. I have written my parents of my feelings for you and they think it's wonderful.

I have enclosed a Polaroid snapshot of me and some of the guys over here. Danny Jackson took it here on top of Signal Hill. Behind us you can see some of Stud below and the mountains surrounding us. From left are Jimmy B. Bryant, a dude from California; my main man Donnie-Boy; me, the runt of the litter; some big guy named Johnny Robert that I'm sure you'll recognize; and Cpl. Chuck Booker, our squad leader. Chuck and Danny are the first colored guys I have really gotten to know and they are fine fellas. Of course, they're not crazy about being called "colored" anymore and say the correct word to use now is "black" when referring to them. I don't know, but I'm having trouble keeping up with all these civil rights changes. All I know is that they're damn good Marines and even better friends.

As expected, our return to the bush has been delayed again. It seems like every time they tell us to get ready to go on a new operation, it gets canceled because of all the crap going on around here. A lot of the guys are glad to be standing lines up here on Signal Hill. But it does get boring, you know. Sure, they keep us busy by sending us out on day-long patrols, but it's not the same. It's just that time passes much quicker in the bush and it means it'll be that much sooner that I come home to you. It's been more than two months since we arrived and about three weeks since we last saw real action. We still get some incoming and line probes, but it's more unnerving than scary.

The rains have slowed down, they don't fall every day and it's getting warmer, much warmer. In fact, it's getting as hot as a...

"Hey, Tuck, I want to ask you something," Donnie-Boy said, nudging his friend on the shoulder with the back of his hand. He plopped down with two warm beers cradled in his hands. "C'mon man, stop. You write that chick damn near every day. I gotta ask somethin' important."

Well, Anna, that's about it for now. I am being summoned by a senior officer with an urgent message and have to go. I'll write again tomorrow. Bye for now, pray for me. Love Tuck.

Tuck folded his writing pad, and then poked Donnie-Boy in the ribs with his pen. "Alright, now what the hell do you want that's so important that I quit writing to the love of my life?"

"The only love, ever, of your life."

"OK, the only love, ever, of my life. Now what you want?"

They sat propped against the side of a sandbagged bunker on the eastern perimeter of Signal Hill. A score of Marine communications personnel and a few Air Force officers manned the outpost overlooking Stud. Kilo's first and second platoons had provided security since returning from Operation Cameron Falls.

Donnie-Boy settled in, leaned back and stretched his long legs onto the red dirt. "Did you put the frog in the chips, or did it just hop in on its own?"

"What the hell are you talkin' about?" Tuck pointed to the two cans of Black Label beer his friend coddled. "You drunk or something?"

"Maybe, not sure." Donnie-Boy smirked and took another sip. "Well, did you?"

"Did I what?"

"The potato chips—when we were four. Did you put the frickin' frog in the chips? You know, the little green mother that pissed in the bag. The ones that we ate, got trench mouth from, and had to go the hospital for and had to get all those goddamn shots for. Those chips."

Tuck paused to think, then nodded with a grin. "Oh, thooose chips."

"Yeah, thooose chips," Donnie-Boy replied with a snort. "Well?"

Delving into his earliest boyhood memories, Tuck wrinkled his brow and scratched at his head with the ballpoint pen. "Not sure, I remember playing with a little green tree frog and that it peed on my hand," he said, shrugging his shoulders. "When it did, I brushed it off. It might have, kind of like, fallen in the bag by accident, you know."

"By accident," Donnie-Boy nodded as if his neck were a spring.

"Yep, by accident," Tuck replied with a similar nod. "That trench mouth sure was nasty."

Donnie-Boy drained the swill of his first beer and then searched his pockets for a church key. His attention briefly turned to a Huey circling overhead. The helicopter landed at an LZ on the far side of the hill. In less than a minute it lifted off and headed for Stud below.

"Guess we should've noticed the chips were wet. What you think?" Donnie-Boy said with a burp and a laugh. He opened the second can and offered it to Tuck, who waved off the warm, foaming brew. "But don't remember 'em tasting all that bad though."

"No, we ate the whole damn bag." They giggled like the little boys they were back then. Donnie-Boy tapped Tuck on the thigh. They stared into the distance, watching the shrinking Huey find its place on the landing strip far below.

"And then we got the mumps," Tuck added with a chuckle. "Wonder if it was all related? I swole up like a chipmunk."

"At least yours stayed in the neck," Donnie-Boy added without a laugh.

"Yeah, I remember, your little balls got as big as my daddy's."

"Never knew something like that could come back to haunt me."

"What you mean? Come back to haunt you," Tuck asked, surprised by the admission.

"Oh, never mind. Just forget about it."

"What the hell brought all this up?" Tuck asked.

"Don't know, maybe because it's your birthday," Donnie-Boy said, rubbing Tuck's head.

"Hey, thanks for remembering. Where's my present?"

"Offered you a beer, didn't I."

"Touché," Tuck replied, smiling.

"I was just remembering how it's been, us always together," Donnie-Boy added. "Can't remember anytime or anything that didn't include the two of us. And then I was thinking about that LP and what it might have been like if it was you instead of Ron. Heck, I don't know what I'd do without you."

Tuck grabbed him on the back of the neck and shook.

"I'm sure you'd do just fine. Always have. You don't need me, never did. Hell, you're Donnie-Boy Hebert."

Donnie-Boy took the last sip of his beer, crushed the can and then tossed it into a trash barrel 20 feet away. "Never needed you, ha," he scoffed. "Man, I'd never made it through school without you...easy to cheat off of. Never could've dealt with my dad's death without you. Heck, I'd have never made it through basic without you being so damned determined. Finishing off that run when your rifle busted, that was just the most courageous thing I saw in boot camp."

Donnie-Boy leaned his head back against the bunker. "Sure, I've bailed you outta some jams, kept you from gettin' your ass whipped a few times. But you've always been my inspiration, my guide. I really do hope the best for you and Anna when you get back home."

"You mean when *we* get back home."

"No, I'm not so sure of that, little brother. Somehow I feel like this is where I'm supposed to be. I won't be goin' home. But I am going to do my damned best to make sure you get home to that Anna of yours. I owe you that much." Donnie-Boy traced his fingers over his lips, remembering fondly Anna's farewell kiss.

Tuck punched his friend on the chest. "Hey, that's the beer talking now, keep it up and I'll shoot you through the heart myself."

"Yeah, I bet you would at that," Donnie-Boy said. He wobbled when he tried to stand and Tuck put out his hand and grabbed Donnie-Boy's hip to steady him.

Donnie-Boy flashed that knowing smile. "See what I mean. You don't even realize it. But you've always been there for me. Now, get up and let's go."

"Go where?" Tuck asked. Donnie-Boy pulled him to his feet.

"To the LZ. Got word the new platoon sergeant was

choppering in today. Must've been him on that Huey. Let's go meet him and get in a good word, you know, kiss some ass."

They walked passed the adjacent M-60 position where Johnny and Danny busily stripped and cleaned their machine gun. Donnie-Boy tossed a pebble that hit Johnny on top of his head. "Going to meet the new platoon sergeant, want to come?"

"Nah, gotta clean Gertrude first. Maybe later. I can wait," Johnny said, rubbing down his M-60. Danny shook his head and smiled before also returning his attention to Gertrude.

"AWWWK, TWEETWEE, DIE HO CHI MINH, DIE HO CHI MINH," chirped the small gray parrot perched atop its stand outside a nearby Air Force communications bunker.

"Hey, Turd Head, how's it going today," Tuck said.

"AWWWK, TWEETWEE, EAT SHIT AND DIE, GRUNT," the parrot squawked.

"Hey, don't go get Turd Head all riled up," an Air Force officer cautioned. "He's not feeling too good. Gave him a green banana this morning and he's been pukin' it up, eh."

Second Lt. Byner Ridgeman had a wry sense of humor and was a grunt favorite. Tall and lean but saddled with a beer gut, Byner had spent 10 months of his tour atop Signal Hill and specialized in raising exotic pets. A Tennessean with a cracker accent, he had raised snakes, an assortment of large lizards and a couple of monkeys. Most had died or crawled away. Rumor had it that Byner had eaten one of the monkeys. Turd Head was Byner's favorite. A Marine patrol had found the abandoned and nearly naked baby bird shortly after it had fallen out of its nest. The grunts had given it to Byner as a gift.

"Hey, Byner," Donnie-Boy nodded toward the perch. "What you gonna do with that foul-mouthed fowl when you get home? Won't be much of a hit with your mom, you know."

"Yeah, I've thought about that. They probably won't even let me bring it home anyway. Customs, you know," he said, scratching behind his ear as if it would make him think more clearly. "Probably just let him go in the jungle. But, heck, he'll probably just fly right back to his perch right here." He pointed to a five-foot high homemade stand. "Got him trained pretty good."

"By the way," Tuck interjected, "does he cuss anything else."

Byner snorted a laugh. "No, not yet. But I've got some in-country R&R coming up in Saigon and we're working on 'nice tits, mama san.'"

They waved off Byner with a laugh and walked on toward the skipper's bunker.

•

"Yes, sir it is my first tour. Should've gotten here sooner, but the Corps thought I was more valuable elsewhere," they heard the new sergeant say when they approached.

Chuck and Ike had already joined Lt. Smith and were welcoming the sergeant, who had his back to Tuck and Donnie-Boy. The sergeant slowly turned at the sound of their approach.

They froze as Jerry Gaines—bug eyes, bulging neck veins, and crew cut—stared back. His smile looked genuine, something they had never seen before. He seemed less menacing to Tuck. Maybe it was the helmet he wore in place of the DIs' trademark Campaign Hat.

"Staff Sgt. Gaines, I'd like you meet one of my fire-team leaders, Lance Cpl. Hebert, and the best shot in the company, Lance Cpl. Richard," Lt. Smith said.

Gaines extended his hand. They looked down at the

hand, the hand that had so often slapped them silly in boot camp. Tuck returned a tentative shake, as did Donnie-Boy.

"What's the matter fellas, looks like you two have seen a ghost," the skipper laughed.

"No, not a ghost, but maybe something…"

"Wait a minute," Gaines blurted out, pointing at them with both of his index fingers, as if it was a stickup. He was grinning now. "I know you two—2080, right? Cajun fellas. There was a third one of you, too. Uh, uh, no don't tell me, uh, Robert. Really big guy. I don't forget many of my babies, especially the good ones."

They nodded slowly, nervous smiles pulling tight across their faces.

"Ha, you mean these guys were under you at the Island," Chuck laughed loudly, slapping his hands together. Ike used his fist to stifle a laugh.

"No, I mean, yeah. They were, but in San Diego," Gaines explained. "Good Marines, both of 'em. Hebert, you were our Honorman, right?"

"Yes, sir," Donnie-Boy said, quickly sobering up.

"Well, you taught them well, Gaines. They're two of my best young grunts. Already up for combat honors," the skipper added. "I expect that boot camp history won't be a problem with you two and won't be getting in the way."

"No, sir," Tuck and Donnie-Boy replied in unison.

"But it might be a little uncomfortable at first," Tuck admitted.

"Same here, Richard. I just want you guys to know what took place back there in the States was needed…"

Donnie-Boy put up his hand to stop Gaines. "We've already benefited from that training, sarge, and understand. No problems, as long as you remember we're not boots anymore."

Gaines nodded. "Fair enough. By the way, whatever happened to that other big guy?"

"He's here, too. Cleaning Gertrude right now," Tuck said.

"Cleaning who...never mind. How did the three of you manage to stay together so long? It's rare that it happens. But it does."

"So does winding up with your old DI as your platoon sergeant," Donnie-Boy replied.

"I've trained a bunch of you guys. I imagine anywhere I was to go, I'd be with some of my babies," Gaines explained with a smile.

"OK, this old home week talk is nice and all, but I've got more paperwork to do with Staff Sgt. Gaines here. So if you fellas will excuse us," Smith said, ushering them out.

Tuck waited until they were out of earshot. "I just can't believe this. Johnny ain't gonna believe it. This is just too much. I mean, we hated that piece of shit and were glad when he was gone from our lives. Now, he's back. Why couldn't it have been Gunny Hill?"

"Cool it, Tuck. Just cool it. Let the man settle in and we'll see what he's really like. Remember, this is his first tour, too, if I heard him right."

•

"WHO? WHO?" Johnny shouted minutes later. "Not the same red-necked mother who liked to thump my eye and made me spend hours on end on my elbows and toes. Not HIM."

"Yep. HIM. Sgt. Jerry Gaines. Now Staff Sgt. Jerry Gaines. He's our platoon sergeant...again," Tuck said. "Ain't this a cruel world?"

"Hell, I thought the Nam was bad enough with all the gooks and skeeters. Now we got Gaines, too? Aw, man," Johnny lamented. "Well, he'd better not..."

"OK, that's enough, now," Donnie-Boy ordered. "Like I told Tuck, let's give the man a chance. We for sure know he's a good Marine and a tough nut. I say let's give him a chance."

"I say let's stick Gertrude up his DI ass and unload," Johnny replied.

"No, I've got a better idea," Tuck added. "But not now."

"Man, what you boys bitchin' about," Danny interrupted. "I wish my platoon commander was here. He'd whip these gooks single-handed. A regular Chesty Puller, he was."

"Yeah, but this is Gaines' first tour in the Nam, too," Tuck explained.

"Oh, shit," Danny replied. "We's screwed big time."

"Some birthday present," Tuck sighed.

•

March 23, 11:30 a.m.: It was going to be a special meal.

Donnie-Boy had fashioned a field stove by cutting away half the height of a large C-ration can with his sharp, single-toothed can opener—better known to the grunts as a "John Wayne," "P-38" or nonsensical "iddywah." He ventilated the can and chose three heat tabs for fuel. The plastic explosive C-4, which grunts regularly snitched to quickly heat meals in the bush, would flare too quickly and not last long enough to simmer the makeshift Cajun/C-ration gourmet meal.

"You sure you want to go through with this," Danny asked Tuck, who stirred a simmering quart-sized can half filled with pork and beans.

"Yep, no doubt." Tuck added a healthy portion of minced mystery meat—it appeared to be beef—from a C-ration tin and a fresh chopped onion, begged off Byner. He had already added a healthy dollop of Tabasco sauce and a spoonful of garlic salt supplied in his mom's latest package. A special ingredient lay beneath the fiberglass helmet liner at his side.

"How you know he'll join us for lunch?" Danny asked for a third time.

"Oh, he will. He's always snooping around, looking to see what we got cooking," Donnie-Boy advised, sampling the fare with a white plastic spoon. "Not quite but it's gettin' there." He then turned to Danny, "And, he'll compliment us and all, then invite himself in."

The four grunts sat in a semi-circle along a sandbag trench, which led into the bunker currently leased to Tuck and Donnie-Boy. It was a sunny morning with a light southeast breeze and no particular competing scents.

"I mean, the guy's been pretty decent," Danny offered. "You saw how he handled himself on yesterday's patrol. He can already hump with the best of us and didn't bitch about the elephant grass. I know he was sufferin' from all those cuts. Man, he even took a turn on point, and that's unheard of for a platoon sergeant. Maybe we ought to give him a break."

"Look, Danny, if you don't want to be part of this, then just say so, OK," Donnie-Boy asserted. "But it's gotta be done."

"Damn straight, bro," Tuck added.

"OK, if y'all say so. Right, Johnny?" Danny replied, testing his closest friend. Johnny somberly nodded.

Ten minutes later the sauce was bubbling and a succulent message wafted along the breeze. Another five minutes later Staff Sgt. Jerry Gaines—the Butcher of 2080, Sgt. Adolph, Jerry the Hun, as Tuck liked to call him—strutted along the narrow, red-dirt path that separated the communication shacks from the perimeter bunkers. He sniffed the air. "What you guys cookin' there? Smells pretty darn good."

"Hey, sarge, how's it going," Tuck called out.

Johnny baited the trap. "We call it 'grunt gumbo,' but it really ain't no gumbo. Just looks like it a little. It's pretty tasty, though; damn spicy too, I'll warn you."

"I know you Cajuns are pretty good cooks. Mind if I

give it a try." Gaines sat and squeezed in between Johnny and Donnie-Boy—a spot reserved just for him.

Tuck raised the makeshift lid from the top of the can and stirred the concoction with a Ka-bar's long blade. He wiped the knife clean on the leg of his trousers. So much for sanitation, besides there was enough hot sauce in there to kill any surviving germs.

Similar culinary efforts had served up palatable results. The addition of the garlic salt and fresh onion promised considerable improvement. It smelled delicious. "Well, it ought to be better than that damn raw dove you made me eat at the Depot," Tuck growled.

"Oh. You still remember that, huh?" Gaines laughed. "If it means anything to you, you weren't the first one."

Tuck looked at Donnie-Boy and Johnny. Gaines had fallen into their trap. Tuck nodded. The two big men reached out with the quickness of a frog's tongue and snared Gaines by his arms. Danny stepped on Gaines' feet like he was stomping on the worn brakes of an old truck.

"What the hell...," Gaines shouted. The men tightened their vise-like grips.

Tuck pivoted to his right, snatched up the helmet liner by his side and firmly, but gently, cupped Turd Head with both hands. The parrot flapped in protest and squawked.

"AWWWK, AWWWK, TWEETWEE, DIE HO CHI MINH!"

"Open up Gaines, pay-back time is here. And you know what they say about payback..."

Gaines' eyes grew into saucers when Tuck shoved Turd Head nearer to his mouth. "Open wide. Isn't that what you told me?" he hissed. "This is the only lunch you're gonna get today." Its beak brushed the corner of Gaines' mouth and he jerked back his tightly pursed lips.

"AWWWK, AWWWK, TWEETWEE, EAT SHIT AND DIE, GRUNT!"

Gaines shook his head and clamped shut. Crying out would mean a mouthful of bird.

Holding the bird before the stunned sergeant's nose, Tuck glared at Gaines, who again struggled to break the grips of Johnny and Donnie-Boy. "I said, open wide. Or I'll shove this damn bird up your nose."

"Aw, what the hell, do it." Gaines went limp. "I probably deserve it." He opened wide.

"And stick out your tongue so you can get a good taste."

"AWWWK, AWWWK, TWEETWEE, EAT SHIT AND DIE, GRUNT!"

Now it was Tuck's turn to chuckle and his laugh spit from his lips. Johnny and Donnie-Boy loosened their grips and howled. Tuck released Turd Head, which flew off squawking toward its perch. Byner, watching from the corner of his bunker, shared in the hilarity of the moment.

A few gray, downy feathers floated down and landed atop Gaines' head. Danny joined in the laughter.

Gaines scrambled up and pointed consecutively to each of the grunts, "You, you, you, and you are all going on report for this." He spun around and pointed toward Byner. "And you, too, I'm going to report you to your commanding officer."

"Me? I didn't know what they were going to do with Turd Head. They just said he wouldn't get hurt," Byner managed to say between laughs. "Lighten up, sarge, it could've been worse. I've heard of guys like you gettin' fragged, or at least shot 'by accident' while on patrol. You ought to give these guys credit for creativity, and respect. They didn't hurt you, now did they."

"AWWWK, AWWWK, TWEETWEE, EAT SHIT AND DIE, GRUNT!"

"See, even Turd Head agrees," Byner added, stroking his bird.

Gaines rubbed at the red finger marks on his biceps, as red as the anger in his face. "This is a serious breach of respect for a ranking superior. Downright insubordination and...."

"I bet Gunny Hill wouldn't put us on report," Donnie-Boy snapped.

Gaines froze, and then slowly turned. The red in his face faded. His voice seemed strangely pinched when he answered. "No, I suppose he wouldn't."

"Of course, the gunny would've been too big to hold down," Johnny smirked. "And if you write us up, I'm gonna write a letter to Gunny Hill and report how you were such an asshole. Look around, sarge, this is Vietfuckin' Nam, you take your fun where you can find it. OK? Now, if I were you, I'd..."

"Gunny Hill is dead."

Fanned by the gentle breeze, the flame from the heat tabs rumbled slightly, continuing to simmer the grunt gumbo. The flavorful scent pleased the grunts' nostrils but blank stares locked in on their sergeant. They paused, hoping for a punch line.

Gaines' shoulders slumped from confrontation to resignation. He looked down at the red dirt floor. It reminded him of his south Alabama home. "Killed New Year's morning on an ice-slick highway near Houston—round about where he was from. I got the word about three days after. He'd been telling me to get my butt over here to find out what it was like. What we were training guys like you for, and where it was we were sending them." His eyes looked glassy to Tuck.

"A week or so after that I trained my last platoon, lost my heart for it. So, I put in for the Nam. And here I am. Maybe, sooner or later, I'll learn what he meant by me getting over here to see for myself. Maybe today was lesson one."

"I think it's done," Tuck said quietly, He spooned a generous portion of the gumbo into a kidney-shaped canteen cup. He sprinkled a pack of black pepper over it, stood and walked toward Gaines. He held the cup out to the sergeant with one hand and a plastic spoon with the other. "It really is good. Hot and a bit spicy perhaps, but damn good. And no bird," he smiled.

Gaines looked up, a sheen of tears covered his eyes. He took the cup and stirred the contents. He sniffed it, and took a small bite. "Damn, that is good. Mmm, real good, didn't know you could do that with C-rats. Mmm. But, uh, you got some water?"

The gesture had broken the tension, Tuck felt. He hoped it had formed a trust as well—maybe Gaines had a human side, after all.

Johnny tasted the concoction. "Oooo, that's flat good, yeah, Tuck."

"By the way, I was coming over here to tell you guys we gotta patrol at 0500—west about two klicks. A Bronco driver flying that way this morning spotted a bunch of gooks headed southwest. Intel figures they might be setting up camp there for the night. We're going check it out." Gaines nodded and began to walk away before remembering to return Tuck's empty cup. "Oh, and guys, thanks for the meal, and, uhh, for the cooking lesson."

CHAPTER 35

Smells Like a Rat
Signal Hill, R.S.V.N.
March 24, 1969—4:30 a.m. local time

The stars seemed to sprawl forever in the clear, black sky. Dawn's rosy fingers had not yet begun to caress the day. The North Star was difficult to find this close to the equator but the Southern Cross glimmered just above the horizon.

Reporting to Staff Sgt. Jerry Gaines, Cpl. Chuck Booker ticked off a head count. "There'll be a dozen of us. Donnie-Boy's team with our sharpshooter Tuck…"

Gaines interrupted. "You know, I taught him to shoot like that. Back in boot camp, even got him the right rifle to start with."

Chuck glanced at Gaines in the gloom and nodded with a raised eyebrow. "Right…and "Mr. Attitude" Jason, that's three; Jimmy B.'s team with "Rodeo" Steve, "Tall" Paul on the prick and Kenny with his blooper, that's seven—damn I hate bringin' short-timers on patrol. The gun team of Johnny and Danny makes nine. You, me and an FAO, that's 12."

"Fine. Who's our Forward Air Observer?" Gaines asked.

"Oh. Uh, Ridgeman," Chuck noted. "He's done this before, plus he knows all the comm freqs for the firebases, jet jocks and Cobra drivers. He'll be a big plus."

"Yeah, I know him," Gaines said. "Smart-ass guy with the parrot."

Chuck nodded with an agreeing smile then pulled Gaines aside. "Sarge, you outrank me, but stay close and follow my lead this morning. This one could get dicey if the gooks are out there."

Gaines nodded.

Chuck summoned second squad. Fire-team leaders Jimmy B. and Donnie-Boy stepped forward. "Where's Ridgeman?" he called out. "Damn."

"You know those fly boys, not used to gettin' up this early," Steve said, drawing a laugh. "That Byner, hell, he's probably saying a sweet good-bye to Turd Head."

"Make that a tweet good-bye," Kenny said, adding to the laughter—nervous laughter.

"OK, fellas, settle down. We got serious business out here this morning. So listen up," Chuck said. "We're headed due west…"

"Here I am. Hold up. I'm comin', just a sec," Byner said, scurrying up the path, simultaneously trying to buckle a loaded webbed belt and light a cigarette.

"Hurry up, we just started." Watching Byner reminded Chuck of his smokes. "Oh, yeah, the smoking lamp is lit, for now. Once we leave the lines, no smoking on this one, got it.

"Now, as I was saying. We're headed due west about two klicks through tall elephant grass. There won't be any jungle until we get to our objective, right here," Chuck said pointing to his creased combat map in the dim glow of his red flashlight. Each team leader pulled out his map and marked the spot on the laminated grid sheet, which was arranged in a series of one-kilometer squares. Each "klick," as the grunts called a kilometer, equaled approximately six-tenths of a mile.

Byner already knew the destination from an earlier briefing.

"Right there is where the gooks might, I say might, have taken cover for the night," Chuck said. "The area is like a point of woods sticking out in a field back home for you country boys. That point, or peninsula, of woods is surrounded by tall elephant grass on two sides. When we get closer, we'll figure which side we'll approach from. That's when flyboy here takes over."

"Oh, yes," Byner said, still fumbling with his web gear. "If we see a large group, I'll simply call in arty or my fast-mover buddies, whatever it takes to take them out, and our job will be done. But if it turns out to be just a few, well, then it's up to the sarge and Chuck here to decide."

"Any questions?" Chuck asked, taking a deep drag on his Winston. "Get 'em out now."

"Yeah," Steve said. "Me and Paul really gotta go on this one? We ain't got but two weeks left in the Nam. This one sucks."

"Afraid so, man," Gaines said. "I tried to talk the skipper into lending us a pair from first squad but he said he didn't want to break up the continuity of the team."

"To hell with the continuity of the team. I'm worried about breaking up the continuity of my hide," Steve added—without a laugh.

"Sorry, man, can't do it," Gaines added.

"Aww, shit," Steve lamented, turning to look his friend Paul in the eyes.

"Any other questions?" Chuck said.

"Yeah, what's the load and order of march," Donnie-Boy asked, folding his map.

"Light load, full combat. Flak jackets, no packs," Chuck said. "Put a little chow in your pockets. Two canteens, there's a blue line we can refill at if needed. Bring your full loads. Leave your mortar rounds, C-4, illums, Claymores and shit. But take all your frags, Ka-bars and .45s.

"Kenny, Tuck, Danny, Steve, Sgt. Gaines and myself will all hump extra gun ammo," Chuck advised. "Danny take two cans if you can manage."

Danny nodded.

"Jason, you take the point, Tuck's your angel at No. 2, then Donnie-Boy and Kenny. Kenny put a Flechette round in that 79. Johnny and Danny you go next with Gertrude, Sgt. Gaines will follow you. Next will be Paul and his prick…"

"I got their prick right here," Paul said, grabbing at his crotch. Chuck ignored the comment.

"…then Ridgeman, myself, then Jimmy B. and Steve. Now, Steve, watch our six, man, especially when we get close. It won't take long because this ain't a hard hump.

"OK, anymore questions?" Chuck paused. "None? Good. The smoking lamp is now out. And that means roaches, too, you hear Jimmy B?"

"Yeah, yeah, man. I hear."

"OK, fellas, lock and…"

"Wait up, guys, wait up," a short, wiry man yelled, sprinting toward the formation. "Wait up, I'm comin', too."

Chuck quickly surveyed the man's gear. "Skipper didn't say anything about a corpsman."

"Well, you can call him," the breathless man said, arranging his load. "He changed his mind after getting a call from down the hill. The company boss said he'd feel better if I tagged along. Plus, they want me to get some experience in the bush."

"Ain't this a lovely development," Chuck groaned. "I wonder what else they're not telling us. Well, it's a little late to worry about that now."

"What's your name, swabby?" Gaines asked, falling back into his DI style.

"Navy Corpsman Wally Wildman, sir," the FNG corpsman replied, almost snapping off a salute. "Came up the hill late yesterday, been in country 10 days."

"Well—Doc Wild—fall in behind me and stay close," Chuck added. "Make sure your .45 is loaded and chambered."

Doc Wild unsnapped the holster and then pulled out his

weapon but fumbled it in the twilight. It hit the dirt with a quiet thud. "Oops."

Chuck rolled his eyes and put his palm over his mouth to stifle a laugh.

Doc Wild picked up the pistol and brushed it off before slipping a full clip into the heavy weapon. He noisily chambered a round. "Ready."

"And you're going to be walking behind me?" Chuck shook his head. "Sarge, that makes a baker's dozen,"

Gaines nodded, trying not to show his grin. "Thirteen. Got it."

"OK, if there's no other objections, or additions, I say again, lock and load. Safe your weapons," Chuck ordered.

A collective clattering of bolts and charging handles rang out before the fringe of dawn could creep over the peaks east of Stud. Kilo 2 Bravo, with medical and air support, headed west through the three rings of concertina wire encircling Signal Hill.

•

It was routine now that at the onset of each patrol or operation, Tuck's heart, mind and soul focused on one thing. *O, St. Joseph, whose protection is so great, so strong, so prompt before the throne of God, I place in you all my interests and desires. O, St. Joseph do assist me..."*

Tuck had scribbled with a black marker the climactic passage of Uncle Joe's prayer across the right side of his camouflaged helmet cover. *"Press Him in my name and kiss His fine head for me and ask Him to return the kiss when I draw my dying breath."*

The other side of the helmet bore a message more in character with the heart of a grunt, *"When I die, bury me face down so the whole world can kiss my ass."*

Large tracts of saw-toothed Napier grass, better known as "elephant grass," covered most of the region's lower elevations like a vast green, swaying carpet. Its stalks grew to 12 feet and provided concealment for the enemy. The wide, sharp leaves sliced the arms and faces of those who trekked through it. It loomed above to capture the midday heat like an oven. It was alive.

Tuck followed point man Jason Green into the elephant grass. Built like a 55-gallon drum and just shy of 5-feet, 10-inches tall, Jason embodied the ideal point man. He would never be selected for a recruiting poster and admitted he cared little for the Marine Corps way. Indeed, he boasted he had not volunteered and was one of the Corps' few draftees. The brooding Jason mostly kept to himself and had no real friends, not even among the brothers.

Despite Tuck's naiveté about blacks, and Jason's distrust of whites, they had buried their inherent differences and become trusted allies since the LP on Operation Cameron Falls.

Jason's strength as a Marine was that he could walk point with the best in the I Corps. He nimbly worked his way along slippery rock ledges, powerfully whacked his way through dense jungle cover, and effortlessly bulled through towering elephant grass—all without complaint or misstep. Opting to work in only a T-shirt, the razor-sharp grass and thorny underbrush had slashed his strong hands and forearms, leaving them toughened and scarred by the festering crud.

"It's uncanny how quiet that big man can operate," Chuck had told Tuck one night while they stood watch. "Jason might've even been recruited by the NVA had they known his gifts. Hell, and he don't mind walking point. It must make him feel like he's worth something. A strange dude, I wish I could get through to him."

Once, during a break on a short patrol, Tuck asked Jason about his affinity for the point. He simply answered with a smile, "I just want to be the first one there. As long as I have a guardian angel looking over my shoulder that I trust, I don't mind. And I trust you."

The patrol slithered through the grass, covering in one hour more than half of the two-klick distance to the objective. The sun shined brightly on the faces of the hills ahead.

An OV-10A Bronco puttered high in the distance, just above the western horizon. The sun occasionally glinted off the light gray and white paint of the observation aircraft.

"See that." Ridgeman nudged Chuck and pointed to the distant Bronco. "That's mine, and right on time. He'll stay out there until I call him. Don't want to tip off ol' sleepy Mr. Charles."

"What makes you think they're still sleeping," Chuck tersely replied.

Donnie-Boy tapped Tuck on the shoulder and pointed to his map. "Tell Jason to slow down. We're less than a half klick from the tip of the woods."

Before Tuck could relay the message, Jason stopped, dropped to one knee and then held up a clenched fist. Tuck raised his fist, passing on the signal to halt and be alert. Donnie-Boy repeated the signal and then rushed forward to join their side. "What you got?" Donnie-Boy whispered.

"Nothin' yet, but we're at the end of this tall grass and that point of woods ain't but a few hundred yards ahead." Jason pointed to a small clearing. "And for a second, I thought I saw some sun flash off something from just inside the tree line."

"Make way, make way," Chuck said. He and Gaines joined the point. "Brief me."

Jason repeated his message while they scouted the objective with binoculars. "It's the right place alright, map coordinates 948-481. Damn, those fly boys are pretty good," Chuck said.

"Damn straight," drawled Ridgeman, who also joined them at the point.

"OK, now, this is gettin' to be a clusterfuck. Spread out," Chuck ordered. "Jason, you and Tuck move up 10 meters and hunker down left and right. Move it."

"Bingo," Gaines said, his eyes glued to the green field glasses. "I count three, no, four gooks about 50 yards inside the tree line. Hard to tell, but looks like they're just sittin' around eating."

"Let me see," Chuck said, raising his binoculars. He spotted the enemy within seconds. "Yep, I make it four, and yes, it looks like they're having a leisurely breakfast. I don't like it. Charlie is too smart to be doing that."

"Think it might be a trap?" Gaines guessed.

"Could be." Chuck adjusted the glasses and scouted the remainder of the woods. "Don't see anything else. Could be some left behinds, making sure the main group's tail is protected. Or just lost. Could be deserters? Who the hell knows? Let's get on the horn and call the skipper."

"Kilo 2 Six, Kilo 2 Six, this is Kilo 2 Bravo. Over," Paul said into the telephone style mike of the big field radio. While the PRC-25 was heavy and required different crystals to change frequencies, the prick was reliable and powerful.

"Six here, go Bravo. Over," answered the skipper's radioman.

Paul handed the handset to Chuck. "Yeah, Six, we've got four, I say four November Victor Alpha about 250 mikes out, chowing down in a huddle. Right at our objective. Over."

"Roger that 2 Bravo, any other movement? Over," the skipper, Lt. Smith, replied.

"That's a negative but it just looks too easy, I smell a rat. Over."

"Well, Bravo, you just go on and kill that rat. Over," the skipper ordered.

"Six, they're almost sitting in the open like they want us to snoop and poop along the side of 'em. I'd like to call in some arty or an air strike and see how many fleas jump off the dog. Over."

The handset hissed for about 15 seconds before a reply came.

"Bravo, are the subjects still in place? Over," the skipper asked.

"Roger that. Over."

"Well, just hold one while I check with the boss down the hill. I'll get back shortly. Six out."

"Shit. That pussy," Chuck growled. He handed the mike to Paul. "I just don't like this. He's calling the company commander for advice. You know what that means? Fucked up."

Gaines nodded. "This might be my first time in the Nam, but I've been around the brass long enough to know this ain't good. When they start looking for advice, and that advice keeps getting farther from the problem than you are, the advice probably is…like you say, fucked up."

Gaines turned to Kenny, squatting at the center of the line. "Pass the word, check your gear and your weapons. And sit tight."

The prick hissed back to life. "Kilo 2 Bravo, Kilo 2 Bravo, this is Kilo 2 Six. Over."

"Bravo here, go Six. Over," Chuck replied.

"The boss at Stud says go for it, no need to waste good arty and rockets on four gooks when there's 13 of you. Do you hear me? Over."

"But Six, I'm telling you, this just ain't a good hit. We're gonna have to cross open terrain and slide up a steep finger of that hill. If there are any more gooks lurking we'll be exposed on both flanks. Just give us some prep, maybe some 81 mike-mikes, they can reach us here. Over."

"Two Bravo, we don't want to spoil the surprise. You've got a gun team, a blooper and 13 men, take the hit, now. Over."

Chuck paused. "Six, roger that, but do us a favor, have medevacs ready. Kilo 2 Bravo, out."

"You heard the skipper," Chuck said to Gaines with sweat glistening above his lip and brow. "Let's get 'em moving, real slow like."

Kilo 2 Bravo advanced westward 100 meters in a crouch and, at times, on their hands and knees. The elephant grass, which had loomed overhead and provided good cover, gave way to a shorter variety of thin-bladed grass and a few, almost leafless trees.

Chuck, now following Jason, raised his fist when the patrol reached less than 150 meters from the objective. He signaled Gaines and Donnie-Boy forward along with Jimmy B. and Ridgeman. Gaines checked the area with his binoculars and confirmed that three of the four NVA soldiers still sat in place, while the other stood and stretched.

"OK, the brassholes want us to take 'em out ourselves. Fine. But we're gonna do it by long distance. We'll stay right where we are now," Chuck said, pointing to his map. "We're directly east of 'em and we gotta good view. The sun's penetrating the canopy at a good angle.

"Here's what we're gonna do. Donnie-Boy, set up big Johnny with Gertrude. Jimmy B., see if Kenny's blooper can reach that site with a high explosive round. Sarge, you help Tuck set up, he's going to be our sniper."

Gaines smiled and nodded his approval.

"First, Kenny will launch an HE round," Chuck explained. "And then Johnny will hose 'em wide open just when it explodes. Kenny should just about have another round ready to adjust and launch. Tuck can then pick off survivors. Any questions?"

Gaines raised a finger. "Why not all of us just open fire at once?"

"Because if there's like a whole damn company out in

those woods, I want some backup shooters watching closely and ready to return fire instantly. OK?"

"Gotcha," Gaines said. "Let's do it, five minutes. Kenny's impact will be the signal."

Chuck nodded.

Donnie-Boy placed Danny and Johnny in position and they sighted Gertrude in. Jimmy B. did the same with Kenny.

"Tuck, come with me Davy Crocket. I've got some 'Ts' that need to be crossed," Donnie-Boy said. Tuck smiled, he knew what that meant. "Now Tuck, you're going to have to shoot some sleepy-eyed slopes in a minute. No problem with squeezing off the rounds, right?"

"Piece of cake, only 150 meters or so and I'll be prone with a clear field." He knew that Donnie-Boy was asking about his heart, not his aim. "Probably could do 'em all myself."

"That's what I like to hear. Go get 'em, Tiger." Donnie-Boy smiled. "Shoot straight."

Tuck winked. "Will do."

Gaines looked at his watch and then Chuck, who nodded. He turned to the blooper position and held up both hands, fingers spread wide and whispered, "Kenny, 10 seconds."

Kenny nodded and lined up the sights on his M-79—a 40mm grenade launcher that could do significant damage in the hands of an expert like Kenny.

One of the enemy soldiers unexpectedly walked away from the group. Through his binoculars, Gaines watched the soldier unfasten his trousers and began to pee.

The Marines barely heard the hollow blooping sound made by the M-79. The enemy quartet did not hear it at all. The high explosive round landed 10 yards short of the enemy and did little more than frighten them. The three sitting men stood up to run, the fourth tried to hurry his pee.

Johnny opened fire and two of the soldiers immediately

spun to the ground in a dirt storm chewed up by Gertrude's spit. Within seconds of the M-60's fusillade, Kenny's second HE round found the target and exploded, flipping the third soldier to his death.

The fourth soldier tried frantically to cinch up the fly of his trousers. Tuck squeezed off a well-aimed round, striking him between the legs and he doubled over in agony. Tuck quickly ended the man's horror, firing a second round, which emitted a small puff of red when it exited the back of the man's head. He fell to the ground.

Chuck and Gaines did not detect any other movement in the spit of woods. "Kilo 2 Six, Kilo 2 Six, this if Kilo 2 Bravo. Over," Chuck calmly hailed the skipper.

"Six here, 2 Bravo, go. Over."

"Mission accomplished. Four enemy KIAs, I repeat, four November Victor Alpha KIAs. Advise further. Over."

"What is your pos at this time, 2 Bravo? Over."

"Less than 150 meters from the site. Over."

A brief pause followed. "Go check 'em out, see what unit. Intel will want to know. Over."

"Uh, roger that Six, but again I seek support, it can still be a trap. Over."

"Damn it, 2 Bravo, put that E-6 on the line, it's time someone started obeying orders quicker around here. Over," the skipper shouted.

Chuck turned and handed the mike to Gaines. Chuck shrugged and shook his head.

"Six, this is Bravo. What are your orders? Over."

"Take over that damned patrol and follow orders like a goddamn Marine. Go to that enemy pos now, and check out those KIAs for intel. Over."

"Roger that Six, but we really could use some support out here, it does look fishy. Over."

"Bravo, am I going to have to chopper out there and run

the show, or what? Now you get those men moving right now and check out that pos. Do you hear me, 2 Bravo. Over?"

"Acknowledge, Six. Moving now. Kilo 2 Bravo, out." Gaines handed the mike back to Paul and looked toward Chuck.

"You got the ball now, sarge, what's the plan?" Chuck asked.

"No way, Chuck. I might be new, but I ain't stupid. I've been training men long enough to know a leader when I see one. I may have the ball, but I'm hiking it to you. Call the play."

Chuck checked his map for what seemed like the hundredth time, and then looked toward the enemy camp. There was no movement. The four enemy KIAs were just that, killed in action.

"OK, gather round," Chuck sighed. "The real objective of the mission now is CYA, cover your ass, as in saving our asses. So we'll free lance a bit.

"I'm going to lead a group straight into that pos to check out those KIAs. Jason you lead. "Rodeo" Steve and Kenny will join me and Jimmy B. And, Kenny, be sure to change to a Flechette in that blooper," Chuck ordered. "Paul, you stay here with Ridgeman and the radio.

"Ridgeman, it seems the skipper doesn't want to know what's happening out here until it's over, so put the prick on your freqs and advise your buddies what's going on, OK."

Byner nodded. "Will do, Chuck."

"Sarge, I'd like you to cover our left flank. Take the gun team along with Tuck and Donnie-Boy. We won't move in until you're just about in position at the southern crest of the hill. That should be in about 30 minutes. Set your watch. When you get there, spread out and wait while we come in and search. That way we can get any survivors, or their friends, in a cross-fire."

Gaines nodded.

"And take Doc Wild," Chuck added. "Let's just hope you're a casual observer, Doc. But just in case, be ready to use that .45. And, don't drop it. Now, let's go feel up the dead."

Jason stood and took his position at the front of the five-man column. Passing Tuck, he winked and smiled, "Sure wish you'd be over my shoulder, bro."

"I'll keep my sights on you."

"Good enough," Jason said, reaching out to slap Tuck's palm. It cemented their friendship.

When Chuck walked past Donnie-Boy he grabbed him by the flak jacket pocket and whispered in his ear. "Sarge is gonna be a good one when he gets some experience. Watch out for him. You got the stuff, too. See you on top of the hill."

Chuck's team walked slowly westward toward the site, their weapons at the ready. Other than pray, there was nothing he could do about the exposure on his right flank.

Gaines hustled his group down the longer route to the south and west to get in position to protect Chuck's left flank. A steep climb up the southern side of the eastward-jutting jungle awaited. Fortunately, taller jungle grass to the south concealed their initial movement.

Donnie-Boy checked on the new medic. "You doing OK back there, Doc. Bet you didn't think your first patrol would turn out like this?"

"No, not really," Doc Wild said, panting hard. "You guys ever slow down?"

"Don't worry, it'll all be OK. You should have been with us our first day in the Nam," Donnie-Boy said, drawing snickers from Tuck and Johnny.

"Save your breath, fellas," ordered Gaines, who suddenly lost grip of his M-16 after he hopped over a small log buried in the tall grass. The rifle hit the fallen tree with a loud clang.

"Hey, don't drop your rifle in the grass, dick-brain," Tuck said to remind Gaines of a certain day back at the MCRD.

Gaines looked back and grinned. "That was you, wasn't it?"

"Yep," Tuck replied.

Gaines stopped the team for a brief rest at a small stream at the hill's base. "By the way, you guys bought a lot of respect from Gunny Hill that day. Me, too."

"Thanks," Tuck said, trying to catch his breath. "By the way, do y'all, DIs I mean, ever give a shit about the boots? I mean, really."

"More than you'll ever know. It's part of the reason I'm out here. Trying to find out how all that training and discipline ends up being used."

"Ever be a DI again?" Donnie-Boy joined in, his breathing even and unforced.

"Don't know. Maybe. If I do, I'm sure I'll be a better one. Probably tougher."

"Tougher! Shit, man," Johnny added, shaking his head. *"Cher, peche."*

"But first, I just want to learn how to survive this shitty place, hell, this patrol."

"Well, we ain't been here a whole hell of a lot longer than you, but we can give you some tips. Keep your head down and watch for the fireflies. Their grenades fizz and flicker when they flip 'em at you. They don't have much shrapnel, but they pack a wallop," Donnie-Boy advised.

Gaines nodded. "Thanks, let's get going, ain't got much time. This hill looks like a bitch."

Crossing the blue line on the map, a ravine with a clear stream flowing over algae-covered stones, stole precious minutes from their approach. The slick rocks provided treacherous footing and twice caused Johnny and Danny to slip into the waist-high waters. Donnie-Boy and Tuck, meanwhile, having skittered across the ravine like giant water bugs, forged ahead into the jungle.

•

Chuck halted his group in the low grass at the edge of the tree line near the enemy camp. He looked at his watch. It had taken them only 15 minutes. He waited another 15 minutes, and then another five to make sure Gaines was guarding his left flank.

•

"This is a lot steeper than we thought and the jungle's a shitload thicker," Donnie-Boy told the group when it again stopped for a brief respite.

"Yeah, Chuck should have sent Jason with us to blaze a trail. Hell, I bet we're not half way up yet," Tuck said, looking up the hill. "If that." They were immersed in a thicket of small, thorny trees that blocked the sun above and to the front. Patches of innocent blue could be seen behind them, but only a quiet and foreboding darkness lay ahead. The trembling began early.

"Well, let's go. We're late for a very important date," Donnie-Boy sang out.

•

Chuck's group entered the enemy camp, each man rotating slowly at the waist. Dense brush and small trees surrounded the small clearing. Jason stomped on the necks of the two KIAs mowed down by Johnny's M-60. They did not respond. No use checking out the M-79 victim—little remained of the man. The victim of Tuck's sharp shooting was an obvious KIA.

"OK, they're dead. Check 'em for papers." Chuck opened the breast pocket of Tuck's victim. He found nothing.

"Nothing here," Jason shouted. Steve looked up and shook his head.

Chuck spun around. Something was amiss. "Weapons? Where's their weapons?...Deserters!"

"Deserters? Yeah, I've heard about the gooks using deserters as bait," Steve joined in. "They used to call it something like, like 'tethered goats' if I remember right."

"Oh, shit," Chuck cried out. "Fellas, fellas, quick, form a perimeter. I don't like this..."

•

Tuck flinched and nearly lost his step when the top of the hill erupted in gunfire. Explosions shattered the peace of the gorgeous morning for a second time.

Gaines estimated they were at least 100 meters from the crest. "Double time, double time, let's go, go, go..."

Tuck tore carelessly through the trees, not feeling the thorns that pierced his fingers and forearms. The terrain ahead promised nothing but darkness.

•

Jason Green, point man extraordinaire, and "Rodeo" Steve Rodriguez—two weeks shy of his flight back to the World—first fell victims to the enemy ambush. Both men, shot through the head, died before they hit the ground.

"Pull back, pull back, get the hell outta here." Chuck shouted. He emptied a magazine into the dense jungle to his front and right. He looked to his left flank, hopefully. The enemy, unseen and only yards away, popped up and fired from camouflaged spider holes. More than an ambush—it was a firing squad. "The little shits have been waiting all along, damn it."

Fighting back-to-back with Jimmy B., Chuck slapped another magazine into his M-16 and silenced one enemy rifle when the soldier inexplicably stood in full view. He then tossed a grenade into a spider hole, taking out another NVA soldier. An intense burning sensation in his right thigh dropped him to his knees. A dull thud hit him in the left shoulder; his arm no longer functioned. He held his rifle with his right arm and continued to fire at random targets. The enemy popped up from the ground like some shooting gallery at a cheap carnival.

"Jimmy B., Jimmy B., give me a hand, man! Jimmy B. help me, damn it, I can't walk," Chuck cried and fell to a seated position. Jimmy B. did not reply. Chuck reached around to his friend and best fire-team leader. He wasn't there. "Jimmy B.?"

Jimmy Bryant lay on his back, eyes staring into the brilliant blue sky. Ten AK-47 rounds had ripped apart his chest. Jimmy B. hadn't needed to return to the A Shau Valley to die.

•

From 150 meters away, an ashen-faced Paul shrieked into the prick. "Kilo 2 Six, Kilo 2 Six, this is Kilo 2 Bravo. Can you hear me? Over. Can you hear me?"

"Kilo 2 Bravo, this is Six. Over."

"They're butchering us down here, we need support," Paul shouted. The ground around him erupted in sheets of dust and heat. The NVA had spotted the pair left behind and mortar rounds were marching toward their position.

"Nonsense, 2 Bravo, how can four gooks fight off..."

"Ahh, screw it," Paul muttered, slamming the mike into Byner's chest. "Here. To hell with that idiot. Call in your flyboys, and hurry. Those mortars are crawling up our ass."

Two more rounds landed, spraying them with hot shrapnel and dirt. Both men cried out.

•

"I'm coming, Chuck, I'm coming," Kenny yelled,

running toward his squad leader. He slapped another Flechette round into his M-79 and fired into a cluster of muzzle flashes. A score of deadly darts tore through the brush. A pair of enemy cries briefly enthralled him. Kenny reached for another Flechette round. "Aw, shit!" The pouch was empty.

Kenny drew his .45 with his right hand and grabbed the collar of Chuck's flak jacket with his left. While trying to drag his squad leader to some semblance of safety, Kenny emptied his pistol into the brush. Chuck struggled awkwardly to reload his rifle with one hand and then returned fire until a searing pain in his right side joined the burning in his leg and shoulder.

Out of ammunition, Kenny cast his pistol aside, fished a grenade from his pocket and then heaved it into the brush. Again, enemy cries drew a brief smile. Before he could fetch another frag, however, Kenny's eyes and mouth formed a grotesque mask. He watched with dismay when his muscular black arm disappeared below the right elbow. "I'm too short for this shit," he shrieked only a second before a sledgehammer-like blow struck his left knee. He dropped Chuck and fell to the ground beside him. Kenny could take it no longer. He crumpled into a fetal position and began to sob. Kenny Charles' misery soon ended after two bullets slammed into the back of his head.

Young enemy soldiers, inexperienced but emboldened by the success of their ambush, abandoned the seclusion of the jungle and charged the surviving Marine. Chuck could no longer aim and opened fire with his M-16 on full automatic. Two soldiers toppled onto the bodies of Jason and Steve.

Chuck struggled to determine his condition. Confused, he gazed down at his wounds. Tuck. Tuck and Donnie-Boy would save him. The sarge would be here shortly. He'd know what to do. And, that new medic, uh, what's his name, Doc Wild, yes, he'd be here, too. But when Chuck looked up he stared into the face of his executioner. The soldier, no more than a child, grinned and pulled the trigger of an AK-47. Chuck gasped. His heart nearly leapt out of his body when the bullets smashed through his chest.

An artisan would some day carve Charles Booker's name on a long, dark-gray granite wall in Washington, D.C.

•

Two minutes, perhaps three, had passed since Tuck heard the first shots. The volume of fire meant only the worst for Chuck's group, he knew. They drove up the hill, still moving quietly. Crawling, Donnie-Boy broke through the thicket and reached the crest first. It took him only seconds to assess the situation.

"Sgt. Gaines," he said with a hoarse whisper, sliding down the hill. "They're all wasted, sarge. I count five dead Marines. Chuck's gone, too."

The faces, and hopes, of the small group faded. Their lids blinked rapidly before vacant eyes. A wave of nausea washed over Tuck when a pungent aroma drifted down the hill. He briefly mourned the passing of their mentor. His insides quivered with grief and fear. Perhaps they should retreat.

Donnie-Boy's voice startled him. "There's about 30 gooks—mostly kids, believe it or not—celebrating up there. Maybe more. And we don't have a damned radio."

Gaines took over. "OK, naval tactics. We advance up the hill and just before we reach the crest, we spread out abreast and broadside 'em. Doc, you make your way around the crest back toward the east and look for wounded," Gaines said hopefully, pointing Doc Wild in the right direction. "We'll take out as many as we can, as quick as we can, and then hightail it toward where we think you'll be. Got it?"

Doc Wild tentatively nodded and then sprinted to the east.

The five grunts ran up the hill. The din of rejoicing

enemy enabled the team to quicken its pace. They reached the crest within minutes and Johnny and Danny took positions in the middle. Gaines flanked them on the left, Donnie-Boy and Tuck on the right.

Half of the NVA soldiers huddled in the middle of the site, firing into the air and looting the bodies of the dead Marines. Gaines raised his arm, and then slowly lowered it and nodded.

Most of the enemy didn't understand at first, mistaking the noise for celebratory gunfire. In reality, a large American was kneeling off to their side firing an M-60 machine gun, while yelling and cursing in a strange French dialect. The popping sounds of M-16s joined in.

The young NVA panicked. Their high-pitched screams cracked like the pubescent changing voices of teen-agers. Those who survived the wall of fire fled into the jungle. At least 15, maybe more, of their comrades lay snuffed out.

"Move it," Gaines yelled, pointing toward the east while hurling a grenade that sent two more soldiers twisting into a heap. "Let's get the hell outta here."

Four of the five men began sprinting around the crest of the hill, in search of Doc Wild and the radio team. Donnie-Boy stayed behind to cover their rear, dropping three more enemy soldiers with his rifle and a grenade.

Tuck looked back and stopped running. Anger suddenly replaced the trembling. "Damn it, Donnie-Boy. Get the hell out of there, let the flyboys take care of 'em."

"You keep running, little brother, I'm covering our ass like Chuck said to do. Now go."

Tuck turned and ran a short way, but stopped, turned back and dashed up the hill in time to spot an NVA soldier, who had made his way behind Donnie-Boy. Tuck fired two rounds. The soldier rolled to his death no more than 10 feet behind his friend.

"If you can CYA, I can, too, damn it," Tuck shouted,

ripping off a half dozen shots toward the hill. Suddenly, a score of NVA, regrouped under a veteran soldier, stormed toward them.

"Oh, shit. Let's get the hell outta here," Donnie-Boy shouted.

The two Cajuns ran as fast as their hearts and legs allowed. The NVA gained ground. "Run, Tuck, faster," Donnie-Boy shouted, passing him.

In a flash, the world behind them erupted in a brilliant sheet of flame. Breathing became difficult when the flames tried to suck the oxygen from their lungs. They inhaled quickly and deeply and then held their breaths. The heat on the back of their necks felt like a homecoming bonfire. They continued to run. An arm reached out from the elephant grass and tripped Tuck. "What the hell?" He fell hard and lost his breath. Donnie-Boy also tripped and fell. Another sheet of flame lit up the bright morning sky. A roar accompanied the heat.

"Phantoms, see." Gaines pointed toward the sky while sitting on Tuck's chest. He looked up and saw Danny sitting on Donnie-Boy's back.

The F-4s—called in by Byner when the enemy first sprang the ambush—dropped fiery canisters of napalm atop the hill. Whatever NVA soldiers remained were now crispy critters, Tuck thought with a smile. The flames, he knew, were also cremating the remains of his friends.

Paul sat quietly in the matted grass with a large pressure bandage tied around his forehead to stop a badly bleeding scalp wound suffered during the mortar attack. "Tall" Paul would be going home two weeks sooner than expected, but without his friend "Rodeo" Steve.

"Damn, there goes all the fun on R&R," Byner laughed nervously while Doc Wild finished bandaging shrapnel wounds to his left hip and right buttocks.

"Guess you'll have to settle for blow jobs," Doc Wild

quipped. "Now, let those two up over there so I can look at those burns."

Tuck reached around to the back of his neck and grabbed a handful of seared skin hanging from just below his hairline. Doc Wild poured water from his canteen over the burn. "Aye, yie yie," Tuck hissed

"Second degree, that's all. A week or so and you'll be OK. You, too," Doc Wild said, turning to Donnie-Boy, whose crisped hair on the back of his head smelled of singed chicken. "More painful than harmful. You two were lucky."

Donnie-Boy stared toward the top of the hill. "Yeah, lucky."

The two Phantoms spotted more fleeing NVA and made another pass. Two more loud explosions, like thunderclaps, ripped into what remained of the hilltop. Byner then got on the prick and received confirmation that the F-4s were heading back to Dong Ha. "Thanks a bunch fellas, y'all saved our ass, out." The pilots waggled their jets' wings and sped to the northeast.

"Better give me that thing, the skipper's gonna want a report," Gaines said.

"What you gonna tell him?" Johnny asked in a demure voice. "The truth? That he screwed us over and got five grunts wasted, whose bodies ain't even bodies anymore, just charcoal. Is that what you're gonna tell him?"

"The truth? Right now? No. First I want the stupid ass to come get us," Gaines said. "Kilo 2 Six, Kilo 2 Six, this is Kilo 2 Bravo. Over....Then I'll tell him what I think."

"Go 2 Bravo, this is Six, what's your sit rep? Over."

"Six, we need a medevac and body bags at coordinates...
"

CHAPTER 36

New Orders

Northern Quang Tri Province, R.S.V.N.
March 26, 1969—6 p.m. local time

"It doesn't sound too good. There's been trouble for our sister group just to the south," Louie explained, sitting to eat his evening portion of rice. "The colonel's been on the radio for 20 minutes and there's been much cursing. Something about a bad ambush that cost us 50 men—mostly boys like yourself, actually."

"Was that what the bombing was about? Two mornings ago, remember, we saw the napalm clouds and you said..."

"Yes, I remember what I said. I just hate to be right."

"You also said this operation wasn't working out the way Bui and the others had planned and we ought to consider deserting," Doan Tien pressed on. "We can't run now, I haven't accomplished my mission. My uncle is still breathing the same air he stole from my family."

Louie dropped his rice bowl to the ground and peered at Doan Tien. He snapped. "To blazes with you and your mission. Look, I've agreed to help you. But it's not worth getting us both killed in the process."

"But you promised."

"Yes, yes, I know I did, Trai...Doan Tien. Listen, this crusade can go sour. If we're going to do anything, we need to do it soon. Understand?"

Doan Tien gulped. "How soon?"

"I don't know, but damn sure before he finds us out, or before the Americans kill us first. It has to be the right time.

It just has to be the right set of..." Louie paused and turned toward the top of the hill, from where a sergeant hailed them.

"Louie, the colonel wants all of you to join us up here. He has some announcements," the sergeant shouted with both hands cupped around his mouth. Doan Tien's sharp eyes noticed that the sergeant's right hand lacked a little finger.

They put aside their meals and jogged up the hill. Pham stood in the midst of a compact circle of troops. "I am sure you have heard the rumors by now," he began. "For the most part, they are true. Dozens of our comrades, new conscripts and most so very young, died a few days ago. But that will neither deter our immediate mission, nor dampen our drive to rid Vietnam of the damned Americans.

"However, we have had some changes in our plans and tomorrow we will march southwest toward Khe Sanh. There we will wait for hundreds more of our comrades coming down from the north. Together we will move east to the Da Krong Valley and begin month-long preparations for a massive attack, from the south, on the Marine base called Vandegrift."

Listening, Doan Tien remembered how Louie had told him how he thought Pham often shared too much information with his troops. The American "chieu hoi" or surrender program successfully siphoned off disgruntled NVA troops. Such troops from this company could provide a wealth of information. It was this trust that Pham placed in his men, however, that fueled his fiery charisma. His men never charged blindly into battle, but they fought blindly for him.

"What does all this mean, Louie?" Doan Tien whispered. "Does it mean more danger for us?" He again anguished over the thought of killing Americans.

"Shhh, listen, he's not finished."

"Now, because of our heavy losses over the past weeks,"

Pham continued. "And until we can gather in greater numbers, we will avoid all contact with the Americans. It will give us time to get stronger and move faster toward our final destination and ultimate goal. Thank you for your attention."

Returning to their squads, the troops murmured and nodded their heads.

"Damn, things must be going bad for him to be that courteous," Louie said with a sigh. "It means, my young friend, that we've bought some time. Or should I say he's bought himself some time."

"Unless. Unless the right time presents itself. And it may," Doan Tien said, fingering the .25 caliber automatic hidden in his pocket.

"You just remember, it will be me who decides when, and if, the time is right," Louie cautioned. "Or else, you are on your own."

"Of course, Louie, of course."

CHAPTER 37

Martyrs and Newbies
Vandegrift Combat Base, R.S.V.N.
April 2, 1969—10 a.m. local time

Kilo Company boss Capt. G. "Butch" King fumed while waiting for second platoon's commander to arrive. "You see him comin' yet?" he called out to his aide.

"No, sir. Not yet."

"Damn."

From the outside, King's K Company command center resembled most tents on the east side of Stud. Inside, however, it included a communications table, two cots, a folding dining table, and an ice chest full of honest-to-goodness ice, a small desk, two oscillating fans, a basin for washing, and a beat-up couch. Yet, it was still a tent with a plywood floor, entirely too thin for King's penchant for stomping when upset. The needless deaths of five of his Marines merited stomping.

He was a tall, burly Texan with salt-and-pepper hair that prematurely receded from his leathery forehead. A permanent tan reflected his love of the outdoors. Not enough game ran wild in the jungles of the Nam for King's taste—a fact he noted in a letter home early in his first tour in '65. It was no different in this, his third tour, probably worse. The continual bombing had scared off much of the game.

Known as Butch to his friends and family back home, he paused from his pacing and sat at his desk. He chomped and rolled back and forth over his lips a half-smoked, unlit cigar while shuffling through a small stack of papers, re-reading the detailed contents. "This is unbelievable. It had better not screw things up for me," he mumbled to himself. The "boss," as his men referred to him, had been a late entry into the officer ranks. He had spent a dozen years climbing to master gunnery sergeant, and, at 38, was thought to be too old to be a captain. But he now hovered only weeks away from pinning on gold oak leaf clusters. As a major, he might secure an appointment on the battalion level, which could jump-start his stalled career.

Second Lt. Hank Smith counted his steps while approaching the boss's tent.

A wiry sergeant with black rim glasses waited outside the flap of the tent. "You're late. He's inside. Waiting," the gnomish sergeant said with a smirk. "And he ain't happy, lieutenant."

"Look, I ain't no lifer. I just want to finish this tour and get back to the World without a limp and my pecker intact," Lt. Smith replied in a menacing tone and then brushed past the sergeant.

"Lt. Smith reporting as ordered, sir," he said smartly from the entrance while attempting to smooth out his wrinkled blouse.

"Come," the boss snapped.

Smith approached and stood at attention in front of the beat up desk. Cluttered with the usual reports and assessments, it also included a framed, 5 x 7, black and white photo of the captain posing with a deer he'd killed. A small strip of paper indicating "12-point buck, San Antonio, 1962" was glued to the bottom of the frame.

The boss slowly pushed back his wooden chair, its legs stuttering on the plywood floor, and stood, easily towering over Smith. He stared at the slight lieutenant and then vented. "What in the hell were you thinking? To turn down three requests for support from your leader in the field is unacceptable. You knew those men needed air support, or at least some arty, and you forced them to take that hill without it. And now five of them are dead and several others wounded."

"But, sir, I called you about it, and you said…"

"I know you did, lieutenant. But that was the first time they requested support, and before their taking out an exposed enemy. You never contacted me about the second and third requests; that they were positive it was a trap. Had I known they were still requesting such…hell, I'd have nuked that hill if I'd had too. And, you surely should have trusted the judgment of one of your best squad leaders, who is now dead, and a new, but one damned fine E-6."

The boss now loomed inches from Smith's face and the smelly stogie filled the lieutenant's nostrils. Shifting his weight to another foot, Smith tried not to let his anger show. "But we did kill 63 enemy soldiers, sir."

"Yeah, but only because the FAO was smart enough to call in his jet jockey buddies and put them in a holding pattern. And that was after you got five guys wasted. Hell, and now I'm in a position to have to recommend this, this…" the boss said, looking down at the papers rolled up in his fist. "This Lt. Ridgeman for the Bronze Star for 'sound combat thinking under duress.'"

The boss turned and threw his cigar butt into a trashcan, then sat on the corner of his desk. He paused to spit out a small piece of tobacco, before again looking at the sheaf of papers in his right hand. "Battalion has been studying this mess for several days now. It's all been one big CYA, and the shittiest thing about it all is the fact that battalion can't see beyond body counts. And 63 *is* a big number, especially when they see we only had 13 of our guys out there. So battalion says they want *me* to put *you* up for a medal for planning this disaster and put you on a fast track to first lieutenant." King slapped the papers on his thigh. "Damn, what a war."

Smith stifled a smile.

"I've got to do it, so don't think you're some kind of

hero. Whatever it's gonna be, you can bet it won't be with a V. Because we both know there was no valor on your part," the boss said. "You're just lucky a frag hasn't found its way under your rack yet."

Again the boss looked at the papers and glanced at the casualty list. "By the way, what was the name of that corporal again? The one that led them in there and paid for your medal with his life? Booker wasn't it?"

"Yes sir, Cpl. Charles Booker, sir. But I don't think he…"

"Battalion may like the numbers but I don't give a damn what you think. I'm putting that kid up for the Silver Star, posthumously, of course, and the other four dead Marines for the Bronze, with V's on all them. I had better have some glowing-ass letters of recommendation from you by tomorrow. Understand?"

"Yes, sir."

"That's all, you can go," the boss said with an abrupt wave of his hand.

Smith did an about face and headed for the exit flap.

"Smith, come back here. I almost forgot," the boss added. His voice was calmer and more business-like. "Intel says a lot of gooks are moving south and west again. They think they might be headed back into Khe Sanh to start up some new trouble. They also have reason to believe our friend Col. Pham is one of the honchos out there. So it must be important. Tells me it is. Especially after the number he did on Firebase Douglas last year during Tet. That bastard knows what he's doing."

"Firebase Douglas, sir? I'm afraid I've only heard the name. No details."

The boss returned to his straight-backed chair and sat with his hands clasped before him on the desk. He paused for a moment with his eyes closed. "If you don't know, lieutenant, you need to know. It was about the worst ass kicking we ever took around here."

He again paused and then recalled the details. "It was during the siege at Khe Sanh and I was on the tail end of my second tour. Firebase Douglas was located about six miles northeast of Khe Sanh and about six or so due west of here," the captain said, gesturing in the general direction. "It was a big firebase, had a 155 battery and took nearly a whole company of grunts to defend. Well, our friend Pham, he was Major Pham back then, pushed nearly a whole company of NVA up Hill 691 where Douglas sat. He created some minor diversions and shit on either side of the hill early one morning and then came charging up a narrow, unguarded ravine on the other side. Caught most of the grunts just waking up and slaughtered 'em like pigs. Heck, most of the guys didn't even know the gooks were there until they were inside the wire. Heads would have rolled had any of the brass on that hill survived.

"Lost nearly 50 Marines. About that same number were pushed into the bush. Only three live grunts were found atop Douglas after the gooks had done their business and our flyboys had done their damage. To add insult to injury, Pham had his troops turn two of the artillery pieces around and fire 10 rounds at Khe Sanh before he left. Now that's balls, and smart."

The lieutenant's face screwed up with confusion. "But sir, how do you know it was this Col. Pham, or whatever his name is? I mean, it could have been one of a number of NVA officers working the I Corps."

"Because, lieutenant, this guy left a calling card," the boss said, reaching down to open a worn leather briefcase. He pulled out a crumpled envelope containing a faded color photo, slightly dog-eared on one corner. He laid the photo on the desk and slid it toward Smith. "I snapped this while heading up the reaction team that was choppered in to help look for survivors. Not too many NVA officers scalp their enemies and then leave a note with their name on it. Now do they? Notice the way he left the message. That's an American-made Bowie knife, son, not all too unlike what I use to skin game with back home.

"Intel says Pham's becoming a legend among his troops—some kind of super patriot, or something. And if he's who we're gonna be up against out there in the Da Krong, we'd best be ready for a fight."

Smith nodded. "I'll surely give this some thought, sir." He handed the photo back to King, who paused to look one more time at the dead Marine.

"Within the week Kilo will be spearheading a battalion-sized operation into the Da Krong River valley. They'll be choppering us out to Firebase Shepherd and we'll free lance from there when we get more intelligence. There'll be a company meeting on this tomorrow at 0900. You can get those letters of recommendation to me then. You're dismissed. Go get some rest with the grunts. Y'all are gonna need it."

•

April 3, noon local time:
Dear Dad,

Happy birthday there April Fool (sorry I'm a little late with this). I wish I could say that I, too, was happy today. It has been a grim week.

It's taken me that long to get up the courage just to tell you of our latest troubles. Last week, while on some sort of screwed up patrol we lost five guys from our squad, including our squad leader, Chuck Booker, whom I have so often written to you about.

Chuck, Steve Rodriguez, Jason Green, Kenny Charles and Jimmy B. Bryant were KIA in an ambush atop a small hill just west of Signal Hill. Donnie-Boy and me were slightly wounded during a napalm attack on the hill. But don't worry mom the burns were second degree and are healing nicely. The doctors at Charlie Med said they wouldn't leave permanent scars. We were very lucky. Johnny and Danny came out of it OK as well, just a few scratches.

We also learned of more bad news from the States, when we were told of the death of Gunny Hill. I'm sure you will remember that name. He was my platoon commander in boot camp. He was killed in an auto accident near Houston on New Year's Day.

It is even stranger the way we learned about it. You see we have a new platoon sergeant here and you would have never guessed that it is Sgt. Jerry Gaines. Yes, one of our boot camp DIs. He was a real asshole back in the World. But out here he is proving to be a decent guy, we think. Strange world.

Because of our severe losses, our squad, what's left of it, and first squad were pulled off Signal Hill and brought back down to Stud. I am writing to you now from on top of a sandbagged trench in the tent area.

Now for some really good news, my promotion to lance came through. Happy birthday, Dad, your son is no longer a private. I have also been named a fire team leader. Too bad I don't have a team. Right now our squad consists of me and our new squad leader— CORPORAL Donald Hebert. That's right, Donnie-Boy is moving up the ladder pretty quick. But like me, he doesn't have much of a squad to lead.

Sgt. Gaines has attached us, along with Danny and Johnny, to Cpl. Ike Likens' first squad (Kilo 2 Alpha) until we get some replacements in. Heck, Ike didn't have but little more than half a full squad himself.

Shit, incoming. . .

•

Wow, that was something. Several rockets hit within a couple of hundred yards of our tents about an hour ago, two about 60 yards away. Two guys in another platoon were hit, but not bad, I think. I hate incoming, there's no way to fight back. It's been getting more intense and more often in the past few days. Two days ago we got hit by about 30 rounds in 90 minutes. You don't need to be an intelligence officer to know the gooks are up to no good. Some short-timers around here fear another Khe Sanh may be brewing.

As for the near future, scuttlebutt has it we're going on a short operation south in a few days or so. It's been quiet down there recently and this is supposed to be a routine security sweep. But I bet we're going look for who's responsible for all this incoming.

This place, this war, is so hard to define, other than it stinks. We were once told that war would be hours upon days upon weeks of boredom, only to be punctuated by seconds or minutes of sheer terror. Man, whoever said that sure knew what he was talking about.

Funny, but I already seem to be getting over the deaths of my friends, if that's possible. But I'm not so sure if that's true. It's all so confusing. Death has a place here. It's easier to accept. I hope it's not wrong of me, but it just seems that I'm so glad that it wasn't me, or Donnie-Boy. Dad, I think you know what I mean. Maybe some day, years maybe, it will all catch up with me.

But that's all for now from your bored, and sad, but loving son. Please give my love to all the right people and pray for me, and my fallen friends. Your loving son, Tuck

P.S. Mom, please send another package with your homemade fudge, packs of unsweetened Kool-Aid, a bunch of cookies and any other junk food you can think of. And pack it all in popcorn. We'll eat that, too, even if it is stale. Also, send some small bottles of iodine for our elephant-grass cuts, Band-Aids and more film.

Tuck stuffed the letter inside a dirty envelope, and then jammed it into the side pocket of his rucksack along with several spare C-rations accessory packs. He regularly exchanged his cigarette four-packs for Chiclets chewing gum and "shit disks"—chocolate candy.

He popped a pair of Chiclets into his mouth. They would have to do until Swamp Rat made his chow rounds, or until they decided to hike up to the mess hall. Some grunts in a nearby tent had their radio tuned in to the Armed Forces

Network and the sounds of "Aquarius, Aquaaaareeeeeeusss…
" droned on.

"Damn, is that the only song that station plays," Tuck complained before hollering over his shoulder. "Hey, guys, put that damn thing on Hanoi Hannah. At least she plays some real rock, not that crap. Find some Stones or the Doors."

"Eat shit and die." The distant reply made Tuck smile.

"Looky, looky here at what we got coming," Danny said, nudging Johnny. "Fresh meat."

Johnny grunted, waking from a morning nap. "Hamburgers?"

Tuck looked up and saw Ike and Donnie-Boy leading a trio of newbies down the path from the skipper's tent. Fresh from Quang Tri, their camouflaged utilities were brightly colored and their jungle boots still had black polish on the toes.

"Look alive, fellas, we have company," Ike said. He waved back to the replacements. "Tuck, these guys will be your new team members, so get 'em squared away. For now, you'll still be attached to my squad. Donnie-Boy here will be my assistant and he's going to run things. I'll be working more closely with Sgt. Gaines. It's a little unorthodox, but we don't have enough people for two full squads. Besides, I'm going on R&R in two weeks."

Ike turned toward the replacements. "These guys here, these Cajuns from Louisiana, are already real pros. They haven't been in the Nam for but, what, about four months?" he said, turning back toward Tuck, who shrugged. "But they've been in beaucoup shit and know more than any 11-month asshole in the rear. So listen to 'em and y'all just might make it your first four months."

"I guess we ain't the newbies no more," Johnny said, slapping palms with Danny.

"OK, guys, y'all put your gear down in there," Tuck

said, pointing to one corner of the tent. "Then come back out and introduce us."

Donnie-Boy walked over and sat on the sandbagged wall next to Tuck. "I saw you writin' again. Telling Anna how you'd like to slip your Nam-dirtied dick in her clean little…"

"Aw, go screw yourself, Donnie-Boy."

"Did that last night. Man, was I ever good," Donnie-Boy laughed.

Tuck shook his head. "Nah, was writin' to Dad, his birthday. Told him about Chuck and them gettin' KIA'ed. Also wrote about our promotions. Asked Mom for another big package."

"Alright," Donnie-Boy shouted, turning to Johnny and Danny. "Tuck here is sendin' off for another package." They cheered on cue.

"Hope she don't forget the fudge," Danny added.

Tuck waved toward the three newbies, who were still stirring inside the tent. "Y'all get out here most ricky-tick and gather 'round."

PFC Alex Miller was the first to emerge. He was a slim, shy boy from Kansas City and had qualified as expert with both the M-14 and M-16 rifles. He, too, had turned down offers to join a sniper unit. "Me and you gotta have a talk later," Tuck told him.

PFC William Dominic was a big red-haired fellow who lifted weights for a hobby. His 6-foot, 2-inch chiseled physique matched Donnie-Boy. Willie, as he was called, hailed from farm country west of Omaha. He had thrown the shot put and discus at the University of Nebraska for two years until poor grades caught up with him. "You see these two guys right here." Tuck said, pointing toward a grinning Johnny and Danny. Willie nodded. "Those two guys are gonna take good care of you." The combination of

Cornhusker, Crimson Tide and Fighting Tiger would prove interesting.

"I guess you want to know all about me, too," PFC Mike Mayerinski said, cocking his cap back on a shaved head. "Chicago, South side, mama dead, no goddamn idea where my old man is. No brothers, no sisters that I claim. It was either the Corps or jail. Figured the Nam was better than the slammer. But by the looks of you fellas, I might've been better off in the slammer."

"Well, if you've got a death wish, too, you've come to the right place," Donnie-Boy answered Kilo 2 Alpha's newest smart-ass.

Ike, who had been sitting back and observing, cut into the conversation. "That's enough grab-assing for now. Listen up. Skipper and the sarge met with the boss and other platoon leaders this morning and here's what's goin' down…"

"OK, you slimy maggots, drop your dicks and gather 'round, here's what's going down," Gaines blurted after sneaking up on the group from behind.

Tuck figured there was still a lot of DI coursing through those bulging neck veins. "You know what they say, 'you can take the boy out of the DI, but can't take the DI out of the boy,'" Tuck whispered to Donnie-Boy.

Ike smiled at Gaines' interruption and nodded. He signaled Gaines to take over.

"First of all, let me say the Skipper caught a bit of the boss' wrath over what went down last week. Let's just say I don't think he'll be ignoring our suggestions in the future. We'll just leave it at that, OK?

"Now, the boss wants us to get some rest, because at the end of this week we'll be heading south, just as the scuttlebutt suggested. It also seems we may be out there a while, maybe a month, maybe more. Intel says there's too much incoming around here just to be an accident and they smell a rat, and they don't want that rat to turn into another Khe Sanh-sized dragon. So we're the ones who..."

SSSST!

Tuck leaped and tackled Gaines and Mike Mayerinski, toppling them into a ditch.

WHAM!

The enemy rocket had left little warning time—just as Chuck had once described—before exploding about 15 yards away. Shrapnel and dirt clods peppered the area. The grunts were nestled safely in the bottom of the trenches when the second and third rockets impacted barely more than 20 yards away. Tuck counted another six explosions in the next minute while the rockets walked their way across Stud. A half dozen more long hisses, bound for the far reaches of the western perimeter, streaked overhead. The rocket attack ended after another two minutes and 10 explosions.

"OK, Lance Corporal Richard, you can get your ass off my head now," Gaines groaned from beneath. "Yeah, me too," Mayerinski added. "It smells awful down here."

"It ought too," Tuck replied with a nervous laugh. "I knocked y'all into our latrine."

"Aw, man, I'm all full of piss, now," the muscular Mayerinski said.

"Good, goes with you being full of shit, too," Donnie-Boy quietly growled into Mike's right ear. "The man, here, just saved you from a quick trip back to the World...in a body bag. I think a little thanks is in order. Don't you?"

Mike nodded toward Tuck and walked away, wiping pissy mud off his cheek.

"Owe you one, Richard, thanks," Gaines said, brushing himself off.

"Counted 23," Tuck noted soberly.

"Make that 25," Donnie-Boy added. "This shit's gettin' too regular."

"Now you guys know why we're headed south next week," Gaines said.

"Owww, shit, Danny, that hurts, man," Ike groaned when Danny pulled Ike's trousers down to examine the shrapnel wounds in his buttocks.

"Don't look too bad. Two pieces, I can feel 'em in there, too. Not too deep," Danny said, massaging the left cheek of Ike's rear end. "But just like ol' Byner last week, your R&R just took a hit in the ass, literally."

The quip drew a chorus of laughs, even from the newbies, who were still stunned and shaking from the attack.

"Like hell, too, I'm gonna postpone that damn R&R. I'd rather be humpin' in the bush with you guys than be on R&R knowing I wasn't goin' to get to hump any bush in Bangkok."

Alex Miller, the K.C. newbie, was sitting on a sandbag wall with his right trouser leg pulled up. "Sarge, think I got hit. Doesn't hurt much, just a little stinging. But it's bleeding pretty bad."

"Hold on, Marine. Doc Wild's comin' up the road now." Gaines nodded toward the corpsman, who always seemed to have his motor revved up. He arrived in a trot with his medical kit dangling from his shoulder.

Doc Wild first examined Ike's butt and applied a heavily padded dressing. He then checked out Alex's leg and wrapped a pressure bandage around it to stop the bleeding. "It's going to be OK, just a flesh wound. Check with me later today and then again tomorrow morning so I can change the bandage. Sgt. Gaines, this man will be OK, but you'll want to get Cpl. Likens here up to Charlie Med. They might have to cut those out."

"Aw, shit, man. I've already got two purple hearts for little shit like this. I don't need another one," Ike lamented. "The squads too short-handed already. I need to be in the field."

"Well, you're gonna get one whether you want it or not, corporal," Doc Wild told Ike, before turning to Alex. "You, too, private."

Tuck walked up to Ike and lightly slapped him on his healthy bare cheek. "Pull up your pants and wait a bit, Ike. Swamp Rat and Skeeter'll be here in a few minutes with chow and he'll give you a ride up to Charlie Med."

"Excuse me," the corpsman said. "Did you say Swamp Rat? Is that the big friendly grunt who delivers the food and mail? Funny Southern accent?"

"Yeah, that's him," Donnie-Boy confirmed. "And he's late, too. Why?"

"I pronounced him dead just a few minutes before I got here, about a hundred yards that way," Doc Wild said, nodding to the northern perimeter. "He and the mule he was driving took a direct hit. He probably never knew what hit him. There wasn't a whole lot left.

"Boss' tent took a hit, too. Boss is fine, but that silly sergeant that works for the boss, he got hit pretty bad. Don't know if he's gonna make it. They're gonna have to send him down to Da Nang to put him back together."

"Shhiiiit," Johnny sighed. "Man, I liked ol' Rat. He was funny."

"Mike, Willie, Alex, y'all come on. We've got some digging to do. If we're gonna live till next week, we're gonna need some more holes to hide in," Donnie-Boy ordered.

First Chuck, their mentor, and now a fellow Cajun, Swamp Rat, were gone. The war was starting to get too personal for Tuck. He looked around. Who was next?

CHAPTER 38

Out to lunch
Mamou, La.
April 7, 1969—Noon local time

Wilfred Robert looked at his watch. "Damn." He was late for his weekly luncheon date with Curtis Richard. The two Marine dads dined on Mondays to trade letters and thoughts about their sons. In addition to their Saturday morning visits, it gave them another chance to talk LSU football with another dyed-in-the-wool Tiger fan.

Wilfred reached out to flip the sign on the front door of the repair shop to CLOSED just as Anna came running up to the entrance, smiling and waving. Wilfred smiled broadly and pushed the door open for his niece.

"Hey, Uncle Wilfred," Anna said cheerfully while entering. She gave him a hug and a kiss.

"Mmmmm, girl, what's that you got on that smells so good."

"It's called *Ambush*," she said, holding up the underside of her wrist for him to smell.

He grinned. "Girl, that stuff's a sin. You gonna make me have to go to confession, yeah. So, what brings you here today? Haven't seen you in a few weeks, *cher*. Was beginning to worry you had forgotten ol' Wilfred."

"I can't forget you. You're the only uncle I have. Plus you're too cute to forget," Anna teased. "I just came by to see what you've heard from that big, dumb cousin of mine. He's quit writing those three sentence letters, and I haven't heard from Tuck in a while, either."

"Ahh, now I know why you're here. It's not ol' Wilfred you want to see. It's about what that beau of yours is doing." Wilfred waggled his finger.

"You got me," she said with a blush. "Well, what is going on with those boys?"

Wilfred took Anna by the arm and gently guided her out the door. He turned, pulled the door shut and then locked it. "Now, you just come with me."

"Where are we going? I've got a 3 p.m. class at LSU-E. It's algebra, can't miss it. Cindy and Charlene are comin' to pick me up."

"To Eunice. I've got a lunch date with Tuck's dad," Wilfred replied, smiling. "I'm sure he'll have all the latest on your boyfriend. You can call Cindy and tell her you'll meet her at school. Could use the company. Plus I just washed the truck. Believe me, Curtis will be thrilled."

Anna wrapped her arms around her uncle's elbow. "You've got a deal."

•

My dearest Tuck,

Today was a great day. I had a wonderful lunch with my Uncle Wilfred and YOUR dad.

I went over to see Uncle Wilfred and he convinced me to go to Eunice and eat lunch with them at the Pelican. I'd already met your dad a couple of times but this was the first time I got to sit down and really talk. He's great and now I know where you get your charm.

We must have talked for two hours. He told me all about you and about how you and Donnie-Boy grew up and were like brothers. I had no idea that y'all were that close, like getting the trench mouth together and all. He also told me how Donnie-Boy gave you the nickname Tuck, though I think it embarrassed him a little. It took him a long time to explain it. Now I know why you never got around to explaining it to me. But, heck, I know what THAT word means.

I'm a big girl. I got the joke right away. I can understand why your mom doesn't like that nickname.

But from now on it's also going to give me some naughty thoughts about you each time I hear your name. I hope this letter is not getting to you too much, know what I mean. But I kind of hope it is a little bit. I miss you so much.

Like I said, it was a wonderful meal and they paid for the whole thing, of course. Your dad also told me how he and Miss Mary worry about you so much. You, Johnny and Donnie-Boy's names are often mentioned at Mass both in Eunice and Mamou. I say extra prayers for you each night, including the one to St. Joseph you sent me a copy of. I almost have it totally memorized.

Cindy, a friend of mine from Ville Platte that you never met, goes to LSU-E with me. She, too, is dating a soldier in Vietnam. He's a gunner on a helicopter. She and I have a lot in common and often find ourselves defending what y'all are doing over there. We get left out of a few things at school because of y'all. They say y'all are fools for being over there. But that's OK. We figure the two of you are worth it. Cindy's boyfriend will be back in less than six months. I still have to wait on you for another nine months. But, yes, I am willing to, and will, wait. You just make sure you come back in one piece…and with no pieces missing. You hear?

Some of the guys keep asking me out, especially that Timmy Tate. But I just remind him of the night back at the Peacock and he backs off.

Tuck, darling, if there is anything you can hold on to over there, a reason you need to persevere, it is this…my love for you. I have to go study now, big algebra test tomorrow. Just wish you were here to "tuck" me in. Love and kisses from the World, Anna

P.S. You've said before that if I don't hear from you for a while, it is because you're in the bush. If so, keep me in your heart. The letters can wait. But I'll keep writing. Also, please try to get Johnny to write to Uncle Wilfred more often. He is so lonely and needs them.

PART 3
The Crucible

He knows of their fear in the forthcoming fight.
Soon there'll be blood and many will die.
Mothers and fathers back home they will cry.
Sky Pilot, The Animals

CHAPTER 39

The Da Krong Serpent
FSB Shepherd, R.S.V.N.
April 10, 1969—8 a.m. local time

The swarm of twin-bladed locusts rose from the steel floor of Vandegrift Combat Base. The angry horde gained altitude and swung to the south, carrying in their bellies the elements of Kilo and Mike companies of the Third Battalion/ Ninth Marine Regiment.

India of 3/9 would join their sister units in the bush the next day. Battalion command, led by Lt. Col. Roy "Chief" Schiefer, also rode along on this one—Operation Utah Mesa.

The departure of the more than two dozen CH-46 troop carriers had required precise timing and swiftness because of the daily rocket attacks, which had increased in occurrence. The brass feared a major assault on Stud was imminent.

"It's going to be OK, it won't fall apart," Tuck shouted to Alex, the newbie from Kansas City who sat to his right. "These 46s are tough birds but rough on the butt."

Alex smiled and adjusted the quick-release straps of his frame pack.

"How far we going?" Willie shouted to the man seated next to him.

Donnie-Boy looked up from his map. "Oh, about 8 to 10 miles southwest as the crow flies. That's all. We'll be there any minute...fire support base named Shepherd, a little more than five miles southeast of Khe Sanh."

The flight would take less than 30 minutes from the time the Marines ran onto the back ramp of the rumbling chopper at Stud until they hopped into the elephant grass of the landing zone.

"The LZ's been a little hot lately. So they're not going to land, just hover a few feet off the ground. We'll have to hop off," Donnie-Boy shouted back.

"Doesn't sound too bad," Willie replied, buckling his helmet's chinstrap.

"Ever do it with 75 pounds of gear on your back?" A three-foot jump was like a 20-foot leap when saddled with a full field load.

"No."

"Piece of cake." Donnie-Boy grinned and pointed out the small round window. "Coming up on it now. See the yellow smoke?"

A dozen grunts below were bailing out of the back of a CH-46 like the one carrying Ike and Donnie-Boy's squad of 12 grunts. The Marines below jumped awkwardly into the swaying elephant grass, awash in the downdraft of the helicopter.

Tuck tapped Mike on his shoulder and looked over the newbie's gear while their chopper circled the LZ. It all appeared to be in place: four bandoliers filled with 300 rounds of ammunition, most of them jammed into a dozen magazines; six grenades—four frags, one illumination and one smoke. There was a two-and-half pound Claymore mine in a pouch; a three-pound, 60-millimeter mortar round strapped to the top of his frame pack; a pound of C-4 plastic explosive and six canteens full of water around his waist. He also toted an entrenching tool and a rucksack filled with a poncho and Snoopy blanket, up to six boxes of C-rations and other personal items. He held in his arms a black, 5.56mm, M-16 assault rifle. And at some time during the operation, Mike would have to carry a can of 200 rounds of 7.62mm machine gun ammunition for Johnny's M-60 and an M72 LAAW—a Light Anti-Armor Weapon, best described as a telescoping one-shot, throw-away fiberglass and cardboard bazooka.

The bittersweet part of it all was that Mike's water and C-rations would get lighter when he got thirstier and hungrier.

Temporarily designated as squad radioman, Willie's load was even heavier. His powerful build allowed him to shoulder the extra 25-pound burden of the PRC-25 field radio.

Ike stood at the rear of the chopper on final approach. "Remember, when you hit the ground follow your fire-team leaders and di-di the hell off the LZ. There'll be others on the ground to direct you up the hill to the firebase."

The pilot of the CH-46 had been in Vietnam only a week. His palms sweated and his eyes flitted while they searched the tree line near the LZ for muzzle flashes. He pulled back on the cyclic and flared the Sea Knight's nose. The chopper descended to the small grassy hill about 200 yards north of FSB Shepherd. He lowered the ramp of the Sea Knight, but failed to notice it was still eight feet off the ground.

Ike paused and waited for the ramp to draw closer to the ground, but the chopper did not move. The men gathered closely around Ike and the additional swaying of the chopper forced him to lose his balance and jump. He landed on his wounded butt and let out a yelp, along with a string of epithets. He reached up saluted the pilot with one finger.

Next off went Tuck, Mike, Willie and then Alex. All fell to their knees upon landing. Willie forced himself to roll with the heavy prick on his back. The squad's other fire team—Matt Gonzales, Glenn Auburn, Carl Kyle and Tony Blake—along with Johnny and Danny also fell to the ground in an ungainly fashion. Kilo 2 Alpha lay sprawled across the LZ.

Donnie-Boy was the last to make the leap and glided like a leaf on a fall breeze, landing gracefully on both feet. Tuck shook his head and simply wondered.

"Welcome to the bush, fellas," a grinning Donnie-Boy shouted to the newbies, sweeping his arm in the direction of the firebase. "Well, come on, get off y'all's ass and move it."

The squad responded. "Ow, shit," Matt cried out and fell back. He grabbed his right ankle.

Ike rushed to the fire-team leader's side. "OK, man?"

"Crap, I don't know. I felt something pop but it didn't hurt too bad until I tried to get up. Now it hurts like a bitch, man."

"Aw, shit," Ike shouted, shaking his fist at the disappearing swarm of locusts. "Damn you, you ignorant cab drivers. Get him up. Carl and Glenn, help him up the hill. Doc Wild's gonna have to look at that. Can you make it, Matt?"

"Sure, I'll make it up the hill, but I don't know how much farther. It feels like it's swelling up real bad. My boot's getting tight." Matt grimaced. "Might be broke."

"Shit, shit, and double shit." Ike spun around, lamenting his squad's continued bad luck. "Before y'all came along, I'd already lost three guys. One got malaria and ain't comin' back for a month or more. Another went on R&R, fell out of a whorehouse window, and broke his shoulder. And another guy rotated back to the World, the lucky shit. Now this."

"Jay Mac?" Donnie-Boy asked.

"What?"

"The guy that fell out of the window. That was Jay Mac, right?"

"Yeah, how'd you hear about that?"

"Story like that can't be kept a secret." Donnie-Boy smiled, slinging his M-16 over this shoulder. Ike laughed and slapped Donnie-Boy on the arm.

"Well, with the gun team, me and you, and the others, that makes 11, if Matt can't make it....Willie, come here, I need to radio up ahead and tell 'em to find Doc Wild," Ike said.

Kilo 2 Alpha limped its way single file up to FSB Shepherd.

•

It was larger than most firebases. It boasted two batteries of 105mm artillery and was often the jumping off point for Marine operations in the area. Shepherd sat atop a 200-meter hill overlooking the headwaters of the Da Krong River, which picked up the flow from the Quang Tri River that looped in from the north.

The Da Krong River fed a valley bordered on the east and north by dense tropical rain forests that covered steep mountains. Grassy hills and relatively smoother terrain lay to the west and south.

The valley, and Shepherd along with it, possessed a mix of strategic values. Not only was Shepherd five miles east of Khe Sanh, but it was also about seven miles north of a portion of Laos that jutted a nose of its country into Quang Tri Province. That geographic advantage provided the NVA with yet another way to smuggle supplies from the north. Intel believed that an extensive tunnel complex honeycombed the valley. They surmised these tunnels contained and provided the stage for the rocket attacks on Stud.

"Well, just as I figured, our bad luck is holding," Ike told the members of Kilo 2 Alpha which gathered on the edge of Shepherd for a noon squad meeting with Sgt. Gaines. "Doc Wild says Matt's ankle is broken and he's going back to Stud. He'll be out up to six weeks. Shit."

Ike took the last drag on his unfiltered Camel cigarette and tossed it onto the red clay. He ground it out, twisting his foot with a grunt. "Tony, you take over the team."

"Sure thing, Ike," said the short but powerfully built black Marine who liked to shave his head. Tony Blake was quick with a smile. "But can I keep my blooper? Really like that thing."

"Yep, not going to change weapon assignments now. But do me a favor, start training Alex over in Tuck's team on how to use that grenade launcher, just in case."

Tuck shook his head while taking a sip from his canteen. "Don't think so. Alex is too good a shot with the 16 to waste on a blooper. I'd rather he train Mike on the 79."

"I roger that, Tuck. Tony, work with Mike. OK, fellas, listen up. Sarge, they're all yours."

Tuck looked at Donnie-Boy and whispered. "That's a bit odd." Donnie-Boy shrugged, bringing his finger to his lips.

Gaines shuffled his contour map and oriented it with the river and hills surrounding the firebase. He knelt and then laid it on the ground, anchoring the four corners with clods of red clay. Kilo 2 Alpha circled around Gaines, who picked up a short stick to point out the features.

"Intelligence figures the rockets peppering Stud—about 10 miles to the north right up here—must be located in the northern and central portions of the Da Krong Valley, down here where we are now." Gaines tapped on their current position. "They also figure the NVA must be moving in beaucoup troops through the Khe Sanh area over here and through the tunnels from nearby Laos down here. They think the gooks might want to do a Khe Sanh number on Stud.

"Kilo's job is to sweep from here to the east about three miles, where intel feels the rockets are located. Mike Company will be working parallel to us about a mile or so to the south. Together we'll sweep several of the larger peaks in the area, and then we'll all come back here in a few days and jump off to the south toward Laos. After that, it'll be a matter of going where ever the gooks show themselves," Gaines explained. "India 3/9 is going to be on battalion reactionary alert in case we get in it over our heads. Any questions?"

"Sarge, these hills look awfully rugged," Tuck noted, pointing to the closeness of the map's contour lines. "How long they figure this op's gonna take?"

Ike jumped in. "They don't get much steeper and tougher in the Nam. This one's gonna be a bitch, Tuck, humpin' like you never humped before."

"As to how long," Gaines said. "As long as it takes, the skipper told me."

"And it ain't gettin' no cooler," Donnie-Boy said, taking a swig from his canteen.

"Fellas," Ike, an Atlanta native, advised, "the monsoons are over now and it was a dry year already. From now on it's gonna get hotter'n a skeeter's ass on a matchstick. Those of us from the South have an idea of what it's gonna be like. You Yankees, well, let us know how you're doing. We have to avoid heat casualties on this big hump, but at the same time, try to conserve your water and don't forget to take your salt tablets."

"Any other questions?" Gaines added.

"Yeah, what's the order of march?" Donnie-Boy mumbled, expecting bad news.

"Afraid you might ask." Gaines hesitated, then stood. "Second platoon on point."

"Oh, *la merde.*" Johnny groaned. "*Fils putain.*"

Except for the newbies, groaning heads shook in disgust.

Ike elaborated. "The boss wants to look good because he wants his gold leafs and the skipper wants out of the boss' doghouse, so they volunteered us to take the point. Right, sarge?"

"I can't be saying things like that about my superiors, but your logic can't be argued. Fellas, I hate to say this. But the reason I met special with you guys and explained this mission personally is because…"

"Oh, shit, here it comes," Tuck said, lacing his fingers behind his neck. His skin was still tender and he recalled briefly the searing explosions that caused the burns on the last mission that went awry.

Gaines folded his combat map and slapped it on his knee to clean it off. "Because we need our best squad on the point, and that's you guys. Ike, you've got some of the best shots and gunners in the platoon."

Ike nodded, shook his head and then tilted his face toward the sky with eyes closed. "Any chance of replacements. Squad's short-handed."

"Sure, I'll do what I can," Gaines advised. "But we're moving out in one hour. The skipper wants us to make a couple of klicks before sundown, mostly grass to start. Probably will be tomorrow before I can scare up a few grunts for you."

It was Ike's turn to do the dirty work—having to pick the man, or men, who would walk point for a company headed into Indian country.

"Donnie-Boy, Tony, Tuck, come with me," Ike said, waving for the trio to join him off to the side. They found shade near an ammo bunker and sat.

Walking away, Donnie-Boy shouted to the other squad members. "Y'all start checking over your gear and weapons. Make sure your boots are on snug and don't have any rocks in 'em. Change your socks, if you got any. Then get over to the water bull to fill your canteens."

Ike took out his small carton of Camels and offered them to the trio. Tony thanked him, took a cigarette and lit it up. Donnie-Boy and Tuck shook their heads. "Oh, yeah, forgot, you guys don't want to ruin your health. But here you are, volunteered and in the Nam. Ha."

They laughed at Ike's perverse logic.

"OK, who's the best point man you got?" Ike asked and lit up. "And I don't mean some newbie who'll wake up the whole jungle and die trying to hack away the entire bush."

"Jason was the best," Tuck offered. "I was his guardian angel most times."

"Yeah, well, Jason ain't here no more, now is he? But

from what I remember Chuck telling me, Jason was teaching you pretty good. So, how about you taking the point? I know you're a team leader and all, but I sure would like someone I can trust up there, and a sure-shot at that."

Tuck hesitated and glanced at Donnie-Boy, who glared back with a mixed look of concern and confidence. He nodded. "Yeah, sure, but I want Alex over my shoulder. He's almost as good of a shot as me, plus he needs to learn some time."

"I'll be glad to walk third and spell Tuck some," Tony offered. "I used to walk some point and I'm used to the big hills back home in the Shenandoah. I can pace him."

Ike turned to Donnie-Boy. "How about you? We're short-handed and I'm having to improvise. I need experience up front. Can you walk No. 4 with the map?"

"I was hoping you'd ask—sure thing," Donnie-Boy said, winking at Tuck.

"OK, Donnie-Boy, let's have that newbie Mike follow you and then the gun team, big Willie with the prick, and me. Glenn and Carl can protect our rear. Damn, we sure could've used Matt.

"Sarge says he'll be walking between us and Redman's third squad. The skipper and his radio man will be near the front of Lightfoot's fourth."

"Wonder where Doc Wild's gonna be." Tuck said. "I hope close by."

"Humph, anywhere's my guess. He's a good doc, but he's still a flaky little squid," Tony said with a laugh, nearly choking on a drag from his Camel. The trio shared the laugh.

"Doc'll be just behind us with third squad—just about the middle," Ike advised. "Now get to your guys and make sure they're ready; we move out in little more than a half hour. And Tuck, thanks, buddy. We'll be watching out for you."

•

The first 90 minutes proved easier than Tuck first thought. The long Kilo Co. column had already marched a klick to the northeast before turning due east. Donnie-Boy passed the word up that Mike Co. was holding its parallel course slightly more than a mile to the south. Knowing where friendlies humped in the area was of obvious importance.

Tuck swatted at a swarm of swirling gnats. "Little shits, they never go away," he complained while struggling to brush away the elephant grass. "Just like the gooks. You might not always see them, but they're there. That's what the gooks are—gnats."

Walking point in elephant grass was physically exhausting but not a mental challenge. After Donnie-Boy pointed him in the right direction, Tuck started pushing aside the saw-tooth blades with his rifle. A few whacks with the machete cleared the thicker grass. The feet of a few dozen grunts trampled the path. Soon there was a neat trail for the remainder of the company to follow.

But perils loomed.

Tuck leaned forward to push aside a clump and tumbled into a large bomb crater hidden by the grass "Aaaaaaaah, shit," he cried out. He came to rest at the bottom of a 20-foot wide by 6-foot deep crater—scooped out by a thousand pounder.

The Da Krong area resembled a sort of zit-scarred lunar landscape since the siege at Khe Sanh. Artillery, B-52s, Phantoms, Cobras, Hueys and other weapons had annihilated anything that moved within a five mile radius of Khe Sanh.

"You OK," Alex shouted from the lip of the crater.

"Yeah, think so. Nothing broken. Just tangled up in all my gear," Tuck hollered from the bottom of the saucer-shaped depression. "Go on back and tell Ike I'm gonna need a break. And tell Donnie-Boy to get down here. I'm gonna need to get my bearings again."

"Gotcha." Alex turned back, leaving Tuck alone.

Tuck slouched on his back in the center of the crater where the tall grass had not yet taken over. Ten feet of red dirt separated him from the looming grass. His rifle sling, frame pack straps and bandoliers had ensnared him like a gnat in a spider's web. He needed help and decided to wait on Donnie-Boy. A gentle breeze drifted across the crater and caused the tall grass to sway gently. It gave Tuck a misplaced sense of contentment.

His machete had gone its own way when he began to tumble, and was stabbed into the dirt at a shallow angle about four feet to his right. He half rolled and reached out toward the sharp knife when he saw out of the corner of his right eye something slither. Tuck froze.

A thick, brownish-green snake about six feet long with a large, sinister head and yellow belly slid inches past Tuck's right arm. The viper slinked into a loose coil near his shoulder and he watched its flicking tongue sample the air. From pictures he remembered in a library book, he thought the serpent looked like a bamboo viper. Or was it a Russell's viper? At least it wasn't a cobra, they were much longer, darker and hooded. But didn't bamboo vipers also inject neurotoxin? Maybe. He could not remember now.

He wanted to call out, but he might startle the snake. What to do? The snake's head settled upon its body and appeared to want to take a nap. Tuck then noticed that he and his pack had created a small patch of shade. Perhaps the viper was seeking a cool spot to escape the afternoon sun. Heck, then why didn't the damn thing slink its ass back into the grass?

"Tuck, don't move, little buddy. There's a big ol' ass snake curled up right next to you," he heard Johnny holler from above.

"No shit," Tuck slowly said through gritted teeth.

"Why you think I'm just lying here like a frozen Popsicle and sweating buckshot?"

"Yeah, there it is," he heard Danny add. "Right next to his left leg."

"What?" Tuck nearly shouted, turning his head toward his left where he saw an even bigger green and yellow viper beginning to coil. "Oh, shit," he sighed.

"Hey, there's another one on the right side of him, too," Danny said, pointing. He shouted. "Hey, Donnie-Boy, come over here man. Tuck's in a world of shit."

"Shhhhh, damn it," Tuck hissed. "Don't spook 'em."

"What's the hold up here?" Donnie-Boy asked. "Alex said Tuck fell and...oh, shit." Suddenly, another viper slithered out of a small hole in the ground. It crawled over Tuck's right boot and took up residence. "Shit, he must be sitting on a nest, or something."

"O, St. Joseph whose protection is so great, so strong, so prompt..." Tuck whispered rapidly. *"Oh, shit, St. Joseph do assist me..."*

"What's all the commotion about?" Alex said, returning to the crater. "Oh, shit." He paused, and calmly counted. "One, two, and three of 'em. Well, I can take care of that."

Before they could turn to hush Alex, the Kansas City sharpshooter had flipped his M-16's selector switch to semiautomatic and taken aim. POP! His first shot picked off the head of the snake near Tuck's right shoulder; POP! The second round blew in half the serpent coiled near his left leg; and the third POP! lifted the remaining snake off the ground and away from his right boot. POP! A fourth shot ensured the third snake was dead.

Tuck sprang to his feet, despite the tangled mess, grabbed his machete and hacked at the still squirming serpents. "Take that you goddamned, slimy bastards. Die, you green pieces of shit...die, die, die."

Donnie-Boy slid into the crater and fired a half dozen rounds into the snake hole. It was over within seconds of

Alex's well-placed shots. Tuck's legs went limp and he fell back onto his knees. Donnie-Boy knelt beside him, and joined the grunts in nervous laughter. Unaware of the reptilian misadventure, the other grunts of Kilo Co. scrambled to seek targets. Some opened fire on imagined enemy; an exploding frag rocked the quiet afternoon.

Ike and Gaines sprinted to the crater. "Snakes, snakes—three of 'em. Big ones, but it's cool, it's cool," Danny shouted.

Tuck turned and hugged Alex, who had joined them in the crater. "Man, where did you learn to shoot like that in Kansas City?"

"I was born in K.C. But spent most of my life in Arizona. I used to shoot rattlers on the edge of an old golf course for extra money during the summer. The cash was good."

"Man, if I had a buck, I'd pay you right now," Tuck said, knowing he had found his guardian angel.

"And, by the way, snakes are deaf," Alex added.

•

Da Krong Valley, 6 p.m.: The shadows grew long when the sun settled into the hilly horizon. It would soon be time to stop and form that night's defensive perimeter. Six sent word to the lead element to steer its way up a narrow ravine flanked by two small but steep and heavily forested fingers. Once at the top of the hill, the company would routinely dig in for the night.

Two full squads of NVA soldiers waited in ambush along either side of the ravine. An enemy lookout had spotted the Marines coming from nearly a klick away and they hastily assembled their trap. Doan Tien and his mentor, Lt. Louie, lay on their bellies half way up the finger to the right. They had spent the better part of two weeks maneuvering into position along with the other elements of Col. Pham's battalion-sized force. They had reached the Da Krong Valley via an extensive tunnel complex, the likes of which Doan Tien had never imagined. Soldiers' quarters, mess halls, aid stations and vast weapons stores of rockets were hidden in the tunnel complex, which stretched for miles.

Although he felt guiltier each day for participating in the operation, his personal quest for revenge possessed his mind. Nor was he willing, however, to give his life in exchange for Uncle Bui's wretched soul. He simply had not found the right time or proper place.

Today, Doan Tien's dread of killing Americans reached a bewildering state. The Marines would be only yards away and it would be a slaughter. It was a sweetly laid trap. "Louie?"

"Shhh. They're less than a hundred meters away," Louie whispered. "What is it now? Worried about killing Americans again?"

"Yes. How is it you always know my mind?"

"Just don't get in the way of me killing them. That's good enough for now," Louie grunted, then cautioned. "Doan Tien, don't hesitate to protect yourself."

Doan Tien slowly nodded, his eyes fixed on the Americans.

The Marines entered the ravine. They joked among themselves and their weapons were not at the ready. Grouped too tightly, they would be easy pickings.

Fifty yards. Forty yards. "Let them get closer," Louie ordered.

Doan Tien looked into the boyish face of the first Marine in line. He bowed his head and thought of his father's words and of the courteous Marine captain who had paid them for the loss of Trau Gia. He could not allow the slaughter. He slammed an elbow into Louie's ribs, stood to expose their position and fired a short burst safely over the head of the point man.

"You stupid little shit," Louie hollered. He reached up, grabbed Doan Tien, pulled him to the ground and then shouted, "Open fire." Two dozen AK-47s stuttered to life and a score of ChiCom grenades rained upon the Marines.

Despite Doan Tien's warning, the point squad for Mike Co. 3/9 withered in the crossfire. The first four grunts—fully exposed in the ravine—died before they hit the ground. Two more died within seconds in the hail of grenades.

None of Doan Tien's comrades had suffered as much as a scratch.

He watched and admired the Marines advancing despite the murderous hail. They had reached within 20 meters of Doan Tien, when Louie called a retreat.

Doan Tien stood and then sprinted toward the camouflaged entrance. His foot caught on a vine and he tripped, falling face-first to the ground. Stunned, it took him several seconds to shake off the daze. He rolled over and looked back. A large, black Marine charged toward him with his M-16 blazing. Soil kicked up along Doan Tien's side and sprayed red dirt across his face.

Doan Tien knew what he had to do—what he must do. He sat up, brought his AK-47 to his shoulder and fired. The short burst carved a large hole in the chest of the Marine, who made no noise but fell hard to the ground. The American did not move again.

Suddenly, he found it hard to breathe. His body jerked helplessly backward. "I said let's get out of here. That means your stupid ass, too," the powerful Louie growled. He dragged Doan Tien toward the tunnel opening. Louie fired a long burst toward the Americans and then threw Doan Tien into the hidden entrance.

Louie quickly followed, shoving at Doan Tien's back. "Keep moving, they're going to blow every entrance they can find around here."

He ran. His mind alternated between the haunting image of the fallen Marine and the fear of what Louie might do to him when he stopped running.

Doan Tien ran on.

CHAPTER 40

The Hump
Da Krong Valley, R.S.V.N.
April 11, 1969—7:30 a.m. local time

Still on the point, Kilo 2 Alpha—the first squad of second platoon—hacked its way 30 minutes into a hump up the steep northern slope of Dong Cho. Reports from Mike Co. had trickled in since the previous evening. A four-minute firefight had claimed 10 KIAs and 6 WIAs. The casualty list included a platoon sergeant and commander, but no enemy kills.

The news had also kept Kilo 3/9 on full alert throughout the night. With no more than two hours sleep, the tired grunts were short tempered.

Topping off at 824 meters, Dong Cho was among the highest peaks between Stud and the mountains of the Da Krong Valley. Intel believed the reverse slope, or southern side of Dong Cho, harbored the rockets and thus targeted it as the main culprit.

Marine F-4 Phantoms and Cobra gunships had pounded the lush Dong Cho for several days, but as Kilo's Boss King liked to say, it needed to be "tidied up a bit." Intel had advised them that when they reached the summit, they'd be able to see all the way to Stud on the north, and as far as Shepherd and maybe even Khe Sanh to the west.

Tuck was not interested in the panorama. He only knew that he had started the morning at the 144-meter level and would have to climb another 700 meters by nightfall.

Alex's eyes swept the dense jungle ahead. "Kind of spooky, huh?"

Tuck chopped off the long leaf of a banana tree lashing at his brow and threw it aside. He then grabbed the trunk of a smaller but sturdier tree to pull himself up one more meter.

"Well, what you think?" Alex asked again.

"What? All those guys in Mike buying it yesterday?"

"Yeah, that, and the fact you know Charlie's out there watching us, too. Right now, even."

"I try not to think about that," Tuck sighed, scouting ahead. "I'm just trying to hack our way through this shit and at the same time keep us going in the right direction. I leave that kind of thinking and worrying to you, my guardian angel," he lied.

Donnie-Boy caught up with Alex and Tuck and pulled out his map. "Hold up just a second fellas. Tuck, come see." He pointed to a small blue line on the map. "Listen. You hear it?"

Tuck cupped his ear, and then smiled. "Yeah, sounds like a waterfall."

"Yep, right over this finger here about 200 meters or so. Sounds like a big one, too." Donnie-Boy checked his compass heading. "The jungle's gonna clear out in just a bit now. I'll get Mike and we'll walk two abreast until we get past this thing. Y'all go on ahead now and keep your eyes peeled."

Tuck and Alex hacked and clawed through thorny trees and ancient vines for another 15 minutes before reaching the top of a fingerlike hill, where they were treated to one of Vietnam's natural wonders. The waterfall cascaded for nearly a hundred meters, twice splashing on jutting rock ledges that ever so slightly veered nature's faucet off its centuries old course. It would have made a grand postcard—if only Tuck had not run out of film. The moving water's white sound also masked the ringing in his ears.

"What a sight this must be during the rainy season," Alex observed.

"Wow," Mike added when he caught up with the pair. "Never saw anything like this in Chicago. Except maybe when someone ran over a fire hydrant."

"Yeah, too bad it's wasted on such a shithole of a country," Tuck said. "You know, Alex, if I live through this mess, I just might come back here some day, just to visit. It really is a pretty country, you know." He took another long look. "OK, let's get on down to the stream."

With a 75-pound load strapped to his back, going downhill required almost as much of Tuck's energy to keep him from toppling forward as it did struggling to hump up. Yet, downhill had never won a debate over which was tougher—up always won, hands down.

Gawking at the sights, Tuck waded into the cool, knee-deep stream. He noted the parrots were squawking their normal insults, meaning they were probably the only ones in the area. An ambush was unlikely now because the NVA would probably wait until later in the day when the grunts were too exhausted to effectively fight back.

"Ohhh, shit," Tuck cried out when he stepped into a hole that swallowed him up to his eyebrows. He stuck his rifle over his head and sought stable footing. His feet slipped on the rocky bottom, and he felt his helmet, buoyed by captured air, begin to float off his head. He knew not to panic, but he needed help, and needed it fast. He simply wasn't going to float up and couldn't swim with his heavy load.

Nearly as fast as he had submerged, Tuck exploded to the surface like a rocket spurting into the sky. He sputtered and spit, hearing laughter through his draining ears. Donnie-Boy had a hold of the back of his flak jacket and was standing there—with that knowing grin.

"Th-thanks, Donnie-Boy," he managed to say, spitting. "At least there were no snakes."

Laughter erupted again. "OK, that's enough, fellas. You OK?" Donnie-Boy asked. "Still want the point? I can call Tony up for a while."

"No, I'm alright. Thanks again." He checked out his M-16. It was still dry. "Let's go, Alex."

Alex and Tuck had taken three more steps toward the waterfall when the stream roiled up between them. "Yiiiiiee, what the shit," Tuck shouted, and Alex also screamed. What looked like a four-foot crocodile with a long skinny snout bolted toward the bank and scurried into the brush.

"Shit, shit, shit. Who needs the damn gooks," Tuck shouted, entering in the throes of a tantrum. "We got hidden craters, we got snakes, we got bottomless pits and now we got goddamned gators. What next? Tigers? They can shoot me, Lord. Just don't let 'em eat me."

Tuck waded to the bank and slumped to the ground. He put his hands over his eyes and began to quietly sob.

"Tony, take over the point for a while," Donnie-Boy ordered.

"Will do," Tony replied, looking back at Tuck. "He's just played out."

"What's going on up here?" Ike said. He, Johnny and Danny had caught up.

"Nice waterfall," Johnny said.

"It's OK, Ike, I got it under control. I'll fill you in later," Donnie-Boy explained. "Just a little too much pressure over the last 24 hours, that's all. I'll take care of him. He'll be fine."

Donnie-Boy knelt beside Tuck and put his arm around him. He pulled him closer and whispered in his ear. "It's the fourth quarter, little brother, suck it up. The team needs you. And I don't think Anna would like to see you like this, either."

Tuck laughed uneasily. "Yeah, I'm OK now, thanks. Just had to let it out. Chuck, Jimmy B., the point, the snakes, that deep water, the...whatever that was. Just building up. I just had to let go for a minute. I'm fine now."

"I know you are. Now, get all your shit together and get on up there and walk third behind Tony and Alex. I'll be right behind you," Donnie-Boy added. "We got a long hump ahead, and it's getting hotter. But before you go, turn around."

"Yeah, what is it?"

"Leeches."

"Leeches? What about leeches?" Tuck said, his eyes widening. Donnie-Boy reached out toward his neck.

"You can now add leeches to your bitch list," Donnie-Boy said. "Two big black ones right here on the side of your neck."

"Awww, shit." Tuck was on the verge of giving up.

"Hold still, little brother, hold still," Donnie-Boy said. He borrowed a lit cigarette from Mike and touched the bloodsuckers with its fiery tip. "Oooh, look at all that blood."

The two leeches released their suction, but their anticoagulant saliva caused Tuck's blood to briefly flow. The suckle marks had swollen and left a pair of welts. It looked like a vampire had bitten Tuck. "St. Joseph, I hope leeches are on your protection list," he mumbled.

Cautiously climbing the algae-covered rocks alongside the waterfall had taken nearly an hour. Three grunts had fallen, suffering extensive bruises, but no broken bones or serious cuts. By 1500 hours, Tuck had returned to the point and was making good time because the jungle grew sparser at 500-meters. But Dong Cho had also gotten steeper. Still, he picked up the pace.

Alex and Donnie-Boy were close by, ready to assist. But Tuck had another helper. *"O, St. Joseph do assist me,"* he quietly repeated his mantra each time he grabbed another tree and willed his way up the mountain. With strength-sapping swings of the machete, he hacked away at clumps of vines and overhanging branches. This part of the hump had been so draining that Tuck, Tony and Alex alternated 20-minute shifts.

"Hey, Alex, ready for a little more point?" Tuck called down to his guardian angel.

"Sure, can't wait," came the sly reply.

Tuck moved over to the side of the trail and reached down to hand the machete to Alex when Donnie-Boy warned. "Get down, quick." He put two fingers to his eyes and then pointed to the east. They followed the signal. "About 200 meters over, just below us. Two gooks running."

"Got 'em. Bet they're scouts," Tuck said. "Alex, think we can take 'em out from here?"

"Yeah, but..."

"But, you never shot a man before, right?"

"Yeah, that's right. Don't know if I..."

"You two talk ethics later," Donnie-Boy growled. "Right now, I want y'all to do like the Greeks and Romans used to do and kill the messengers. Pass the word down the line to the skipper for them not to freak out when we open fire."

Tuck and Alex crouched behind a tree with low, sturdy branches to use as supports. The fleeing soldiers were about 250 meters away and crossing a chemically defoliated area.

"On my mark, Alex, count of two, OK?"

"I'm ready, I got the one on the left."

"You bet. It's a turkey shoot," Tuck said calmly. "One and two."

P-POP! The two shots nearly went off as one. They were the only shots needed because the man on the left fell after a small puff of smoke exploded from his back. Alex had killed his first man. The second man died at the same instant when a spray of pink spewed from the right side of his head.

"Good time to take a break," Ike said, joining them. "Donnie-Boy get four guys down there to check out those good gooks. And send some guys with experience, make sure they're dead before checking out the bodies. Look for a radio, too. See if they're carryin' papers."

Tuck watched Glenn and Carl lead the four-man team down the hill. Partly sprinting and sometimes sliding, they arrived within minutes and began searching the bodies.

"Nice shooting, cowboys," Ike said, turning to Tuck and Alex. "Tuck I'd heard about you, Chuck bragged on you enough. But Alex, I thought you just shot snakes, podnuh."

"Me too," Alex said, his voice cracking and his eyes glazed. "My whole family's real religious, heck, I've got an uncle who's a priest and my aunt's a nun. I even tried the seminary for a year myself. There's a piece of me that feels... well, you know, kinda guilty," he added, wiping his eyes. "Don't worry, I'll do my part."

"Yeah, I'm sure you will," Ike said, nodding toward the dead men. He patted Alex on the back. "Good job, Father Alex."

Tuck flinched when Carl unexpectedly ripped off a burst of automatic fire below. Glenn and the other two men joined in. "There, there, he's over there," they screamed and pointed farther down the hill. They fired again. "Shit, shit."

"Damn, he must have got away," Ike cursed, and then stood up and hollered. "Get their radio and then get your asses back up the hill. Hurry up, damn it."

Ike turned to Donnie-Boy and Tuck. "I'm goin' back to fill in the sarge and the skipper. We still got a mountain to climb. So let's get moving when those guys get back up here."

Tuck looked up toward the crest of Dong Cho. "Only got about another 100 meters or so. Steep, but looks like we ought to be there in less than an hour. What you think, Donnie-Boy?"

"You the point man. Let's go."

CHAPTER 41

In the Genes
Da Krong Valley, R.S.V.N./Tunnel complex
April 12, 1969—11 a.m. local time

"What in the hell were you thinking about yesterday?" Louie asked. Even though they were crouched against a wall in a secluded part of the tunnel complex, he chastised Doan Tien with arms flapping and head bobbing like an angered goose. "Did you think you were going to spare a few Marines by jumping the gun? They didn't have a chance no matter what you did. You're lucky none of my men were killed. If one had died because of your antics, you wouldn't be breathing today and still having a chance at your precious revenge. Do you understand me?"

Doan Tien raised his bowed head, stared Louie in the eye and nodded. "Yes, I understand completely. I also understand I killed an American."

"Yes, you ended up killing one of them yourself," Louie continued. "But it looked to me like self-defense. If you had just done as I said, you wouldn't have had to shoot anyone. You could have saved all your bullets for good ol' Uncle Bui. Damn, you are hardheaded, son."

Doan Tien's skin flushed upon hearing Louie refer to him as "son." Louie had always been a friend, but never had he endeared himself. It struck a chord in his heart. Louie was indeed becoming his surrogate father, and as such, he would honor him like he had his father.

Louie reached out and pulled Doan Tien to his side. His voice mellowed. "Just listen to me, son, I'll get you the revenge you crave and then I'll get you out of this mess. OK?"

"Mess? What do you mean, Louie?"

"Doan Tien, when all this Bui stuff is over, I want you to 'chieu hoi' and give yourself up to the Americans. You'll be much happier with them."

"And what of you? Are you going to desert also?" Doan Tien's question was more of a pleading. "If I do, please do yourself. You're too old to continue fighting."

Louie scoffed at the observation with a snort.

"Maybe there, you, too, could confront your demons and find another means to deal with your hatred. Louie, I am honored to be your friend, perhaps more than a friend. I don't want to see you hurt for my sake."

Louie pulled him closer. "We'll see, son, we'll see when the time comes."

A muscular young corporal, one of Pham's bodyguards, approached. They looked up. The man was staring at them with a smirk. "Lt. Louie and Pvt. Doan Tien?"

They nodded.

"Come with me," he ordered. "Col. Pham says he has business with you. Now."

Louie looked at Doan Tien. "*La merde*, this is not good."

They rose and trotted hunched over, following the corporal in the semidarkness. They padded through the damp passageways for 200 meters, taking turn after unfamiliar turn until they reached the entrance of a room twice as large as normal rooms in the complex. Better ventilated, the room did not emit the familiar dank smell, but cigarette smoke hung thick in the air and layered itself close to the high ceiling. Smoking in the tunnels was reserved for staff officers.

Two guards with AK-47s blocked the entrance. Doan Tien craned his neck to see above their outstretched arms and spotted another pair of guards gripping a young private by his upper arms. Pham stood in front of the boy, brandishing his Bowie knife and puffing on a hand-rolled cigarette. The putrid smoke drifted across the young captive's face and he coughed.

Major Chen, a Chinese Communist adviser who had joined the battalion when they had rendezvoused near Khe Sanh, observed from a short distance. Handsome in a Western sort of way and a full head taller than Pham, Chen stood with one leg propped up on a straight-backed, wooden chair. His elbows rested on his raised knee and he passively smoked an American cigarette that smelled slightly less odorous than Pham's hand-rolled weed.

"So, tell me again. Why did you leave the area without the radio? Were you not sent to observe the Americans and immediately report their movements via radio and not in person, as you chose to do," Pham asked. He pressed his knife against the young man's bowels. "Because of this we have lost valuable time, and obviously, an element of surprise."

"Comrade colonel, I've told you snipers killed the sergeant and corporal who operated the radio," the private stammered. "I didn't know how to use the radio. I'd never been schooled in its use. I went along for security. So when they were killed, I knew my only chance was to run back here as fast as possible and report."

"But why didn't you bring the radio back with you?" Pham shouted. "Your stupidity has left in the Americans' hands a radio tuned to our battalion frequencies. Do you have any idea how much trouble it is to set up new frequencies and coordinate them with all our units?"

The youth, no more than a year older than Doan Tien, sobbed.

"Aahhhh," Pham said, shoving the soldier's forehead, "I have no more use for this one. Chen, what are we to do with him?"

Chen smiled crookedly with one side of his mouth, raised his right hand and then waved with his little finger. Pham nodded and turned to his restraining guards. They tightened their grips while Pham slid the pointed tip of his knife to the boy's throat. "You are fortunate. I cannot afford to lose any more men. But just to make sure you'll never forget such a thing as a radio again..."

Pham reached out and grabbed the forlorn soldier's right hand. With a quick slicing motion, Pham amputated the boy's little finger, dangled it in front of his face and then placed it in the breast pocket of the soldier's khaki shirt. A small red spot spread slowly across the bottom of the pocket while the dying digit bled out. The youth did not cry out. Only a loud gasp escaped him and he doubled in pain, tearfully grabbing at the bloody stump.

"Now, go, get out of my sight," Pham bellowed. "Go to the aid station."

The soldier scurried past Louie and Doan Tien without looking up.

"Come," Pham commanded, waving toward the guards blocking the entrance. Terror filled Doan Tien's eyes and heart. He looked at Louie, searching for hope in Louie's eyes.

Pham pointed to Doan Tien. "Take him," he ordered the two torture-chamber guards.

Doan Tien glanced about the room, from one soldier to the other. His eyes fell upon Louie, they begged for assistance. Louie stepped forward but an armed guard halted him.

"This is not about you, Louie," Pham growled in Doan Tien's ear. "Stand fast and watch how we deal with cowards and traitors."

Pham turned and looked at Chen. The sneer still pasted to his face, Chen watched the smoke of his cigarette curl upward until it reached the ceiling.

Pham stared into Doan Tien's eyes. "You are sure we've never met, my stupid young friend? I am so sure I know your face."

The smoke from the colonel's mouth engulfed him. "No, sir, I do not think so," Doan Tien said, coughing.

"I've been told by those who were there that you intentionally tried to foul up an ambush yesterday. They say you stood up in full view, giving our position away, before impotently firing over the Americans' heads. Is this true?"

"Col. Pham, I...I..."

Louie forced himself forward. "Col. Pham, it was my fault," he shouted. "My instructions to him were not clear. He fired too early, yes, but it was my fault—not his. He is not a traitor. Did he not kill an American Marine himself? I saw him do so."

"Is this true, private? Did you kill a Marine?"

Doan Tien labored to breathe. He could not speak, but nodded and then looked into Louie's eyes.

"But you did foul up an ambush that could have been far more successful had you not been so stupid. Stupidity is in-bred. It's in a family's genes. Maybe I shouldn't let you pass on that stupidity to someone else," Pham said, once again wheeling to face Chen.

Doan Tien furrowed his brow and looked toward Chen, wondering just who it was that was in charge of the disciplinary chamber.

Chen's smile grew into a full, haunting grin. He puffed on his cigarette, and then held out his right hand, palm down. He let his middle finger dangle, and then wiggled it.

"Good idea," Pham scowled. "Grab him and hold tight."

Pham pulled loose the belt holding Doan Tien's trousers. He reached inside with his left hand and grabbed Doan Tien's penis. The youth struggled without success.

"What a shame, such an ample source of pride," Pham laughed. He raised his big knife in a chopping fashion. Doan Tien's face blanched and his terror-filled eyes grew wide like boiled eggs on a pale platter.

"No, you cannot," Louie cried out. He pushed past the guards and dove toward the knife. He grabbed Pham's right arm and held it high over Doan Tien's head and exposed penis, still in the grasp of Pham's left hand.

Louie was much stronger than Pham, but the colonel was a wizard with his blade and schooled in the martial arts. With a simple twist of his wrist and a bob of his knee and head, Pham pirouetted and rose with his blade ominously pressed against Louie's throat.

Louie froze.

"Maybe it's you who should die today. I don't care how valuable you are to me. I will not tolerate such insolence and assault," Pham shouted. His spittle sprayed the face of Louie, again restrained by the door guards. A small drop of Louie's blood trickled from beneath the knife's blade at his throat. Pham pressed harder and Louie jerked backward.

"No, Uncle Bui, you must not!" Doan Tien shouted. Tears streamed down his cheeks.

Pham's head spun toward Doan Tien, his eyes bulged in disbelief.

Chen reacted slowly. The smirk faded from his face and he stood erect behind the chair.

"What's this you say, private? A lie to save your friend's life, maybe? For if it is, he will die this minute and you will lose more than just your dick. Tell me more. Now."

"My name is not Doan Tien. I've been living a lie for all these months. Yes, you do know my face. My real name is Pham Thuc Trai, third son of your late brother, Pham Van Loi, and my mother, Pham Tri Minh. We lived in Cam Lo before the Americans slaughtered my family."

Pham slowly turned back toward Louie. "Did you know this, too?"

Louie nodded, and then smiled and shrugged. "He said he wanted it to be a surprise."

Louie sighed when Pham slid the blade away.

Doan Tien collapsed into the arms of the guards.

"I just might believe you, if you can tell me..."

"I have been counseled by my Aunt Linh. She's told me much about you and has even confided in me about your special relationship. She also said that you are good in..."

"Enough," Pham ordered. "I am beginning to believe you...for now." He looked at the guards. "Release them. And you, young Pham Thuc Trai, pull up your pants." He looked down and grinned. "I guess I should have recognized such a prominent family trait."

Pham Thuc Trai pulled up his trousers. He tucked in his shirt, and looked at Louie, who was wiping blood from his neck with a rag handed to him by a guard. Trai saw Louie struggling to disguise his outrage.

"OK, nephew, so tell me why you have not come forward before today?" Pham asked, now courteously blowing his cigarette smoke in another direction.

"When I first joined the raiders, I immediately identified myself to Lt. Dang," Trai lied. A dead Dang would be a perfect scapegoat. "When I told him how my family had been killed by the Americans, he said that I should not speak of this and not tell anyone who I really was. He suggested the name of Doan Tien, a dead private he had known."

"How did you know that the Americans had killed your family?" Pham carefully probed.

"I was not at home when it happened, but Aunt Linh told me of it and showed me the evidence. See," Trai reached into his blouse pocket and pulled out a folded envelope containing the foil wrapper from the chocolate disk and several fibers of blond hair.

Pham smiled, recognizing the scalped hairs that he had planted at the scene. "Your Aunt Linh was always a smart one. It was proof enough for her, so it was proof enough for you, eh?"

"Yes, uncle, it was. Plus, Lt. Dang admitted to me that

he, too, had heard about the murder of my family through intelligence sources," Trai continued to weave his tale. "He said that some day, when it benefited both he and I the most, he would tell me more about his information. But until then, he told me to keep my identity a secret. So I did.

"I almost told you who I was the night after the battle near Cam Lo—after you executed Lt. Dang. But you were so furious, I dared not disturb the situation more."

Pham nodded. "And, did Lt. Dang ever share his secret information with you?"

"No, he died too soon."

"I see. Go on."

"It was not long after that night that I confided in Louie. He encouraged me to continue the charade because you were under great pressure in trying to lead this operation. He also suggested that I wait until I distinguished myself in battle, so as to impress you even more when I revealed myself to you." Trai laid it on thick. "And that is what I had in mind yesterday when I stood up and fired the first shots. But, now, I must admit, my soldiering—and aim—may not yet be up to that standard. For all of this I am sorry, my uncle."

"Is this all true, Louie?"

"As true as I'm hearing it now," Louie rasped, still holding the towel to his neck.

Pham glanced at Chen. "One more thing, nephew, do you know how your brothers died?"

Caught off guard, Trai hesitated. The truth might be helpful now.

"We never knew for sure. My father always insisted you had something to do with it. Honestly, there were times when I believed him and hated you. But, again, Aunt Linh counseled me." Time to lie again, Trai figured. "She explained that you had nothing to gain from killing them and that you had assured her, intimately assured her, that you had nothing to do with it. She said my father, and I hope I do him no dishonor with my words, was always jealous of you and your success."

"You do him no dishonor by telling the truth," Pham said, offering his own lies. "Your father was a great man and I grieved the news of his death. I even put a bounty on the heads of the Americans responsible for this atrocity."

Trai realized where his ability to lie came from.

"Nonetheless, I'm standing here before you now, honored to be your nephew, and ready to accompany you to your grave, if need be," Trai concluded, telling not so much of a lie.

Uncle/Col. Pham Van Bui hugged his nephew, Pham Thuc Trai. "Come. There is much more we have to talk about. You are my son now, perhaps even my aide," he said, glancing toward Chen, who shrugged and nodded his approval.

"But what of Louie," Trai asked when they turned to walk away.

Pham stopped and turned. "Louie, I have wronged you. You may return to your unit. Sorry about the neck."

Louie nodded acceptance and turned to go. "*Fils putain,*" he muttered.

●

An hour later Trai returned to the dark haunts of the tunnel complex and found Louie quietly squatting alone against the same wall they had shared hours before. He sat beside him.

Other soldiers sat close by but Trai knew that the worldly Louie spoke four languages. He whispered in the English he had learned as a child. "He make me corporal. I am to be aide." Tears welled in his eyes. "And he say he grieved for my father. Yes, I will kill that son bitch."

Louie looked up, rubbed the wound on his neck and replied in French-accented English. "But you only have one obstacle, *my* son." He paused. Trai looked into his eyes and waited.

"I just might kill him first." Louie reached out again, and pulled Trai closer to him.

"My dick still hurt." They shared the laugh.

CHAPTER 42

Assault on Sanity
Da Krong Valley, R.S.V.N./Atop Dong Cho
April 13, 1969—6 p.m. local time

Breathless and soaked with sweat and drizzle, Kilo 3/9 reached the summit of Dong Cho two days before on the afternoon of April 11. It settled into a defensive perimeter that evening. Its sister company, Mike 3/9, surrounded Dong Ta Ri, a peak two klicks to the south.

A fog bank formed the next morning on April 12 to "sock in" both mountains. When the eerie carpet of clouds crept up to within a hundred meters, the peaks of Dong Cho and Dong Ta Ri rose up as might volcanic islands in a placid sea. The fog's surreal visit continued for two days.

"It looks like a fuzzy white lake down there, like we could almost walk across it," Tuck said to Donnie-Boy while they prepared an evening meal of C-rations. He heated a can of pinkish pork steaks with a side order of something resembling white beans. He gently stirred and tasted. "Man, am I gonna fart tonight."

"Glad you warned me. Now I know where I'm gonna sleep—upwind," Donnie-Boy said. He opened a can of beans and franks. "Hmm, but I may outdo you. I'm having a can of fruit cocktail for dessert."

Tuck looked down into his can of pork and sighed. "Sure wish I had some good hot boudin or cracklins."

"Yeah, some good Johnson's Grocery boudin," Donnie-Boy added.

Danny's head popped up from his rucksack. "Boudin, what the hell's that? Sounds nasty."

"Ahh, but no way, *mon ami*," Johnny interjected. "It's some spicy rice dressing made with ground pork and stuffed into a casing to look like a sausage—a food fit for the Cajun gods. Umm, mmm. And damn you, Tuck, for making me think about it."

"And boiled crawfish wouldn't be bad either," Tuck added, fully knowing the impact.

Donnie-Boy tasted his beans. "Shit. Man, don't get me thinking about all the good stuff we're missing. That's worse than not seeing any round-eyed women for the past three months. Come to think of it, we've hardly even seen any women, period."

Tuck shrugged. "I know what you mean. Like, where's all the villages with the whores and all? And, where's all the marijuana everybody told us about back home?"

"I don't know, but it sure ain't up here," Donnie-Boy shrugged, waving his arms toward the peaks of the Da Krong Valley. "We've been in the bush too damn much. Ain't seen no mama-sans out here. I guess the women and pot stuff is down south or something."

It began to drizzle. "At least it waited until we were almost finished eating." Tuck looked up. "Thank you, God, now send me some boudin."

Donnie-Boy laughed. "We were supposed to get re-supplied today, but this weather's gonna screw everything up. Probably won't eat good for a few days. And I doubt if there'll be any boudin on the next chopper."

Danny and Johnny retreated to their hole when the shrouded sun settled behind the peak.

Darkness loomed and Tuck felt an uneasiness drift up from the artificial sea below.

"Donnie-Boy, tell me. Why haven't you ever settled on one girl? I know you can get any girl you want," Tuck asked, gobbling his bland C-rations. "By the way, got any Tabasco sauce?"

"Yeah, sure, here," Donnie-Boy said. He tapped out a few drops of the fiery hot sauce into his food and then tossed the small red bottle back to Tuck.

"Thanks." Tuck caught the bottle, juggled it and caught it again. "So, well, why not?"

Donnie-Boy nodded toward the little bottle. "Like that sauce, I like my women hot and spicy. Just never found one to suit my taste."

"Aw, bullshit, Donald Charles Hebert. That's a load of crap. What about Tina? What about Claire and Gail, or even Celeste or Cathy? They were great catches, real Sweetpeas. You could have had 'em at the snap of a finger. Sherry and Judy, all of 'em, Debra, hell I could make a list."

Donnie-Boy paused for a few seconds. He took a bite and then scraped at the bottom of the empty can of beans. "Maybe. Maybe they wouldn't want me. Ever think about that?"

"But you…"

"But nothing. We're close. OK? Like brothers even." He crushed the can and threw it aside. "Still, there are things you don't know about me. OK? And, no, I ain't queer."

His reaction surprised Tuck. It was a side of Donnie-Boy he'd never seen.

"Oh, never mind. Look, Tuck, you've got your Anna. And I'm happy for you." He knitted his fingers together. "Some day, if I'm lucky enough to leave this place alive, maybe I'll find my Anna. Until then, let's concentrate on getting you home to her," Donnie-Boy added. He stood and brushed off the back of his trousers. "I gotta go check on the others. Be back in a few minutes."

"Doesn't have anything to do with when you used to stick marbles up your butt and fart 'em out in the bathtub, huh?" Tuck called out. Walking away, Donnie-Boy whipped his arm behind his back and flipped him the bird.

"Guess not," Tuck shouted with a shrug, then tried again, in a quiet, serious tone. "What about those mumps?"

Donnie-Boy stopped in mid stride, paused briefly—and then continued on his way.

•

When Capt. King had ordered his exhausted company to set up temporary camp, he had also seized the opportunity to conduct a thorough search for the enemy rockets and tunnels.

The fog had brought with it a disquieting calm in the two days since Alex and Tuck killed the NVA scouts. An ambush by third platoon the night before had come up empty, and now Tuck watched 12 men from first platoon exit the perimeter on another ambush. The dozen Marines departed to his right and soon disappeared down the south slope.

The remaining squads and platoons linked to form a 100-man perimeter atop Dong Cho's oblong summit. Sgt. Gaines, along with the skipper and his radioman, dug in approximately 40 yards up the hill from Tuck's position. Boss King's company command post settled in another 50 yards up, near the peak.

"OK, fellas, same plan as last night," Donnie-Boy began when meeting with Tuck's fire team at about 10 p.m. "You and your team set up right here on the east slope. I'll be to your right 20 yards with Danny and Johnny. To your left about 20 will be Tony, Glenn, Carl, and Cpl. Ike. Y'all try not to shoot 'em."

Tuck waved off Donnie-Boy's dig and then briefed his team. "Willie, take first watch till midnight. I'll relieve you, then Mike and Alex will finish up." They nodded. "Now, try to get some sleep and hope this is another quiet one."

MY DYING BREATH

•

Tuck lay on his stomach on a chaise longue on the back patio of his dad's house. Anna, wearing a flak jacket, rubbed sun tan lotion on his bare back. Her small hands kneaded the tense muscles in his neck. "Tuck, Tuck," she cooed, "It's your turn to shoot the gooks. They're in the back yard, now. Here's your 5.56mm, gas-operated, semiautomatic M-16 assault rifle, silly."

"Tuck, Tuck, wake up, man. It's your watch. C'mon wake up," Willie quietly urged, gently squeezing the back of Tuck's neck.

"What gooks? Anna?" Tuck almost shouted. He bolted upright and saw Willie's silhouetted face. "Oh, uh, sorry about that. Man, I was back home."

"Yeah, I know the feeling. Hope to go there in a few minutes myself." Willie laughed softly and patted Tuck on the shoulder. "You awake? You OK?"

"Yeah, I'm OK. Any movement?" Tuck asked, rubbing his eyes.

"Nope, nothing at all, except for a few LSU Tiger snores from the house to the right. Sounded like Johnny." Willie laughed again. "G'night"

"G'night, Willie—and put your helmet on that big red head of yours."

Tuck, shivering in the thick fog that chilled the night, shook his head and again rubbed his eyes. He reached over and pulled his camouflaged Snoopy blanket around his shoulders. It amazed him how this thin, damp blanket could keep him so warm. And some grunts said it was a magic blanket. As long as you were wrapped in it, nothing could hurt you.

After reciting the prayer to St. Joseph, he focused on the task of standing watch—no sleeping, no letter reading, and no pulling on the ol' pud, he reminded himself. The business of living—standing watch—took precedence.

Tuck wriggled to get comfortable while sitting on the

back of his fighting hole. His feet dangled into the 3-foot deep by 4-foot wide pit. He surveyed the area directly in front of his position, which watched over a sharp slope covered by elephant grass. It looked so different in the daylight. He wished his team had trampled the high grass a bit farther out. The edge began only 10 yards away. He made a mental note to expand the inadequate field of fire the next day.

A nearly full moon shining above the ground fog cast elongated shadows across the elephant grass. It reminded Tuck of a scene out of a Saturday afternoon horror movie.

On any given night, the sounds of rain, rats and other nocturnal movements drifted from the grass and jungle underbrush. The clanking of metal or unusual rustling often signaled a visit by the enemy. It took grunts several weeks of intense listening to discern a creepy crawler from a stealthy sapper. Even then, the most experienced grunts didn't always catch on.

Forty-five minutes into his watch, Tuck noted a rustling in the grass about 20 yards to his right front. The seconds ticked furiously in his mind. He strained to listen. Two minutes later the elephant grass emitted a deep, guttural rumbling.

"Mike, Alex, wake up. Wake up," he hoarsely whispered after turning back to where the grunts slept. "Hurry up, come on down here. I think we've got a tiger outside our pos."

"Tiger. What you mean a tiger?" Mike almost shouted.

"Shhhh!"

"Aw, come on, don't shit us, man," Alex added.

"I shit you not. I'm telling you, it sounds like a damn tiger. Listen." He picked up a small clod of dirt from the damp parapet in front of their fighting hole. He tossed it in the direction of the phantom. The clod startled a large figure, which scurried forward about four feet and let out a low growl, and then paused again.

"Think we ought to frag it?" Mike asked. "The guys on the South Side would love to see a tiger paw, man.

"Hell no," Tuck spat. "If we miss, we're gonna have one mad tiger on our hands."

"Yeah, but we're armed to the teeth," Alex said.

"Right, but it's armed *with* teeth. And I ain't gonna take a chance of gettin' a piece of my ass bit off by a pissed-off tiger."

"Yeah, you right, man," Alex agreed. "Want to wake up Willie and the other holes?"

"Not just yet. Let's see what it does. Lock and load and unsafe your weapons just to make sure," he ordered the newbies.

The tiger continued to prowl and approached the edge of the high grass. The dark form, now more distinctive in the moonlight, took the shape of a large cat. It twice circled itself like a house cat on its favorite chair, plopped into a semi-reclining position and began to lick its paw. Its throat again emitted a low idling, growl. Tigers can't purr, Tuck remembered. "Oh, shit," he whispered. "Looks like he wants to camp out with us."

The grass to his right suddenly rustled again. He gasped and swung his M-16 in its direction. "Whoa, there. It's me— Donnie-Boy. Don't shoot," he said holding up his hands.

Tuck dipped his head in relief and sighed. "Have y'all heard it, too?"

"Yeah, it's a tiger alright," Donnie-Boy confirmed. "It's been prowling all around the perimeter. The company's radios are going nuts. They think there might be two, a mating pair or some shit like that. Boss King gave direct orders not to shoot 'em. He said if we have to kill them, he wants to do it himself."

Tuck pointed in the direction of the sound. "Well, I don't know if it's girl-san or boy-san, but one of 'em just took a seat about 15 yards that way."

"Y'all just sit tight, too. I'm gonna go see what the sarge and the skipper think. Remember, don't shoot unless it attacks. OK?"

The three grunts nodded. "And don't wake up Willie unless you have to."

Donnie-Boy returned less than five minutes later. "He still there?"

"Yep, you bet. It's lying down now," Tuck explained. "I think its mate might be close by, too. There was more growling just a few yards away from that one."

"OK, here's the plan," Donnie-Boy began. "The boss don't want us to allow the tiger, or tigers, to sleep over. So, on my order, we're going to each fire a three-round burst over them and see what happens. Hopefully, he and his friend will haul ass. If not, then we'll have to think about it a little more. Which means, we don't know what the hell we'll do next."

The four grunts readied their weapons and on Donnie-Boy's signal, each fired three shots above the tigers. The big cats leaped up with a loud roar and sprinted into the dense grass.

While the grunts relieved themselves with laughter, dozens of distant shots split the quiet evening. "Oh shit, the ambush got 'em," Tuck surmised.

"No, too far out. Plus, the ambush is on our right. The damn tigers must have flushed some gooks," Donnie-Boy figured. "Get ready, this might be a long night. I'm goin' back up the hill."

Ten minutes passed—nothing. Willie, roused by the gunfire, fussed at them for not waking him. "I wanted to see those tigers, man."

Four sets of eyes and ears scanned the elephant grass. The night's agenda no longer included sleep. A light rain began to fall from what Tuck had thought to be a clear sky.

The first shots erupted to their right at about 1 a.m. Unlike the distant shots fired earlier, they came from the site of first platoon's ambush. A staccato of M-16 and AK-47 fire tore into the darkness; an M-60 ripped the night. The dull thumps of ChiComs and the crisper whams of American fragmentation grenades punctuated the small arms chatter.

The firefight flared, then died out. The sudden quiet struck the grunts with as much terror as relief. Tuck heard panicked shouts—American voices—approaching the perimeter.

"I don't like this. Not one bit. That ambush should have held longer. Unless..."

"Unless what?" Alex asked, hastily slipping into his flak jacket.

"...there were too many. Overrun," Tuck whispered. "Fellas, get ready. Make sure you can get to your frags real quick. I'll stay in the hole. Y'all back up a few yards. We're too close to the grass. Now, go. And keep down." He motioned with a jerk of his thumb and shed his blanket. He pushed his helmet tighter onto his head. He closed his eyes. *"O, St. Joseph..."*

The gunfire roared in like a tidal wave, working its way from Tuck's right, across his front and then to his left. Explosions simultaneously flashed across at least one-third of the perimeter.

Like he had on the LP on Cameron Falls, Tuck saw the telltale sparks of two ChiComs flitting toward him. One landed 20 feet to his front right, the second only 15 feet to his direct front. They exploded in unison without harm, but rang his ears. He dropped into his hole and ripped a burst of automatic fire along the path of the ChiComs. A third grenade landed a scant six feet to his front left. The warm, concussive winds blew past his face, but again without harm.

"Get back here, Tuck, you're too close to the grass. Get out of that hole," Willie, the big Cornhusker, shouted. He lobbed a frag into the elephant grass. "Move it, so we can open fire."

"Roger that," Tuck shouted back. He crawled out of the hole to his left. His peripheral vision caught a glimpse of a fourth, and then a fifth ChiCom homing in on his position. One found its intended mark—his fighting hole. The other lit four feet to the left of him. The simultaneous explosions lifted him into the air and hurled him backward six feet. Several small bits of shrapnel stung his right side. It was like he had stirred-up a wasp nest. His helmet flew off.

Dazed, Tuck sat straight up. Confusion set in and his ears rang even louder. He struggled to focus. A large arm reached across his chest from behind and pulled him flat to the ground before two more ChiComs exploded within 10 feet. He then felt himself being dragged up the hill.

"Hey, you're OK, little brother," Donnie-Boy screamed into his ear. "Snap out of it."

"Huh, wha...?" his world was a giant whirring whistle of confusion. He was unsure if he wanted to return to the world of the lucid. Oblivion might have its advantages.

Donnie-Boy yelled again. "Come on, Tuck, get back into it."

"Uh, OK. OK. I'm OK, now." Tuck shook his head, looked around and blinked hard twice. His team busily returned fire while Donnie-Boy tended to him. "I'm OK now, just stunned a bit. Those damn things pack a wallop. Get on back to what you were doing."

Tossed from near the perimeter, the ChiComs combined with the rocket propelled grenades and mortar rounds landing atop the hill to rip the earth all around. Russet smoke, mingled with the light drizzle and fog, drifted past carrying with it the sweet smell of Composition-B—a main ingredient in high explosives. Like diesel fuel and gasoline, the pungent aroma had an intoxicating lure, a sort of acrid sweetness.

Donnie-Boy sprinted off to check the positions to the left and Tuck rejoined his team. Lying flat on their bellies, they fired in the direction of the deadly green tracers coursing overhead.

"Man, I gotta pee something terrible," Mike announced. "And I'm shaking all over inside, man. I'm so goddamned scared."

"Me, too," Tuck smiled. "You know, these gooks are surely trying to kill us tonight."

Mike managed a laugh before Willie cried out, "Ahhh, MOVE, left."

Two ChiComs exploded where Willie had been crouching. He leaped clear of the explosions. So did the remainder of the team. "Damn thing hit me in the head and bounced off."

"Next time wear your helmet," Tuck shouted.

"I ain't got it. Fell off when we were moving up here. Man, that's gonna leave a bump."

"You should be so lucky," Alex added.

The night suddenly brightened after the mortar team fired an illumination round. The incendiary burned with a loud hiss while it descended from the end of a small parachute. The attack tapered off. Only short bursts of automatic fire and sporadic explosions punctuated the night.

"They're gonna get down and hide now that we've got some good light. But God help us when that flare goes out," Tuck told the former newbies, now combat veterans.

"We'll be getting more illum coming from artillery out of Shepherd soon," Sgt. Gaines said, again having sneaked up on Tuck. "That'll give us even more light and it'll keep their heads down until Spooky gets here. Then that's their ass."

Gaines' explanation ended when the first flare flickered out. "Good luck, I'm headed to the Boss's position. Need to know more about what's going on." He was gone as quickly and silently as he had come.

The enemy attack resumed, as did Tuck's trembling. The explosions lessened on the perimeter but small arms fire intensified. Green tracers zipped overhead, making a popping noise when they split the air only inches above the prone Marines. "They must be running low on ChiComs," Tuck guessed. *"O, St. Joseph, whose protection is so great, so strong, so prompt before the throne of God..."* he prayed with his heart. His mind and body reacted as trained.

For another 40 minutes—an eternity in combat—the enemy pressed the Marines' lines but could not penetrate. Danny and Johnny coaxed their M-60 mistress, Gertrude, to bring down a murderous curtain of fire. The fusillade helped expose the enemy to the well-aimed fire of Tuck and Alex. Strong-armed Willie hurled more grenades. Mike blazed away on automatic.

"The gun team's OK. But why haven't we heard from Donnie-Boy or the guys to our left," Mike asked. "Think they're all dead?"

"Don't know, but I doubt it. The gooks aren't breaking through anywhere that I can see," Tuck said. Donnie-Boy couldn't be dead, he wondered with a shudder.

Suddenly, two bright artillery illumination rounds shrieked in from FSB Shepherd and burst overhead—again silencing the attackers. Tuck glanced at his watch—2:15 a.m. "Damn, we've been at it for nearly two hours," he whispered through gritted teeth. Will it ever end?

Tuck rolled onto his right side and then quickly back onto his belly. "Still need to pee?" he asked Mike, who lay beside him.

"Yeah, bad, too."

"Look, you're laying in elephant grass matted down nearly a foot thick. Just roll over, whip it out and let it go... like I'm doing right now," Tuck said. Relieved, he forced a smile. But the grin couldn't hide the dread in Tuck's eyes and heart. Anna, stay with me, please, he begged.

Mike returned the smile, fumbled with the fly of his

trousers and dug in. He smiled again. "Ahhhhh. Man, pissin' never felt so good."

"Well, better hurry up, the flare's about to go out."

Two more artillery flares exploded with dull thuds overhead. The area again grew brighter while the illumination rounds floated down, burning through the smoke and mist. Tuck caught a glimpse of at least three bodies inside the boundary of the elephant grass and less than 10 yards from his fighting hole. The flares dimmed again, but the enemy did not attack. Instead, he heard bustling and strange whispers throughout the grass.

"Shhh. Listen. They're out there talking gook, man. Damn, they're still out there. Regrouping, shit." The realization that the enemy had not yet given up chilled Tuck. The full-body trembling, that had momentarily ceased, returned. He could hardly swallow.

Shadows and voices suddenly turned into targets. Sprinting toward the fire team, a trio of NVA banshees wailed and blazed away with AK-47s. Four more rushed Danny and Johnny's position. At least two, maybe more, headed toward Ike's hole to the left.

The small men charging Tuck's position barely cleared the tall grass before Willie and Alex each fired a burst to drop two of the enemy. Tuck and Mike together blasted the head off the third man.

"Take that, you little pricks," Mike screamed, pumping a few more rounds into the lifeless bodies. "You don't mess with Chicago."

The four soldiers attacking to the right died just as quickly as the M-60 reached out and nearly severed them. Tuck heard Danny hollering, "Get some, Gertrude. Get some."

The NVA soldiers charging Ike's position on the left fared better, reaching the middle of the Marines. Two explosions erupted amid screams. Several more shots rang out before the attackers died. Dull thuds overhead brought new light.

"Help me. Hellllp me," a weak American voice whimpered from Tuck's left. He did not recognize the sobbing. How could he? He'd never heard his comrades' cry, only their laughs and curses. "Please, help," another Marine moaned. This time he recognized the voice—it was Ike.

"Oh, please, God, help me. Mama, mama, please," the first voice pleaded again. It had to be either Glenn or Carl—not Tony.

"We've got to get to them. They need help," Alex shouted.

"No, stay down. Don't give your position away," Tuck ordered.

"But they need us."

"That's what Doc Wild is for. He'll get to them," Tuck said, adding hopefully. "At least, I think he will."

"What if Doc Wild is hit? Then what?" Mike said, rising to go for help. Tuck reached up, grabbed the bottom of his flak jacket and pulled him down just before two AK-47s opened fire. The bullets churned up the matted elephant grass surrounding Mike.

"Damn it, I said stay down," Tuck ordered. "All of you. There's still a bunch of those bastards out there. It ain't over yet."

The wounded moaned again. Tuck squeezed his eyes shut. "Shit." A tear rolled down his cheek. His mind reeled. Where in the hell is Donnie-Boy? When is this shit going to end?

The darkness again thickened and sporadic gunfire chattered from around the hilltop. Several single shots whizzed over Tuck's team. One bullet struck Alex's canteen and another pierced Willie's stray helmet with an odd metallic ring.

Tuck did not notice the three running grunts until they

dove to his left side. "How's it going, little brother?" he was relieved to hear Donnie-Boy say. "Understand we got some wounded over here. You OK?

"I'm OK," Tuck sighed and then pointed to his left. "But I'm afraid Ike and those guys are hurt real bad. Mike tried to go help them but the gooks had him spotted. We liked to lost Mike."

"I got Doc Wild and Sgt. Gaines with me. We're going to check them out as soon as Spooky gets here. That'll be any minute. They say it carries big time illumination."

"Glad to hear that. This shit's startin' to get serious," Tuck said, his grin quickly wiped away by yet more moaning. "Y'all get on over to 'em quick. OK, Doc?"

Three more artillery flares exploded overhead and washed the area with fresh light.

"Sure thing, Tuck. Sure thing," the Navy corpsman nodded before tilting his head to study the side of Tuck's face. "You been hit?"

"Yeah, I took a little shrapnel in my right side. I'll be OK, don't think it's bleeding anymore. You can check it out in the morning—if I'm still here. Now get on over and help those guys."

"How about your head, it OK?" the medic pressed.

"Yeah, why?"

"How about your ears?"

"A bit fuzzy and a lot of ringing. Why?"

"Tuck," Gaines joined in. "Wipe the side of your face."

Tuck set his M-16 aside and wiped the sides of his face with both hands. He looked at them under the man-made sun. Dark blood filled his hands. He stuck his index fingers into his ears and wiggled them. He felt and heard liquid squishing within.

"Bleeding from the ears; a couple of those ChiComs must have gotten real close," Doc Wild said to Gaines, who nodded back as if sharing diagnoses.

"Yeah, too damn close," Tuck confirmed.

"Tuck, you might have something internal busted, eardrums maybe. Be sure to check with me at first light," Doc Wild ordered. "You hear?"

"Yeah, sure, I hear you," a dismayed Tuck replied. He noticed a small but bloody bandage wrapped around Doc Wild's upper left arm. This was one tough little squid. Doc was one of them now. "Anybody else we know hit?" he asked, turning to Gaines.

"Yeah, the Boss. Capt. King bought it. His new aide, too. An RPG hit their pos right in the beginning of this thing." Gaines then nodded toward Donnie-Boy. "Me and Hebert here have been all over the hill. Trying to patch holes and keep the guys focused. Our skipper's in charge of Kilo right now. We've been hit pretty hard, fellas, the ambush just about got wiped out."

Tuck looked at Donnie-Boy and reached to touch his shoulder. "Donnie-Boy, I just want to let you know..."

"Listen. What's that?" Gaines interrupted. "Props. A plane. Must be Spooky."

Tuck looked up. Though muffled and ringing, his ears detected the deep drone of two large engines circling overhead. Spooky then announced its arrival when two small suns erupted in the night sky, flooding Dong Cho with artificial daylight.

"Wow," Gaines remarked.

"You ain't seen nothin' yet. Just wait," Donnie-Boy advised. "We saw Spooky work out about a month ago near Signal Hill."

"Yeah, but he wasn't this close," Tuck added. "We better lay low and hope that guy knows what he's doing."

The World War II vintage aircraft was an AC-47 transport fitted with a platform of three 7.62 mm, rotating mini-guns—modern day Gatling guns. They each fired 3,000 to 6,000 rounds per minute and rumor had it they could place one round in each square foot of a football field. Lord help whoever might be caught beneath Spooky's blazing red breath, Tuck imagined.

The silhouette of the twin-engine plane was barely visible while it circled above, braving the threat of small arms fire. Without warning three streams of closely spaced, red tracers—one in each five rounds fired—spewed from the craft. Faster than a long string of New Year's Eve firecrackers, the sound of the mini-guns buzzed. The pilot waggled the plane's wings. The effect was an even distribution of bullets.

A few screams echoed from beyond the perimeter, but the deadly chainsaw circling above chewed up even the mournful cries of the enemy.

"They say he's going to be on station for a good half hour. Nothing's going to move in our direction while Spooky's here. Let's get to the wounded," Gaines ordered. He and Doc Wild moved on. Donnie-Boy remained, choosing to stay by Tuck's side.

The fire from Spooky's flanks paused briefly while its pilot positioned the plane for another pass. Rounds landed just yards outside the perimeter. None ever threatened the grunts within. Tuck marveled at the precision of the firing plan and the spectacle it created. This was part of the excitement of war that he had always imagined. If for only a while, the trembling abated.

"Now I know why they call this thing Spooky. It really is SPOOKY, man," Mike observed, craning his head to take it all in.

"Some call it Puff the Magic Dragon because it looks like it's spitting fire," Tuck said, continuing to gaze upward. "By the way, Donnie-Boy, how's Danny and Johnny? I heard Gertrude working out most of the night. They must be OK."

"Oh, yeah, they're just fine. Talked to 'em just before I came here. Danny burned his hand pretty good while changing Gertrude's barrel and Johnny was bitching about a blister on his trigger finger. Other than that, not a scratch between them."

Relieved, Tuck laughed. Oddly, two of his friends lay only 20 yards away, yet he had had no contact with them throughout the firefight. "What about you?" he asked.

"What about me?"

"Were you hit?" Tuck asked again.

"A few little pieces of shrapnel. Nothing much, certainly no more than those neck burns our own flyboys gave us back in March," Donnie-Boy replied. "Heck, I'm indestructible. Remember? Hell, those gooks'll have to blow me apart before I report to sick bay."

Spooky made his last pass at 4 a.m. He hovered on station for another 30 minutes dropping the remainder of its 50 flares.

Donnie-Boy looked around the hill and over toward Ike's position. "Two more hours until daylight. Two more long, dark hours before this one's over."

Tuck cleaned more blood from his ears. "This one, I'm afraid, will never be over."

CHAPTER 43

The Day After
Atop Dong Cho/Da Krong Valley, R.S.V.N.
April 14, 1969—7 a.m. local time

"What happened?" Tuck asked Tony in a reverent tone. They were standing over the body of PFC Glenn Auburn. A charred, 18-inch hole cupped the earth where Glenn's head had rested. The searing explosion left little blood to stain the singed grass.

Staring at his friend's body, Tony slowly shook his head. "Got his head blowed off. ChiCom, one of the first ones. At least four hit at the same time, know what I mean."

Tuck nodded, again trying to clear his ringing ears with his fingers. "It was a bitch alright."

"We all rolled left to avoid 'em and he just rolled right into another one. And, boom, he was gone," Tony droned on. "I don't think he ever got off a shot."

"ChiCom hit Willie in the head, too," Tuck offered. "But it didn't blow right away. He was lucky. Got a hell of a welt."

"I'm sure ol' Glenn would trade for a bump right now," Tony added. Tears trickled down the smudged face of the brawny black Marine. "Came to the Nam together, you know. We both from Virginia. He was a D.C. kid, tough guy." He squatted, pulled Glenn's poncho liner from his rucksack, and then laid it over the body. "They didn't want me to cover him up until they had proper I.D. and all. Heck, didn't have no more head. But I knew my Glenn...rest easy buddy."

"How about the others?"

"Oh, uh, yeah, the others," Tony said, returning to the action report that Gaines had ordered Tuck to obtain from his flanking positions. "Carl caught a lot of shrapnel down his left side. I think the doc counted 40 something hits. A few went deep. Real painful, Doc Wild said."

"Yeah, we heard him crying. It was tough. Glad you were with him," Tuck said, scribbling a note on a sheet of paper from his writing gear.

"I tried to keep him quiet. But between Glenn gettin' wasted, Cpl. Ike gettin' shot and the gooks trying to kill me, too…well, it got hairy. But Carl, he'll be OK, and he might even get a ticket back to the World. He's outta the bush for a long time, that's for sure, and he's only got about five or six months to go. So I figure we've seen the last of him."

"And what about Ike?"

"That ol' Georgia Marine is a tough bird." Tony smiled. "He took some shrapnel to the leg early but kept on shootin' and fraggin' away. He kept saying he wanted to leave and check on the rest of you. Then with Carl gettin' hit and all, well, he knew he couldn't leave us. Fought with me shoulder to shoulder before he caught a bullet in the gut when the gooks rushed us."

Tony paused and looked away, again choking back tears. "He just grabbed his gut and kept on fighting. Wouldn't let me touch him. Then, just before Spooky got here, when everything kinda got quiet, he started hurtin' bad. And he started crying. Thought I was gonna go crazy. Cpl. Ike was crying. Carl kept beggin' for his mama. And I couldn't think about nothin' except Glenn didn't have no more head," he struggled to report. "And…and, I was scared shitless, man, peed in my pants twice…but you don't go puttin' that in your report. Hear?

"It don't mean nothin' bro," Tuck assured.

"Anyway, Ike's gonna make it, too. Gotta ticket straight back to the World." Tony dried his eyes. "I just kept shootin' and fraggin.' Seven dead gooks right there in front of our hole."

"And you? You hit?" Tuck asked, gazing about the hill. A half dozen Marines kept busy pushing down the elephant grass further away from the perimeter. Three grunts chopped away at the soil, deepening their fighting holes. Yet another dozen began forming up for a sweep and body count. Atop the hill, Marines carried filled body bags and laid them out for evac along with the moderately wounded. The critically wounded had been choppered out at first light.

Tony tittered, looked down and shook his head. "Not one damn scratch. Imagine that. Not even a flash burn. God must have something big in store for me. Or, I'm a walkin' dead man."

"I'll check with Donnie-Boy, he's the head of the squad now. He's probably gonna want you to either take over my team, or join us. Don't know yet. We're a bit scuffed up, but intact." Tuck patted Tony on the shoulder. They would "tag and bag" Glenn's body soon.

Tuck walked up the slope and through the matted grass to where Danny and Johnny huddled over Gertrude, meticulously cleaning and oiling "her" moving parts.

"Ain't no way LSU gonna beat Bama in Baton Rouge. Ain't gonna happen," he heard Danny boast. "Didn't happen last year, ain't gonna happen this year. Get over it, big boy."

"Screw you, you black Crimson Tide sonbitch. You dumb ni…"

"Oh, no, don't be goin' there again. You hear? I'll bust your ass with this barrel right here," Danny said, feigning a club-like blow.

"Hell, I oughta shot your black ass last night, too. Then I'd had an even dozen," Johnny growled back, tossing an oily rag into Danny's lap.

The bantering brought a needed smile to Tuck's face. He cleared his throat. "Uh, fellas…"

"What the hell you want, Tuck? You Tigers want to gang up on the Bama boy here? Well, bring it on," Danny intoned, slapping at his chest with both hands.

"It's OK. Never mind, catch you guys later." Tuck held up his hands, and then noted: "All's well and normal at the gun hole. No apparent serious wounds and spirits are high."

With a pleasantness that belied the night's horror, the mid morning brought a gentle southeast wind that cleared much of the cloud cover and allowed the sun to peek through and burn off the fog layer below. Its refreshing warmth felt good on Tuck's face. The smell of explosives and congealing blood still filled his nostrils. "Pretty soon, when it gets hotter, this is all gonna stink pretty bad."

"Yep, I imagine it will. A feast for the flies," Doc Wild declared while probing Tuck's right side for embedded shrapnel. "I count nine wounds, none serious. I can feel a couple of good-sized pieces right under the skin here just above your hip. They'll work their way out."

"When?"

"Hard to say, several hours, some in days, some even over the years. Nothing to worry about, except you may have to do some explaining when you take X-rays. But it's those ears that concern me. Any headaches?"

"What the hell do you think? Everything aches this morning," Tuck said. Doc Wild pulled at Tuck's left ear to inspect it closely. "Oww, that hurts," Tuck grimaced.

"Still ringing?" the corpsman asked.

"Yeah, some. Not as bad as last night, though. When's it gonna go away?"

"Hard to say. Maybe never if its noise-induced tinnitus."

"Tenni-what?"

"Tinnitus, medical talk for persistent ringing in the ears. It can become chronic if the nerves are damaged by loud noises. Half the rock singers in the world have it," Doc Wild explained.

"How come you know more than the average doc?" Tuck asked while Navy Corpsman Walter Wildman washed out his blood-caked ears.

"Two years medical school at the University of Texas before I joined the Navy."

"Well, you don't sound like no Texan, podnuh," Tuck said with an exaggerated drawl.

"Grew up in Oregon, but got a full scholarship to UT."

"You don't look like no athlete, non," Johnny interrupted, walking into the middle of the conversation.

"They do give scholarships for other things," Doc Wild chided. "Dumb ass jock, jarhead."

They laughed, but neither too long nor too loud. The horror of the early morning lingered.

"OK, you can go now," Doc Wild said with a wave. "Just keep me posted about those ears."

"Doc, one more thing. Why'd you quit? You know, quit medical school," Tuck asked, bending over to pick up his flak jacket. He donned it and awaited a reply.

Doc Wild paused, folded his arms, grabbed his chin and looked around. He'd never been asked. "I want to be a surgeon. And, I figure I can learn from the books, the labs and the hospitals on how to become a surgeon. But here," he paused again, stretched out his arms and looked around the battlefield. "Here in this war, in the Nam, is where I know I can learn how to be a physician. Look around. I could work a dozen years back in the World and not see the variety of trauma I've seen today. Humph, you're sending me to school. Now, I gotta go...podnuhs."

Tuck watched Doc Wild approach Glenn's body. He paused, squatted, and then pulled back the Snoopy blanket covering it. He briefly examined the remains, scribbled in his notebook, closed it and then bowed his head. He crossed himself as Catholics do at the end of a prayer. He stood and moved on to his next patient.

"He's gonna make somebody a good doc, yeah," Johnny offered.

"He already has," Tuck replied, slapping Johnny on the back. "He already has."

•

By noon, Kilo Company had swept the area just beyond the perimeter. Then after a hasty lunch, Lt. Smith briefed his squad and team leaders.

"Only one wounded NVA soldier was found and he soon joined the ranks of the 98 dead when he resisted," the skipper began. "We also found scores of blood trails, meaning they drug off a lot of wounded. Intel says a battalion of nearly 300 NVA hit us. About 40 died at or within our perimeter. We figure Spooky got the rest.

"Also be advised we suffered heavy casualties. As you know, Kilo commander Capt. Butch King, the boss, was among our 14 KIAs—six of whom died when the gooks overran first platoon's ambush. We also had 42 WIAs. Fortunately, only 17 of those required medevacs. That leaves us with about 75 able-bodied Marines on the hill.

"Now, I have been placed in temporary command of this company and I will not let it fall behind its intended mission. We will remain here one more night and..." A groan rumbled through the ranks. "I said...I said we will not fall behind in our mission and we will be here again tonight. And we'll again send out an ambush. This time we'll be more successful. Sgt. Gaines will brief the ambush party later. Until then, get back to your squads and teams and get those fields of fire pushed back even further and those fighting holes dug even deeper. You can bet they'll be back tonight. That is all."

The skipper closed his notebook and returned to his

position to meet with two of his four platoon sergeants. One was on a chopper headed to Charlie Med back at Stud. The other was zipped up in a body bag, awaiting a solemn trip back to the World. The skipper outlined the night's assignments to Sgt. "Hannibal" Sierichs, dismissed him, and then turned to Sgt. Gaines.

"Gaines, get your first squad ready for ambush. I want my best out there tonight," he nonchalantly ordered the former drill instructor without looking up from his map.

"Begging the lieutenant's pardon, sir. There's not much left of first squad. They've taken quite a beating. I'd rather go with third squad. They've got more bodies. In fact, sir, I'd say we could probably get along without an ambush tonight. We'll need all the able-bodied men we can get to defend the perimeter."

"Sergeant, you're not here to dictate policy or strategy to me. You are here to carry out my orders. Is that understood?"

Gaines snapped to attention. He replied through gritted teeth, "Sir, yes sir. I'll get the ambush together." He turned and walked away, his neck veins throbbing.

"Sgt. Gaines?"

"Yes, sir?"

The skipper waved Gaines back and handed him a small sheet of paper with scribbled notes and a rough sketch of the area. "You know that gook radio we got off that patrol the other day? Well, it seems before they could change their frequencies one of our Kit Carson scouts heard reference to a Col. Pham. If it's *the* Col. Pham then we could be in for some tougher nights ahead. I need my best out there to give us a heads up. I trust you understand."

"Yes, sir," Gaines replied, looking down at the notes.

•

The remnants of first squad lounged about 50 yards

from the perimeter. Working to expand holes and push down elephant grass had added to their fatigue. Donnie-Boy stood when he saw Gaines approach. "Well, what's the word? I bet we got the assignment, right?"

"Yep, you got it," Gaines replied, pausing to swat away a fly, one of thousands attracted by the smell of decaying flesh. "OK, fellas, look alive, I've got a job for you."

Gaines briefed the eight grunts on the skipper's orders. Donnie-Boy, Tuck, Johnny, Danny, Tony, Alex, Willie and Mike moaned on cue, but none objected further.

"Eight? Just eight of us out there? *J'amie la vive*," Johnny questioned before Gaines began.

"That's all we can spare. I'm sorry," Gaines replied. "Skipper says he wants his best out there and you're it."

Donnie-Boy looked over his map and compared it to the lieutenant's outline. "Basically, the ambush they want us to run is the same as that of last night. Right?"

"Yeah, I don't like it either, but..."

"But what if we go here," Donnie-Boy said, tracing his finger east to map coordinates 019-396. "Our ambush got slaughtered because the terrain gave the gooks room to maneuver and surround our guys. But look here. See this ravine? It's deep, steep and narrow and comes to an abrupt end right here, about a hundred yards out. Anything comin' up this ravine can just about walk into our perimeter unseen. I'm surprised the NVA honchos missed this last night. If they had come up this way, we might all be eating fish eyes and rice balls."

"Go ahead, I'm listening," Gaines replied, pointing to the map.

"Now, if we position ourselves here, at the top of the ravine," Donnie-Boy explained. "We'll have the high ground and even eight of us can cut to ribbons just about any size unit comin' up. If they don't come this way, well, we've got a nice night off. And if things get dicey, we've got a straight route right back to the perimeter."

"You've sold me," Gaines said. "I think I can sell it to the skipper, too. Give me a bit and I'll be right back. And I think I'm gonna do this one with you guys. Y'all can use an extra hand."

Tuck was writing a letter to Anna when Gaines approached a half hour later. Gaines' neck veins were bulging like they had in boot camp. "What's the verdict, sarge?"

Gaines held out his hand signaling Tuck to wait while the squad gathered around.

"Donnie-Boy's plan is a go," Gaines snapped. Donnie-Boy and Tuck exchanged their knowing smiles. "He told me to tell you good work and that the gook honcho we might be up against out there is known for using a ravine like that. He also said good hunting. But he…"

"But, he won't let you go along. Right?" Tuck interjected.

"Nope. Says he needs me back here in case they hit us again, or if they get past you," Gaines said, dropping to a knee. "But I promise that I'll have reinforcements ready to go if you get in trouble. You have my word. Just holler."

"Holler like you did at us all through boot camp. Right?" Johnny quipped.

"Yeah, just like that," Gaines said with a grin.

Gaines rarely socialized with the men, but at times he wanted to share in the comfort of camaraderie. Their DI sat among them for the first time since Signal Hill.

"By the way, sarge" Tuck began. "Why did you get on my ass so early when we arrived at the MCRD? We didn't have our hair cut yet and you were already all over me."

"Look, Tuck, I didn't know you from Adam, and I didn't care. I didn't even pay particular attention to you until the day I fed you that bird and when you fell on the run. Then the job you did on the rifle range was amazing. I really took note then."

"What about me?" Johnny joined in. "Notice me?"

"Hell, yes, the first minute. We don't get 'em much bigger'n you. And Gunny Hill liked you from the start, especially after he slapped the snot out of you and you took it like a man. We picked up on Donnie-Boy pretty quick, too. We knew you three guys would be special Marines."

"What part of Bama you from?" asked Danny, the Tuscaloosa native.

"Around Mobile, actually a little beach town called Gulf Shores," Gaines replied.

Tuck paused to think about the answer. "Didn't you say Gunny Hill was from Houston?"

"Yeah, but more like closer to Beaumont?"

"You ever been to New Orleans?" Tuck continued.

"Sure, several times. Even saw your LSU play a game in Baton Rouge back in say, oh, '61 or '62. Why?"

"So with Gunny Hill being from east Texas, and you being only a few hours from New Orleans, the two of you knew all along about coonasses and Cajun names. Right?

"Oh, hell yes. We've had plenty of Cajuns go through the MCRD and most make damn fine Marines. All that name harassment shit is just a routine—a pretty good one, too. Gunny Hill made up most of it, REE-TARD."

"Well, I'll be damned," Donnie-Boy said, shaking his head. "The way y'all acted, I thought we were the first."

Gaines stood and brushed off the seat of his faded trousers. "Well, I'd like to stay and talk about old times, fellas, but I gotta go. I'll see y'all again when it's time to saddle up. Check out your weapons again and make sure you got enough frags. And we've got plenty of gun ammo, so I recommend everybody carry an extra can."

When Gaines walked past, Tuck reached up, grabbed Gaines' sleeve, and then nodded with a smile. Gaines looked down. "You know, Tuck, Gunny Hill once told me that I was a good Marine and a good DI. But he added that I could be a damn fine one if I knew a little more about what y'all were gonna face out here. Well, Gunny Hill was right." He paused, then turned toward the elephant grass and nodded. "And now, I just wish I knew a little more about what y'all are gonna be facing out there tonight."

CHAPTER 44

Calculations
Da Krong Valley, R.S.V.N./Tunnel complex
April 14, 1969—3 p.m. local time

Trai sat quietly in the same dimly lit room in which he had earlier feared for his manhood. Now, as an aide to Col. Pham, he watched his uncle spar with the Chinese advisor Major Chen.

The two officers leaned over from opposite sides of a small wooden table, their arms outstretched over a combat map illuminated only by a low-wattage bulb hanging naked from the ceiling. Their stark shadows crisscrossed the map.

Pham heard the cries of the wounded soldiers who overwhelmed the complex's small infirmary and its few medics. Their bloody and dying scent saturated the corridors of the dank tunnels. Their moans echoed at every turn. He winced and dropped his head, Trai was surprised to notice. Chen also heard, but ignored them.

"What in the hell were you thinking when you sent 300 of my troops rushing up to that perimeter?" Pham lashed out. "You got more than 100 of my men killed and scores more wounded. If you would've used the ravine..." He paused to jab his finger to a specific point on the map. "Here, as I had planned, it would have succeeded."

Chen coolly took a drag on his cigarette and turned his head to blow a slow vent of smoke from the side of his mouth. "Our plan was working perfectly and we would have easily overrun the Americans had we not, unfortunately, been tipped off by a pair of amorous tigers." Wisps of smoke escaped his lips when he spoke.

"Little has gone right for our regiment since you were assigned to me and I'll be damned if I'm going to let you destroy it with your continued ineptness. Tigers? That's *bullshit*," Pham growled, using the American word. He wiped cool sweat from his brow. "Is that understood? And be mindful of your rank, major, before you reply."

"As you wish, colonel, I'll be sure to mention your feelings in my report." Chen's smile faded.

"You do that. And, be sure to mention to your superiors about your liking for young Vietnamese soldiers," Pham said, spitting onto the damp clay floor. He put his right hand to his big knife's scabbard.

The large vein tracing down Chen's forehead throbbed. "Let us get on with our, no, your plan for tonight, please."

Trai let out a slow, quiet sigh.

"Yes, perhaps we should turn our attention to the matters at hand—the American Marines," Pham agreed, returning his focus to the map. "Tonight you will take our remaining battalion of 300 men and attack here, atop Dong Ta Ri. I estimate there are about 120 Marines there, maybe more, and you will need all the support we can give you."

"And I will need a diversion as well, something to counter that damned flying battleship they use," Chen said, alluding to the effectiveness of the Spooky gunship. "It caused half our casualties last night."

"We'll create your diversion when I take my remaining 100 men and again attack the Marines, here, on Dong Cho two kilometers to the north," Pham explained. "Only this time we will approach via this ravine, which exits very near their perimeter. It'll provide excellent cover."

"If you get ambushed in there, it could be a disaster. You do know this?" Chen cautioned.

Pham nodded. "Our scouts have reported seeing many

helicopters ferrying out their dead and wounded and we think their numbers to be below 80 men. They will need all hands to defend their perimeter. Maybe a listening post, but I can't see them risking an ambush until they get replacements. Plus, how will they know where we might strike?" He stroked the map and his plan like an artist in the midst of painting a masterpiece. "We should just about be able to walk right in and slaughter them. Remember, they're tired and Americans like their sleep. Just like last spring...like our successful assault atop that firebase."

Pham took a sip of water from a canteen dangling from one of the chairs. He turned and winked at Trai. "I will also send two small teams of men to either side of their perimeter. Should we be discovered in the ravine, they will then create diversions to give their officers something else to consider. We should also be able to use our mortars—what's left after last night's waste—to keep the Americans busy atop the hill as we move up the ravine."

Chen nodded excitedly. "The plan is, indeed, a good one. I like it. But the timing, that's what worries me. If that gunship is able to open fire on my..."

"Forget the dragon gunship. Ours will be a quick strike and we'll be there only long enough for them to call in that damn thing. I plan to have my men out of the kill zone before it spots us. I've watched how it works. It will finish its mission whether it sees us or not. And, after it finishes and returns to its base, then and only then will you strike on Dong Ta Ri."

Pham paused to fetch a cigarette from his blouse pocket. Chen flicked his American-style lighter to life and lit Pham's cigarette. Trai felt the anger in the room ebbing.

"Chen, if we pull this off tonight we'll be able to continue with our plan to strike at their Vandegrift Combat Base. We must hurt these two companies of Marines. We need to get them off our backs. If we fail..."

"If we fail, we'll do little more than run from these same Marines for the remainder of the spring," Chen said, completing Pham's thought.

•

Trai found Louie, his eyes closed and shoulders hunched up against the tunnel wall in his favorite out-of-the-way place. He gently tapped Louie on the shoulder.

"I'm not sleeping. How can one sleep when so many of his comrades lay dying?" Louie sighed deeply. "Trai, my son, I think it's time for me to get out. I can't take it much longer."

"Well, tonight, you just may get that chance, Louie."

Louie's eyes opened wide and he quickly turned to Trai. "Eh?"

"I've just been listening to my Uncle Bui's conversation with Major Chen and how they plan to attack the Americans," Trai said, nestling closer to his friend's side. He told Louie of the confrontation he had witnessed.

"So how does this figure for us, except that we might be killed in the attack?" Louie asked, slipping his right hand behind Trai's neck.

"Louie, you must be getting old. Think. As his aide, I may finally be left alone with him in the jungle. And I may not even need your help."

"But I want to help. Don't you see, it's personal with me now, too," Louie added, using his other hand to rub the not-yet-healed knife wound on his neck. "Besides, he'll still have those behemoths by his side, as always."

"Yes, they will be a problem. But I'm sure you'll come up with something."

CHAPTER 45

Orders

Da Krong Valley, R.S.V.N.
April 14, 1969—8 p.m. local time

A brisk west wind had swept the clouds away, and by evening a full moon was creeping upward to meet the stars.

"You ready, Tuck?"

"Yeah, sure, why not?" Tuck replied with a shrug, hoping to hide a dread coming upon him.

Donnie-Boy slapped Tuck on the helmet, spun him around and checked his combat gear. "You know, we're best friends and all, but tonight might get rough out there. I may have to make some tough calls. So just remember, orders are orders, no matter who gives them."

"Sure, I know what you mean." Tuck looked up at the moon. "It's gonna be a clear one tonight. That's good and bad."

"Yeah, we can see Charlie better. But he can see us better, too—a Sapper's Moon," Donnie-Boy said. He turned and called out to his squad. "Everybody got a can of gun ammo?"

The chorus of affirmatives ranged from "yep" to "you bet."

"Well then, lock and load. It's time to roll."

The head of the ravine lay slightly more than 100 yards east southeast from the Kilo Company perimeter. Gaines stood at the departure point when first squad passed—Tuck on the point, followed by Alex, then Tony with the blooper and Donnie-Boy.

"Bring 'em all back alive. If you get in a fix, call me and I'll have a team ready to haul ass and bail you out," Gaines told Donnie-Boy with a nod and pat on the shoulder.

"Aye, aye, sir," Donnie-Boy replied. Willie hauled the radio behind Donnie-Boy, then came Danny and Johnny with a well-groomed Gertrude. Mike brought up the rear.

"O, St. Joseph whose protection is so great…" Tuck prayed while leading the team into the darkness, where the uncertainty that gripped his mind resided.

Donnie-Boy counted his steps, keeping track of the distance. Mostly elephant grass and a few bare trees made up the downward slope. At 50 yards, the team arrived at a bomb crater. Tuck outwitted the depression this time and dropped to his butt before he could tumble into it.

Donnie-Boy followed suit and put his hand on Tuck's shoulder and then pointed. "Doing a good job. Keep straight ahead and we should be at the ravine in a few minutes. Keep this crater in mind. If things go to shit, this'll be a good rally point. Pass the word back, Alex.

"Willie, hand me the mike." Donnie-Boy took the phone and keyed the handset twice. He turned to survey his surroundings.

"Kilo Six here, sit rep please," a whisper replied.

"Large crater, 50 yards, rally point, do you copy? Over," he reported.

The prick hissed. It was Gaines. "Copy, out."

Donnie-Boy handed the phone back to Willie, then motioned Tuck to move on.

Tuck soon reached the edge of the elephant grass where it gave way to an expanse of knee-high grass with narrow blades. It resembled a pasture where cattle might graze on a spring morning. Spotting two jagged boulders jutting up like oversized garbage cans, he signaled for a halt. He knelt, then crawled through the grass toward the rocks and the sound of trickling water. He had reached the head of the ravine. Once again he felt the trembling return—his insides began to shiver. He looked back and felt, despite the full moon overheard, that the darkness was stalking him.

Donnie-Boy, standing at the edge of the grass 20 yards away, watched for Tuck's signal, then rushed forward and dropped to his side. Deeply anchored, the twin rocks rose about four feet high. The rim of the ravine, also bordered by the shorter grass, lay only 10 feet away. By the moon's light, they estimated the ravine to be about 30 yards wide at the most and stretched downward into the darkness. Steep, rocky sides 20 feet high walled off either side. It was as if the gods had gouged the hill with a swipe of a spoon.

The water trickled from a small spring, which leaked from just below the rocks. How many thousands of years had it taken for the spring to carve the ravine?

"I was right. This is a perfect conduit to our perimeter," Donnie-Boy whispered. "We'd never see 'em coming. Now, whether they're coming tonight, or coming this way, is another thing. We'll see if the skipper's right about that gook colonel."

"It's an A-1 ambush point, that's for sure," Tuck observed. "The rocks will protect the gun team real good."

Donnie-Boy motioned for the phone, and then keyed the handset twice. Not waiting for a reply, he said, "On site, out." He signaled for Johnny and Danny to set up Gertrude. Each gunner carried two cans of ammo each. The remainder of the squad carried another 2,000 rounds.

Except for Tony and Johnny, each squad member carried an M-16, several hundred rounds of ammo and six frags. Tony carried a .45 along with his M-79 and dozens of extra Flechettes to go with his High Explosive rounds.

Donnie-Boy, moving briskly among his men, aligned the squad along the lip of the ravine in a shallow crescent around and in support of the gun team, which stared down the gullet of the kill zone. Tuck, Tony and Alex fanned out to the right. Donnie-Boy, Willie and Mike went to the left. "Get about five yards apart," Donnie-Boy instructed. They soon covered all practical exit points.

Alex and Mike, at the outermost points of the crescent, crept to the edge and set up four Claymore mines. Kilo 2 Alpha bristled with deadly teeth.

"Now, we wait," Donnie-Boy whispered at 8:45. The mosquitoes began their feast.

•

The NVA's trek to the mouth of the ravine proved more arduous and time-consuming than expected. The 100 men had climbed much of Dong Cho, threading their way through dense underbrush. Pham's men needed rest.

"Trai," Pham summoned his nephew. "You and Louie come here, now."

They sprinted to the colonel and slid to their knees.

"Louie, you'll spearhead this operation," Pham ordered. "You make sure the men push through to the top. Even if we run into trouble, I still want to push over the top. I don't want you in the front. But I want you in there to inspire the men. Do you understand?"

"Yes, sir. Completely," Louie nodded.

"You want me to go with him, Colonel?" Trai asked.

"No. Absolutely not. You stay with me at all times. Right here by my side. We will go up the ravine when it is safe."

"Yes, sir, Colonel," Trai replied disappointedly.

"Ah, you can call me Uncle Bui if you like tonight. I can tolerate such a small breach of protocol," Pham said in a fatherly manner.

"Yes, sir, Uncle Bui," Trai replied, his lips tracing a fake smile in the moonlight.

"You men, over there," Pham ordered. "Nguyen, set

up your mortars and be ready to fire on top of the hill. And conserve your ammunition."

Pham turned to Trai and Louie. "Lt. Louie, get the troops ready—four groups of 25. Prepare to move."

"Yes, sir." Louie turned, looked into Trai's eyes and then nodded before sprinting off to shepherd the first group into the ravine.

Though the dry season had provided the ravine with only a trickling of water, thick green algae covered the rocky bottom. Several soldiers slipped and banged their knees when the climb began. Most muttered oaths to themselves, but a few couldn't stop their rifles from clanging off the rocks. The sound echoed off the sides of the steep ravine.

Trai grimaced at the sound.

•

"Did you hear that?" Tony asked Tuck, who lay to his right.

"Hear what? I didn't hear anything," Tuck replied, cupping his ear.

"I heard it," Alex said. "There it is again. Sounds like metal hitting something."

"Yeah, I got it now," Tuck whispered excitedly. "Johnny, think we got movement straight on down the ravine. Listen up."

"Yeah, we heard it, too. Now keep quiet," Donnie-Boy ordered before grabbing the handset from Willie. He squeezed twice, and then whispered, "Got movement, out."

Tuck's trembling seemed to worsen. Not since the convoy ambush had he felt such fear. He hoped Donnie-Boy would not notice the sweat beading along his forehead. For a moment, the darkness was his ally.

•

"Pass the word up that I'll gut the next man that makes

a sound," Pham chided the leader of the second 25-man team, which was lining up for the climb. He turned to Trai. "Of course, I doubt if there is anyone between us and the top of the hill."

Another soldier fell on the slick rocks and sprained an ankle when his boot caught between two jagged boulders. He cried out, and then dropped his rifle.

•

"I damn sure heard it that time," Tuck said.

"They're out there all right, little buddy," Donnie-Boy whispered. He looked at Tuck; they locked glances. Donnie-Boy nodded and smiled. Tuck's insides now shook as if gripped in a feverish chill, Donnie-Boy's assurance offered no relief, indeed it only worsened his dread.

"Everybody get set," Donnie-Boy cautioned. "Get ready on those Claymores."

•

"Move quicker. Quicker," Louie called out while trying to keep his voice down. "If there's anybody up there with ears, I'm sure they've heard us now. Faster."

The lead element of the first two 25-man groups, carrying ropes with grappling hooks, neared the lip of the ravine. It met with two brilliant flashes.

•

"Fire!" Donnie-Boy cried out. The exploding Claymores smothered his voice. The four mines drove thousands of red-hot ball bearings down the ravine at supersonic speed. The first dozen soldiers, forced together by the narrows, fell mute after the pellets perforated their bodies.

Johnny jerked his M-60 machine gun to life. Playing her like a musical instrument, Gertrude spit fire. Two soldiers in the lead element reacted too slowly and fell backward.

Tuck and Alex sighted in on shadows and joined the massacre. Tuck's trembling abated. His training took over. He no longer thought; no longer felt; he reacted.

A survivor of the first group maneuvered in close and hurled a ChiCom toward the lip, but the grenade fell short and rolled back into the ravine. A blast from Tony's M-79 shredded the brave soldier's body with a dozen steel darts.

All eight Marines fired into the ravine. Tuck wondered how anyone could survive.

Johnny drew a bead on three soldiers clamoring up the right side of the ravine. He raked Gertrude's fire across the wall at shoulder height. The men spun into the rocks.

Suddenly, a loud SWOOSH leapt from below. Trailing fire, the Rocket Propelled Grenade struck the jutting rocks with a loud roar. Sparks flew among the rock chips and shrapnel.

A steady breeze dissipated the thick gray smoke. Tuck saw Johnny and Danny lying on their backs, motionless. Gertrude was silent. He leapfrogged over Tony and rushed to their sides. Donnie-Boy also moved in, grabbed the machine gun and pulled the trigger. The M-60 answered with a long burst of fire that sent four soldiers diving for cover. The enemy soldiers swelled in number and hugged the walls rather than trying to run up the middle.

"They're alive, just knocked out," Tuck shouted to Donnie-Boy.

"Get 'em out of here. Now!" Donnie-Boy shouted back, feeding another belt of gun ammo into Gertrude.

"I can't leave you," Tuck cried out. "I won't leave you."

"Move it!" Donnie-Boy hollered. "You get 'em back up to that crater and tell Willie to radio for backup. We can hold them till you get back. That's an order," he yelled before repositioning himself behind the rocks.

"OK, but I'll be right back," Tuck hollered, struggling to obey an order that had him abandon his friend's side.

Willie began shouting into the handset.

•

"Skipper, it's getting hot down there. We need to saddle up a team, ASAP," Gaines said. He relayed the urgent call. "That ravine is lousy with gooks."

"Just hold on a minute there, sergeant. They're holding their own. No use risking..."

WHUMP, WHUMP, WHUMP!

Mortar rounds exploded atop Dong Cho, sending Gaines and Lt. Smith diving. The cracking sound of AK-47s and the popping of M-16s erupted at two points on the perimeter. The muffled sound of ChiCom grenades also burst along the defensive lines.

Four more enemy mortar rounds landed atop the hill. Pham's diversion was under way.

•

Two NVA soldiers reached the head of the ravine but their efforts failed when Tony stood and fired a Flechette round into their faces. They toppled backward, rolling down the steep bank.

Firing Gertrude from the hip, Donnie-Boy rose to his knees and raked the sides of the ravine. Two more soldiers tumbled. "Tuck, what's taking you so long, damn it?" he yelled. "Get these guys out of here."

Tuck stared at Danny and Johnny lying by his side and then looked at Donnie-Boy. It wasn't fear for his life, but the living darkness and fear for Donnie-Boy's that froze Tuck into inaction.

"Damn it, Marine, I said move. Now!" Donnie-Boy screamed. "Now, Tuck!"

A ChiCom landed atop the ravine and exploded six feet from Tuck. His world reverberated like a giant gong. The concussion shook him from his melancholy. He rolled and fired a three-shot burst. One of his rounds caught an NVA soldier in the lower leg.

Tuck scooted toward Johnny—unconscious but breathing. He pulled Johnny's .45 from its holster and shoved it into his right thigh pocket. He tossed aside his M-16 and rolled Johnny over onto his right side. He wriggled his way beneath the big Cajun and lifted with a grunt. He grabbed Johnny's left arm, and then crawled up the hill.

"O, St. Joseph do assist me..."

Tuck found solid cover in the elephant grass 20 yards up the hill. He strained and stood with Johnny straddled across his back and shoulders. Living in the Nam had lightened Johnny since Tuck lifted him during their horseplay at Staging in California. Spurred on by a rush of adrenaline, he moved quickly, reaching the crater within minutes. "This is for the lift you gave me in boot camp, big buddy," he said to his unconscious friend.

He knelt, and then rolled Johnny over onto his back. He examined him. Johnny was bleeding from his oft-injured shoulder and Tuck couldn't rouse him. Ignoring the sudden twinge in his back, Tuck darted back to the ambush site. The firing had slacked off. Donnie-Boy should be safe. He hoped he wasn't too late.

•

Louie scurried down the ravine and reported to his commander. "Colonel, this is a senseless slaughter," he pleaded between pants. "We can't get over the lip because of that machine gun behind those rocks and the sides are too steep and slippery to outflank them. They have the ravine covered like vines."

"How many men have we lost?" Pham calmly asked, though Trai noted a hint of desperation in his uncle's voice.

"All but six of the first 50. The third group is setting

up to try a bull-rush now. But I don't think that will work either. You must call it off," Louie begged.

"If Louie says it's so, then it must be doomed, uncle," Trai added.

"Silence, both of you," Pham shouted. "I'm in command here. And I say we will take this ravine and then enter their perimeter in strength."

"Colonel, please, the element of surprise is long past," Louie continued. "I fear their reinforcements will arrive soon and annihilate all our men."

"No! I won't tolerate failure," Pham ordered. "Louie, you go back up there and get those men over that ravine..."

"Then I will go with him," Trai blurted out.

"No, you will stay with me. Here," Pham commanded. A bit of spittle oozed from the corner of his lips. "Louie, get back up there. That's an order,"

"Yes, sir," Louie hissed before turning to whisper to Trai, "The time has come."

•

Tuck dove beside Donnie-Boy, picked up his M-16 and peered into the ravine. "How's Danny?"

"Still out, but breathing," Donnie-Boy replied. "Alex and Tony each took a bit of shrapnel in the hip, and the gooks are either running out of troops or thinking this thing through. Either way we've got a break. Where'd you leave Johnny?"

"At the crater. He's still out, but he's alone, too."

"Get Danny up the hill," Donnie-Boy ordered. "I'm gonna talk to Six and see if I can get us some help."

"OK," Tuck said with a deep sigh, unable to shake the ominous feeling. "Take care, hear?"

"You bet. Now get going," Donnie-Boy said with a smile. "Willie, get on the horn again. Better yet, give it to me."

Willie used his left hand to pass the handset. His right hand dripped with blood. "I'm OK, just a scratch," he said. Donnie-Boy nodded and then clicked the handset twice.

"Six here, how's it..." Gaines replied before Lt. Smith grabbed the handset. "What's your sit rep, 2 Alpha, over?" The skipper's voice quivered.

"Two men down, unconscious and need immediate attention. Two, no, make that three more hit. Six, there must be a hundred gooks trying to get up this ravine and our ammo's gettin' low. We need..."

The skipper interrupted. "Look 2 Alpha, can't you hear what's going on up here. We've got gooks on the perimeter and we're taking beaucoup mortar fire. I'm afraid you're on your own for now. You're probably better off than us."

"What the hell do you mean?" Donnie-Boy shouted into the mike. "Come down here and look at the pile of gook bodies, you stupid ass, and you tell me who's knee-deep in shit. If we don't stop them right here, it'll be your sorry ass that's in danger up there! Get us some fuckin' help, now. Out!" Donnie-Boy slammed the handset to the ground.

"Skipper, I think this stuff on the perimeter might be a ruse," Gaines assessed. "We haven't taken any casualties. I think Charlie doesn't want us down there.

"Let me take three volunteers and a medic," Gaines pleaded. "You know he's right. If we don't stop them there, we could be putting the whole company in jeopardy. At least call in Spooky for support."

"Sgt. Gaines, you will do as I ordered and stand down until I say otherwise. That's probably Col. Pham out there and I can't risk pulling more men off the perimeter. Is that understood?"

WHUMP, WHUMP!

"See, see what I mean," the skipper cried when two mortar rounds landed inside the perimeter.

"Yesss, sirrr," Gaines sarcastically replied. "Now, if you'll excuse me sir, I'll be at the departure point in case you change your mind. Sir."

•

Compared to hauling Johnny up to the crater, Danny seemed no heavier than a case of C-rations. Nonetheless, he struggled up the hill with Danny tossed over his right shoulder. Danny began to regain consciousness and unwittingly fought back.

"Calm down, bro, we're almost there," Tuck said, trying to calm his friend while wondering who just might calm him. "I'm not gonna let you go. I promise. I won't let you die."

Trudging up the slope and slapping away the elephant grass, Tuck thought about men like Danny. Twice he slipped to the ground and felt something in his left knee pop. He fought on, for Danny, for Chuck, for Gunny Hill—black men who with their very lives had taught him lessons in humanity and pride. Lessons Tuck never knew he needed to learn, until now.

"Just a few more yards. Doc Wild will be there and he'll take good care of you."

"Whaaa...Where am..." Danny struggled to say. Blood oozed from a large gash on the side of his head.

"Hold on buddy. We're there," Tuck said. He knelt and laid Danny next to Johnny. He hurriedly checked Johnny's neck for a pulse. It pumped strong and regular but still no sign of consciousness.

Tuck shook Danny. "Come out of it man. Corpsman!" he yelled. "Doc, where are you?" He fought off his panic.

"What happened, man?" Danny asked groggily. Pulling himself up on one elbow, he put his hand to his head. "Oww, my head hurts bad. I need a doc." He fell back onto his side, noticing Johnny for the first time. "Is he dead? Not Johnny man, ohh, not Johnny."

"No, he's just knocked out, like you were," Tuck

explained. "An RPG blast. Rocks saved you. He'll be OK." He looked around. "Damn, I thought they'd be here for sure. Willie was calling for 'em when I left." He looked around the crater again. No one approached. "Shit."

They were alone.

"OK, look now, Danny. I gotta go back. The gooks are gonna hit us again real soon. You shake it off and see about Johnny. Come on, bro, wake up and see about your buddy."

Danny nodded, pulled himself closer to Johnny and then looked back at Tuck. "Go get 'em, little bro."

"Here, take this—just in case," Tuck said, handing Danny his M-16. "Wish me luck."

He sprinted down the hill along the dark trail he now knew by heart. In less than a minute, he slid to the side of Donnie-Boy, who was slipping another belt of ammo into Gertrude.

"I can hear 'em maneuvering down there," Donnie-Boy advised. "I think they're either gonna rush us, or maybe send some guys around the top of the ravine to flank us.

"But that's gonna to take some time," he added. "How's Johnny and Danny? OK?"

"Danny's coming to. Johnny's still out, but breathing," Tuck said. "Why aren't Doc Wild and Gaines there? I thought we had help coming."

"Me, too, but the skipper says he can't spare anybody because they're getting hit up there and 'cause *we* have this situation in hand," Donnie-Boy said with a laugh. He pointed to the bodies of three NVA soldiers 10 feet away.

"Listen up, fellas," Donnie-Boy spoke up. It was one of those moments that defined a leader. Turning toward Donnie-Boy, Tuck memorized the look on their gallant and determined faces. The moment etched itself into his mind. This was valor. "So far we haven't had to use many frags. But this time I want you to each get three frags ready to throw on my command."

"I got only one left," Mike announced, holding up his remaining hand grenade.

"Here," Tuck said. He tossed two frags toward Mike. "Make 'em count."

"Now guys," Donnie-Boy continued, "I want you to throw them as far as you can down there. We need to get as many gooks as we can in the middle and at the end of the charge. That'll confuse them and allow us to cut down the closest ones with our rifles. Got it?

"And let's hope the Skipper comes to his senses, because if this don't work we're gettin' the hell out of here."

"What do you mean, Donnie-Boy?" Alex asked. "We're just gonna run?"

"Hell, no. If I yell 'sky' I want all of you, except me and Tuck, to head back up to the crater and defend that position. We'll stay here as long as we can to cover your retreat," Donnie-Boy said, then paused. "If any of you have questions, get 'em out now."

"You the boss. Let's kick some more gook ass," Willie agreed. He lined up his frags and inserted a full magazine into his M-16.

"Good, now let's see if we can stir 'em up a bit," Donnie-Boy said. "Tony, drop a couple of HE rounds way out down the ravine. See if we can catch 'em in a huddle."

"Will do," Tony said. He extracted the Flechette round from his blooper and pulled out two High Explosive rounds from his ammo pouch. He inserted one. "Ready."

Donnie-Boy looked Tuck in the eye. "All set, little brother?"

"Let's do it." Near Donnie-Boy's side, Tuck found a new calm.

•

"The third group is ready to rush them now, Colonel," Louie reported to Pham. "But, first, I must recommend we send a half dozen men around the ravine to flank them. It will take time. But it will also give us time to get the remainder of the fourth group in place."

"Nonsense. We're out of mortar rounds and time is short," Pham explained. "We have to hit that main perimeter in time for the Americans to call in their gunship on our position. That'll take the pressure off Major Chen's assault on Dong Ta Ri."

"What?" Louie shouted. "You want that dragon to pounce on us again—like last night. What are we? Bait? This is madness."

"Lt. Louie, you will not..."

"No, I'm not finished. I've fought for the cause for more than 20 years. But never have I heard such insanities as tonight. First we're told to attack a ravine that is nothing but a vision from hell. Now, I'm told we are hoping their gunships attack us while we're in the open, just so your chink adviser can make good his attack. This is all bullshit. Fils putain."

"That's enough, lieutenant. You're a good officer and I need you. But that is enough," Pham shouted before drawing his big blade. His two bodyguards stepped forward. "Now, get back to your men and prepare to attack."

Louie stared Pham in the eye, and then turned and spat on the ground. He looked at Trai and nodded. "Yes, colonel, I will do what is needed."

"And, Louie, take my bodyguard, Manh, with you," Pham ordered, gesturing toward his nephew and the remaining bodyguard. "I've still got Trai and Bao here to protect me. I'm sure you can use another strong hand.

"And, Manh, you keep an eye on Lt. Louie," Pham added.

"Are we really just bait for Major Chen's bidding?" Trai asked after Louie and the bodyguard began trotting toward the ravine. "I heard you and the major discussing similar plans. But I had no idea it involved our being slaughtered, either in the ravine or atop the hill by a dragon gunship."

"Fear not, Trai. We will not be slaughtered. We won't even be here when Louie figures out that the cause can't be won here tonight. So, prepare to leave when this final rush begins."

"But we cannot betray Louie and our men so easily," Trai said, his brow knitting with bewilderment. "Surely we can't."

"My young Trai, you will soon learn that you can betray anyone, even family, when the time comes for you to act so that you can prevail. In war, there is no honor in one's own death, only in the killing," Pham seethed. "Now, come. There is still work to be done."

"Yes, uncle. I do understand, now."

BOOM!

The ground beside Pham and Trai churned, spraying the colonel's bodyguard with shrapnel. But before Bao could cry out—BOOM—another round exploded and spun him to the ground.

•

"That ought to shake 'em good. Nice shooting, Tony," Donnie-Boy praised his M-79 man. "Look alive, fellas. They'll be a comin' soon. Remember, hold the frags till I say, then let 'em all loose as quick as you can."

No sooner had Donnie-Boy said it, a shrill whistle split the night and the shouts of men rose from the ravine like the screeching of brakes on asphalt.

The shouts grew closer. "Hold on. Hold on. Pull those pins, but hold on," Donnie-Boy cautioned, ticking off in his mind the distance an armed soldier can run up hill in 10 seconds. "Now. Frag 'em!"

The six grunts threw their grenades as far as their strength allowed. Donnie-Boy's frag reached the middle of the ravine and landed near where Louie stood directing his troops. The explosion knocked Louie and Pham's bodyguard off their feet and laced Louie's left side with shrapnel. He let out a loud cry and fell between two large rocks.

An advancing junior officer soon stopped and pulled Pham's legless bodyguard from atop Louie's limp body, which was soaked with blood. He hastily examined Louie and felt no pulse. "They've had it. Let's keep going."

The grenade thrown by Willie, the Nebraska shot-putter, also landed near the rear of the enemy formation. The other four grenades landed in the midst of the charging NVA. Two more soldiers fell dead and landed atop Louie and the bodyguard.

The second salvo of six frags also landed in the middle of the ravine, taking a heavy toll on the soldiers who bunched in confusion. The third salvo, thrown by weakened arms, did not travel as far but caused significant damage. Less than half of the third group of 25 soldiers survived.

Gertrude returned to action. Her barrel now cooled, she sprang to life with Donnie-Boy traversing the ravine with short, aimed bursts. Two more soldiers spun to their knees. Alex squeezed off well-aimed shots in the moonlight—as if shooting rattlers back in Arizona.

Two soldiers reached the lip of the ravine and barely crawled over when Tony killed them with a single Flechette blast. A hush followed.

Donnie-Boy looked at Tuck. "Hear anything? All I hear is moaning."

"No," Tuck yelled. "But my ears are ringing so bad I can hardly hear you."

Another loud cry erupted from the ravine when the fourth, and last, group of NVA soldiers charged. A chorus of SWOOSHES accompanied them. RPG explosions erupted around the six Marines but most overshot by 20 yards.

"Time to go," Donnie-Boy cried out, "Sky! Sky now!"

Alex, Mike, Tony and Willie turned to retreat to the crater when three RPGs landed nearby. Tony fell to his knees and cried out. The others did not see him fall and continued up the hill.

"Tony," Tuck hollered. "I'm coming."

"So are the gooks, goddammit," Donnie-Boy said, pulling the pin on a grenade and heaving it as far as possible.

•

"Skipper, enough is enough. We gotta help these guys," Gaines again pleaded with the lieutenant, who had joined him at the perimeter and knelt by his side. The few NVA who had created Pham's diversion now lay dead. "They can't even radio us anymore. They're getting cut to pieces."

"No, we just can't risk it," Smith replied, pensively jabbing at his chin with his thumb. "The gooks may attack us again and first squad is still returning fire with the 60. You can hear that. They're still in command of the situation. And I am still in command of this company. So stay put. I'm going back up to my pos and call in Spooky. That'll take care of them. Take care of them; all of them."

Gaines waited until the skipper reached the top of the hill. "What would Gunny Hill do? He liked the Cajuns because they stuck together," he said aloud, as if sorting through a thousand thoughts. "Private, come here," he hollered, grabbing the closest Marine. "Get Doc Wild down here immediately. And I need two volunteers."

A half dozen voices responded.

•

Two RPG rounds exploded near the boulders when Tuck reached Tony 10 yards up the hill. Donnie-Boy cried out. But Tuck heard the M-60 continue to fire and looked back to see three soldiers fall when they topped the ravine.

"Help me, Tuck. I hurt bad, man," Tony murmured. He knelt and held his stomach.

Tuck looked down at Tony. He looked over at Donnie-Boy. He looked back down at Tony.

"Please man, help," Tony begged. "I can walk...just can't run."

"OK, let's go," he said, throwing Tony's arm around his neck. Stumbling up the hill, they heard three more blasts erupt near Donnie-Boy. But Gertrude continued to fire. Another blast erupted behind Tony and Tuck, who again felt the sting of shrapnel in his back.

Ten yards before they reached the crater, Willie joined the duo and grabbed Tony's waist. Together, they carried Tony the remaining distance and laid him in the crater.

"We can't carry all these guys up the hill," Alex quickly explained. "Mike's goin' up to get help. Go on back and get Donnie-Boy. Me and Willie will take care of things."

Tuck had no time to reply; seconds were precious. He grabbed Tony's M-79 and ran back to Donnie-Boy. The explosions continued, but the return fire from the machine gun lessened.

"Aw, shit, Gertrude, now's not the time to freeze on me, damn it," Donnie-Boy cursed. Two enemy soldiers topped the ravine and closed at the same time. Donnie-Boy, lying in the grass, emptied his .45, killing them.

A small soldier scurried over the lip when Tuck reached Donnie-Boy. Tuck fired a High Explosive round from the M-79, striking the man in the chest near the shoulder. The blast spun the soldier wildly to the ground. A final NVA soldier came over the edge. Tuck pulled Danny's .45 from his thigh pocket and fired, shattering the man's face.

The night suddenly grew deathly silent. The assault was over but Tuck's trembling returned as violently as before. Donnie-Boy's voice validated his dread.

"Oh, Tuck, ohhh, man...I'm hurt bad...real bad," Donnie-Boy moaned haltingly.

Donnie-Boy lay at the feet of Tuck, who let his focus slowly break away from the edge of the ravine. His eyes widened at the horrid sight. The darkness that had stalked his mind now flowed past him and engulfed his friend.

"Tuck, come here man...I need you," Donnie-Boy wept. Little more than twisted and blackened stumps remained of the athlete.

Tears rolled down Tuck's dirt-caked cheeks. "Donnie-Boy, Donnie-Boy...Donnie-Boy, what...how..." He slumped to his knees beside his friend.

"They finally got over the top...too many RPGs...But I got some," Donnie-Boy cried—his words punctuated by gasps.

Tuck scooped Donnie-Boy's head and shoulders into his arms. "Let me see, um, let me see. Man, I can help you. Let's see. Damn, Donnie-Boy, what do I do first? Help me."

Donnie-Boy's limp left arm lay unnaturally twisted by his side. Splintered bones protruded from both legs just below the hips. Rather than gush, the blood oozed from his mangled legs—cauterized by the heat. Small shrapnel wounds peppered the left side of his face and blood filled his left eye.

"Don't hurt much, now...Least it won't when you finish it." His breathing was shallow but his voice grew calmer. "I'd do it myself, but that'd be suicide. Nuns said...couldn't go to heaven..." he laughed before a cough forced blood to trickle from the corner of his mouth. "Plus...ain't got no bullets...See?"

Donnie-Boy held up his .45 with his right hand. The pistol's slide was locked back. He pulled the trigger but nothing would happen. He threw the pistol aside, and then grabbed the back of Tuck's neck. He pulled Tuck forward and kissed his forehead, leaving a bloody smudge.

"I can't kill you," Tuck rebelled tearfully, his trembling replaced by a knotted pain in his stomach. "You're like my brother. You are my brother. I won't do it."

"Tuck, look at me..." Donnie-Boy yelled—his voice again halted by his labored breathing. "I ain't goin' back to the World...like this. I'm worse than...a cripple. I'm a freak." He grabbed Tuck's hand and forced it to his crotch. Tuck felt nothing that should have been there. "Tuck...they blew 'em all off, man," Donnie-Boy cried.

Tuck's stomach revolted. He turned his head and vomited.

"Who's gonna want me back in the World?" Donnie-Boy sobbed between gasps. "Who's gonna...want me now?"

Hopelessness gripped Tuck. He struggled to breathe and gasped in unison with his friend.

•

"Well, I hope you're pleased. They're all dead...or dying. All of them," Trai shouted.

"But we're not," Pham shouted back. "And that's more important. Now you come with me. We can just make the tunnels before the gunship arrives."

"Gunship? What gunship? There's no gunship coming here. There's nothing left for it to kill. God, I hope it goes to Dong Ta Ri and slaughters Chen and his men."

"That is treasonous talk and I will not hear of it. You understand?" Pham shouted back. He turned and began to walk away.

"Treason? You speak to me of treason?" Trai spat out. He grabbed his uncle by the shoulder and spun him around. "What's worse than betraying your own kin—murdering in cold blood your brother and all his family."

Pham stared in disbelief. "What do you mean? The Americans killed my brother. Do not play games with his memory."

"Why, you hypocritical old man. I've known the truth for months. You killed my entire family and made it look like the work of the Americans. And now you've gone and sent my friend to his death."

Pham stood silently for several seconds. Then, with eyes dancing madly in the moonlight, he smiled thinly and seethed. "So what are you going to do about it, eh? I should have cut your dick off. You're no soldier, not even a man. You don't even carry a rifle. My aide, ha! At one time, I thought I needed you. But look at you. You're pathetic.

"Yes, I killed your cowardly father and his whole sniveling family. Your little sisters were so sweet to my touch," Pham said. He spat on the ground and again pulled out his Bowie knife.

Trai quickly stepped back, reached into his pocket and drew his parents' pistol. He pointed it at his uncle's heart.

•

"No, no I can't do it. I won't do it," Tuck cried, cradling Donnie-Boy's torso in his arms and refusing to give in to what he knew he might ultimately do. "Doc Wild can fix you up, man. They can do a lot. And, I'll be there for you."

"Tuck, you're here for...me now," he sobbed, trying to flash that Donnie-Boy smile.

Tuck rocked back and forth like he had done with his little brother Winston not too many years before. He pulled Donnie-Boy's head close to his chin. His tears dripped onto Donnie-Boy's bloody cheek, where they mingled.

"Can they put...back together again? Can...help me love...woman...again?" Donnie-Boy strained and pleaded between increasing gasps. "I'm not gonna make...It's hurtin' again, Tuck. It hurts. Oh, mama, I'm so sorry...I'm so sorry."

He watched Donnie-Boy take another deep breath and appear to grow calm. "Look, damn it," Donnie-Boy suddenly hissed in a hurried whisper. "Either there's gonna be more gooks coming out of that ravine and we'll both be dead. Or, someone's gonna come to my aid and..."

"No, Donnie-Boy, no," Tuck whispered. He wiped the blood from his friend's face with his palm. He rocked while memories of soggy potato chips, summer evening baseball games, double dates and touchdowns in the fall flashed through his mind.

A strange, weak voice from several feet to the left of Tuck's shoulder startled him.

"Lam on, ban toi di. Lam on, ban toi chet di," a young NVA soldier cried in his native tongue. Tuck turned and saw the boy's pale face illuminated by the moonlight. The battle had torn away the soldier's left arm and a massive piece of his chest. Tuck noticed the soldier's right hand was wrapped in gauze where his little finger should have been. The soldier did not move except for his glassy, pleading eyes and lips that trembled as if chilled. "Lam on, cho toi chet di," the soldier again begged. His eyes then shifted toward Donnie-Boy. "Va cho no nua."

Tuck did not understand the words but he recognized the tone and the look in the soldier's eyes—they were the same as that of Donnie-Boy. He now saw a different face of his enemy—no longer menacing, no longer mysterious. He saw only another soldier in agony.

"Lam on," the soldier begged a last time.

Tuck nodded, raised the pistol with his left hand and fired. The bullet silenced the soldier's plea, but not Donnie-Boy's.

"Tuck," Donnie-Boy's voice rattled. "Tuck." He looked into Tuck's eyes, trying again to flash that Donnie-Boy smile. "I'd do it for you. Kiss Anna for..." He closed his eyes and waited.

Tuck looked at the smoking .45 still gripped tightly in

his hand. Pressing the muzzle against Donnie-Boy's heart, he wept. "Nooooo," he quietly groaned.

"Damn it, Tuck...it's an order," he hollered, and then coughed and vomited blood.

Tuck's primordial scream ripped the fabric of the night. A scream so loud, only the sound of a bullet being fired through a friend's heart could suppress it.

Tuck slumped over the body of his friend. It was done. His trembling ceased. But he now feared the darkness would come after his very soul.

•

"With my family's pistol, I do this for their honor," Trai spat. He pulled the trigger.

The bullet struck Pham in the chest, spinning him to the ground. He grabbed Trai's ankle and then fell onto his side. He gasped twice and looked up into his nephew's eyes. His breath hissed into silence. His body grew limp.

Trai stared at the slumped body of his uncle, and then pushed him away with his boot. "Revenge is ours, Father, but not as sweet as I'd hoped," he whispered with tightly closed eyes.

The eerie silence in the ravine startled Trai as much as the cacophony had overwhelmed him before. "Louie." Trai said quietly. "Louie!" he turned and shouted up into the ravine. "Louie!"

He slipped his father's pistol into his pocket and sprinted into the ravine. Struggling over the slippery rocks, he hurdled dozens of bodies. He checked the uniforms and faces for Louie. The search was maddening in the sharp lunar shadows. He sorted through the piles of bodies—none were Louie's. "He's got to be alive. He must be," he mumbled, looking up toward the lip of the ravine. If anyone had reached the top it was Louie.

A single gunshot, accompanied by an unnerving scream,

rang out from atop the ravine, causing Trai to flinch. Someone was alive. But who? He hoped it was Louie.

Trai scurried up the ravine and soon reached the top and peeked over the lip. Two large rocks limited his view, but he could see more than a dozen bodies littering what looked like a meadow. He pulled himself up by the trouser leg of a fallen comrade. The body's hand was bandaged. Despite the large hole in the forehead, Trai recognized the body. It was that of the boy Pham had earlier tortured. He paused briefly to recall the incident in the tunnels. It reinforced Trai's feeling of triumph over his uncle.

Quiet sobbing quickly captured Trai's attention. He stood and looked from behind the rocks. Trai saw a single American seated with his back to him. He was holding the body of a man. The American, not much older than he, Trai judged, held a pistol in his hand while slowly rocking back and forth.

With Louie gone, and his family's vengeance complete, Trai no longer feared death. His desire was now only to know the face of those he had once called the enemy. Trai spoke haltingly, searching for the English words. "He...fren to you?"

Tuck spun to face the sound of accented English behind him. He tried to bring his pistol to bear on the target. But when he twisted, the weight of Donnie-Boy's body forced him to his elbows.

"No shoo...G.I. No shoo," Trai said calmly, raising his hands above his waist. Suddenly the need for his father's pistol re-entered Trai's mind. He felt its weight in his pocket.

Tuck watched the soldier, also just a boy, slowly walk amid the bodies, turning them over as if searching for someone—perhaps a friend or maybe a weapon. He looked down at Donnie-Boy's bloody face but kept his pistol pointed in the direction of the soldier.

Trai sighed and examined the last of his comrades'

bodies—again, none were Louie's. He wiped away a tear, and then returned his attention to the grieving American. "He dead?" Trai asked, pointing with his head toward Donnie-Boy.

Tuck nodded somberly. The pall was like some Requiem Mass in a jungle cathedral.

"You...OK?" Trai pressed on, hoping to learn more from the encounter.

"No, I'm not," Tuck replied quietly, struggling to split his attention between Donnie-Boy and the soldier. He allowed his aim to droop. He regarded this unexpected visitor, who appeared unarmed and nonthreatening. Like the young soldier he had put out of his misery minutes earlier, he harbored no hatred for this man. Indeed, he found himself strangely comfortable with the soldier, as if he could sit on the steps of a porch and discuss the way things should be between them. For that moment, there was no war. "And you?"

"No...I look, for fren. He not here," Trai replied, shaking his head. For several seconds he stared into the American's eyes, which also glistened with tears in the moonlight. He studied the face and sought the menace, but only found the familiar. Yes, his father was right, he now believed. The Americans were not their enemy—surely not this young man who held his fallen friend in his arms. The war was their enemy.

Tuck suddenly changed position to shift the weight of Donnie-Boy's body off his injured knee. The movement forced the pistol's aim to rise higher and toward the soldier's face.

Startled, Trai reacted. He jammed his hand into his pocket and grabbed his pistol. He cocked the hammer with a loud click and began to draw the weapon, but stopped.

Tuck froze at the sound of the click. He slowly shook his head. "Don't do it." Their eyes again locked for several seconds. "We've killed too much tonight."

Trai nodded, released the pistol, and slowly slid his hand out of his pocket. He again lifted his empty hands above his waist. "Someday...maybe we mee again...as fren."

Tuck raised his pistol and nodded. The soldier stepped backward and bowed.

Trai slid down the lip of the ravine and was gone.

•

Tuck sat cross-legged with Donnie-Boy's body in his arms and the .45 still in his hand. His friend's face was peaceful now. He no longer hurt. Tuck sobbed even though his eyes had no more tears to offer.

Suddenly, a strong hand touched his shoulder. Tuck did not react this time. The hand shook him. "Come on Marine, shake out of it. Come on, Tuck, it's time to go," Gaines whispered. He helped Tuck to his feet, steadied him and then pointed him in the direction of the bomb crater.

"Wait, wait, I can't leave him like this," Tuck mumbled. He removed his flak jacket and covered Donnie-Boy's face and torso.

"I'll make sure they get down here ASAP and bring him on back up. That I promise," Gaines said. He looked around the ambush site and counted a score of bodies.

"How long you've been down here, sarge?" Tuck asked, glancing toward the lip of the ravine. The young soldier was gone.

"Long enough, Tuck. Long enough, Marine."

•

Trai walked gingerly through the rocks and twisted bodies to the mouth of the ravine. All that remained were the dead and the dying. The few survivors of the slaughter had fled. He was alone now and his thoughts centered on the young American and the loss of Louie. Perhaps he could call out one more time for Louie. He turned to shout Louie's name but was suddenly tackled and knocked backward.

Trai shook his head and looked up into the eyes of Col. Pham. A large bloodstain filled the area of the colonel's left shoulder and blood trickled from his mouth. "Thought you could kill me, eh? You pitiful little nothing," Pham wheezed. He reached for his big blade.

Strengthened by his days of carrying ammunition, Trai shoved his uncle away and reached in his pocket for his pistol. Pham lunged again and slashed his nephew on the right forearm. The pistol flew from Trai's grasp and Pham grabbed the teen's legs. Trai again managed to push his uncle away and crawled toward the pistol.

Pham pulled at his nephew's foot and dragged him away from the weapon.

With knife in hand, Pham rolled the smaller Trai over onto his back, leaped atop the young man's stomach, and then raised his knife high with both hands, as if posing for some ancient sacrificial rite under a full moon. Trai threw up his arms to shield his face from the strike.

CRACK! CRACK!

Pham's eyes bulged. His chest exploded with a gush. He gyrated and fell to the ground in a heap. His body convulsed onto its back and his leg twitched once. Col. Pham Van Bui died slowly—his eyes open, fixed and staring at the night sky above.

Trai pulled his hands away from his eyes and saw a smoking AK-47 fall by his side. A pair of strong hands pulled him to his feet.

It was Louie.

•

"I told you the right time and the right place would come," Louie smiled, pulling the shirt off Trai to treat his knife wound.

"But, but I thought you were dead," Trai said, helping to hold the gauze in place. Louie wrapped it around the wounded arm.

"So did I, for a while, especially when my head banged into that rock. Here, feel this lump," Louie said, guiding Trai's uninjured hand to the large welt. "When I came to, everyone around me was dead. Three men, including that big bodyguard, were on top of me and had me wedged between two boulders. It took all I had to claw my way out.

"When I did get out and saw all the dead around me, I didn't have to ask who had won the battle," Louie sighed. He tied off the dressing with a tug. "There, now. That'll heal up nice, but you'll have a nasty scar.

"This is all madness. I've had enough. Son, I've had enough." Louie bent over and picked up Bui's big knife. "Here. Here's a nice souvenir. I imagine you're the heir apparent. Just call it...a trophy."

Trai took the knife. He looked up at Louie and nodded. "Don't need it. I've made my peace." He hurled the knife as far as his injured arm would allow. It clanked off the rocks in the ravine. His eyes then drifted toward the top of the ravine and he wondered, he hoped, that the young American might also find peace.

Trai leaned up against Louie, who wrapped his arm around Trai's shoulders.

"If we get going now, I think, with a little luck, we can make it back to Cam Lo in a few days," Trai advised. "And there'll be plenty of chances to *chieu hoi* along the way."

"Ah, yes. But first, tell me more about this Aunt Linh of yours. The one with the big..."

Trai laughed like a boy again. "Oh, you'll like her. She has hair as black as a raven's feather and creamy skin as white as porcelain. And she's smart, too..."

"Yes, but what about her ass? She's got to have a nice ass. You know I like women with..."

CHAPTER 46

All Alone
Da Krong Valley, R.S.V.N.
April 15, 1969—7 a.m. local time

The backwash from the helicopter's twin rotors whipped the cool breeze into a gale, chilling the morning air atop Dong Cho.

Tuck squatted in the matted elephant grass, his arms wrapped around and pulling his knees tightly against his chest. He stared ahead, his eyes unable to focus on the present. A long night of tears had traced crusty rivulets across his smudged and bloodied face. The tears no longer flowed, yet he grieved within. Donnie-Boy was dead. Danny, Johnny and Tony were wounded. All were gone—carried away by the departing helicopters.

He was alone.

Doc Wild approached and knelt beside him. He put his hand on Tuck's shoulder and whispered as he might to an ailing child. "How you feeling, Tuck? Sorry I didn't get to you sooner, had to see about those guys," he said, titling his head toward the disappearing chopper.

"Hmm?"

"Tuck, I said how do you feel? Physically that is?"

"First, how about them?"

"They'll be OK," Doc Wild said, pausing to watch the CH-46s drop behind the nearby hills. "Johnny has a really bad concussion and a few shrapnel wounds to his shoulder. Danny also has a concussion and a nasty gash on the side of his face that's already showing signs of infection. They're taking them to Stud and then I suppose out to the hospital ship, maybe Da Nang.

"As for Tony, that gut wound is pretty severe. I'm sure it's stateside for him after Charlie Med," the corpsman continued. "By the way, speaking of gut wounds, I got some good news for you. Ike is going to be OK, but no more Marine Corps for him. I also hear Matt's ankle is healing up nice and he may be back in a week or so."

Tuck stared ahead, his eyes and head not moving. "What about the others?"

"Minor stuff, really. Shrapnel, no bullet wounds," Doc Wild quickly added, then paused to open his notebook to two full pages dedicated to Tuck's previous wounds. "Tuck, it's you I'm worried about now. The platoon's really going to need you and I have to know how you are."

He turned toward Doc Wild and rested the side of his head on his knees. Newfound tears flowed again. "I rocked him in my arms and watched him die. Now I know why they don't let family members serve together. He was more than just like a brother."

Doc Wild nodded and sighed. "You want me to come back later?"

"No, don't leave me. I can hardly move."

"I'll take that as an invitation." Doc Wild removed Tuck's blood-soaked blouse and shredded green T-shirt. "These day-old shrapnel wounds look like they want to get infected."

"Ssss, yie," Tuck winced when Doc Wild probed the sores.

"These three in the back look fresh."

"Yeah, took those hauling Tony up to the crater. The RPGs were raining all around us." Tuck again winced while Doc Wild cleansed the wounds. "I can hardly straighten up, must have pulled a back muscle or something while running with Johnny up the hill. And, I wrenched the hell out of my left knee when I fell twice while carrying Danny to the crater, too."

Doc Wild paused. "Let me get this straight. You carried three men to that crater last night?"

Tuck nodded slowly. "Donnie-Boy ordered me to."

Doc Wild scribbled a note in his book.

"But the worst part is this damn headache and ringing in my ears."

"Not getting much better, huh?" Doc Wild read over Tuck's medical history. "Says here this'll make your fourth Purple Heart—three I've recorded and one before I joined you guys. Creased left thigh, right?"

Tuck nodded again.

"Well, I wish I could've put you on that chopper but the skipper's orders are to keep as many men here as possible. We're staying another night. Sorry. But there is something I can do to help you feel better for now."

Doc Wild dug in his bag and came up with a small, dark plastic bottle of pills. "Here, take this. It's penicillin. I'll make sure you get the daily dose. You should be feeling much better in a few days." The aspiring surgeon handed Tuck a canteen. "As for right now..."

Tuck flinched when the small needle pierced his right thigh. A rush of pleasure coursed through his aching body. He gasped.

"Morphine. It'll kill the pain and help you rest. I'll tell the sarge and skipper to leave you alone. Now you get some sleep...doctor's orders." Doc Wild helped Tuck unfold from his crouch and lie down. He then covered him with a poncho liner. "I'll get you a new T-shirt, too."

Tuck nodded and closed his eyes. The soreness in his side and back immediately subsided, then the aching in his knee. Sliding into oblivion, the headache and tinnitus also succumbed.

•

"Tuck, Tuck, wake up, Tuck. Come on now," he heard. A firm hand grabbed his shoulder. Tuck bolted upright and looked from side to side. "Donnie-Boy, that you? Donnie-Boy?"

"No. It's me, Sgt. Gaines. Sorry, man. Come on, it's time to wake up. You've been out for about 10 hours now. Doc says you need to start moving a bit to get the stiffness out."

He turned, looked at Gaines and blinked, trying to make sense of his surroundings. His headache had subsided, as had the ringing in his ears. Physically, he felt refreshed. With the return to consciousness, however, Tuck's heartache also returned. Donnie-Boy was gone. Life would never be the same.

Tuck yawned and stretched, trying not to be obvious about his long rest. "What have I missed?" he said, shakily rising to his feet. Gaines grabbed his arm. The morphine had left his grasp on reality slightly askew.

"Not much, but the skipper wants to see us. I'll fill you in on the way up." Gaines handed him a new T-shirt. "Here, Doc Wild says this is for you."

Tuck unwrapped himself from his poncho liner and donned his new T-shirt, then his camouflaged blouse. He looked around. Something was missing. "Seem to have lost my rifle. And my flak jacket."

"Yeah, don't worry, we picked them up during patrol this afternoon. Alex and Willie led us back down to the ravine," Gaines said, pointing him in the right direction.

"By the way, where are the guys?"

"Doing what you just did, getting some extra sleep, skipper's orders, imagine that." Tuck again stumbled and Gaines grabbed him. "You OK?"

"Damn knee feels awfully sore, a little weak, too. So what did y'all find?"

"We went all the way down to the mouth of the ravine. Counted 86 KIA gooks, legit, too, including a full colonel—

shot in the back by an AK. His own guys, we figure. We also found four wounded and medevaced them out. Intel will try to milk them for info I guess." Gaines paused. "Word about what you guys did last night spread damn quick. Battalion's going nuts. Head of 3/9, ol' man Schiefer, even let the press get wind of it."

"Hell, I didn't do nothin' I wasn't told to do," Tuck replied absently.

"That's not how Alex and the others tell it, and how the brass now sees it. You haven't heard it all, yet," Gaines said, pointing toward the skipper, who busily chatted on the PRC-25.

Lt. Smith nodded and smiled cheerfully. Holding a large knife, he enthusiastically waved for Tuck and Gaines to join him. "Roger that, I sure will. You'll be getting my full report and recommendations in the morning. Thanks much. Kilo Six, out."

Tuck stared at the knife. The sun's reflection glinted across his face.

"Like it?" the skipper asked, holding his new souvenir like an amateur swordsman. "One of the guys found it down in the ravine this morning. Had to promise him in-country R&R for it."

Tuck shrugged at the silliness of the skipper.

"That must be the fourth time I've talked with the ol' man today. It seems we hit a gold mine with the papers we found on that gook colonel." The skipper flipped the knife to the ground and clapped his hands loudly. "You, my young Marine, and your buddies may have stopped, temporarily at least, a major assault on Vandegrift. That colonel *was* the notorious Pham Van Bui and was carrying full operational orders for this area's campaign.

"That, coupled with my small part, has dealt Charlie a severe blow," Lt. Smith added.

"Your part?" Tuck asked, no longer caring about the

ramifications of his tone. "What did you do, other than hang us out there as bait?"

"Now, let's not get snippy today there Corporal Richard. Yes, I said corporal—my newest squad leader," Smith said, dismissing the insult and putting emphasis on Tuck's new rank.

Gaines, quietly standing by Tuck's side, shrugged and shook his head slowly.

"It appears there will be a lot of promotions going around in the next few days—not to mention mine to first lieutenant, according to the ol' man here just now." Lt. Smith nodded toward the radio. "And he's putting me up for the Silver Star for having the foresight to call in the gunship before it was too late."

"What? What do you mean? Spooky never worked out last night. We had no help at all."

"Ah, but you're wrong there new corporal. You see, when the gunship arrived last night your ambush had already done its bang up job. But Mike Co. was just starting to report movement all around Dong Ta Ri. So Spooky just slid on south and caught a whole battalion of gooks on the move. They slaughtered them in the moonlight. Last count was nearly 280 gook KIAs plus a dead one that might be a Chinese adviser," Smith exclaimed with a cackle. "That's damn near 400 dead gooks in one night. Hell, Mike Company didn't have but three minor casualties. And all we had was only one dead Marine and less than a dozen wounded."

Tuck stepped forward with balled fists. Until now, Doc Wild's shot of morphine had done its job of sedating him. Gaines reached and grabbed Tuck's shirtsleeve and held fast. Tuck's face grew red with anger, as red as Gaines' face had ever grown during boot camp.

Smith noted Tuck's reaction. "Oh, yes, of course, Cpl. Donald Hebert. He was some kind of friend of yours. Right? Well, I am sorry for his death. But, that is war, isn't it? For whatever it may mean to you, I am recommending him for the big one, the Medal of Honor, posthumously, of course. Lt. Col. Schiefer has already assured me of his support in that matter.

"And from what the remainder of your team members tell me, as well as Sgt. Gaines here who tells me he witnessed the final shots of the whole affair..."

Stunned, Tuck quickly replayed the final moments in his mind, all the way until the final shot fired through Donnie-Boy's heart and his subsequent visitor.

"...and of course Corpsman Wildman's report on your wounds and own descriptions, I am recommending you for the Navy Cross. Hell, I'm guaranteeing all of you at least a Bronze Star."

He listened attentively but did not otherwise react. "Lt. Smith, any other time, any other place, such news would have overwhelmed me with pride. Today, I'm sorry. I just can't share in your jubilation—perhaps tomorrow. Right now, I have letters to write," he calmly said. "Thank you, sir, may I go now?"

"Carry on corporal," the skipper added. "Sgt. Gaines, remain here for a few minutes so we can go over tonight's plans, which by the way, do not call for an ambush."

Tuck returned to his position and found the members of his new squad, albeit a small one, asleep. He chose not to wake them and quietly removed his writing gear from his rucksack. He noted his rifle and flak jacket laying beside his rucksack. The jacket bore a large but dried bloodstain from the remains of Donnie-Boy's torso. He pulled it close to him and touched the stain with his cheek. New tears silently flowed again. He sat and wrote.

Dear Mom and Dad,

I am well but my heart is crushed beyond belief. My Donnie-Boy is gone. All is dark and I feel all is lost. We are still in the bush and in harm's way. I'll write when I'm able. Please give me time. See to it

Anna sees this. Dad, you explain it to her. Pray for my soul—Your loving son, Tuck

CHAPTER 47

The Visit
Eunice, La.
April 17, 1969—4 p.m. local time

Mary Richard swept the freshly mowed grass from the front sidewalk while Dave mowed the last few strips of the lawn. The work kept her mind busy, more so than it kept the walk neat. Every waking moment not involved in some activity found her mind wandering across the far reaches of the Pacific. She continually calculated her son's world of 13 hours ahead and wondered what he might be doing at certain times of the day. Right now, at 5 a.m. in his world, Benjamin must either still be sleeping, or preparing for another day's long trek in the jungle.

Mary had only a few more feet to go when the lawn mower stopped and Dave trotted toward the house for a drink. "Want me to bring you a glass of cold water," he hollered. "Mama?"

Mary did not hear her son's offer. She gripped her broom and stared—her eyes wide and mouth slightly agape—while the beige Ford sedan made a slow left turn at the corner and drove up their street. The military vehicle, bearing the official Marine Corps emblem on its door, cruised to their driveway. Mary's knees buckled but she steadied herself with the broom's handle.

"Mama, you OK?" Dave shouted and rushed to her side. "Mama, what is it?"

The car stopped and the driver rolled down his window.

"Excuse me, ma'am. Can you tell me where I can find the Hebert residence? I'm from out of town and not sure..."

Mary feebly pointed to the house next door.

"Thank you ma'am," said the polite young driver. A second uniformed Marine on the passenger's side shuffled through a stack of papers. A city police patrol car closely followed the Marine Corps vehicle, which turned into Grace Hebert's driveway.

"Get your daddy, now," Mary ordered. "Tell him...tell him, just tell him to come next door. Something terrible's happened to Donnie-Boy."

Dave met his father at the door. "Mom said get over to Miss Grace's right away," he said, his face confused and bewildered.

Curtis marched toward the house where Tuck had lived much of his childhood as Donnie-Boy's best friend, neighbor, classmate and teammate. He thought of them as inseparable. He could not fathom Tuck's world without Donnie-Boy. His mind raced. Maybe Donnie-Boy was only wounded, or was missing. Did the Marines come out in person for anything less than that dreaded acronym for death—KIA? What of Tuck? He would've been with Donnie-Boy.

Curtis caught up to Mary when she reached the front porch. He placed his arm around her and together they walked up the three short steps. Tears filled Mary's eyes when the shriek of Grace's voice reached them. No longer just dread in the middle of the night, their nightmares had grown into terrifying reality—darkness engulfed their world on a sunny afternoon. It was a Thursday, Curtis noted. One does not forget such things.

The two Marines stood on the front porch. "No, no. You're not coming in," Grace wailed from inside the screen door. "Go away! Please?"

"Mrs. Hebert, we need to speak with you," the younger Marine pleaded.

"Nooo, please, nooo."

"Excuse me, son," Curtis said to the Marine, a second lieutenant, but hardly more than a few years older than Tuck and Donnie-Boy. The officer nodded and stepped aside. "Grace, Mary's coming in to meet you."

She stepped back from the door. Mary entered and Grace fell into her arms.

Curtis, his chest suddenly trembling, turned to the Marine. "We're the next door neighbors, the Richards, lifelong friends of the Heberts. Our son is in the same combat unit with their son. Her husband is not yet back from work. Can I be of assistance?"

"Yes, sir. But I will eventually have to speak directly with Mrs. Hebert and her husband."

"I understand," Curtis nodded, choking out the words.

"Mr. Richard, it is with much regret that I inform you that Corporal Donald Charles Hebert was killed in action on the evening of 14 April in Quang Tri Province in the Republic of South Vietnam. He died from explosive injuries and hostile gunfire. It is also noted that his death involved extreme valor. Details will be forthcoming. Now I will need to speak with the family so that the scheduling of funeral arrangements can be made," the Marine said in a proper tone.

"Thank you, lieutenant. You have acquitted yourself well this afternoon and I will pass my commendation on to your superior. Thanks again," Curtis said in a military manner. The young Marine nodded in appreciation. "Now, let me go inside and pave the way for you. OK?"

"Thank you, sir. That would be appreciated."

"Give me five minutes." Curtis prepared to enter the front door but he paused and turned. "Would you have any information on Benjamin Richard, by any chance."

"Sorry, no sir. We only received notice in Lafayette of Corporal Hebert's death. I'm sorry I can't help you."

Curtis nodded and then entered the home. Grace and

Mary huddled on the sofa in the living room. Grace looked up at Curtis with hope in her eyes. "Please, tell me no."

He knelt in front of her and took her hands. "Two nights ago, Donnie-Boy was killed in action. He's gone, Grace. I am so sorry."

Mary looked into Curtis' eyes. He returned the look and didn't need to be asked. He quietly replied. "No word." Mary briefly closed her eyes and sighed before returning to Grace. She felt a strange mixture of elation and grief. Guilt flushed over her.

"Grace, these two young men need to come in and speak with you now. I'll call John," Curtis said. "Mary, I'm also goin' call Willie. He may need us now as well."

Mary nodded and Curtis signaled the two Marines to enter. He stepped out onto the porch, where Chief of Police Vidrine waited. The chief put his hand on Curtis' shoulder. "If you're going look for John, don't worry, we've already contacted him at work and he's headed home with a friend. If I can be of more help, well, just give me a call at the station. You hear?"

Curtis nodded. "Thanks, chief. I gotta go make some calls now."

The sight of the familiar blue Ford pickup froze Curtis in his steps. Parked in his driveway, it meant only one thing—Wilfred. "Oh, my God, not Johnny, too? No."

Wilfred and Anna walked out of Curtis' house, following Dave who was leading them toward Grace's home. They met at the sidewalk and Dave continued on his way. Wilfred's red eyes met Curtis' tear-streaked face. Anna slumped to Curtis' side, sliding her arms around his waist. Wilfred momentarily took them both into his huge embrace.

Wilfred then pulled a telegram from the breast pocket of his western-style checked shirt. "Says here, Curtis, that Johnny's been wounded—pretty bad, too. He's been brought to a hospital ship. It says his wounds aren't life-threatening and that he'll be contacting us."

"Anything about Tuck?" Curtis asked.

"No, not a word," Anna said with a sniffle. "I can't believe Donnie-Boy is gone. My poor Tuck. He's all alone."

Wilfred shook his head. He turned toward the Hebert home. "We didn't know about Donnie-Boy until your boy Dave told us just a minute ago. I suspect they must've been together."

"Yeah, looks like it. I just wish we knew something about Tuck."

Dave came running out of the Hebert house. "Gotta get something for mom. Be right back."

Curtis nodded his approval.

"Well, Curtis, you got no telegram and they haven't paid you a visit," Wilfred said, nodding toward the Marines, who headed back to their sedan.

"I suppose so. It also means the boys are in some deep shit. We'd better keep an eye on the news for a few days," Curtis replied, feeling the warmth of Anna's soft arms. Her damp face was buried in his shoulder.

"Look, Curtis, I came right over when I got this." Wilfred held up the telegram. "I wanted to see how everything was over here. But I gotta go back home in case I get a call, you know."

"Sure, I know. Give me a call if you hear anything. OK? Anything at all."

"You bet, little buddy. Please give my sympathy to Miss Grace. I don't think I can handle goin' over there right now." Wilfred turned to walk back to his truck. "Anna, you comin' home with me, *cher?*"

She shook her head.

"I'll drive her home later," Curtis said. "You sure you don't want to stay here tonight? Y'all are both welcome. We got the room."

"Naw, gotta be home in case he calls," Wilfred said with a big wave. "I'll be OK."

Curtis' dabbed at his eyes with the back of his hand after Wilfred drove away. He gave Anna a fatherly kiss on the top of her head and pointed her in the direction of Grace's home.

"Tuck, give us a sign of some sort. Dear God, give us a sign," Curtis mumbled.

Dave hurried out of the house carrying a Catholic daily missal in his hand. "What was that, Dad? You say something?"

"Uh, nothing, Dave. What you got there?" Curtis held out his hand.

"Oh, Mom wanted her prayer book for her and Miss Grace, see," Dave said, handing the black missal to his father. Curtis reached without looking and fumbled the leather-bound book. It fell open with its spine to the ground. The pages fluttered in the warm breeze and stopped near the end of the book. He picked it up, brushed away a few grass clippings and then looked at the prayer on the dog-eared page and smiled.

"*O, St. Joseph whose protection is so great...*" he read. "It's Tuck's prayer. He's OK. Thank God, he's OK."

•

May 7, 10 a.m. local time: Steve Soileau shifted his truck into low gear and slowed. He sifted through the mail for Amazon Street. Mail to the Hebert home over the past three weeks mostly included official-looking stuff from the U.S. Government and Marine Corps. Sympathy cards poured in as well, even though they'd buried their son more than two weeks ago.

Nearly half of Eunice had attended the funeral service, which featured an open casket to the surprise of many. Rumors had hinted of a horrendous death. A glass seal and the artistic hands of a government mortician had made Donald Hebert's body presentable.

Rumors also abounded that the fallen Marine had died heroically and that high honors would be coming his family's way. The town buzzed with curiosity.

But the excitement that once gushed from the Hebert household was missing. Grace, often waiting at the mailbox each morning, never met "Mr. Steve" at the roadside anymore. Townsfolk whispered that Grace's husband, John, had taken an "extended vacation" the afternoon of the funeral. He hadn't been seen since.

The Richards' son, Tuck, was a prolific letter writer. But in the past few weeks, Mr. Steve had delivered only one thin envelope about a week after the Heberts learned of their son's death.

Until now.

"Whoa, what's this? A fat letter from Cpl. Tuck Richard. Aha, I knew he'd come through sooner or later. Think I'll bring this one down myself," Mr. Steve mumbled. Too often he was the only person around to listen.

Mr. Steve ran his route as quickly as possible, jamming more sympathy cards into the Heberts' mailbox, along with another officious looking letter from the USMC. He paused a second to make sure Grace wasn't coming out to greet him. She did not.

He hurriedly fished through the stack to make sure he had all the Richards' mail and magazines, and most importantly, Tuck's letter—it was dirty and mangled as usual. He pulled his truck into the driveway and then briskly walked to the carport entrance, kicking aside an unattended football. He rapped hard on the door.

In a matter of seconds, Mary Richard peered out the kitchen door window. Mr. Steve was grinning and holding an envelope up to his face. He nodded almost comically.

Mary flung the door open and yelled, "Curtis, come quickly. Hurry."

"What is it, Babe? You OK?"

"Oh, yes, I am. It's a letter from Tuck." Mary heard the desk chair fall to the floor. Curtis rushed to meet her. He found his wife hugging and kissing the mailman.

"Oh, thank you, thank you, thank you. You're such a dear to bring it to us. You know how much this means. Oh, thank you."

She hurried to tear open the letter.

"I just hope it's full of great news. Knowing Tuck, I'm sure there'll be more coming soon. Y'all have a great day because days like these make my job all worth it," Mr. Steve said, smiling and with a tip of his hat.

Curtis settled Mary and guided her to the kitchen table. "Take it easy now, Babe, don't rip it apart. It looks like it's been through the mill."

Together they read through a sheen of tear-filled eyes.

Dear mom, dad and family,

I am alive and well. At least as well as one can be after nearly 30 straight days in the bush (when you receive this) and we are not going back to Stud anytime soon.

I fear I may never leave the bush.

We have the gooks on the run and the battalion commander wants us to flush these vermin totally out of this area.

My many minor wounds have mostly healed and I feel stronger now than I have in weeks. Our contact with the enemy has been sporadic and light. We haven't had a combat casualty in more than two weeks. Still, we hump the mountains of the Da Krong Valley. The Nam's heat and humidity are our real enemy now.

I have received a field promotion to corporal and am a squad leader now. But as always, my squad is a small one. We hope to get reinforcements soon.

I don't know just how much you know about what happened to Donnie-Boy. I don't know how much the Marines tell families. I am just as sure there have been rumors. It is not easy. Indeed, it is impossible for me to convey the horrors of that night and many other nights we have suffered through.

So where do I start? Do I say that he was a hero? Or, do I say he died in my arms?

Re-reading the words, Mary's breathing grew rapid and shallow.

His death haunts my every waking moment, and even my dreams. There is no peace for me.

On the night of April 14 we were on an eight-man ambush led by Donnie-Boy. We ran up against an entire company of NVA regulars and pinned them down in a ravine. It is a long story, but Donnie-Boy directed a firefight in which we killed nearly 90 gooks over two hours or something like that. Donnie-Boy also held off the enemy single-handedly with a machine gun while I carried Johnny and Danny to safety. They had both been knocked out and wounded during the battle.

"We heard about that battle on the 5:30 news, remember? We wondered if that was around where our boys were. They called it a victory with huge strategic implications," Curtis said.

"Shh, I'm still reading," Mary sniffed, dabbing her eyes with a soaked tissue.

When I returned to Donnie-Boy's side, he had been wounded terribly. He had lost both his legs. But he was still alive and firing away. Suddenly the fighting stopped. I guess we had either killed all of them or they had had enough. Anyway, he looked up at me and grabbed me and pulled me close. We both cried, as I cry now as I write.

Mary and Curtis' tears mingled with Tuck's on his letter. "I don't know if I can read on, Babe," Mary admitted.

"He wouldn't have written it if he didn't want us to share his grief."

He said he hurt so much and that no one would love him back in the World. Mom and dad, the explosions had castrated him. All that was left of him was but a stump of the great athlete he had been. I took him in my arms and rocked him. I rocked him in my arms, Mom, like you did for me whenever I was hurt as a little boy. But his pain was too great, and I could do nothing more for him. Then, he smiled at me in the moonlight. You know, one of those Donnie-Boy smiles. Soon after that, his suffering ended and mine began.

I loved Donnie-Boy so.

I feel so alone now. So alone. I've written to my beloved Anna but I haven't yet been able to tell her everything about how Donnie-Boy died. I suspect someday I might be able to. But not now. Anyway, the company commander hailed us as conquering heroes and I have been recommended to receive the Navy Cross. And if you haven't heard yet, Miss Grace and them will be notified soon that Donnie-Boy has been recommended for the Medal of Honor. Dad, I'm sure you can grasp the full meaning of these awards.

Curtis let out a slow, low whistle. "Babe, this is big-time stuff."

Still, they mean nothing to me. Perhaps someday, if I survive, I will wear it proudly. But for now my mind is filled only by the thoughts of Donnie-Boy and my own survival. I pray to St. Joseph all the time now. I think he may be the only one who can get me through this war.

Please pray for me, and my soul. I hope my next letters are more cheerful.—Your loving son, Tuck

P.S. Please send more Kool-Aid.

CHAPTER 48

A World Gone Awry
Southern Da Krong Valley, R.S.V.N.
May 15, 1969—5 p.m. local time

A gnat had lodged itself in the corner of Tuck's right eye and he could not blink the pest away. He fished a small round mirror from the depths of his rucksack. A rouge-filled crack ran down one side of the glass. It had been one of his mom's old compacts that she had sent to him in a package.

He looked into the mirror and dabbed at the gnat with his little finger. "There, got it," he said, flicking away the black spot. Tuck again looked into the mirror and stared, hoping to find his mother's latent image within. Instead, the bright blue eyes that once could light up a room and steal the heart of an Anna Carlisle now stared back at him as vacant gray orbs. His nose, sitting upon sunken cheeks, no longer seemed to fit his face. His mouth sat below, drawn tight into a line by lips that neither curled into a smile nor sank into a frown.

•

Tuck sat in the matted elephant grass and shared a bitter tin of coffee with Sgt. Gaines. "I've been in the Nam 'bout five months and already it seems like a lifetime," Tuck said somberly. "Lately, when we've finished humping for the day, I just sit, like this, and stare toward the east, back toward home. And I wonder, where's the glory and the patriotic music swelling up in the background when we charge up the hill?" He took a sip. "War wasn't supposed to be like this.

"At times, I ask myself is all of this just a nightmare and I'm really tossing and turning in my rack back home? Or worse, has everything that happened to me before this time just been a dream, and that Vietnam, this war, Donnie-Boy's death, the only realities there are?"

"Oh, it's real all right, Tuck; all of it—before and since," Gaines said, pausing to drain his cup. C-ration coffee, at least, offered a caffeine lift. "I also think maybe, no, hell I know now, that this is what Gunny Hill meant about me getting my butt over here. He wanted me to actually feel what you guys were going to feel, to know what it was like to hump the hills, feel the aches and lose friends. Damn, he was right. I had no idea it'd be like this. Sure, I knew it'd be tough. But not like this. I only wish I could tell him he was right."

Tuck crushed their tins and buried them with two quick swings of his entrenching tool. "So, you think you still want to go back and be a DI again?"

"Damn straight, more than ever now. If I make it outta here, I'm goin' home on leave and then straight back to the MCRD. I'm a lifer, Tuck, and I'm a good DI, even better now. I'll be able to do it with feeling and conviction." Gaines grinned. "When I jump a turd's ass, it'll be for a reason."

Tuck hesitated, his head bowed, unable to look Gaines in the eye, "Tell me, sarge, uh, just how much did you really see that night? That night...last month when Donnie-Boy died. Things were kind of crazy, you know."

Gaines also hesitated. "I saw two Marines doing their job. Two good friends being friends, one in need, the other obliging. I saw two of my boots doing my Marine Corps proud." A single tear formed in the corner of his eye. "It was the most courageous act I've ever witnessed, an act I will keep close to my heart and take to my grave."

Tuck nodded with a thin smile, and then asked, "How about that young gook who walked up on me? See him?"

"What do you mean?" Gaines asked. "I didn't seen any

gook, just you and Donnie-Boy. But I did go back up to the crater for a while to help with the wounded. I figured I'd give you a few minutes alone with Donnie-Boy, you know. What gook you talking about?"

"Aah, never mind." Tuck nodded. "Must've been seeing things."

The afternoon air suddenly whirled and the elephant grass bowed when a CH-46 circled close to the hilltop, swinging its re-supply sling only a few yards overhead. The powerful Sea Knight flared and unleashed the mesh sling, dropping the boxed contents softly to the ground.

"We'd better get up there and give those guys a hand." Gaines stood and motioned Tuck to follow. "Come on, let's go."

"Oh, one last thing, sarge."

"What's that?"

"Thanks."

"You bet." Gaines smiled. "Let's go, Marine."

Instead of heading northwest toward Stud, the chopper circled, waiting for the grunts to clear the cargo from the LZ. "Must be bringing in replacements," Gaines shouted. He looked up, shielding his eyes from the sinking sun and downdraft. "About damn time."

"Hope they're for my squad," Tuck hollered back.

The helicopter lit and three grunts charged down the ramp and hopped off. For the first time in a month, a real smile danced across Tuck's face.

Gaines looked toward the chopper, grinned and gave Tuck a gentle shove. "Go ahead. I'll get some other guys to help with this stuff."

Johnny and Danny trotted toward him with renewed vigor.

"Hey, hot damn, look at what we got here," Tuck said with a newfound grin and clasped hands. "Are you guys ever a sight for sore eyes? I thought I'd never see you two again."

He jumped into Johnny's mitts and Danny wrapped his long arms around the pair.

"Good to see you, too, but I can't say I'm happy to be back out here in the bush, you know." Johnny laughed, letting Tuck slip to the ground.

"Yeah, but at least we'll be keeping good company again," Danny chimed in. "I was getting sick of all those squids back on the ship, not to mention this big oaf."

"I bet. Look at you, both of you guys have put 10-15 pounds back on. Don't expect me to be humping y'all's ass out of trouble now," Tuck chortled. "Man, it's so good to see you guys. It's been tough without you and..."

"And Donnie-Boy?" Johnny finished the sentence. "Yeah, we figured you were pretty much tore up inside over here without us. But here we are, back in the middle of Viet-fuckin'-Nam."

"Aw, c'mon, man, you were the one tellin' all them round-eyed nurses about how you were a killin' machine and was ready to get back in the shit," Danny redressed Johnny with a smile.

"Hey, it's my new pitch, man."

"Did it work?" Tuck asked.

"No," Johnny emphatically replied with a scowl, and then a grin.

The three grunts hugged again and slapped one another on the back.

"Guess you guys will want Gertrude back."

"Bet your sweet ass," Johnny replied.

"Two guys over in third squad's got her now, but the sarge is making new arrangements. Those two guys are new and having trouble handling her anyway," Tuck said, leading them back to the squad.

"Man, they had better not have messed with our gal, or there'll be hell to pay, yeah," Johnny warned. "Bet she can't wait for me to give her a good bath."

"Hey, Matt," Danny turned and shouted. "C'mon, man, we're headed to the squad area."

"Be right there," replied the former squad member, who had broken his foot near Shepherd. He still walked with a slight limp but insisted to the medics he could hump.

"Good, Matt's back, too. Damn, I don't know what I'll do with half a squad." Tuck said.

"You our new squad leader?" Johnny asked with some surprise.

"Yeah, even promoted me to corporal after Donnie-Boy went down. They gave me his squad, or what was left of it," he said, pausing. "Is that gonna cause a problem?"

"No, not at all," Danny replied. Johnny shook his head and grinned.

"Good, because, Johnny, you're going to get Gertrude back. But Danny, I'm sorry, I'm making you a team leader. And the sarge got the skipper to agree that if y'all ever got back, that you'd both be promoted to lance corporal." Tuck winked.

The big men slapped palms. "All right, brother lance!" Johnny shouted.

"Likewise, bro."

Matt caught up with the trio after they reached Kilo 2 Alpha's position. He slipped his gear to the ground, and then slapped Tuck on the back. "Glad to be back with you guys. But can you bail me out? Just where in the hell are we anyway?"

"Well, let's see," Tuck said, retrieving Donnie-Boy's combat map from his thigh pocket.

The returning trio traded greetings with Willie, Alex and Mike, plus the M-60 team temporarily assigned to Tuck's squad. "You two dudes can di-di on back over to third squad now," he heard Johnny admonish them. "The boys are back... and just lay my lady Gertrude gently on the ground."

"I'd say we're about right here, Matt." Tuck pointed to

map grid 87-36. "We're only about eight klicks southwest of Shepherd, where you broke your foot, right here." Tuck added, tracing his finger up to map grid 93-41. "We're also about nine miles southwest of Dong Cho mountain and right around 15 miles from Stud, way up here."

Tuck turned and pointed over his left shoulder to the west. "Heck, Khe Sanh is only about two miles over that way where all the bomb craters are. Laos is about five miles that way, too."

"So what's up?" Danny asked. "What they got planned for us now?"

"Our orders are to stay here tonight. Tomorrow we've got a bitch of a hump ahead, they say about 10 klicks to the south, southeast, mostly elephant grass. The objective is a mother of a climb. The map says a 908. It's called Co Yan, less than a mile from Laos."

"Shit, some welcome back, huh?" Johnny sighed.

"Don't mean nothin', bro," Danny added.

"Yeah, it's the shit alright. But it's never been easy, guys. Why should it change now?" Tuck answered.

Danny shook his head and punched Tuck on the arm. "No, guess not, little Tiger."

"Oh, and Tuck, uh, we, Danny and me, never really, uh, got to thank you," Johnny stammered. "We didn't get to see much of the fight down at the ravine. And never heard about Donnie-Boy and how he really got it. Just rumors from back home. So, sometime, when you get the chance, maybe you'll fill us in. Oh, and congratulations."

"Congratulations? For what?" Tuck asked, folding his map "Making corporal?"

"You mean you didn't hear? We heard it when we got back to Stud two days ago. Looks like they're gonna give you the Navy Cross for hauling our asses up the hill, Tony's too, and helping knock off all those gooks," Danny said. "It just needs to go through all the channels and shit."

"And Donnie-Boy's family is gonna get the Medal of Honor," Johnny added. "My ol' man says the Marines are givin' Donnie-Boy the Congressional, some bronzes and a possum..."

"That's posthumously, dumb ass," Danny corrected.

"Oh. Anyway, Miss Grace is going to be invited to the White House later this year. That's big stuff back in Eunice," Johnny added.

"No, I hadn't heard. The mail's been real sparse up here," Tuck said with a grin. "But thanks, fellas. I was just doing what y'all would have done. Plus, Donnie-Boy ordered me to do it, else I would have left your silly asses on the ground."

"Yeah, sure, Tuck, sure," Johnny replied, slapping Tuck on the shoulder. "And, to show our gratitude, me, Danny and Matt have agreed to stand all y'all's watches tonight. We figured y'all might be pooped out a bit."

"Now, that is gratitude, and something I will take y'all up on," Tuck replied with a point and a smile. "We've been humping hard the past month and we could use the rest. Gooks have been pretty quiet lately. But be careful, we're still getting a lot of night probes on the perimeter.

"Now go on and get re-acquainted with Gertrude. Danny, we'll set up your fire team tomorrow. I'm going fire off a quick letter to Anna. There's something I've got to ask her."

The days in the bush were mounting and the words were harder to find. Nearly a week had passed since he'd written and told her all she needed to know about Donnie-Boy's death. He sat next to his rucksack and fished out his writing gear. Just enough sun remained in the western sky. Before beginning, he paused and watched Johnny and Danny gleefully tear into Gertrude. They stripped her naked and squealed. They checked her out like a Saturday-night conquest. Oh, how they loved their M-60 machine gun.

"Darlin', if I had you in Tiger Stadium, that damn Bama

would never have a chance," Johnny said, caressing Gertrude's black plastic stock.

"Yeah, that's about what it'd take for you Tigers to beat the Tide, a damn machine gun."

"Get outta here, boy."

"Hot damn, Johnny, there you go again, how many times am I gonna get on your ass about calling me boy."

Tuck smiled. They made him laugh again.

Dear Anna,

It's been a month now since Donnie-Boy's death and I still can't shake him from my waking mind, even though the hurt has turned to a sort of numbness. I guess it's supposed to be like that, when you've lost your best friend. But it's the nightmares that haunt me most. I can sleep no more than a half an hour before I see his smiling face. I fear they may never go away. And in a way I hope they never do.

However, today a tonic that might ease my suffering arrived in the form of your cousin, Johnny, and Danny Jackson. I knew there was a chance they might return but never believed it. I feared so much that I was doomed to be alone out here.

I pray to St. Joseph that we three can survive this war. And if I do survive, the first thing I plan to do is get down on my knees and thank the good Lord for his blessing, and while I'm down there, I guess I'll also just go ahead and ask you to marry me.

I believe we've always taken it for granted that marriage is in our future, but neither has wanted to officially mention it first. Maybe it's the war and the fact I might not have another chance, so I will say it now. Anna Carlisle, I love you, will you marry me?

I know it's all kind of corny. But when you're sitting alone atop a hill in Vietnam, sounding corny is the last of your worries. Well, gotta go now, need to check on the guys before dark sets in. I look forward to your reply. I love you so much, pray for me.—Your loving Tuck

P.S. Tomorrow we again have a long hump ahead. Someday soon I hope I can say the same to you (ha, ha).

•

10 a.m., May 16: "Heard the latest scuttlebutt?" Sgt. Gaines said, collapsing next to Tuck when Kilo Co. halted for a short break.

"Nope." Tuck took a swig from his canteen and thought, thank God and mom for the Kool-Aid that made the halazone-treated water more palatable. Gaines fetched a cigarette, lit it and took a drag. Kilo 2 Alpha's days on the point had luckily ended before the weather had kicked into high heat. "Another hot one today, and its just 10 o'clock," Tuck lamented. "Must be in the 90s already. And this damn elephant grass doesn't help either."

"Well, the trees are just ahead a few klicks," Gaines advised. "Unfortunately, so is about 700 more meters up Co Yan. Name your poison."

"So, what's the scoop?"

Gaines laughed while nodding skeptically. "Heard the skipper on the net just before we left this morning. He was real excited, too. After he finished, he got off and told me it was a secret. 'Don't tell the men, I don't want them to not be focused on the task at hand.' That kind of bullshit. Anyway, the word is, we may not be long for the Nam. It seems, the skipper says, that President Nixon is determined to start pulling us out of here and start turning the war over to Marvin the ARVN. They're calling it the 'Vietnamization' of the war."

"So, how does that affect us? And why not tell the guys? The Army will be the first to go anyway, the worthless shits."

"No, that's not what the skipper hears. Seems 3/9 was the first combat unit to reach the Nam back in '65. Nixon says it's fitting Ninth Marines be among the first to go. How about that?"

"You mean?"

"That's right. If, if there's any truth to it, we could be headed home sometime in August, according to what the skipper hears. But like I say, it's all scuttlebutt." Gaines strained against the shoulder straps of his rucksack and stood up. "Make the skipper happy and keep it quiet today. I'll try to find out more before tonight and pass it on."

"Thanks, appreciate the word."

•

Tuck reached back, grabbed Matt's hand and then pulled. Slowly the fallen grunt scrambled to his feet. The northwest slope of Co Yan provided as steep a challenge as any of the Da Krong hills. Its triple canopy shaded the climbing grunts from the glaring 3 p.m. sun but captured and focused the heat like some enormous oven.

"How's the foot?" Tuck asked Matt, who trudged up the hill behind him.

"Oh, the foot's fine. All healed up. It's the thighs and lungs that aren't back to 100 percent. About has my ass kicked, but I'll make it somehow," the panting Marine said. He pressed on.

Two hours later, the snaking line of grunts halted less than 100 meters from the Co Yan peak. The arrival of the point squad at the summit signaled the end of the ordeal— nearly 10 klicks in 10 hours and in temperatures nearing 100 degrees.

"It'll take another 30 minutes until we all get up there and they set up the perimeter," an exhausted Tuck told Danny, before he collapsed into the brush. "Man, this was the worst. I'm bushed. Actually, I really don't give a damn how I feel. Just glad it's over."

Danny huffed and placed his fists on his knees. Sweat poured from his head as if giant hands were wringing his face dry. "That hospital ship didn't exactly keep me in shape, either."

"Fils putain, c'est chaud," Johnny exhaled in his best Cajun French.

"Son of a bitch, it's hot," Alex added.

"That's what I just said," Johnny explained.

"Don't guess you guys are going to offer to stand watch tonight again, huh?" Tuck said with a hopeful laugh.

"No, way, man," Danny said. "Don't even wake me up before it's my watch. Not even a minute early."

An eerie hush, almost a pall, fell over the grunts for the next 15 minutes while they sought their second wind. Eyes barely exchanged glances. The exhausted Marines' thoughts and feelings turned inward.

"OK, let's go. Line's movin' again." Tuck moaned and forced himself to his feet. "C'mon, let's go, get up."

Helping one another to their feet, Kilo 2 Alpha grunted and groaned.

•

By 9 p.m., the skipper had assigned Tuck and his squad to the southeast slope of Co Yan, where the elephant grass grew closest to the jungle. They dug their fighting holes just inside the tree line and about 20 yards from the elephant grass, which they had routinely trampled.

"Danny, you, Mike and Alex set up with me," Tuck ordered. "Matt, take Willie and that loaner from third platoon and get with Johnny over there to the right so Gertrude can cover that grassy area."

Darkness returned after the half moon disappeared beneath the horizon. An hour later, Tuck felt a light touch on his shoulder. "How's it going over here tonight? Haven't heard much chatter around the perimeter," Gaines said quietly but not in a whisper.

"Well, let's see. It's hotter and humid as all hell. We ain't stopped sweating since today's little climb. We've been in the bush for 40 straight days. The chow's gettin' low. And I..."

"And, I get the idea, Tuck. I know it's lousy. But

this'll cheer you up. That scuttlebutt we talked about this morning?"

"Yeah?"

"Well, it looks like it's on the up and up. Skipper talked to battalion and they're confirming that we could be headed out of here and on the way to Okinawa by August."

"Oh, dear God, let it be true," Tuck said, making the sign of the cross.

"And there's more. Skipper says if contact stays light over the next two days, they're gonna call an end to this op and bring us back to Stud. Another battalion will finish the Da Krong sweep later," Gaines added. "What you think about that?

"If I wasn't so exhausted, I'd jump up and kiss you."

"Well, glad to know something positive came out of that hump today," Gaines said, looking to draw a laugh.

"Want me to pass the word to the guys?"

"No, not tonight. Let 'em be. Skipper's right this time. News like that just might get 'em too pepped up and they'll get careless. You tell 'em first thing in the morning," Gaines advised. "Oh, by the way, I'll be on the other side of the hill tonight. So keep an eye on things for me. OK?"

Tuck nodded, and then pointed to the ground. "Hey, sarge, look at that. Bet you've never seen one like that." He motioned toward a glowing foot-long centipede crawling down the phosphorescent trail stirred up only hours before by the Marines.

"No, I can't say I have. Wonder if it glows on its own, or if it's just all full of that decaying crap on the ground."

"Don't know, but I'd kind of like to catch it and put it in Donnie-Boy's pack. He hates big bugs, and little green frogs. Let me see if he's watching, and then I'll..." Tuck caught himself and bowed his head. "Don't guess that would work, would it, sarge?"

"It's OK, Tuck. That's what I mean about the excitement of the moment. Just get some rest, if you can."

"Sure, sarge, thanks for the good news."

•

The memories—the nightmares—returned, cascading into his subconscious. Tuck's mind drifted back to that haunted April night while he stared into the darkness.

"Hey, Tuck, you OK, man?" Danny squatted quietly before him. "Snap out of it, dude."

"Ohh. Uh, OK. Danny? I'm sorry. Just can't shake Dong Cho sometimes, you know." Tuck pulled up his stiff T-shirt and wiped the sweat from his brow and the tears from his eyes.

"Yeah, I know. Like that for me, too. Back on the ship they had some Navy shrink aboard for us to talk to, though. Helped us some—Johnny, too," Danny explained. "How you want to set up the watch? I'll take first watch if you want."

"No, I'm OK. Just tired, like y'all. I'll take first watch till 12, you do the next two hours, and then Mike and Alex can wrap it up." Tuck looked down at his watch. "Let's see, hell, it's almost 10 already. Go get some sleep, I'll slide on down to the hole closer to that elephant grass."

Tuck stretched and yawned, then shook his head. He slipped on his flak jacket and placed his helmet and a full canteen under his arm. In a crouch, he quietly scuttled 10 yards past where Mike and Alex slept. Mike snored gently and rhythmically. Danny spread and smoothed his poncho liner like a giant bird fashioning a cozy nest for his chicks.

Tuck pulled in his heels and sat cross-legged. He checked his M-16, inserted a full magazine with a barely audible click, chambered a round and propped the rifle against his thigh. He looked at his watch, the glowing hands showed 10:10 p.m.

He watched and listened.

The always-thick air seemed syrupy. He had to breathe deeply to satisfy his lungs. Try as he might to concentrate, the heat and exhaustion seduced his mind into wandering. The night. So quiet, so still. No noise. So tired. Donnie-Boy would have been up with him right now. No. Push Donnie-Boy from the mind. Anna. Yes, that's it. Concentrate on Anna. What is it going to be like after you marry? Where are you going to live? Go to school? Kids? One? Two? Three, four...I love the Marine Corps. Wake up, Tuck. Don't drift. You're drifting. Concentrate.

"Ouch!" Twin bites to the cheek by the invisible devils of the night snatched Tuck from his reverie. He slapped at the humming near his ears. It reminded him that the continual ringing never really stopped. Doc Wild said the tinnitus could be permanent.

His head slowly began to droop again when the elephant grass suddenly rustled to life. His head snapped up. He listened long and hard. "A rat," he decided.

In a rush and a blur, yet an eternity, Tuck's world exploded and he found himself lying on his back confused—staring at a star-filled sky. Danny hovered over him. He couldn't breathe.

"O, St. Joseph..."

CHAPTER 49

My Dying Breath
Southern Da Krong Valley, R.S.V.N.
May 17, 1969—12:05 a.m. local time

"Corpsman! Get your ass over here, my man's down. Hurry the hell up," Danny shouted to Doc Wild, who had sprinted from the far side of the hill.

Trying to catch his breath, Doc Wild dropped to his knees and ripped open the T-shirt he had given Tuck a month before. His eyes narrowed and stared at the neat round wound in Tuck's upper left chest. The blood seeped slowly. The flak jacket had provided little protection.

"Help me now, gently, gently," he told Danny. A half roll and a probing hand beneath Tuck's torso confirmed Doc Wild's guess—an exit wound spread blood across his back.

Small bubbles formed when the air gurgled in and out of the entry wound. Tuck's chest heaved. "Doc, hellllp," he wheezed. A frothy red trickle oozed from the corner of his mouth. "Please."

His eyes focused on no particular point. They blinked slowly. With every gasp the wound stole his breath, and life, away. But, he couldn't die. Anna said she would wait.

"Sucking chest wound. Shit, this ain't good," Doc Wild cursed quietly to Danny and Johnny. He sighed heavily and then rummaged through his kit. Tuck's friends prayed.

"Don't go shitty on me, Tuck. You're not gonna die on my watch. Stay awake," Doc Wild commanded. He sought a piece of plastic to seal the hole. Blood continued to seep from the wound. Jackson?"

"Yeah, Doc?"

"This man needs to get to Charlie Med ASAP. If we don't get a medevac here in the next 15 minutes, I'll be toe-taggin' him." Doc Wild bit into the plastic that covered a sterile gauze wrap and then placed it over Tuck's wound with the palm of his hand. "Now get your ass up the hill and tell the skipper he's about to lose another squad leader down here if he don't get moving."

"Aye, aye, doc." Danny gently laid Tuck's head down. "You ain't gonna die, Tuck. You hear? Just keep sayin' that prayer of yours."

Tuck nodded weakly. *"O, St. Joseph do assist me..."*

"Alex, here, take this," Johnny said. He flung Gertrude to the ground and crouched in Danny's place, hovering over Tuck like a huge mother hen. "We got him, Tuck. Blowed him the shit away, yeah," he said with a hopeful smile. Tuck's labored breathing allowed scarcely a pause between gasps. "Just one guy, one lousy gook. Must've been a line probe, just like you warned us, and couldn't pass up the shot. He paid for it, though, yeah."

Rallying under the care of Doc Wild, a faint laugh punctuated Tuck's effort to breathe. He then smiled, peacefully. *"...I never weary contemplating you and Jesus asleep in your arms..."*

•

12:08 a.m.: His slung M-16 flapping at his side, the fleet Alabama halfback cleared the distance between the perimeter and the platoon commander's position in less than a minute. After dodging rocks and logs as if they were would-be tacklers, he arrived breathlessly. "Skipper, Doc Wild says it's bad, real bad. Tuck's been shot bad and can hardly breathe. We need a medevac chopper ASAP. Man, Doc Wild means quick." Danny, too, now gasped for air. Sweat poured from his closely cropped head.

"OK, there, Marine. I'll see what we can do. With the night and jungle canopy and all, I don't know how quick..." Smith curtly replied, his voice trailing off. He turned to hear a report from his aide on the confirmed kill of the enemy sapper.

"No, there's no 'don't know how quick' shit about it," Danny shouted.

"What's that you say, Marine, you don't..." the skipper shot back.

"Pick up the damn radio and call in a chopper, NOW. There's a clearing just 200 yards from where Tuck, I mean Corporal Richard, is down. We can have him there before the chopper gets here," Danny started loudly, before tempering his remarks.

"Jackson, you're not running this..."

"NOW, damn it! Sir." Danny raised his M-16 to bear on the skipper's dog tag, dangling like a target over his heart. "NOW!"

His eyes fixed on the rifle, the aide picked up the field telephone and called battalion. Danny clicked the selector switch on the black rifle to fully automatic for emphasis.

Suddenly, Gaines stormed in from the north side of the perimeter. "Jackson, what in the hell do you think you're doing here?"

Smith snapped, "Staff Sgt. Gaines, place this man under arrest, I want..."

"Tuck's down, sarge. He's hurt real bad," Danny hurried to explain. "That shot a few minutes ago, it got Tuck in the chest. And this asshole won't call in a medevac."

"Tuck's hit? How bad?" Gaines nearly shouted. He reached out and gently turned the barrel of Danny's rifle away from Smith's chest. "Slowly now, what's goin' on?"

"Doc Wild says he's *got* to go, now." Danny's face contorted with anguish. "Doc says it's a sucking chest wound, and, and..."

"It's OK, get back on down and get him ready to go to that LZ near the clearing. I'll take care of it here. Go on."

"Aye, aye, sarge." Danny turned and sped down the hill toward his wounded friend.

"Sergeant I want that man arrested and..."

"Lieutenant," Gaines interrupted. "If you don't want me to shoot you myself, you had better get on the horn and find a chopper. And like the man said, now."

The skipper turned and looked to his aide, who was already speaking softly over the battalion net. "Yes, that would do fine, perfect. Ten minutes? Yes, I have the coordinates..."

Smith turned and looked incredulously at Gaines.

"Now what was so damn hard about that?" Gaines, again the DI, said through gritted teeth.

"Thanks much." The aide hung up the field phone. "We got lucky. Battalion patched me through to an army Huey making an emergency medevac run this way up from out of the A Shau—a place called Hamburger Hill. They said the 101st Airborne's been taking a shit load of casualties down there all week and have been flying them 'round the clock to field hospitals all over the I Corps. This one is inbound for Stud right now."

With the information he needed, Gaines nodded and raced toward Tuck's position. He caught up with Tuck's squad. They were rushing him on a folded poncho toward the LZ. Doc Wild trailed closely, holding an IV bag high like an Olympic torchbearer.

"Tuck, can you hear me? Hang in there. You hear? Like you did back on the run at the Depot. You can make it, gut it out, Marine." Gaines then sprinted ahead to the LZ and heard the distant but distinctive popping sound of the approaching Huey and began organizing the dust off.

•

12:20 a.m.: The Marines hoisted Tuck onto the floor of the chopper while its skids barely hovered above the sloping ground. Doc Wild hopped onto the skid and saw three bloodied and bandaged men leaning against the inner walls. Two filled body bags lay next to them. He shouted above the whipping sound of the Huey's blades. "Who's the medic in here?"

"I am," a mustachioed man answered loudly. "What you jarheads giving us here?"

"Sucking chest wound, left side. Bad one."

"Never seen a good one," the medic shouted back. He secured Tuck into place.

"Yeah, know what you mean. He's kinda special to us, though."

"They all are. We'll take good care of him, sailor. Heck, he'll be at Charlie Med inside of 15 minutes." Doc Wild reached up, pulled the medic close to him and then whispered into his ear.

"No shit?" The medic looked at Tuck, then scribbled a note on his medevac tag.

Johnny reached out, grabbed one of Tuck's boots and gently squeezed. Listening to his Cajun buddy's continued gasps, his eyes became filled with tears.

Danny rubbed Tuck's leg. "Hang in there, little Tiger."

Unsure, Tuck thought he heard his friends cry out to him. Donnie-Boy? The confusion grew. Strong vibrations shook his topsy-turvy world. Is this what death is like? He felt himself rising toward the heavens.

The Huey quickly lifted off and the pilot spun its nose toward the northeast. Tuck did the only thing he could think of. *"...But I dare not approach while He reposes near your heart..."*

•

Charlie Med, Vandegrift Combat Base, 12:22 a.m.: Dr. Jimmy DeSchott sat atop his favorite sandbagged wall outside of the field hospital. He took a long, last drag from a Lucky Strike and exhaled the blue smoke into the starry sky. Smiling, he flicked the butt into the red clay. How beautiful Vietnam could be when its combatants weren't struggling for their lives on a table before him.

He rubbed his face and eyes. He hadn't shaved for three days and the stubble was like sandpaper against his delicate palms. The Marine sweep of the Da Krong Valley and the slaughter atop Hamburger Hill had kept Charlie Med busy 24 hours a day.

The popping sound of an approaching Huey robbed him of his peace.

"One minute out, doctor," Nurse Binh said in stilted English. She seemed to have suddenly appeared from nowhere. "They say four wounded, they say one chest, two bad legs, possible amputees, one gut."

"Thanks. Set me up for the chest wound, get Doc Kenny on the others."

•

12:26 a.m.: Tuck struggled to remain conscious. Gasping gave him focus and the air he desired. Somewhere he'd been taught the importance of remaining conscious. Maybe it was in basic training; at school back in Eunice, Louisiana, U.S.A.; or was it on "Ben Casey"?

The vibrations and noise stopped. He could now feel a hard, cold surface beneath him. The sun above shone so brightly in his face, but it was not hot. His confusion grew. Where were the stars? Was it not night? Who is that masked man? Somehow he knew, but, but—shit, no, shoot, no, shot. The shot. DeSchott? Yes, Doc DeSchott. He must be back at Stud, Tuck struggled to deduce. He battled with oblivion. He gasped and again retreated to his refuge, *"...So press Him in my name and kiss His fine head for me..."*

•

12:30 a.m.: "I think I recognize this one," DeSchott said, preparing Tuck for surgery. "Lift up the sheet."

Nurse Binh looked at DeSchott quizzically and then complied.

"I thought so," he said, examining the raised red scar on the outside of Tuck's left thigh. "I sewed this Marine up a few months ago when he first got in country. By the looks of all these fresh shrapnel wounds, I'd say he's been a busy lad. Let me see his chart. Hurry."

Nurse Binh spun and grabbed the chart from a nearby table and held it up for the surgeon. DeSchott glanced through the scant remarks made by the admitting nurse. "Whoa, here's something. The chopper medic must have scribbled this on his tag. 'Navy Cross.' Well, let's see if we can save this young hero. Put him under, Nurse Binh."

Tuck felt a prick on his arm. Can't be any skeeters in here, he mused. But he could no longer fight it. Consciousness began slipping away. *"…and ask Him to return the kiss…"*

•

12:48 a.m.: "Damn, I just can't stop the bleeding. The lung is OK, got him breathing. But there must be something I'm missing. Aorta, OK. Pulmonary? Anterior pulmonary, oh, shit…"

"Pressure dropping fast, fast, doctor," the nurse advised. "Breathing too shallow."

"Get ready we're gonna have to crack him open. This one's gettin' shitty."

•

Tuck no longer gasped. The fatigue drained from his body. The ringing in his ears waned. He slept without nightmare. Anna lay next to him in his heart. Chuck and Jimmy B. beckoned.

He could feel Donnie-Boy's smile again, radiant like the sun on his face.

And, as always, there were the words to St. Joseph. *"...when I draw my dying breath."*

EPILOGUE
Eunice, Louisiana
April 15, 1972—2 p.m. local time

A north wind chilled the spring afternoon, and the scent of freshly mowed clover greeted the big man when he hopped out of his pickup truck. He joined his waiting friend. They shook hands and embraced.

"Come on, they're over here." Johnny cocked his head toward a nest of chalk-white headstones. "I come out here regular, at least twice a year, particularly on this day. Sure am glad you could finally come down. I've been waitin' for a long time, yeah."

"Yeah. It's been, what? Nearly two years since we last met, bro?"

"About. Since up in Tuscaloosa."

"College's been keeping me busy. Get my degree next fall," Danny said quietly. They were drawing closer to the site. "Then I might try law school, too."

"No, shit? All right, my man, Danny," Johnny tapped him on the shoulder with his fist. "Didn't talk to the Bear like I told you, did you?"

"No, they've got real good running backs out there now. You oughta know. Bama's Wishbone's been kicking everybody's ass in the SEC. Including your Tigers."

"I know. I just like to hold on to the old days sometimes. Like they were before the Nam."

Danny nodded.

"Oops, look out!" Johnny grabbed Danny's arm. "You almost stepped on my aunt's foot."

"Whaat?" Danny cried out, hopping aside. "Aw, man."

The two men laughed.

"You still the fastest boy I ever saw, too."

"Damn, you still into that. How many times do I have to tell you that I'm not a boy."

"Gotcha," Johnny said with a smirk and a point.

"Man, you something else. You know that? But I love you," Danny grinned and slapped Johnny on the back of the neck. "And you? Still running the repair shop for your dad?"

"Yeah, Pop's stroke last year set him back some. But Wilfred's gettin' stronger. He hopes to be walking regular again by this time next year. Mind's still good, though. Gives me shit all the time."

"I imagine you deserve it."

"That's what he says, too. Also says I ought to go back to school, be a football coach."

They arrived at the knot of headstones near the center of the cemetery. "Look at that. They got 'em all lined up like a little Arlington," Danny said. He scanned the area. Several other military markers stood behind the pair of radiating tablets. "Would you look at that? 'Donald Charles Hebert, Medal of Honor.' So they really went ahead and gave it to him. Damn, that Donnie-Boy was one fine Marine."

"Yeah, and so was the fella next to him," Johnny added, swiping his eyes with his sleeve.

"Hey, guys, over here," the pretty young woman shouted. She waved from the window of her silver Stingray. "Y'all wait up."

"Fine car," Danny observed. "Fine girl."

"You're late, as usual, cuzz. Hurry on up," Johnny shouted with a grunt and a long wave of his arthritic shoulder.

The driver's side door slowly opened. "Hey, wait a minute..." Danny turned and sprinted toward the sports car, easily hurdling the rows of white markers. He threw open his arms.

The young man grinned and leaped into Danny's strong grasp.

"Oooo, not too hard, the old lung's not what it used to be." Tuck laughed. Danny swung him around.

"I'm so sorry, man, that I never came before now. I just couldn't. The memories. That last night I saw you in the Nam, it was just too much for me," Danny cried. "I like to never snap out of it, I..."

"Hey, it's over, OK, I'm fine. That doc back at Stud really knew his shit," Tuck said, rubbing his friend's back. "He said he thought he'd lost me for a while. Would have if I hadn't gotten good care back in the bush. Plus the quick response time, thanks to you."

"I caught a lot of flak from the skipper for that one, but ol' sarge ran interference for me. But the harassing, it didn't last long, cause Nixon stuck to his word and pulled our ass out of there." Danny hugged Tuck again.

"And you missed all the fun in Okinawa, Tuck," Johnny added.

"Yeah, yeah, I've heard all those stories over and over again." Tuck dismissed Johnny with a playful wave. "Oh, Johnny tells me you saw Sgt. Gaines earlier this year. How is he?"

"Who?" Danny teased. "Oh, you must mean Gunny Gaines. Yeah, I saw him when I was in California on vacation. It seems, sarge got assigned another tour to the Nam after we rotated back to the World. Got his arm shot up, too. But he's back at the MCRD in San Diego, harassing more boots, I suppose. But he's a gunnery sergeant and is bossin' his own recruit series now."

"How about the skipper?"

"Don't know and don't give a shit, either."

"I know what you mean," Tuck laughed. "I phoned Doc

Wild about a year and a half ago after one of my surgeries. He went back to med school at Texas and last I heard he was doing his residency in heart surgery in Dallas. Told him if he needed a reference I'd be happy to oblige."

"That was close that night. Wasn't it?" Danny remembered. "Lucky Doc knew what to do."

"Lucky I had that prayer," Tuck added. He nodded toward the wrought-iron arch spanning the white shell lane. "You notice the name of this cemetery?"

Danny turned and then shook his head slowly. "St. Joseph's Cemetery. Guess he didn't want you in here just yet. Prayer must have worked."

"You bet it did—still say it every night."

Anna hugged Tuck's arm. "How about all those other guys you always talk about, Alex and Willie and Mike and Ike..." she said, nodding her head, the names rolling off her tongue.

"Oh, we're always talking about a reunion. But you know how those go, Babe? We were the best of friends back then. But now, well, we have our own lives to get on with."

They all nodded. "But, here we are together, again," Danny said.

"Yeah, fuckin'ay, bro," Johnny added.

Danny turned to Anna. "And you must be the famous Miss Anna Carlisle, excuse me, Mrs. Anna Richard." Danny took her hand, bowed and shook it delicately as if meeting royalty.

"Oh, Danny, I, too, so much wanted to meet you, to thank you for helping my Tuck. Thank you so much." Anna stood tall to kiss Danny on the cheek. "Forgive my husband. He's never been one for formal introductions. It's probably because he never wanted to tell me just how handsome you are. Tuck was right, you are an ebony angel."

"OK, OK, that's enough, you two." Tuck steered the trio

back toward the monuments. "Have to pay my respects to Donnie-Boy. Don't do this as often as I should."

"Tuck, how's your parents? OK, I hope," Danny asked while they meandered through the cemetery.

"Watch my aunt's feet," Johnny called out from ahead.

"Oh, fine. Ever since the Arab's started their oil embargo, Dad's client has been raking it in. They made him a full partner and now Curtis and Mary are rolling in dough. They're touring France and Germany right now. Dad said he was going to try to find some of the places he bombed back in WWII, maybe even try to find some old Luftwaffe pilots," he laughed.

"And what about you, Tuck?"

"I'm finally gettin' over it some, needed more surgery to get my lung working right, though—nightmares still pretty bad. And, I'm going to the local LSU campus here, shootin' for a journalism degree. Anna here is expecting, too."

"No?" Danny said. "A little Tucker?"

"Hey, man, you didn't tell me," Johnny complained. "Anna, why didn't you tell…"

"Calm down, T-Johnny, we just found out yesterday." Anna patted him on the shoulder after they arrived at the graves.

Four abreast with arms around one another's waists, they stood vigil before the markers. Danny nodded toward the headstone next to Donnie-Boy's grave. "Who was that other Donald again, that Donald Etienne?"

"A good friend of ours from back in school. A Marine— killed at Khe Sanh during the siege." Tuck wiped a tear from his eye. "You would have liked him."

A gust of wind rushed past the markers and rustled day-old flowers. It caused a shiver that nearly stole the breath away. Danny and Johnny bowed their heads in prayer. Tuck, however, focused on the heavens where a jet's contrail traced a fine silver thread across the blue sky. Anna gazed at the tears in her husband's eyes.

"So, Tuck, if it's a boy, what you gonna name him?" Johnny pleaded, breaking the pall.

"That's easy enough." Tuck knelt to touch the headstones. "Donald Curtis. I figure they earned it."

"And if it's a girl?" Johnny eagerly asked.

"The hell if I know." Tuck said, rising up. "Then it'll be up to Anna and the grandmas."

Johnny turned to Anna with a hopeful glance. "How about Gertrude?"

"Aw shit, Johnny. They ain't gonna name their kid after a machine gun," Danny scolded. "Damn."

"Well, it's better than the BEAR," Johnny shot back.

"That'd be better than TIGER," Danny responded.

"Oh, yeah, well how about…"

While strolling to their vehicles, Tuck turned and looked back toward the markers. He pulled Anna close and tenderly kissed her cheek.

"What was that for, silly?" She gently brushed the spot with the back of her fingers. "It was so sweet."

"Just following one last order."

Tuck could feel Donnie-Boy's smile again.

THE END

Glossary

50-caliber—An American heavy machine gun.

51-caliber—A Russian heavy machine gun.

60 mm—American light mortar.

81 mm—American heavy mortar.

105s—105 mm howitzer (cannon)

155s—155 mm howitzer (cannon)

Ao dai—A traditional, long white dress worn by Vietnamese women.

ARVN—Army of the Republic of Vietnam (South Vietnam)

A Shau Valley—Region infamous for numerous bloody engagements throughout the war. Located in the I Corps and Thua Thinh Province. The NVA used the A Shau as a supply conduit into the country after leaving the Ho Chi Minh Trail in Laos. Among some of the operations fought there were Operation Dewey Canyon and the battle for Hamburger Hill.

AK-47—A durable and respected assault rifle of Russian design that fires a 7.62 mm round. It was used by the North Vietnamese Army.

CH-46 Sea Knight—Primary Marine Corps troop and supply helicopter (twin-bladed).

CH-47 Chinook—Similar in appearance to CH-46 but larger and more powerful (also twin-bladed).

CH-53 Sea Stallion—Large heavy duty, single-bladed helicopter used by all branches of the service for various missions.

Camp Pendleton—The Marine Corps' largest base; located between San Diego and Los Angeles.

Charlie—Nickname for enemy soldiers; also, gooks, slopes, and dinks. Over the radio it was November Victor Alpha.

Charlie Med—Location of the M.A.S.H. unit at Vandegrift Combat Base.

ChiCom—Stands for Chinese Communist but also refers to a grenade used by the NVA which leaves a telltale spark or "fizz" when used in the darkness. Unlike American-made fragmentation grenades (frags), Chi-Coms rely primarily on concussive forces to do their damage.

Chieu hoi—A program in which NVA soldiers were allowed safe passage through American lines if they possessed a leaflet declaring their intentions to "chieu hoi" over to U.S. forces.

Claymores—An antipersonnel mine that fires hundreds of pellets creating a wide kill zone. It was highly effective in defensive perimeters and ambushes. The explosive plastic, C-4, is used to ignite the mine. Grunts often cannibalized the C-4 from Claymores to quickly heat their C-rations.

Deuce-and-a-half—A heavy-duty, 10-wheel military truck (M-35) used for hauling supplies and troops. Also called a Six-by.

DMZ—Demilitarized Zone. The 17th parallel, a political boundary and buffer zone between North and South Vietnams.

F-4 Phantom—The world's elite air superiority fighter of its time. Its droopy nose cone and wilting tail made it an icon of the air war in Vietnam.

FAO—Forward Air Observer. A junior Marine or Air Force officer, who sometimes accompanied ground operations and calls in air strikes. Also called an FAC for Forward Air Controller.

FNGs—Fucking New Guys, also known as "newbies" or "cherries," are green troops first arriving in Vietnam.

Firebase or FSB—A forward artillery base or Fire Support Base; usually located atop a hill, high ground or in a relatively secure area. Defended by an infantry unit.

Grunt—Term used to describe a Vietnam-era infantry soldier of both the Marines and Army. Endearing if used by a grunt; sometimes derisive if used by another military occupation.

Gunny—Short for the rank of Gunnery Sergeant. Often used as a term of respect.

I Corps—Military designation for the northern-most theater of operations in South Vietnam. Started just south of DaNang and covered several provinces northward to the DMZ (Demilitarized Zone).

Iddywah—A single-tooth can opener used on C-ration cans. Also called a

"P-38" or a "John Wayne."

Ka-bar—Optional issue jungle knife of legendary strength, sharpness and balance.

KIA—Acronym for Killed in Action; also WIA = Wounded in Action and MIA = Missing in Action.

Khe Sanh—A Marine combat base abandoned following a two-month siege in 1968. Located about 15 miles southwest of Vandegrift Combat Base (Stud).

Kilo 2 Alpha—Designation for Kilo Company, Second Platoon, First Squad. Kilo 1 Bravo would be Kilo Co., First Platoon, Second Squad. The unit designation plus the attachment "Six" would refer to the commander of that unit. (e.g. Kilo 2 Six would be the call sign for the commanding officer of the second platoon of Kilo Co. The company commander would be Kilo Six).

Klick—Military speak for a kilometer (0.6 mile).

LAAW—Light Anti-Armor Weapon. Basically a

fiberglass and cardboard, one-shot, throw-away bazooka; effective against tanks and bunkers.

LP and OP—Listening Post and Observation Post.

M-16—Introduced into combat during the Vietnam War, the American-made M-16 fires a 5.56 mm or .223 caliber round. Improved versions remain the most popular assault rifles in the world.

M-14—An improved version of the venerable M-1 rifle used in World War II and Korea. It was used in Marine Corps training until phased out in the 1970s by the M-16. Extremely accurate and durable, the M-14 fires a 7.62 mm or .308 caliber round.

M-60—A much-heralded machine gun that fires a 7.62 mm round. An icon of the Vietnam War along with the M-16.

M-79—A single-shot, breech-loaded weapon that fires 40 mm high explosive (HE) and Flechette (steel darts) rounds, making it an effective weapon both from afar and up close. Also called a "blooper."

MCRD—Marine Corps Recruit Depot located in San Diego. It's East Coast companion is Parris Island, South Carolina.

Medals—Military awards for valor given to Marines (in descending order): Medal of Honor, Navy Cross, Silver Star, Bronze Star, and Navy Commendation Medal. The Vietnamese Cross of Gallantry was also given for valor and regarded just below the Bronze Star. The Purple Heart is given for wounds suffered during combat operations.

Mikes, mike-mikes—In radio talk, mikes refers to minutes if used singularly (as in 5 mikes or 5 minutes). If used as a pair, mike-mikes means millimeters (81 mike-mikes refers to an 81-millimeter mortar).

MOS—Military Occupation Specialty. (e.g. 0300—infantry, or more specific 0311—rifleman, or 0330—machine gunner).

NVA—The North Vietnamese Army.

Op—Operation; an extended, long-range patrol by a large unit usually lasting more than a week. Normally given names by senior planning officers. (e.g. Dewey Canyon, Hastings, Scotland, Kentucky, Allen Brook, etc.)

OV-10A Bronco—Light, fast and highly maneuverable observation aircraft. Also carried machine guns and light rockets.

PT—Marine lingo for physical training.

Pos—Military talk for "position," pronounced "paws."

PRC-25—Heavy but dependable field radio carried on the back of an unlucky grunt. Often called the "prick 25" of simply "prick."

Puff the Magic Dragon—A C-47 cargo transport plane converted to a minigun platform carrying a trio of rotating, 7.62 mm machine guns. Also referred to as "Spooky" or "Snoopy." It was normally summoned as a matter of last resort to prevent installations, etc. from being overrun by the enemy.

R.S.V.N.—Republic of South Vietnam

R&R—Rest and Recuperative leave. At least two weeks vacation taken during the middle of a grunt's 13-month tour of duty. Bangkok, Thailand; Hong Kong; Honolulu and Sydney, Australia, were among the more popular destinations.

RPG—Rocket Propelled Grenade. An anti-armor, bazooka-type weapon used by the NVA.

Radio talk—Sample language used on a combat frequency: Pos = position; Nathaniel Victor = NVA soldiers; fast movers = jets; that's a negative = no; ASAP = As Soon As Possible; mikes = minutes; mike-mikes = millimeters; arty = artillery;

Route 9—A main highway winding roughly northeast to southwest through Quang Tri Province.

Slang—A sampling of grunt terms: "I shit you not" =

"I'm not kidding;" di-di, pronounced deedee = hurry; most ricky tick = as fast as you can; short-timer = grunt with little time remaining on tour; Skipper = immediate commanding officer; beaucoup = a lot; movement = enemy in area; "watch your six" = "look out behind you;" bush = jungle; World = anywhere but Vietnam; in country = in Vietnam; creeping crud and jungle rot = festering sores; No. 10 = very bad.

Squad—Upward of 14 Marines when fully manned. Included three four-man fire teams, a squad leader and radioman; rarely fully staffed.

Quad-50—Four .50 caliber machine guns mounted on a rotating platform and linked to fire in unison.

Quang Tri Province—The northernmost province of South Vietnam. Includes Khe Sanh, Quang Tri City, the villages of Cam Lo and Dong Ha, Vandegrift Combat Base, the Rockpile, Con Thien, Camp Carroll, and the DaKrong Valley.

Tet Offensive—Some of the most intensive fighting of the Vietnam War occurred during the Tet Lunar New Year in the spring of 1968. The battle of Hue City, the siege of Khe Sanh and the assault on the U.S. Embassy in Saigon are among the more infamous incidents of this period.

UH-1 Huey—Light assault helicopter used by the Army. It emits a distinctive popping sound created by the design of its rotors. Another popular icon of the war.

Uniforms—Marines call: pants = trousers, shirts = blouses, caps = covers.

Vandegrift Combat Base—The staging area for the Ninth Marine Regiment. Also known as **LZ Stud**, or simply "Stud." Located approximately 12 miles south of the DMZ and 15 miles northwest of **Khe Sanh.**

Vietnamese quotations—"Lam on, ban toi di. Lam on, ban toi chet di." = "Please, end it. Please, end it for me."

"Va cho no nua." = "And for him, too."

ABOUT THE AUTHOR

Bernard A. "Ben" Reed has been a journalist in south Louisiana for the past 27 years. He currently is the assistant state editor at The Advocate newspaper in Baton Rouge, where he has worked since 1990.

He has also worked as managing editor at four Acadiana newspapers: The Jennings Daily News (1975-79), The Eunice News (1979-84), the Ville Platte Gazette (1984-85), and The Abbeville Meridional (1985-90).

Born and raised in Eunice, La., Ben is the son of Rosemary Bergeron and the late Curry Reed. He is married to the former Clarese Soileau of Ville Platte and they live in Baton Rouge with their three daughters, Lesley, Allison and Kayla.

Ben enlisted in the U.S. Marine Corps after his graduation from St. Edmund High School in Eunice in 1968. He trained at the MCRD in San Diego before embarking for South Vietnam in March 1969. As an 0311 "grunt," he served with Kilo Co., Third Battalion, Ninth Marines of the 3rd Marine Division. He was wounded in combat in June 1969 while on Operation Utah Mesa near Khe Sanh in Quang Tri Province.

Upon returning home in 1970, Ben enrolled at LSU and was graduated from the LSU School of Journalism in 1973. He has since earned more than 30 writing and editing awards from the Louisiana Press Association. He is an ardent LSU football fan.

My Dying Breath is his first novel.